FALLING FOR MR. WRIGHT

A CHRONICLES OF A DANCING HEART NOVEL

BOOK ONE

Falling For MR. WRIGHT

OLIVIA BOOTHE

Three Brothers Press

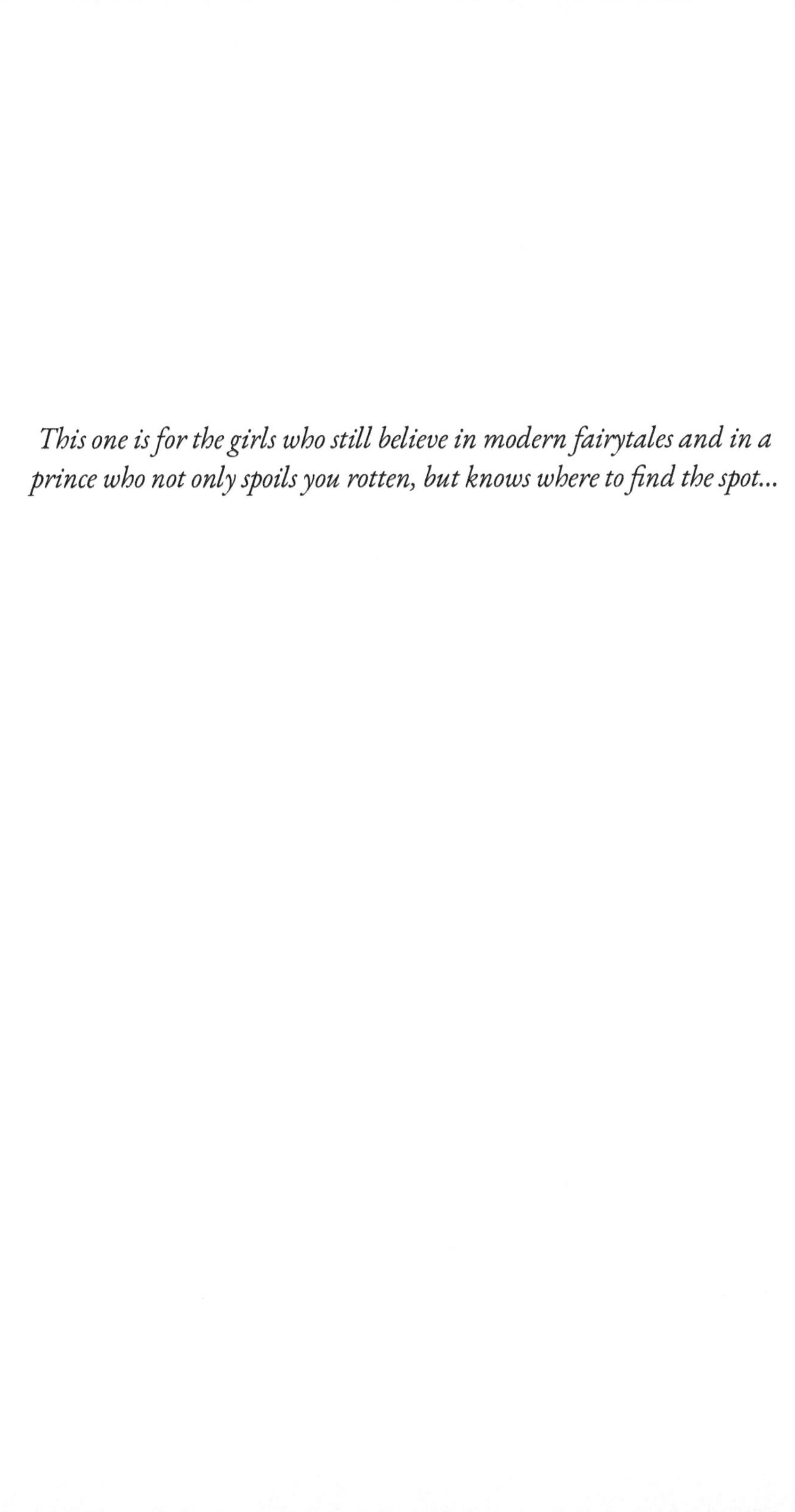

This one is for the girls who still believe in modern fairytales and in a prince who not only spoils you rotten, but knows where to find the spot...

Previously published as Wicked Dance in 2017, Falling For Mr. Wright is the 1st book in Olivia Boothe's completed contemporary billionaire romance duet. The bulk of the story remains untouched. However, this edition contains fresh edits, reimagined scenes, spicier romance, and additional chapters from the MMCs POV.

Content Advisory

**For audiences 18 years+, explicit sexual scenes, war veteran, PTSD, depression, mention of death, grief, mention of substance use, foul language, depictions of sexual assault (not gratuitous and not by the hero), workplace harassment (not by the hero), some physical violence.**
**Reader discretion is advised**

One

SARA

Going to work at the Rebecca Fitzgerald Dance Company was like stepping onto the set of a horror movie instead of a dance studio. And it didn't help that I was going to be late for the third time this week. Every day was a new torture scenario specially crafted for me by my boss, aka Satan, aka personal tormentor, aka Rebecca, the Artistic Director for the dance company. She and her minion, Alexei Voronov, the resident choreographer, schemed daily to make my life a living hell.

Every night I'd lay in bed, my left eye twitching while my mind tried to shutdown, unable to get the day's shenanigans out of my head, haunted with thoughts about going back the next day.

Last night hadn't been any different.

Black pumps beating fast against the concrete, I hustled down West 49th street toward Rockefeller Center. Gracefully bobbing and weaving through the morning masses in a choreographed dance, I slithered through the amplified horde of morning commuters, racing against the clock and knowing only divine intervention was going to get me to work on time. My feet burned from the long city blocks I'd trekked in heels, but I'd rather have throbbing sores on my toes than get mushed between strangers in an underground sardine can.

I took a deep breath, praying no new dancers had been fired from the company and that I wouldn't have to scramble to keep the whole performance from ripping at the seams. My heart kept pace with my feet, making me damp with sweat. Instrumental music piped through my ear pods, blissfully drowning out the cacophony of indistinct chatter, honking horns, and hasty traffic vibrating off the streets.

Le Café Au Lait, my favorite French bakery and everyday morning stop, was in the complete opposite direction of the dance company, but regardless of the hail storm waiting for me, nothing would keep me from getting my a.m. fix. Not to mention if I showed up without my boss's latte, the fire-breathing dragon would definitely char my body and feast on me for breakfast.

Just one more block...

I jacked-up my stride and hurried past a herd of suits then dodged slamming into a delivery guy who was carrying boxes. As he teetered on one foot, he called out after me in brightly colored words. I shrugged in a half-hearted apology and kept rushing toward the cafe.

"Yes..." I hissed with a smile as I finally reached the bakery's doors and pulled on the handle.

The door didn't budge.

"What the hell?" I peeked inside, but the glass windows and doors were covered in construction grade paper, the words *Closed for Renovations* blasted across in checkered patterns.

I reached up and yanked out my ear pods, leaving the concerto of the morning chaos free to assail my ears.

The signs mocked me. Unamused, I rubbed the butt of my palm

on my temple. My barista warned me the day before they'd be closed for a few days. I'd completely forgotten about their plan to revamp the interior. Catching my breath and holding my right rib in pain, the soles of my feet burned while I absorbed what happened. With my jaw dropped and hands on my hips, I caught my reflection on the golden-framed glass doors. I stood cemented, eyes wide open, as if staring at the doors long enough would make the place not-closed.

I shook my head and let out an exasperated breath. Did they really have to be closed today, of all days? I'd barely slept, there was a mountain load of work waiting on my desk, and now this? What the heck was my caffeine-addicted body supposed to do without my quadruple-shot cappuccino? And with the way things were going at the office, today was not the day to mess with my morning routine.

Trust me.

Okay, so yes, it wasn't the only cafe around, but to me, that French boulangerie was supposed to be my every-morning-ten-minutes-of-sweet-heavenly-delight on my way to work. Even though I was chasing the clock, skipping my usual coffee and scrumptious chocolate-almond croissant was not an option. I needed to be fully armed with an indulgent breakfast before heading into the inferno to face Lucifer.

I looked down at my watch and frowned. Eight-thirty a.m.

Thirty minutes late. Just great.

Rebecca was surely going to rip my head off. There was no possible way I was going to face that demon without caffeine in my system. No fucking way. All my pent-up frustration with this woman would certainly erupt.

Time for plan B.

The Int'l House of Java was located right inside Rockefeller Center, and while it would make me even later, I needed coffee ASAP. I rushed toward the busy cafe, almost getting knocked over as I was pushed forward by a rushing bike-messenger.

"Watch it," I yelled after him, but with headphones plugging his ears, my complaint went unheard. He stopped short in front of me and dismounted before slinging his track-bike over his shoulder and opening the door to the coffee house—not bothering to hold it open out of courtesy.

It smacked me right on the forehead. "Ow."

Take a deep breath, Sara. Just breathe.

I rubbed my head as I pushed through the heavy door, praying for some grace, but as I peered up, I choked on my prayer. Every New Yorker in a three-mile radius was cramped into this tiny place.

Decked out in the usual protective gear, the sweaty bike courier bounced to music piping through his headphones. I waited in line behind him, my scrunched-up nose only inches away from getting hit by one of his cycle's wheels. The waft of roasted beans barely masked the musty smell of body odor emanating from him.

More people piled in from the street, herding us forward and causing someone's elbow to jab me in the ribs. I huffed and puffed while I shifted on my feet and checked my watch again, wishing somehow that time could move backward.

When I finally made it to the register, I brushed a hand over my head, trying to smooth away one escapee lock of brown hair. It sprung back up. Apparently, it was determined to add to my rattled nerves. I kept trying to tame it down as I ordered my cappuccino quad and gave the girl my name. While I tapped my toes, my eyes followed as the female barista moseyed around, preparing my coffee.

Why did everything seem to take longer when you were rushing to get someplace? The instant my coffee was placed on the counter, I snatch it up, turned on my heel ready to book out of there, when my foot twisted, jerking me forward.

Dammit.

"Watch it, lady," the young fashionista standing behind me shouted as coffee splashed on my shirt and some spilled onto the floor by her feet. Her mouth agape and with scorn in her eyes, she checked her designer shoes for splatter. I could have apologized, but I'd left my manners back in front of Le Café Au Lait's entrance.

She earned a glare with my response. "It was an accident," I barked.

The angry woman rolled her eyes and walked past me to pick up her order.

Of course, feeling like a complete idiot, my face radiated with humiliation. Cursing the coffee gods, I wiped down my stained white blouse, then, with frustration smeared across my face, when I looked back up, my body froze.

There, blazing like fiery suns, and staring at me while their owner waited in line to place an order, was the most mesmerizing set of olive-colored eyes I had ever seen.

Then I saw the rest of him, the man who owned those eyes. My heart stopped. No, I mean it. It really did stop. All the oxygen was sucked from my lungs. Stunned, my body was boneless yet stiff at the same time. Flustered face aflame, my cheeks burned as our eyes locked for an eternity.

Fine. It was a mere second, but it'd been a cosmic second. One in which I was weightless and lifted off the floor in a trance. As my disembodied-self floated toward him, he glanced away and headed straight to the counter, deflating me and planting me back on solid ground.

Yep. As quickly as the spell was cast, the enchantment was broken.

Or so I thought. As soon as he spoke, the hands on the clock stopped spinning once more.

"An iced double. Large," he said to the barista. His voice was like velvety chocolate melting on my tongue, smooth and sensual.

Motionless, I gawked at the mysterious stranger as if I was some high-schooler ogling her crush.

I should be flying back to the dance studio.

And peel my gaze off that man? Good luck. Broad shoulders,

definitely over six feet tall and golden brown mussed up hair—yeah, you didn't see many such fine specimens around here. And the fragrance trailing behind him? It had to be some foreign cologne I wouldn't know how to even pronounce. Dressed in what looked like a ludicrously expensive, tailored gray suit, no doubt he was the CEO of a very important corporation. This guy oozed of success and power.

They didn't take long to prepare his coffee. Figures.

He retrieved his order and turned to leave.

Oh, crap. He's coming back my way.

"Excuse me, miss," he said as he stopped in front of me.

Everyone freeze-framed around us, all sound completely muted. Even the dust particles dancing in the sunlight were suspended in time. I peered up into the deep, green ocean of his eyes, my eyelids batting in slow motion, entranced by some unknown force. I curled a smile at the corners of my mouth, expecting that he was experiencing the same thing—that we were spellbound in a magic universe and were sharing a moment.

Then he smiled. "Um, do I know you?"

The room came alive again—very quickly.

"I ... don't think so."

"Oh?" A glimmer of disappointment settled over his eyes. "You always block the door for random strangers, then?" he asked, a sparkle returning to his gaze.

As he spoke, I could barely keep my eyes off his mouth. I fumbled through my words, realizing I was keeping him and the patrons behind him from leaving the coffee house. "Oh, um...yes. I mean, no. Sorry, I just—"

His lips stretched into a crooked grin, perhaps amused at my stutter. Or maybe he knew the effect his body had on me, but before I could say another word, he leaned down and whispered in my right ear, "While I'd love nothing more than to gaze into your pretty brown eyes, you are going to have an angry mob on your hands in about two seconds." I shivered as his breath tickled my skin. He locked eyes with me, winked and with one look, nudged me to the side. Speechless and dazed by the melodic chime of his sultry voice, I slid to the side and let him pass.

"See ya 'round," he said with a playful smile as he rushed out the door.

Okay. Who was that and what the hell just happened?

Compelled to know, I followed after him but lost him in a sea of corporate suits. My heart squeezed in my chest, and for the briefest second, I was sad he was gone.

My phone rang, shaking me out of the bewitchment, the office number bleeping on the screen.

Probably Pinhead.

"Um...hello?" My voice nearly trembled.

"Sara, girl, where are you?"

"Martha? Oh, thank God. I thought you were—"

"The Witch? No, but if you don't get your ass over here, the gates of hell will open. Alexei is at it again."

"Why am I not surprised? I'm on my way. Be there in a few minutes."

Rebecca wasn't by the reception desk tapping her foot and waiting for my late ass to arrive.

Martha's head popped up as soon as she saw me push through the glass entry of our office. "Girl, Alexei is on a rampage."

"What's he done now?" I whispered, leaning over her desk, trying to keep my late arrival quiet.

"What do you think? He fired two more dancers. Before rehearsals even started. He's got Rebecca running around like crazy trying to put out fires."

"Fantastic." A frosted smile traced across my lips.

"Good luck today. You're gonna need it."

"Thanks." I stealthily scurried off to my office and hurried to fire up my computer, plopping my butt on my swivel chair, pretending I'd been working all along.

A big sigh of relief blew out of my lips.

Then it dawned on me.

Shit.

Rebecca's iced latte. How the hell did I forget the most important reason I was rushing this morning? I was so preoccupied with Le Café Au Lait being closed and with running into Mr. Iced Double, I completely forgot to get her damn latte.

Fuck it. There was nothing I could do. She would be furious, but the universe was determined to keep messing with my day, so whatever. I leaned back on my chair, waiting for my computer to finish loading, and finally took a sip of my coffee only to gag. There was nothing worse than cold coffee when it wasn't supposed to be cold.

Annoyed, I slammed the cardboard cup down on my desk causing some to spill over onto the stack of mania envelopes waiting to be opened.

Shit. Shit. Shit.

Quickly cleaning it off, I took a breath to settle myself. Coffee or not, I needed to focus on work. New applications arrived every day, whether we solicited them or not. As the artistic director's assistant, it was my job to sort through the hundreds of packets we received weekly. The competition was fierce. Choosing one dancer out of the myriad of hopefuls looking for a spot on the company was a daunting job, but if there was something I was good at, it was finding true talent.

Still, while I somewhat enjoyed what I did, I couldn't tolerate my boss, and to top it off, according to Martha—our receptionist and daily gossip buzz-feed—Alexei had fired two more dancers. It was his modus operandi. Soon, we'd be running out of bodies to fill the stage.

As I opened up my email, Rebecca's screechy voice echoed down the hall from my office. Martha said she'd been on the phone with the dancer's union doing damage control since before we opened.

Good. At least Alexei is keeping her busy.

And off my tail.

For now.

Fifteen minutes later, my eyes were still glued to the initial line of my first email. I'd read it a million times and still didn't know what it said. Every time I tried to focus, my imagination went elsewhere. Well, not exactly elsewhere, but more toward someone else. I wasn't drinking coffee, but it was still on my mind—Mr. Iced Double that is. I couldn't forget the searing look of those olive eyes. And the way he smelled? My body shivered thinking about inhaling his scent. It was a mix of fresh mountain rain wrapped up in golden delicious honey. I know, it didn't make sense, but my nose understood.

God, and those lips. Taking a deep breath, I pinched the bridge of my nose, trying to eradicate the unbidden images taking over my mind. How the hell was I supposed to make it through the day when Mr. Iced Double was running through my veins? Talk about caffeine addiction. This guy could send me to rehab.

I leaned on my chair and threw my head back, exasperated that with all the crap piled up on my plate, I couldn't get anything done because all I could think about was the man I almost met that morning. Almost, because like an idiot, I missed an opportunity to—

Wait. That's where the nonsense had to stop. I shook my head, rotated my shoulders and cracked my knuckles. I was not going to allow myself to be carried away by conjured-up mock scenarios of how I could run into him again. First of all, men had been off my radar for quite some time, and second of all—there was no second of all. I simply wasn't interested in dating anyone. Ever.

I tried to convince myself of that, but with the heat radiating from my chest and nether regions, my body told me something different.

As if on cue, Rebecca stormed into my tiny, square office, her frizzy red hair flaming around her angry face. "Sara," the demon bellowed, "the show is in six weeks and I still don't have enough dancers. Where are my auditions?" Before I could answer her, she crossed her arms and eyed my coffee. "Where's my latte?"

"I'm sorry, Rebecca. Le Café Au Lait was closed and—"

"And you went to Int'l but couldn't bother to buy me a latte? Sometimes I wonder if you care enough about this job, Sara. It's one simple task and you can't even bother?"

"I'm your assistant not your personal punching bag or your coffee runner, Rebecca."

Her eyes bulged as she gasped.

"Don't look so shocked. You know you abuse me and I let you, so quit your gall. And in regard to your precious dancers, I'm doing my best to clean up the mess your choreographer keeps making." I grabbed a couple of portfolios and slammed them on my desk. "There's been plenty of applicants, but Alexei's requirements make it nearly impossible to find anyone that fits the bill. Dancers with the experience he wants are hard to come by. Most of the applicants are students fresh out of school. Perhaps if he stopped firing every one of our dancers—"

"He didn't fire anyone," she interrupted, quickly coming to his defense.

Clearly, I'd hit a nerve.

Sneering down at me, Rebecca approached my desk. "They all quit."

When I didn't say anything, she plopped onto the chair facing my desk. She wasn't fooling herself and certainly not me, but that didn't mean she wouldn't try. "Alexei is one of the best choreographers in the business. People should be lining up at the door dying to work with him." The inflection in her tone suggested otherwise.

Still, I'd had enough of her ignorant allegiance to that tyrant. We housed perfectly great dancers, but he always managed to find something wrong with everybody. Biting my tongue, I stood up from my chair and looked her square in the eyes. "They quit because he is an absolute nightmare. Alexei is positively the most pompous asshole I have ever known, and while he may be a renowned choreographer, his attitude also precedes him." I sat back down and looked away from her. "Experienced dancers don't want to work with him. Everyone knows how volatile he can be."

She pointed a finger at me in warning. "Careful, Sara. Your job is on the line here." Arms pretzeled across her bosom, she practiced her typical authoritative arrogance. "I don't care what you have to do, but I want auditions by next week. Get it done." With that, she stomped out my door. After the way I'd spoken to her, I was surprised she hadn't fired my ass on the spot.

I spun on my leather chair and turned to the glass wall behind me. Through the open slits of the dusty, white blinds, I stared out at Manhattan. I stood up and placed a finger between the plastic dividers, and from my third-story window, spied on the busy city streets of Times Square. Each day, countless people trekked past the studio, heading somewhere it seemed, with purpose. Yet, my life was so stagnant.

I glanced toward my desk and sighed. Stacks of paperwork sat untouched. That was not how I had envisioned myself years ago—sitting in front of a computer, sifting through emails. This couldn't be how I would spend the rest of my days.

As I stared at my sad excuse for a career, the portrait photo of a pretty brunette pinned inside an opened portfolio mocked me even more. My heart squeezed as I thought back to my days at Juilliard. Dancing had been my life force, the only thing that made me feel alive.

It should be me up on that stage. If only...

Memories of the fateful night flashed in front of me. The screeching tires, the scraping metal, the broken glass. My mother's screams. Then everything went silent and dark. My body shivered as I recalled the accident that changed everything. Shaking my head, I tucked those thoughts away and sat in front of my computer.

There was no use thinking about the past or about how things could be different. This was the path the universe had chosen for me —the life I was meant to live. After a couple of long breaths, I straightened in my seat and set to work.

Alexei wants dancers?

Sure thing, buttercup.

I took his list of requirements and deleted it from my desktop. Grabbing the pile of portfolios lying on top of my desk, I cold-called all those who could make it to the auditions last minute. Ten unknowing victims took the audition. One might make it out alive.

"If this doesn't get me fired, I don't know what will."

Two

TOM

Coffee Girl. That's what I dubbed her. I ran into the adorable stranger four hours ago at my usual caffeine pit stop and still couldn't get her out of my mind. Like an idiot, I didn't bother asking for her name. Or her number. I should've at least offered to buy her another cup of coffee given she'd spilled hers all over the floor and her blouse.

Damn. *That* blouse.

She must have known how absurdly sexy she looked wrapped in that silky white top, conservatively buttoned to her neck and tucked neatly into her black pencil skirt. My corporate sex fantasies exponentially expanded all in a matter of seconds. The way that blouse clung to her feminine figure made the gears in my brain stop spinning the instant I spotted her waiting for her order two people in front of me. Then her heel twisted as she turned to leave and she nearly fell flat on her face, coffee splattering all over the place.

On instinct, I dashed forward to make sure she was ok, but she managed to stay upright without calling much attention to herself. I stepped back and pretended I hadn't noticed her stumble. She furiously mumbled something incoherent, seeming flustered and annoyed with herself. It wasn't her morning, that much I could tell, and for some reason, I found myself wondering what caused her to be in such a tizzy.

The barista called me to the counter, forcing my attention away, but as I retrieved my iced Americano and turned to leave, Coffee Girl stood by the door, blocking my exit. She was in the process of wiping coffee stains off my already favorite white blouse when her gaze snapped up and met mine. Something in the way her chocolate-colored eyes twinkled made a string pull at my heart. It was as if I'd always known those eyes. Deep and sultry, they looked at me as if they could see into the deepest recesses of my soul.

Needing to shake the uneasy feeling, I rotated my shoulders, wondering if perhaps I did know her. Maybe I'd met her at a business dinner? At one of Jake's roof-top parties? I was terrible with faces, but that face was one I should have remembered.

"Excuse me, miss," I said with a gentle smile as I stopped in front of her. "Um, do I know you?"

She blinked fast several times, as if she too had been trying to place me. "I ... don't think so," she replied, her voice sweet and melodic.

My chest caved a little. A part of me had hoped we did know each other. The sparkle in her gaze dimmed, and I worried I was adding to her troubled morning by being so forward. "Oh, you always block the door for random strangers, then?" I teased, wishing to lighten up the mood. But her brow creased and her eyes flashed with uncertainty.

Snapping out of her daze and fumbling through her words, she said, "Oh, um...yes. I mean, no. Sorry, I just—"

I couldn't help the smirk that stretched across my lips. Christ, the way her mouth twitched in a nervous, uncomfortable smile made my heart melt. She was so goddamn adorable, and she probably didn't even know it. We drew in closer, pulled by a crackling energy I couldn't ignore.

Fuck. If I hadn't been running late for my business appointment, things might have panned out differently. I'd wanted to stay and explore whatever was happening between us, but the presence of other patrons standing behind me waiting to exit made me aware of how long we'd been standing there staring at each other. And instead of pulling her to the side to ask for her name, I leaned down and whispered in her right ear, "While I'd love nothing more than to gaze into your pretty brown eyes, you are going to have an angry mob on your hands in about two seconds."

She shivered as my breath brushed her skin, her face flushing as I pulled away. I drew her scent with me, and it was enough to knock me off kilter. Shit. She'd smelled good enough to lick. We locked eyes and for a brief second, I again contemplated skipping my meeting and standing up my client, the biggest high-rise developer in New York City. I would be giving my firm's most lucrative contract the middle finger. All for this girl. All because I needed to know why my body thrummed with such interest for someone I didn't know.

And right when I was about to ramp up the wattage on my charm, a memory poked at my brain. I wasn't the kind of guy she needed to get mixed up with. I wasn't dating material. For some reason, this girl didn't strike me as the type to be interested in a man like me, and I wasn't about to turn her into one. My dick tried to convince me otherwise.

Thank God I squashed that impending disaster before giving it time to sink its teeth into my flesh. I winked as I nodded for her to let me pass. "See ya 'round," I said with a playful grin as I rushed out the door, leaving my adorable, sexy stranger behind.

Now, hours later, perched up in my steel tower, staring out my office window ninety-three stories above Midtown, I simmered in regret for walking out of there without at least getting her name. I couldn't stop thinking about her. Where she was. Who she was with. What she was doing. Fucking. Hell. This was absurd. Something inside me warred with my instincts to forget about this girl, but I knew I wouldn't be able to stop thinking about her until I kissed her perfect mouth and tasted her silky skin.

And she would hate me for it. I already hated myself.

Shaking my head, I scolded myself for the plan already forming in my mind. I ran a palm down my face. This was not going to end well.

Three

SARA

After a grueling day at work, I finally made it home.

"Good evening, Señorita Hart. Hope you had a good day today," the nighttime doorman said, a bright smile spanning his face.

"Hi, Pedro. Just another day at the office. Um, did you see Ms. Roberts?" I asked, walking through the long, narrow lobby of my apartment building, dragging my feet on the white, tiled floors. When I reached the elevator, I leaned on the wall for support then pressed the call button.

"Oh, I saw Miss Jen go up a little while ago."

I rushed in as the elevator door opened. "Thanks, Pedro. See you tomorrow." Leaning against the mirrored back, I tilted my head up, closed my eyes, and let out a long breath, exhaling the frustrating day out of my body. It wasn't even Rebecca or Alexei who tormented me. Those two I could handle. Not being able to focus on my work because I was day dreaming of Olive Eyes—that was the new bane of my existence.

Drinking coffee was impossible without thoughts of Mr. Iced Double invading my mind. He'd single-handedly highjacked my morning routine and apparently my afternoon and evening as well. With relief, as I entered my apartment, the welcoming aromas emanating from the kitchen greeted me.

My best friend, Jen, had returned from her week-long trip to Boston. She'd been visiting her boyfriend, Marko, and I couldn't be happier she was back.

"Jen?" I called out to her as I walked through the foyer, scooping my orange tabby cat, Skiddles.

"In here," Jen sang sweetly. "Cooking pasta."

I strolled over to the small open kitchen, nuzzling Skiddles' nose while she purred her welcome. Jen's curly blonde locks were pulled up in a messy bun. She wore her hot pink apron, grooving to country music as she drained the raviolis over the sink. My keys and purse dropped on the counter and with a long breath, I plopped on one of the barstools facing the kitchen. Skiddles squirmed out of my arms.

"What's the matter, hon, Rebecca grind you to the bone today?"

"I guess," I grumbled, folding my arms over the counter.

She put the drainer down and looked at me. "You guess?" She seemed incredulous. Continuing to stare me down, she pinched her brows, as if trying to solve some mystery about me.

"What?" I asked.

"I don't know. Usually you have some crazy story about Rebecca or Alexei you can't wait to tell me. Something seems off."

"It's nothing." I shifted on my stool and rested my chin on my hand.

Jen poured the ravs into a big pasta bowl and tossed in the sauce. "Nothing? That normally means it's something."

"Just had a long day."

She scoffed. "You're really trying to feed me that bullshit, as if I haven't known you practically all your life? Something's got you mopey and it ain't work. What happened today?"

"Do we really have to do this right now; can't it wait at least until after dinner?"

She looked up from her stovetop while continuing to stir something simmering in a pot. She raised an eyebrow. Her shimmery blue eyes were determined not to let me slide. "No. Now spill it."

Images of my mom lying motionless next to me in my car clawed at my soul.

Jen could read me so well. I hated it when she did that.

In the four years since the accident, I hadn't talked much about it. I tried not to think about it either. Things were easier that way. It was simply too painful. Now, the memories were resurfacing and I didn't know why.

Mr. Iced Double was a much easier topic. After all, he was the other reason I was in the pits, reminding me how lonely and pathetic my love life was.

Noticing the fruit-filled bowl on the counter, I reached for an orange and tossed it back and forth between my hands. "Fine. I met this guy."

She froze mid stir. "You met a guy." It wasn't even a question.

Straightening up in my chair, I said, "Well, not exactly met him-met him. I mean, I ran into Mr. Iced Double at Int'l and I can't seem to shake him. Don't know why I can't get him out of my head."

She smiled with a glint of triumph in her eyes.

Good. She thinks she cracked me.

"So, who is this...what did you call him, iced what?" she asked as she sprinkled some basil over the pot.

"Who knows. It's not like we talked. And it's Mr. Iced Double."

"You've definitely been giving this guy some thought."

I shot her an icy look.

"Is he hot?" she asked.

"Is he hot?" I repeated, perking up and swiveling on my barstool.

"Molten lava scorching type of hot. This guy is so out of my league." I stopped mid turn to look back at Jen. "I mean, he's probably some high-power executive and I'm...well, we know what I am."

Jen continued to stir.

"He was wearing like a tailored designer suit for crying out loud," I chuckled. "I shop at the local thrift shop."

"Nothing wrong with a thrift shop, honey."

Probably.

But that wasn't really what bothered me. It was the way his gaze penetrated me, as if he saw past my façade. "His eyes were...the kind that can cut through bullshit, you know?"

She laughed. "Thought you were gonna say they were mystifying or some type of fairy sparkly blue."

I inhaled deeply as I remembered the moment we saw each other. "Olive. With twinkly streaks of honey."

She cackled. "Look at you all dreamy-eyed."

What? No. I didn't do dreamy-eyed.

"Don't be ridiculous. I'm not the high-power executive type of woman. I'm more the no-man-in-my-life type right now, so..."

"For a no-man type of woman, this man sure is on your mind." Her gaze met mine, an eyebrow hiked. "Plus, high power executives don't buy their own coffee."

Trying to mask a smirk, I rolled my eyes and shrugged. "Maybe."

The smell of the simmering sauce pulled my attention. "This is my first home-cooked dinner in forever," I said as I nodded toward the pot. "I've been eating crap, not sleeping well..."

"How many times have you seen him?"

God, she's persistent.

"Just this morning."

Jen plopped two meatballs onto my plate. "I made your favorite, by the way. Veal."

"Lord, I've missed you."

After placing a plate in front of me, she took a seat next to mine and tucked a loose strand of hair behind my ear. "You know you are beautiful, right?"

Not saying anything, I stared at my food and took a big bite of one of the moist meatballs. Nirvana hit my taste buds.

"Maybe you should say hello next time you see him. You know, strike up a conversation or something."

I nearly choked on my chunk of heaven and had to take a big gulp of water to clear my throat. "Me? Strike up a conversation? Okay...yeah. I'm not you, Ms. Social Butterfly. I can't just strike up a conversation with this guy. I won't be going there anymore anyway, so it doesn't even matter."

She threw her hands up in the air. "Seriously? There you go again, always running away."

"Running away? What are you talking about?"

"You know exactly what I'm talking about. Ever since Josh left, you bolt at the mere thought of meeting a guy. I don't get it. You can't be alone forever, you know. You're going to have to tear down that wall someday."

"I hate it when you bring him up. This has nothing to do with him."

She popped a few raviolis in her mouth then pointed her barren fork at me. "Yes, it does and you know it, Sara. You need to let go of the past and move on."

"Why? So, I can get my heart ripped out of my chest again? No, thank you. I've got enough problems to worry about. I don't need guy drama to add to it."

"You see, that's just it. Why does it have to be guy drama? We all need love. It's time you let someone in to take care of you." She placed her hand over mine and gave it a light squeeze.

Sliding my hand from under hers, I said, "That train's come and gone. I can't endure another loss, Jen. I can't." I knew she was trying to be helpful. Encouraging, even. We'd had this conversation before. I wasn't ready to let anyone in. Didn't know if I'd ever be.

"You are so afraid people are going to leave you. You can't live life like that. Haven't I been here for you always?" she asked.

"Yes, and that's why I love you. Can we not talk about this anymore? This guy...it's nothing. Really."

"Yeah, well, your eyes tell a different story."

"Stop reading into things. I told you. It's nothing."

She gave up and turned to her plate. "If you say so."

I didn't like to talk about my past, especially Josh. He was the reason I was so fucked up in the head when it came to men. Bringing him up only reminded me of the terrible mistakes I made in dating him.

So, I did the one thing I knew best. Deflecting.

"How was Boston, by the way?" I asked, changing the subject.

After dinner, as I loaded the dishwasher, I noticed the cheap bottle of white wine Rebecca had given me at Christmas still sitting on the counter. I was more of a cabernet type of girl, but with the way my day had gone, I desperately needed a drink. With resignation, I broke the seal and poured myself a glass.

After queuing a jazzy tune on our sound system, I walked toward the tall living-room windows of the high-rise, two-bedroom apartment. They showcased a clear evening over Central Park. I cracked open a pane to let in some air. Only a handful of pedestrians trotted along the Upper East Side. Some walked their dogs while others were out for a night jog. The loud churning sea of yellow cabs had receded and all that remained was the low and steady hum of light traffic. The rustling sound of leaves was carried sweetly through the window, and the cool breeze brushing in caressed my skin.

I tried to enjoy the quiet of my solitude, but the silence of it all eventually made me crave morning so I wouldn't feel so alone.

Resigned, I chugged the rest of the bitter wine and stared at the empty glass cradled in my palm.

"Why can't I stop thinking about you, Olive Eyes?"

I'd promised to never let myself be fooled again. Since then, no one had spurred desire in me—especially after the way my last relationship ended. I was convinced my heart had turned into an unbreakable iceberg. Yet today, one pair of mesmerizing eyes had managed to crack the icy surface.

I could feel my heart again.

The notion unnerved me.

He was out there, somewhere in the concrete jungle, and I was up here, perched in my tower, thinking about him.

"O Romeo, Romeo, wherefore art thou Romeo?"

I chuckled.

Talking to myself. I must be going crazy.

I'd never dwelled on the memory of a complete stranger before. Or hit the replay button so numerously, trying to recall an encounter with someone so badly, I picked it apart to its most miniscule detail. His strut oozed of manliness. His voice was like melted butter, warm and silky. And his lips... I'd never seen lips so full and inviting.

Did I mention they were moist?

Christ, I could've quenched my thirst on them.

Yeah, denying the effect his body had on me was pointless. Warm currents ran up and down my spine every time he made cameos in my mind. I'd been man-less for four years, but I was still human. Yet, it was the drum beat in my chest and the ache I felt in my soul that truly unsettled me.

Maybe I'd blown things out of proportion. Olive Eyes probably wouldn't even be able to pick me out of a lineup, yet I couldn't stop thinking about him.

I shook my head.

What the hell happened to me?

It didn't make sense. And neither did drinking cheap wine by myself on a Friday night while day dreaming about a guy I'd probably never see again.

As I scanned around the room, a part of me couldn't let go of the loneliness curdling inside my chest. My eerily silent, closet-size living room felt as immense and vacant as a black hole. I swallowed a large gulp of air and went to bed. Whatever was making my mind churn with unease would be gone by morning.

At least by Monday. For sure.

I hoped.

Four

TOM

As I readied to head out to work on Monday morning, I snuck a glance at myself in the foyer mirror. A smirk tugged on my lips as I adjusted the collar of my shirt and buttoned my suit jacket. Bax, my chocolate lab, sat at my heel, looking up at me, a goofy dog smile on his face.

You are not seriously considering going back there he seemed to say as if he could read my mind.

I crouched beside him and scratched his head. "I know. Definitely not like me. What are the chances she shows up, though?" I asked him, dumbly hoping he could talk me out of it. He cocked his head, ears perked. "Yeah, I'm confused about this whole thing myself."

Standing, I looked at my reflection again and rubbed at the day-old scruff. Couldn't believe I'd been so preoccupied with thoughts of Coffee Girl I hadn't bothered to shave. I also hadn't bothered to check her ring finger to see if she was even single. Not that the lack of one would mean she didn't have a boyfriend.

This was ridiculous. I had a company to run. Worrying about some girl at a coffee shop was the last thing I needed on my mind. But she wasn't just some girl, was she? She was the girl with the sultry brown eyes and timid smile. The girl with the white blouse that had me fantasizing about what she looked like underneath all that silky fabric. And she had been on my fucking mind.

All goddamn weekend.

Not thinking about Coffee Girl had been a failed mission. It nearly drove me insane. I wanted to see her again. Needed to.

Tiff could make a coffee run. I could order my Americano on the app and have it delivered straight to my office.

Coulda shoulda.

Fuck. I had a feeling I was gonna regret this.

With a resigned breath, I told Bax I'd see him later and grabbed the keys to my Range Rover before dashing out the door of my Hoboken river view apartment. Some days, I took the ferry across the Hudson. Other days, I didn't feel like dealing with crowds and drove in instead. Today, I drove in because I was anxious to get to the coffee house early. I couldn't remember the last time I'd been this eager to get into the city. The amount of times I face-palmed while stuck in tunnel traffic was comical. All for Coffee Girl. Who was likely not even going to be there.

Once I made it in to Midtown and to our office building, I handed the keys to our valet and took off on foot. A block away from Rockefeller, sweaty beads rolled down my back. If Jake saw me now, he wouldn't let me live this down. The man was always trying to drag me to where he claimed were the hottest spots in the city and the easiest places to hook up with beautiful women. I wasn't a tail chaser, though. I didn't like going around town hitting up bars looking for sex. The women who wound up tangled in my sheets were typically women I already knew. Women who didn't care I wasn't looking for attachments but were cool with just a helluva good time in bed.

Yet, there I was, tail chasing at a coffee house.

I arrived at eight on the dot and as always, the place was packed. I nonchalantly scouted the interior looking for Brown Eyes, but was quickly deflated when there was no sign of her.

Idiot. You've now become a creepy stalker.

Bummed I'd rushed there for nothing, I walked up to the counter to place my order when my cell rang. *Speak of the Devil.* "Hey man, what's up?" I said, placing the phone to my ear. "Yeah. I'll be in a few minutes. We got the sale, Jake. Don't worry. I'm telling you, man, we got it. The presentation was seamless…hold on a sec." I looked up at the barista waiting to take my order. "Hey, Em. The usual. And I'll take a blueberry muffin too, thanks." I paid the girl and moved on to the next counter to grab my order.

"Till tomorrow, Mr. Wright!" she said, batting her eyes.

Phone still to my ear, I smiled back as I turned to leave and nearly dropped my phone when I spotted Brown Eyes sitting at a table by the door. She tucked a loose strand of hair behind her ear, shying her gaze away as if she didn't want to make eye-contact with me. She was as stunning as I remembered.

Just ask her, asshole Ask for her name.

But for some fucking reason I couldn't decipher, I kept walking, fingers itching to touch a silky strand of her hair, and berating myself a million times over inside my head for not turning around and ending the game. I pushed through the double doors and immediately reached up and loosened up my tie. I didn't realize how flushed I felt until fresh air hit my face.

"Tom, you still there? Tom?"

Fuck. I'd forgotten Jake was on the line. "Yeah, man. Look, I'll see you in a few minutes."

∼

Located on Fifth Avenue across the street from St. Patrick's Cathedral, our Commercial and Luxury Real State office was situated on the ninety-third floor of one of the tallest skyscrapers in Midtown, offering a perfect Birdseye view of Manhattan. I stood in front of the wall of windows of my private office, gazing out toward the city as I did every day, except, the views of my city no longer hit the same way, not when I knew she was somewhere out there.

My personal assistant, Tiffany, sat in front of my desk, briefing me on my schedule for the day, but I could hardly concentrate on what she said. All I kept thing about was about my brown-eyed Coffee Girl and where she could be at the moment.

Jake stormed through the door, snagging my attention and temporarily distracting me from my thoughts.

"Hey, Tiff," he said, his blonde hair bright as the sun. "Can I have a private word with Tom?" His grey silk suit practically gleamed under the morning rays blasting through my office windows. He looked like a shark prowling the seas for prey. This usually spelled trouble.

Tiff threw him a side glance that spoke volumes of her distaste toward him, but she stood, red hair dancing over her shoulders as she pressed her tablet to her chest. "Call me when you're ready," she said to me as she exited, not offering a word to Jake.

"Dude, what's her problem?" Jake asked, taking the seat she'd just vacated.

"Could be the fact you're a bit of an asshole to her."

He shrugged. "She's a beautiful girl. What girl doesn't like to be told that?"

"When she's made it quite clear she's not interested in you, it's called harassment."

He leaned forward, blue eyes narrowing over me. "Or she's still hung up on you."

I wasn't in the mood to breach *that* topic, especially when that ship had sailed ages ago. "I take it you're here to talk about the Cantanello Developers?"

He nodded, knee bouncing up and down impatiently.

"I told you they are practically ready to sign. It's a done deal."

"Not until Cantanello signs. What the hell is taking him so long?" he asked.

Unbuttoning my suit jacket, I sat on my leather chair and opened up my laptop. "It's a billion-dollar investment. This is standard procedure. You know this. What's really going on?"

He wiped at the sweat beading on his forehead. "I need this commission, okay? Can't have this asshole backing out at the last minute."

I eyed him with suspicion and a bit of concern. "He won't. And if you're having money issues again, that's a separate problem."

Jake jumped from his chair, eyes darkening. "Know what, I don't need a lecture from you. Just let me know when you hear back from Dan, okay? A week to review the paperwork is more than enough time. Either he wants the damn property or not."

"I'll give his agent a call. Nudge him a little if it makes you feel better."

"Good. I'll be in my office." Flustered, he stormed back out.

Pressure built between my shoulders as I watched him leave. I hated seeing him consumed by anxiety, but he wasn't one to listen to reason. Jake was my best friend and we shared a history that went beyond being business partners. We'd been enlisted in the military together and were practically brothers, so I knew when he was being plagued by something. And given his desperation over the commission of this deal, I could only surmise it had to do with his gambling debts.

We'd been down this road before and I'd bailed him out more times than I wished to remember, but this was worse than I had ever seen. Way worse.

I pinched the bridge of my nose and leaned back on my chair

when a text notification popped up on my phone. My brother, James, and I had recently reconnected and he'd been trying exceptionally hard to get me to go up to Lake George and visit him and mom. The thought iced my blood. It's the one place I swore I'd never return to—too many shitty memories. I looked at his text again:

Penny and I are celebrating our engagement this weekend. Mom's letting us use the lake house to throw a small dinner party. Would love it if you could make it. LMK

Fuck. How was I supposed to get out of this one? I wanted to see him and mom. And I wanted to meet his fiancé. I just couldn't bring myself to make the trip to the lake house. Not after everything that happened with my father. With Shayna. Not after the way I left.

I decided to leave the text unanswered. James would understand. He had to.

Expunging a deep breath, I chose to bury myself in work. It was the only way I knew how to keep myself from ruminating about my brother's party or about Jake. Coffee Girl, though?

She was already running through my veins and I hadn't even tasted her. My craving for her was going to be harder to ignore.

Five

SARA

Like a silly school girl, I giggled on my walk back to the dance company from the coffee house.

*The usual...*he'd said to the barista. Mr. Iced Double was a regular and I literally had to hold back a chortle the instant I heard her say *'Till tomorrow, Mr. Wright.*

Mr. Wright. He couldn't have been any more of a walking cliché if he tried. With his ludicrously perfect smile, body built like a tight-end, and a voice that could hypnotize, I mean, who wouldn't drool for the guy? He strutted like a lion claiming his territory, and everyone around him practically parted the seas to let him pass.

I didn't realize how hard I'd been staring at his broad shoulders and sculpted backside until he turned around, almost catching me staring at him. I shielded my gaze like a dumbass because the guy made me so nervous my thoughts turned to mashed potatoes in his presence.

Couldn't deny that a part of me caved when he didn't recognize me from the other day. Though, maybe if I hadn't pretended like he didn't exist, he may have dared to ask me for my number. I shook my head at the dumb thought. The guy was so out of my league.

Still, I couldn't keep my eyes from putting a GPS lock on his bodacious body as he dashed out the door in some type of hurry.

A long breath puffed from my chest, wondering where he was headed to or if perhaps I'd have another chance to see him soon.

Soon...because I was clearly already contemplating continuing to stalk him.

Back at the company, Rebecca ran down the hallway, hair flying, eyes bulging, chasing after three more dancers who were threatening to leave if Alexei didn't change. "You're damned lucky to be dancing at all in this city, you ungrateful brats. With Alexei Voronov, mind you."

After demoralizing Jess, Estella, and Danny, she made me clean up the mess. It wasn't unusual. While I was her assistant, everyone knew I didn't necessarily hold any loyalties to her, so the dancers used me as their pincushion to vent their frustrations.

I played peacemaker—for their sake, not Rebecca's. I knew the endless hours they devoted to rehearsals. Food and sleep were a luxury. These dancers ate and breathed their routines as if their lives depended on it. I wasn't going to allow them to throw their dreams away because of one arrogant, heartless choreographer who arrived late when God handed out souls.

Two hours after stroking their egos and promising them Alexei wasn't always going to be our head choreographer, I managed to convince Jess and Danny this job was only a stepping stone to an even bigger and brighter future. They agreed to stay.

Two down. One to go.

Before calling Estella into my office, I trudged into the kitchen to fetch some of our notoriously stale, afternoon coffee. With lead-laced limbs, I sluggishly reached for the pot, poured myself a cup, and plopped on a chair at one of the tiny lunch tables, hoping to relieve my body of the strain of Rebecca's and Alexie's baleful antics. I needed to summon happy thoughts—anything to help dissolve the mind-twisting problems of the company's circus. As my brain painted a beach getaway in Tahiti, a pair of olive-colored eyes materialized in front of me.

"Girl, what you smiling at, 'cause it sure ain't about that shit you're drinking?" Martha's voice startled me out of my day dream.

"Oh, hey," I said, shaking my head. "I wasn't smiling."

"Yes. You were. Like a big-ass grin. What's his name?"

"Whose name?"

"The guy who's got you all stupefied, that's who."

Jeez, is it that obvious?

I smoothed down my hair and took a sip of the battery acid in my cup. Avoiding her gaze, I said, "You're too funny. You know I don't believe in men."

Martha let out a belly laugh as she walked to the fridge and retrieved a yogurt. She took a seat next to me and peeled off the top to her afternoon snack. Martha's mocha-colored eyes twinkled and her black curly hair cascaded to her shoulders. She looked me straight in the eyes and did her famous head-jiggy, the one she gave people trying to sidestep an issue. "Honey, you ain't fooling nobody. You've been acting strange since last Friday."

"Define strange," I said.

"For starters, you've been walking around all spacey and now you're drinking...that." She nodded toward my cup.

"Well, I need caffeine, and right now I don't give a rat's ass how it tastes." I smiled then added, "And I'm not spacey."

She rolled her eyes.

"What?"

"Fine. Don't tell me. I'll figure it out. Is it the new delivery guy? He's kinda cute, although a bit bony for my tastes. You know I like my men plump and juicy," she reminded me as she licked her spoon.

"No. It's not Adam."

"Ooh, you know his name," she chirped.

"Everyone knows his name, so stop it. There's no guy. You know I'd tell you if there was."

"Right. Anyway, back to work." She threw the yogurt cup in the trash and winked at me before leaving the kitchen. "Say hi to Adam for me."

I laughed.

His name is Mr. Iced Double.

I poured the remaining coffee down the drain and went searching for number three—the beautiful, brunette starlet, Estella. She proved harder to convince and after much deliverance, I was forced to use my last card. "As a Russian immigrant with a pending legal status, finding another dancing job in the city could be difficult, Estella. I guess, you could try your luck back home."

She sat in front of my desk, eyes filled with brimstone, arms crossed in frustration, aware we had her pinned.

It was a low blow, but Rebecca made me use it to our advantage. When Estella sent us her portfolio, we knew we'd hit the jackpot. We immediately offered to sponsor her green card, contingent upon her staying with the company at least for a year after obtaining legal status. Estella would have been picked up by any dance company in Europe, but we knew she wanted to come to the U.S. to be close to her family.

Having to practically coerce her made my stomach churn with disgust. I really despised Rebecca for making me use Estella's family against her, but reminding her of the promise she made helped change her mind. By the time the day ended, I'd saved the company from having one amazing show but no performers. I could have patted myself on the back, instead I felt like I'd sold my soul to the devil.

On my way home that night, I passed Rockefeller Plaza. It wasn't my normal route, and I tried to convince myself it was just a coincidence I'd taken a different way home, but lying to myself was lame. As soon as I spotted the coffeehouse, my chest tightened as thoughts of Mr. Iced Double rushed in. What would be the chances he'd stop for a cup of Joe after work? Maybe if I ran into him again I'd finally have the guts to say hi. Perhaps he'd see me and this time ask for my number?

Summoning courage, I pushed through The Int'l House of Java's doors and noticed Pretty Little Emily was still tending the counter. I ran my fingers across my brow, smoothing away the tension.

"May I take your order?" she asked as I reached the counter. Her eyebrows pinched in the middle as she tipped her salon-perfect, blonde bob, making it swoosh at her neck.

"I'll have a medium cappuccino with skim milk. Two raw sugars and cinnamon powder, please," I replied.

"Will that be all?"

"Um..."

"Hey, Bob," a man said behind me. "Yeah, it's a done deal...I'm serious...drinks at The Pussy Cat's Meow tonight. Eight. See ya later, man."

Iced Double.

My body temperature immediately skyrocketed from cool to scorching. "Actually, just the coffee," I said to Ms. Googly-Eyes.

The counter girl looked up, a smile stretching past her cheekbones. "Evening, Mr. Wright."

My hands trembled and my clothes dampened from all the perspiration.

Sweating like a hog. Oh, yeah, this is attractive.

Not wanting to trip again, I carefully pivoted, but my heel twisted anyway and I went flying.

As I shut my eyes, bracing for the face-plant, Iced Double said, "Whoa, careful there."

When I opened my eyes, my face inches away from his mystic green gaze and luscious lips, I turned to stone in his strong arms.

"You okay?" A short smile pulled at the corners of his mouth as he held me.

"Um ... yeah. Th-thank...you," I stammered.

His crooked smile only widened, melting me in his arms. Goosebumps flared throughout my skin as he settled me back on my feet. I steadied myself, straightened my twill dress, and glanced up as his twinkling gaze once again. Heavens. The man was tall.

"Looks like you keep falling for me," he said with a chuckle, his smile broadening as he waited for me to respond.

My brain failed to compute what happened. My thoughts were a jumbled mess.

Say something witty, you klutz.

All I could muster was a shrug and an awkward laugh.

He frowned.

Iced Double had flirted with me and I'd basically brushed him off.

His glorious smile faded. "Okay..." he droned, nodding goodbye. Then he turned back to the counter to order his espresso.

Mortified, I lowered my head, grabbed my coffee from the counter, and scurried away.

Shit. Shit. Shit. That was not how I'd intended things to go.

Mental note to self—start wearing flats.

Feeling utterly foolish, I stomped out of there determined to never return.

This time, I really mean it.

But when did people actually have a say in how things panned out? And why couldn't I stop thinking about this guy? About wanting to get to know him better? About wanting to experience what it would be like to be kissed by him?

Sara, the hopeless romantic...

Scratch that. I didn't believe in that crap. Not anymore. I was Sara, the one with no hope of ever finding true love.

Yet, if that's what I truly believed, why did I pull out my phone to text Jen?

Me: *Hey, any plans tonight?*

Jen: *Working a double. Why?*

Me: *Just wondering*

Jen: *Why?*

Me: *No reason. Gotta go.*

I didn't like lying to Jen, but I also wasn't up for a lecture. Contemplating a stop by The Pussy Cat's Meow, a nightclub downtown? All by myself? To look for a guy I didn't even know?

Yeah. I'd gone from not believing in soulmates to becoming a total psycho.

Six

SARA

THERE WAS NO PLAN. I WAS GOING TO SIT IN A CORNER and spy on him like some pervert. If Jen found out, I'd never hear the end of it. Our girl's safety code—expertly crafted by her when we turned twenty-one and began hitting the clubs—was to never go out to a bar alone, never go home with a guy you just met, and never get into his car.

Perhaps a part of me wanted a glimpse of who this guy might be outside of his business suit. Maybe if I saw him with another woman on his arm, the childish infatuation would incinerate, allowing me to return to my normal, mundane life. All I knew was that I wanted to see him. The how and what would all play out once I got there.

Dressed in skinny jeans and killer heels, I took the service stairs leading straight to the parking garage. They were steeper than I would have liked to climb down in four-inch shoes, but I didn't want to listen to Pedro comment on my late-night excursion. Given I was already breaking the girl safety code, I opted to drive my beat-up Jeep instead of using the train.

I drove down to Third Street and circled the block about seven times before a spot finally opened up across the street from The Pussy Cat's Meow. Of course, the previous car had likely been a toy car and fitting in there wasn't easy. I had to squeeze the Jeep's fat ass into the spot. It would've helped if the idiot stationed in front of me hadn't taken two spots. If it'd been anything but a beautiful new black Range Rover, I would have accidentally hit the back bumper—a couple of times.

Well, it did have Jersey plates, so that explained it.

The place buzzed with activity as I bobbed and weaved through the crowd, searching for his familiar face. There were several floors and rooms playing different types of music, from hip hop to dance to merengue. I searched the entire club for Mr. Iced Double, but there was no sign of him. A spot by the bar opened up, so I leaned my back on the counter and stared out at the scores of skinny women sipping their overly priced cocktails. They scanned the room for a potential hottie to buy them their next drink. I sighed and hung my head. Things were not going according to plan.

Then again, I never had a plan. Or perhaps somewhere in the deep, unexplored corners of my mind I had formulated some makeshift plan; I might waltz in there and spot him sitting on one of the lounge booths, hanging with two of his buddies. He'd spot me and be lured by my mystical beauty (I could be mystical in my fantasy) and he'd gallantly stroll to my side and say in his sexiest voice...

"Hey, can I buy you a drink?" a man asked in a seductive tone, startling me out of my day dream.

I turned toward the voice, my face contorted in confusion. "Huh?"

A very handsome young man sat next to me on a stool. "Can I buy you a drink?" he repeated. His short-cropped, black hair, sparkly-blue eyes, and chiseled chin made him any girl's dream. With a practiced sexy smile, he waited for my response. On a different night, I may have been amused by the attention, perhaps even entertained it. Right then, I was more annoyed than anything Mr. Hot and Steamy sitting next to me wasn't my Mr. Iced Double.

With a similarly practiced smile, I refused him. "Aw, thank you, but I'm actually the designated driver tonight. And we're just getting ready to leave." I pointed to my phantom friend in the crowd. "Oh, and there she is. Thanks again, bye."

I scurried off before he could say another word. As I tromped out, the cauldron of the club's belly spat me out onto the concrete, the night breeze splashing against my burning face. I jumped in my car and sat there, white-knuckling the wheel for a minute, reflecting on what I'd done.

I remembered my high school days and chasing after boys. Jen and I would stalk our crushes at football games. It's how I ended up with Josh.

Ugh, Josh.

I shook my head.

Time to go.

At least no one knew about my hunting expedition.

As I turned the ignition, my relief switched to anguish. The Jeep wouldn't start. I turned the key, but my engine responded with a fast-clicking sound. "Come on." I leaned back on my chair and growled.

I popped the hood and jumped out of the car. It was pointless. I didn't know anything about cars, but I needed to do something. My automatic door-lock was broken, so out of habit, as I got out of the car, I manually locked the car door and slammed it shut before realizing the keys were still in the ignition.

Shit.

No car, no keys, no phone. And without my handbag, I had no money for a cab. The night could not be any worse. I couldn't even reach the front of my car because Asshole-Range-Rover-Jersey-driver was still parked in front of me.

As I kicked the front wheel of my truck, footsteps approached from behind.

"Whoa there, whatever it is, don't take it out on the car," a man called out.

As I turned around, I was whacked on the side of the head with a sledgehammer.

Then the world faded to black.

Seven

SARA

Okay, so I wasn't actually slugged with a sledgehammer, but I might as well have been. Mr. Iced Double walked toward me and I nearly fainted when I saw him. I came-to as a spike of adrenaline surged from my gut, trying to shoot my heart out of my chest. The sight of him would've knocked me off my feet were it not for the roots sprouting from my feet. Anchored to the ground, I stood solid as an oak tree.

He came closer, and spotting the hood open, glanced over my shoulder.

Afraid any sudden sound or movement would startle me awake from my dream, I held my breath.

"Car trouble?" he asked, his lips curled to one side.

I slowly released the air trapped in my lungs. "Um..." was all that came out. The English language might as well have been a lost ancient tongue. Befuddled and unable to speak, I simply nodded yes.

"Want me to look under the hood for you?"

Blood rushed to the surface of my skin as other thoughts not related to my car flipped through my mind. I ran a nervous hand through my hair, shaking the thoughts out of my head before he could notice.

Get it together, Sara.

I cleared my throat. "Oh, you mean the hood of my car?"

The confused expression on his face said it all.

Dumbass, what other hood is there?

"I...mean...you can't...I mean..." I rambled. As I stared at his weary eyes, I sucked in a deep breath and gathered my thoughts. "What I mean is, you can't look under the hood because the asshole who parked this SUV apparently thinks he owns the streets or something."

His eyebrows pinched into a tight knot. "Asshole, huh?" Iced Double took something out of his pocket, clicked it, and the Range Rover unlocked.

My cheeks turned to hot coals.

Shit. Asshole-Jersey-Driver.

He walked over to the curb, examined his parking job, and placing his hands on his waist, he confirmed my accusation with a chuckle. "I guess I did park like an asshole."

"Look, I didn't mean to call you an—"

He narrowed his eyes. "—hey, you're the coffee girl from today."

Wait. Did he recognize me?

"I'm sorry, what did you say?" I played stupid.

"We've been running into each other lately." He waited for a response. "You almost fell earlier...I caught you..." He slowly tilted his head, his eyes bright with the hope he'd jogged my memory.

The mini-me inside my head did back flips and cartwheels. *He remembered me. He remembered me.* The words echoed in my mind. Thankfully, I knew how to keep my inside voice, inside.

He dropped his gaze, disappointment washing over his eyes. "I'm sorry. I thought you might have recognized me. Now I feel like an idiot."

Great, he thinks I'm an ice queen.

In reality, my beating muscle was on overdrive, pumping boiling blood through my veins. I struggled to stay composed, sweat beading down my back. I needed to break out of the iceberg containing my volcano or the night would end in an epic fail of monumental proportions. "Oh, wait. You're the guy from today? Yeah, I think I remember now. Sorry I didn't recognize you."

Liar.

"Oh." He forced a tight grin, further confirming his disappointment.

"And...here we are running into each other again," I said with a smile, trying to make him feel better. "Or are you stalking me or something, coffee guy?"

Light returned to his eyes, accompanied by that curling lip. "I don't think so, coffee girl. I think you're the stalker."

My eyes widened as I stared in horror.

His smile stretched wider. "Relax, I'm joking. It's a pleasant coincidence though."

I looked away, trying not to turn into a melted puddle of goo. He walked to the front of the Rover and in that velvety voice of his, he said, "Let me move the car up so we can take a look at what's happening under there."

Iced Double was positively stunning in his black, button-down shirt, which he left untucked and slightly folded at the wrists. His dark designer boot-cut jeans sat just below the waist. He finished off his outfit with black leather, tapered-toe boots.

Stepping out of the car, he did a short jog back to my Jeep. He lifted the hood higher and handed me a small silver flashlight he pulled from his back pocket. Olive Eyes folded his sleeves higher, exposing his chorded forearms. They were dusted in fine, dark hair. I couldn't stop staring at his big masculine hands. He tucked his head under the hood and I handed him the flashlight. My hand gently skimmed over his skin, excitement surging through my body.

He poked around the machinery. I didn't know what he was doing, but there was something sexy about watching him work under the hood of my car. After a few moments, he popped his head back up. "It's your battery."

"So, what now?"

"I can jump you."

My saliva caught in my throat and I swallowed hard—down the wrong pipe. "Jump me?" I coughed.

Is there anything he can say that won't cause my mind to head dive into the effing gutter?

"You all right?" he asked, a flicker of amusement dancing in his eyes as I continued to spurt out little coughs.

I forced the frog out of my throat with a fist pump to my chest, blinking away wetness and taking a deep breath. "I'm good."

"I'll get my jumper cables. Just turn the ignition when I tell you."

As he turned toward the trunk of his car, I waved a hand at the Jeep. "Um, actually, I locked myself out."

He cupped the back of his neck with his broad hand and sliced his head to the side. "You're not having much of an evening."

"Nope."

He hiked an eyebrow. "You know, I could give you a ride to your place if you want. I mean, if you have a spare key at home I can bring you back and jump you then."

Shit. There goes my mind again.

"I don't know…" I wavered.

"Look, I know you don't know me, but I promise I'm not some serial killer."

"Isn't that exactly what a serial killer might say?"

"Probably, but I promise you I'm not. I can't leave you here alone. It's not safe. Really. I wouldn't be able to live with myself if I read about you in the paper tomorrow."

"That's morbid."

"I'm serious. I'm not about to leave you here all damsel-in-distress." He placed a hand over his heart. "That wouldn't be too gallant of me now, would it?" His luscious lips thinned into a straight line that curled upward at the ends. The luring smile infected his eyes as well, and before I knew it, I was lost in those dark-green, reflective pools.

Darn. He's good.

I cocked an eyebrow. "So, I'm a damsel in distress?"

"Are you coming or am I gonna have to come over there and sling you across my shoulder?"

I raised my palms and stopped him from coming forward. "Hold your horse, Mr. Knight in Shining Armor. We just met." The girl safety sign zipped around my head, but I quickly swatted it down and walked toward his car. He jogged over to the passenger side, and as he leaned in to open the door, I caught a scent tendril of his cologne. Oh, he smelled so scrumptious. I was gripped by the sudden urge to press my nose against his neck and inhale him.

Stop it. Just get in the car and focus on getting yourself home and safe.

The Range Rover's interior was upholstered in exquisite jet-black leather and wood veneers. It spewed power and masculinity.

Iced Double stepped into the driver seat and buckled up. "Where to?"

"Um, Upper East Side, please."

As he started up the engine, I turned toward him. "So, what's your name?"

"Tom."

"I'm Sara."

"Pleasure to meet you, Sara. What're you doing alone downtown at this hour?"

"I...ah...met up with some coworkers for drinks...we...were...celebrating my coworker's promotion."

Did I mention I'm also a terrible liar?

"I see." He looked briefly at me then went back to driving. "And your friends let you walk to your car alone?"

"I'm a big girl, I don't need a chaperone. It's not like I've never driven alone at night. I know the city pretty well."

"When you drive an older car, you run the risk of breaking down."

"Hey, not everyone can afford to drive a fancy-shmancy car like you, you know," I said smiling at him, sweeping a hand over the dashboard.

He grinned. "Shmancy even a word?"

"Your car is very nice."

"I know," he reaffirmed as his grin hooked at the corner of his lips.

Tom was so blindingly beautiful, my retinas stung. I sat there looking at him, and I could not believe I was in Mr. Iced Double's car. Driving to my apartment.

How's this for not having a plan?

My gaze traveled from his perfectly sculpted face chiseled with a strong jaw and high cheekbones, to his broad hands and the tip of his long fingers. I could not take my eyes off him as he turned the steering wheel. The air grew stuffy and I rolled down a window.

"Are you okay?" he asked.

"Just need a little air, that's all."

He rolled his down as well, and as the cool air brushed through the interior, I was swathed in more trails of his scent. My eyelids gently glided down over my eyes, allowing me to focus on his aroma. The warming tingle traveling up my nose descended into my belly, filling me with searing heat. I opened my eyes, and as we approached my apartment, I broke the sweet silence. "Make a right at the light then half way down the block you'll see my building."

"You got it." He slowed down as he pulled up to the front.

I unbuckled my seatbelt before the Rover came to a full stop and stepped out quickly. "I won't be long."

"I will be right here."

The amused look on his face took my breath away.

I scurried inside so fast I barely noticed who was at the desk. The elevator moved through molasses as it ascended to the fifth floor, but as soon as the doors opened, I took off my heels and bolted for the apartment and frantically knocked, praying Jen was home.

Cellphone to her ear, Jen dug her bloodshot gaze into me as she opened the door. "Oh, my God, she's here. I'll call you back, bye." She hung up, grabbed me by the arm, and pulled me inside, then in one breath bombarded me with questions. "Where the hell have you been? I've been worried sick. Why haven't you picked up your phone? I've been calling you like ten thousand times." Her hands flared and flapped. All I saw was a blur.

"Jen, I'm sorry. I can explain, but right now I'm in a rush." I ran to my room and looked through my drawers.

Jen followed and stood at my doorway with her arms crossed. "Sara, what the hell is going on? Do you have any idea how worried I've been the last couple of hours?"

"I told you, I'm sorry. I will explain everything later, but right now I need you to help me look for my spare key, please."

"Spare key to what?"

"My Jeep."

"Your Jeep? Can you please tell me what is going on?"

"Where the heck is it?" I said to myself as I emptied out my drawers. I scanned my jewelry box—nothing. "It's gotta be somewhere around here."

"Sara, stop. I swear, if you don't tell me what is going on right now..." Her hands were clenched at her sides, and her feet dug into my carpet.

I stopped and clamped my gaze on her. "Jen, it's coffee guy. He's downstairs waiting for me." Then I walked out past her and headed into the kitchen.

Jen followed. "High-powered-executive-Mister-Iced-Double is downstairs?" She ran to the window and peeked below onto the street.

I nodded. "The Jeep broke down and I locked myself out with all my stuff still inside, including my phone. That's why I haven't answered. Tom drove me here to get my spare and he's going to drive me back."

She darted a look at me. "Tom?"

"His real name," I said as I continued to rummage through the kitchen.

"It's in the utility drawer," she replied quickly. "You know, I've been hysterically crying. Why couldn't you tell me you were out with this guy? Not to mention you told me you were not dating anyone. Especially *him*."

"Jen, I'm sorry. I...this night is a big blur." I found the key and ran back to my room to put on a pair of flats. When I returned to the kitchen, I stopped to gather my thoughts, but when I saw Jen, my heart broke. Her usual bouncy curls clung to her face, oily and flat. The sparkle in her clear-blue-ocean eyes was overcast with stormy clouds ready to burst. She'd had a miserable night and it was my fault. I walked over and gave her a bear hug.

She returned the embrace and whispered, "I thought something happened to you. You didn't say where you were going and it's not like you to disappear."

I released her and wiped her soggy eyes. "I haven't really been myself lately. I promise I will tell you everything when I get back, okay?"

She closed her eyes and hugged me once more. "Be careful and don't be gone too long." It was a plea.

"I promise." I kissed her on the cheek before heading out the door.

Out of breath, I jumped back into his car. "Okay, got it. Thank you so much, you're a life saver."

Tom leaned forward over the steering wheel and looked up at my building from underneath the windshield. "So, who's the shmancy one now?"

"I just live here. My girlfriend is the one who actually owns the place."

His eyes widened. "Oh? I...didn't know you...were...I mean...that you had a girlfriend." All teasing was gone from his voice.

As I buckled my seatbelt, what he said finally dawned on me. "Oh, Jen's not my *girlfriend*, she's my best friend, and we're only roommates."

"Well, that's good news."

My breath stilled. "Is it?"

He leaned in closer, and mere inches from my face, stared me dead in the eyes with a smoldering look that fused me to his leather seat. "Yes, it most certainly is, Sara." He breathed the words onto my skin, summoning goosebumps to the surface. The sound of his breathy voice combined with the luring smile of those moist and flushed lips was so hot I could have spontaneously combusted. Our eyes remained tied to one another, the inhale and exhale of our lungs synchronized until the air around us felt humid. My mouth watered as I continued to stare at him then—

The obnoxious honk of a speeding cabby trying to dodge our idling car startled us. We both blinked hard as if awakening from a deep dream, killing our almost-kiss, possibly saving me from death by breathy voice.

Eight

SARA

A JAZZ SINGER SERENADED US AS TOM TURNED UP THE volume a couple of notches and we waltzed through the streets, now diluted of traffic, free as a river breeze. The city never felt so magical and surreal. It didn't take long for my soul to sally off into a daydream, a dance concerto gliding my spirit through a routine of leaps and arabesques. I was so lost in the beauty of the music, before I knew it, we'd arrived back at the club.

As it seemed, my battery was not only drained, it was completely and utterly dead. There was no reviving the damn thing.

"Just great..." I droned behind the wheel of my Jeep.

Tom walked toward me after storing his jumper cables. He stood at my open car door, crestfallen. Perhaps he wasn't used to not saving damsels in distress. "I'm sorry," he lamented.

"Don't be. Not your fault."

He shrugged apologetically. "So, what now?"

"Don't know," I said, shaking my head. "I guess I call a tow truck and have it taken to a mechanic somewhere?" I seldom drove, so I had no idea where to take it. Having a car in the city was a luxury I couldn't really afford, but parting with the Jeep would be carving out a chunk of flesh from my bones.

It was my mom's old car. We beat it up driving up and down the East Coast chasing competitions. That Jeep was as much a part of my life as my childhood home. I'd already lost that one. No way I was losing this, too. Nah-uh. Never. Too many memories lived inside, vibrant as if they happened yesterday. Happy. Sad. They all mattered. People told me the memories lived in my heart not in the car. That I should stop holding on to the Jeep as if losing it meant losing the memories. No. To lose it was to lose my mom all over again. So, fuck 'em. I'd scrape pennies for Asian noodles just to keep paying for the parking garage.

"You don't have a mechanic?" he asked.

"Not one I use regularly. Jen might know a guy." I reached into my purse for my phone but when I pressed the ON button, it didn't power up. "Shit." I threw my head back. "I always forget to charge this stupid thing." A strangled breath strained out of my lungs.

"Hey," he intoned softly as he reached for my face and cupped my chin with his fingers, turning my gaze toward him. "Don't worry about it. We'll figure it out. I promise."

We'll figure it out...

I stared into his green eyes. They shimmered with a twinkle of hopefulness, as if saving my sorry ass tonight was his sole mission. He wasn't planning on abandoning me to my bad luck. I smiled, offering him a silent thank you. Sorrier still was the fact that I wanted him to save my sorry-ass. I wanted to play the damsel in distress, the princess rescued by her knight in shining armor. Anything to keep this night from ever ending, and to prolong the kindling fire deep in my core, blazing like a pyre when he looked at me like this, as if he'd always known me, as if he never wanted to let me go.

He dug into his jeans pocket and retrieved his phone. "I'll give my guy a call."

"His shop is open at this hour?"

"Not his shop. I have his personal number."

"What? No. Don't wake this guy up for me. This is silly. Don't—"

Tom turned from me as I jumped out of the car to stop him from making the call. He smiled as he spun in the middle of the street. "Juan, hey man, thanks for taking my call. I got a bit of a situation." He paused to listen then turned to me.

My eyes bulged as I whispered to him to end the connection. I was mortified.

"For a friend," he went on before another pause. He squinted and crossed his fingers as he listened to the guy. Tom made a rolling motion with his hand, silently urging the person on the other side to speed up the conversation.

Then he turned to me once more and gave me an okay with his fingers, his face beaming. "Perfect. Thanks, man. I owe you one." He ended the call and polished his nails over his shirt with a triumphant gleam in his eyes.

I shook my head. He was absurd. I could have left my car there overnight and figured this out in the morning. But he wanted to be the one to save the day. And there was no denying that I secretly enjoyed every bit of his efforts to impress me.

"So, he's gonna see us tonight?" I wondered.

"I'm good but not that good. He told me to have it towed to his shop and he will take care of it first thing in the morning."

"Where's this shop, exactly?"

Our drive to Jersey was serene. Jazz continued to dance in the background as we crossed the George Washington Bridge, following the tow truck to Juan's Auto Shop located in Fort Lee. I stared out the window, gazing at the evening panorama of the Hudson River. Enveloped in the plush of his seats and the scent of leather mixed with the musk of his cologne, I sat in utter disbelief. How the heck had I ended up in this crazy scenario with this man who only days ago was just a guy at a coffee shop?

Tom shut off the engine as we approached a garage. Unbuckling his seatbelt, he said, "We're here. Gonna talk to the driver. Wait in the car."

I straightened. "Um, wait...wait. I have to pay him."

"I got it, Sara. Don't worry about it. I'll be right back."

As he stepped out of the car and closed his door, a chill from the cool night prickled my skin. I rubbed my arms together and held myself in an embrace. I stared out the car window as he gave the truck driver a strong handshake and patted him on the shoulder with his free hand. The driver tipped his cap and turned to jump back in his truck.

As Tom walked back to the Rover, I gasped. He was agonizingly breathtaking. I salivated at the thought of his body underneath those clothes. I observed every small detail, from the way his golden-brown hair sat soft and wavy atop his head, to the thickness of his eyebrows and the depth of those eyes dusted with long lashes. His lips were full and his square jaw was strong. His perfectly tailored shirt clung to him, and I could only imagine the ruggedness of his arms and the rip and tone of his torso. And talk about those long powerful legs waiting to burst out of his jeans—that I didn't strip down to my birthday suit and wasn't on all fours panting "take me" like a lioness in heat was a shocker even to me.

Christ, the sexual hunger growling inside me was unavoidable. My body tingled at the anticipation of his return. The thought of being savagely consumed by him rocked my senses. Against all better judgment, I wanted to be there trapped with him, hoping to be his prey.

As he jumped back in the car, he noticed my arms wrapped around myself. "Are you cold?"

I nodded.

He leaned into me, and my heart immediately began to ferociously beat against my chest. Blood throbbed at my temple. With a strong inhale, my entire body tensed with fervor. My legs parted slightly as heat migrated to my center. The whole scene played out in slow motion inside my brain. I licked my lips, preparing for a kiss—as if kissing right now made any type of sense.

And just as the cleft of my lips peeled open, he sliced his head to the right and reached for the seat behind me. He grabbed a black leather jacket and handed it to me. "Here, wear this," he said with a smirk.

Damn him.

"Oh...thanks," I said, my voice deflated. I took the jacket from his hands and dropped my gaze, hoping to hide the foolish thoughts probably evident in my hungry eyes, but as I peered up, the gratified look flashing in his told me he knew exactly what I'd been thinking. His lips twitched.

Arrogant sonuvabitch.

He thoroughly enjoyed watching the reaction my body had to his.

The things he did to me without even touching me made my head spin. That he basked in torturing me with such subtleties only made me crave him more. If he could fire me up with a simple look, I could only imagine what having his hands all over me could do.

The jacket was too big for my frame, but I was deliciously warm, and when I realized I was bathed in his scent, I wrapped it tighter around me.

"Better?" he asked, holding back a trembling smirk pulling at the corners of his lips, trying to mask the satisfaction bouncing in his eyes.

He wasn't very good at it.

I shot him a steely gaze. "Much, thank you," I replied coolly, trying to squelch his overheated ego.

He reached across and ran his knuckles over my cheek. "Anything for my damsel."

Christ. Really?

I'd just managed to cool myself down and he went in for a knuckles-over-the-cheek move? What could I do? His touch emitted a calming warmth. I stared at him, trying to figure him out. Hot/cold, hot/cold. Could he make up his mind? He dropped his hand and reached inside his pocket for a piece of paper and pen.

Back to cold.

"You need to leave your name, number, and keys in the drop box." He scribbled down my name then hovered the pen-point over the paper, waiting for me to drop him my digits.

"You know, if all you wanted was my number, you could have asked me back in New York. You didn't have to construct this whole rescued-princess tale."

He swung his head toward me, his eyes unblinking. "*Now* you tell me."

Both of us tried to stifle a laugh, but we failed miserably. I gave him my number and after he left to put the paper and keys in the drop box, he popped back inside.

"So, thanks for all your help. How much do I owe you for the tow?" I asked.

He tilted his head to the side, his forehead lined with offense. "Please, you owe me nothing. This is the least I can do for kidnapping you this evening."

"Is that what you're calling it?"

"Maybe." He chuckled. "It's getting late, and I should bring you home before your *mom* grounds you and I can't see you again."

"You want to see me again?"

"Maybe."

"Maybe?"

A wolfish grin stretched across his lips. "If you're a good girl."

I sat in my seat unable to come up with a retort. My mind swirled. Did he mean good as in good, or good as in bad, in which case being bad was good? I turned from him and simply stared out the window in stunned silence.

A few minutes later, we were driving across the George Washington Bridge again. We drove the rest of the way with bluesy tunes crooning in the background. As we approached my apartment, a sense of loneliness enveloped me. I didn't want the night to end.

"You are home, Sara. Safe and sound, like I promised." He turned to face me as he ran a hand through his silky hair. The lights from the street lamps sparkled in his eyes, lips soft and beckoning. Then he smiled, causing my heart to squeeze in my chest. I was so drawn to him, the feeling teetered on being painful.

Fearful of losing myself in him, I looked away and dropped my chin to my chest. With a sigh, I peered up at my building through the car window, whispering to myself, "Yep, I guess I am home." Then I turned toward him, hoping the charm had been broken. "What now?" I asked.

Eyes aflame with bewitchment, he mystified me, and I realized I wasn't sure if the spell could ever be broken. Tom inched closer, his gaze continuing to arrow deep into me for another brief moment before narrowing slowly over my lips. In a sultry bedroom voice, he uttered, "It was lovely meeting you, Sara. You made an adventure of what would have been an otherwise uneventful evening."

Whatever it was, purposeful or not, his voice did insane things to my feminine parts.

I swallowed hard. "Likewise," I whispered as we both inched closer to one another, eyes focused on the other's mouth. The knock of my heart hammering against the walls of my chest muted every other sound around me. His large hand reached for my jaw, where he carefully outlined my chin with his thumb before brushing its pad over my bottom lip. My breath caught at the tingling sensation. He licked his lips as he watched my reaction to his touch.

As his chest rose with one heavy inhale, his hand lacing through my hair, palming the back of my head and bringing me closer to his lips, I turned away, cutting the tether holding us together, shattering the tension, obliterating the kiss I had longed for all night.

"Um, I guess I will call your mechanic in the morning?" I asked, instantly regretting the question. I didn't know why I did it, but with those words, I dropped an iron wall between us.

It was a mistake I could never take back. His hand fell to his lap, and from the corner of my eye I noticed he lowered his gaze, shaking his head in confusion.

Dammit.

Like a fool, I swiftly maneuvered away from the one thing I wanted most. He leaned away from me to reach into his back pocket and took out his black leather wallet. He pulled a business card out from one of the folds and handed it to me. "Here, this is the contact information for his shop. I'll call him in the morning to remind him."

I took it from him, making sure to touch his hand as I grasped the card. "Thank you. For everything." I stalled, trying to think of something else to say, but he interrupted my thoughts.

"Get upstairs and go to sleep, you have to get up for work tomorrow, and frankly, I need to get my ass home too." His smile lacked the humor he intended.

Yep. I fucked up.

Royally.

I went to open the door, but not before looking back at him. For a few seconds, we were anchored to one another, unable to break free. There was urgency in his eyes, the dancing fire was gone. I wanted to jump across the console and bury myself in his mouth, but I'd blown my chance already.

"Good night, Tom," I said, stepping out of his car and closing the door.

As I climbed the front stairs of my building, I heard his voice call out to me. "Sara."

I stumbled as I turned around.

"Nice Jacket."

Crap. I mouthed I'm sorry and attempted to walk to his car, but he put his hand up, signaling me to stop.

"Keep it."

"Why?"

"As insurance." Then he flashed me those pearly whites and drove away.

Speechless and utterly enchanted, I entered my building.

After gently closing the front door, I tiptoed to my room. Skiddles followed behind me, purring her welcome. "Hey, girl, momma's home." I scooped her up and stepped onto the soft carpet of my bedroom. As I flicked the lights on, my reflection stared back at me through the bedroom mirror. A wide grin creased my face.

Skiddles squirmed out of my arms as I walked closer to the mirror. I reveled in the feel of Tom's jacket. The fine leather was cool and soft and was imbued with the smell of him. I inhaled deeply, wanting to make his scent a part of me.

As I continued to stare, my grin faded, recalling the reason I'd given up on love. My heart throbbed with longing. It was so starved of affection, it now hungered voraciously for passionate, all consuming, dangerous love. I felt so safe and secure inside my iron prison, I didn't bother to feed my heart, believing I didn't need anyone in my life to feel fulfilled.

Deep inside, I knew the truth.

I wanted to fly.

And tonight, Tom bent open the bars of my cage.

I stripped his jacket off my body and changed into a pair of pajamas. As I padded to the kitchen for a glass of water, Jen called my name. Her door slightly ajar, I poked my head through. "Thought you were sleeping."

"I was, but I heard you come in. So, how did it go?" She could never pass up girly gossip, no matter what time it was.

I walked over to the bed and laid under her covers.

"Sara, is everything okay?

"Everything...is...perfect."

She sprang up and switched on the lamp by her nightstand. No longer groggy, she teemed with excitement. Crossing her legs, she sang, "Tell me everything."

Nine

SARA

The sound of my alarm radio echoed into Jen's room, stirring me awake. I took a pillow and placed it over my head.

Jen called from the kitchen. "Sara, you plan on shutting that damn thing off?"

Oh, c'mon. Can't a girl get some sleep around here?

"Sara!"

"All right already," I grumbled.

Is it really time to get up?

With one eye open, I glanced at her clock—six-thirty a.m.

Ah, crap.

With a growl, I sat up and planted my stubborn legs on the rug. I sat there, eyes partly glued shut, refusing to accept it was morning, my brows pinched in denial. I palmed my face as I stood up and marched across the living room to my bedroom. I slammed my hand down on the alarm clock as it was about to blast again. Like a soldier being shipped off to war and forced to leave his lover behind, I stared at my bed with sodden eyes.

"Trust me, I wish it wasn't so," I told my fluffy mattress.

Showered and dressed, as I got ready to head out, I caught sight of Tom's leather jacket sitting on my chaise. Memories of the previous night made me swell with delight. I couldn't wait to see him again.

In the kitchen, Jen packed her lunch.

"Morning," I said as I reached inside the fridge for a bottled fruit smoothie. She barely looked at me.

"What's the matter?" I asked.

"You know what."

"You're still mad about last night? I thought we talked about it."

"I'm not mad, but you broke the code. That's serious. I don't care how hot or steamy a guy is."

"I get it. I screwed up. We don't have to keep having this conversation."

She looked up, her gaze brimming with concern. "What's so special about this one?"

I shrugged, unable to give her a straight answer. "I guess...when I first saw him, a heavy weight settled over my heart. There was this connection, an invisible tether pulling me to him." I paused before continuing. "I don't know. I'm just rambling."

"I'll tell you what the problem is. Your hoo-ha has cobwebs."

"Excuse me?"

Hands on her hips, she raised an eyebrow.

I puffed out a breath. "Okay, fine. I *could* use some action. Can't deny there's a serious physical attraction, but that's not all, Jen. I'm talking about something deeper."

"I thought you didn't believe in that sort of thing anymore."

"I didn't."

"So, now you do?"

"I thought you wanted me to date. Whatever happened to me needing someone to take care of me?" I replied, mocking her words.

"I don't want you getting hurt. You've just met him and already you sound head over heels for this guy. Not everything that shines is gold, you know."

I blinked. "Did you just use a cliché on me?"

She shrugged.

"Look, I know what I'm doing," I reassured her. "I don't plan on making the same mistakes all over again. Trust me."

"I'm sorry for being difficult. I love you, and I can't help it if I worry."

I walked around the kitchen counter and gave her a hug. "You don't need to worry about anything." I grabbed a banana and turned to leave. "I'm running late. I'll call you later."

"Bye, Googly-Eyes," she teased, laughing.

Work was swamped. We were hosting auditions for new dancers and Rebecca made me coordinate the entire thing. I sat at my desk sorting through email when my cell phone buzzed.

Unknown: *You didn't stop for coffee this morning.*
Me: *Who's this?*
Unknown: *You forgot about me already. Crying emoji.*
Me: *Who's this?*
Unknown: *Am I that unmemorable?*
Me: *Depends on who you are...*
Unknown: *Your Knight in Shining Armor*
A smile split my face.
Me: *Didn't realize you'd memorized my number.*
Unknown: *Blushing emoji*
An even bigger smile carved across my cheeks.
Me: *So, what's up?*

Unknown: *You have my jacket.*

Me: *You gave it to me*

Unknown: *I only parted with it because you looked so unbelievably adorable in it. Smiley face with heart eyes.*

Me: *Well, in that case, maybe I'll keep it.*

Unknown: *Or maybe, you'll go out to dinner with me tonight.*

Me: *Was this your plan all along?*

Unknown: *What if it was?*

Me: *Then I like the way you scheme.*

Unknown: *Pick you up at eight. Can't wait to see you. Winky face.*

A few days ago, I was googly-eyed over this guy in a silk suit, and now, here he was, sending me emojis.

Did that really happen?

I read the texts over and over again and couldn't stop grinning.

There were about fifteen dancers from around the world auditioning for a spot in the company. I walked backstage making sure everyone was ready and the music properly queued. The dancers were nervous, each of them encased in their own respected corners, stretching, practicing their sequences.

This was their moment, the culmination of all their years of hard work and determination. Out there, a dancer's body and soul became the music. We feel it in our blood. It's what fuels our existence. Upstage, I watched a young girl, probably not much younger than me, she was beautiful and graceful. Her body was petite, muscular, but lithe. My muscles twitched as I gazed at her movement—an upper back arch, a yield and push, x-rolls. A smile crept onto my face as I thought back to my days at Juilliard. For a brief moment, I was her and life raced through my veins.

"Places, everyone." The director's voice startled me out of my daydream.

Rebecca sat front and center with Alexei at her side. "Let's begin," she commanded.

My job was done. I exited backstage and headed to the auditorium. I could have stayed and watched, but my heart couldn't stomach it. It had been four years since I quit Juilliard, and four years since I gave up dance completely. The emotional wounds from the past still felt fresh every time I gazed up at that stage and those dancers. Becoming a contemporary dancer had been my only dream, but when my mother died, things changed.

I changed.

Before everything happened, dancing was the only thing that mattered to me. I possessed raw talent, promise. They told me I would be a star one day, and I believed every word they said. The biggest audition of my entire dance career was slated for the day after a major snow storm was predicted to hit the city. I was up north in Cape Cod with my mother and sister, visiting grandmother for the holidays, when we heard of the bad weather threatening to assail the tristate area.

I should have listened to my mother when she told me not to drive that night. I was selfish and reckless. The weather people always exaggerate, I told her. It was the greatest opportunity to dance for one of New York's most prestigious companies. There was no chance I'd miss it because of a little snow.

Turned out to be the harshest mistake of my life. Not to mention it should have been just me in the car that night. But who was I to argue with my mother? I inherited my stubbornness from her. And I paid dearly for it. Overcoming the injuries to my spine was a harrowing ordeal. Still, it wasn't what kept me from setting foot on stage.

Guilt. Shame. Regret. They were the deadly trio vice gripping my heart and crippling my soul. I was a shell of who I used to be.

Without my mother, I lost my motivation, and without that, I lost my ability to dance.

As I reached my office and closed the door behind me, I pressed my back against the solid wood, hoping to shut out the sorrow trudging behind me on my way back from the auditorium. How much longer would I be able to ignore it? How much longer could I go on without facing the demons lurking in the shadows? I'd kept my past buried, yet somehow, within the last few days, those dreadful memories seemed to be escaping from their tomb.

I wiped tears bubbling at the corners of my eyes and sucked in a deep breath, stifling the ocean of pain pushing against the walls of my heart. Everything in that place was a constant reminder of my failures, but in the end, I could never purge my body of the desire to dance.

Five o'clock couldn't have come fast enough. I bolted out of the studio not a minute later. On my way, I texted Tom.

Me: *Charming, what should I wear to the ball tonight?*

Tom: *Your attire is being freshly delivered to your humble abode.*

Me: *That's awfully presumptions of you. How do you know I'll like it?*

Tom: *Trust me. You're gonna love it.*

I wasn't sure if I should have been delighted I was being lavished with a gift or insulted he didn't think I owned an appropriate evening dress.

Ah, screw it.

After not being on a single date in eons, it was time I let myself be wined and dined. Not to mention, dressed. At five-fifty, when I walked into the lobby of my building, Pedro greeted me with a nervous smile. He wiped corn muffin crumbs off his trimmed beard and off his navy-blue uniform. His dark eyes lit up as soon as he saw me, creases forming at the corners of his skin.

"Good evening, Ms. Hart." He quickly wiped his hands on his pants.

"Good evening, Pedro."

"A package arrived for you." He ran his hands through his thick block of charcoal-colored hair before reaching behind the desk and grabbing a white, medium-size square box tied with black ribbon. He fumbled for the tag attached. "It's from a...Mr. Charming?"

I smirked and reached for the box. It was heavier than it should be for just a dress. I wondered what other surprise *Charming* had in store for me that evening.

"Thank you, Pedro. I'm expecting a visitor around eight."

"Okay, Ms. Hart."

In the elevator, my hands twitched with excitement. Being swayed by lavish gifts? Pre-Mr. Iced Double, I probably would have scoffed at the presumptuous gesture, but holding the soft box wrapped in delicate ribbon had me feeling exceptionally regarded and I died to look inside.

Jen hadn't arrived home from work, and welcoming the privacy, I dropped my tote on the floor by the entrance, flung my keys on the kitchen counter then kicked my shoes off my feet. By the time I made it to my room, my heart pounded so fast my hands were sweaty. Not wanting to ruin the delicate package, I uncoiled the ribbon and opened the box with gentle fingers.

Wrapped in red satiny material was a pair of exquisite Park & Cliff four-inch heel, black Sicilian lace, peep-toe pumps.

Geez. A pair of these probably cost him more than my entire wardrobe.

Deeper in the box, I found a marvelous Geena Salvatore black, short, strapless, lace dress. It was absolutely stunning and likely twice as expensive as the shoes. I never dreamed one of her dresses would be wrapped around my body. I peeked at the size—four. *How did he know?*

I found a pair of black satin panties in my drawer, and after scrambling to find a strapless bra, I decided to borrow one of Jen's. The dress caressed every curve as if custom made. His taste was remarkable, and I wondered what else he could possibly have in store for me. I tingled with anticipation and couldn't remember the last time my heart fluttered inside my chest like a caged bird.

At eight on the dot, my phone buzzed.

Tom: *Your carriage awaits. Don't keep me waiting.*

Me: *Be right down.*

In the elevator, I texted Jen.

Me: *Got a date with Iced Double tonight. Don't wait up.*

Jen: *Have fun!*

When the elevator opened, my breath caught. *Charming* leaned on the front desk, talking to Pedro. He looked dapper in tailored black pants and matching blazer. Underneath, he wore a crisp white button-down and no tie. My lips parted with an inward breath. Pedro spotted me and nodded to Tom. When he looked at me, his jaw dropped before he glided over to meet me.

"Sara."

"Tom."

He leaned in and planted a soft kiss on my right cheek, feathering his lips against the corner of my mouth. He let the kiss linger and softly brushed his mouth close to my ear. "You are absolutely enchanting in that dress."

His breath ignited my skin, his intoxicating scent making me woozy.

Tom pulled away but stood close and presented me with a single red rose he had been holding behind his back.

"It's beautiful. Thank you."

He turned to his side and put his left arm out for me. "Shall we, my lady?"

I laughed at the continuing joke and hooked my arm around his and let him guide me to the exit. Tom nodded at Pedro as we passed and waved.

"Good night, Mr. Wright," Pedro said to Tom. "Señorita."

The Range Rover sat up front and Tom hurried to open the

door. I stepped inside and the familiar scent of leather mixed with his cologne wrapped around me. Sinking into the seats, I relished in the opulence. When he stepped into the driver's seat, he turned toward me, luring me with his honey-streaked green eyes.

"Are you hungry?" he asked.

"Yes," I replied, half enchanted.

"Good, me too."

"Where are we going?"

He checked the car mirrors for incoming traffic. "To my favorite restaurant."

"Oh?"

He looked at me, then shifted the car into drive. "The Riverview Steakhouse. Ever been?"

I blinked fast. "Celebrities eat there. You can't get a reservation unless—"

"Hush," he scolded playfully as he softly placed a finger over my lips, a smile carving his cheeks. "You're gonna love it."

We pulled out, his left hand on the wheel and his right hand on the gear shift. He looked amazing. Sophisticated, gallant, and with that I-own-this-town type of confidence people dream about. I didn't know if I liked him better like this or in his designer jeans.

"Music?" he asked.

"Um, sure."

"Any particular requests?"

"Surprise me."

He pressed a button and bluesy tunes filtered through. The car was practically sound proof, shutting out the chaos of the city streets. I looked over to him and everything seemed perfect, almost surreal.

Nestled right on the Hudson River with a breathtaking view of the Brooklyn Bridge and lower Manhattan, The Riverview Steakhouse exploded with romance. A quick sweep of the area showcased an array of expensive, luxury automobiles lining the parking lot. Understanding for my lavish gift settled over me.

The valet opened my door and I stepped out into the warm and windy evening. Tom strolled along the front of the car and signaled for me to join him. As I walked up to him, he grabbed my hand, threading his fingers through mine. The gesture caught me off guard. He sensed my tension and looked at me with the kindling embers of his eyes. A tender smile crept to the corners of his mouth as he gave my hand a gentle squeeze, untangling the knot in my stomach.

Hand in hand, we walked, enjoying the evening twilight panorama over the river. The blue hour covered us in all her splendor. The last of the sun's rebel rays scattered in the sky, illuminating the water and casting a hypnotic ambiance to the atmosphere.

The formal host greeted us at the entrance and shook Tom's hand. "Good evening, Mr. Wright." Then he nodded toward me. "Madam. Your table is ready."

"Thank you, Dom," Tom said, patting the host on the shoulder.

Dom escorted us to our table in the main dining room. Piano music hung in the air as we were seated at a cozy table in front of the glass wall of windows facing the New York City skyline. The Brooklyn Bridge and an early moon loomed over us.

"This place is magical," I whispered as the waiter pulled out my chair.

Tom sat back in his seat, unbuttoned his jacket, and leaned forward, his gaze never leaving mine. "Well, it's the perfect setting for dinner with a spellbinding woman like you."

His flattery made me uneasy. As our waiter gave us each a menu and another man filled our water goblets, I glanced to my lap where my fingers twirled restlessly. When the servers left, I peered up at Tom and he tilted his head to the side, his eyes narrowed in confusion. "You seem uncomfortable," he noted.

"I'm overwhelmed."

"What do you mean?"

"This dress, the shoes, this place, Tuesday."

He frowned. "Something wrong with Tuesdays?"

"Most people don't go out to fancy dinners on Tuesdays. Tom, why all of this?"

"I thought you'd like it."

"It's mesmerizing. Romantic. Any girl's dream. But you don't even know me."

He glanced away before answering, his jaw muscles clenching as he took a deep breath. Finally, he locked eyes with me. "Truthfully?"

I nodded.

"I haven't been able to stop thinking about you. Last Friday, at the coffee shop, I couldn't keep my eyes off you...flustered and trying to wipe down the coffee stain from your blouse. You looked adorable mumbling to yourself. If I hadn't been running late for my leadership meeting, I would have asked you to breakfast."

The air inside my chest crystalized at the mention of the serendipitous moment. "I had no idea you actually noticed me."

He rubbed a trembling hand through his hair. "Who wouldn't?" He smirked. "It's crazy, you know, this thing you've done to me. I can't explain it, but when I'm with you, the world stops spinning and all there is...well, you and me."

The blood iced in my veins.

He did experience it.

Tom looked at me expectantly, waiting for me to say something. And there was so much I wanted to tell him, but I struggled to make sense of the words sitting at the tip of my tongue.

The space between his eyebrows twisted into a tight knot and his shoulders slacked as he leaned back on his chair. "You don't feel the same."

I reached over to grab his hand. "No, it's not like that at all. It's just—" But I couldn't finish my sentence. I couldn't tell him how my world wasn't the same anymore or that the battle inside my chest raged with savagery. A part of me wanted to give into the magic of something we could not explain, and the other part of me quivered in a cold, damp corner, afraid to come out—timorous to embrace the warmth of a promise of love.

He squeezed my hand gently. "I know it sounds crazy, but for a guy like me, this sort of thing doesn't happen. And now, I can't ignore this unrelenting pounding in my chest."

He put his hand over his heart and peered at me, perhaps wanting to find confirmation in my eyes of my feelings for him. I was attempting equally hard to hide them. When I said nothing, he let out a rankled breath, running his hands through his hair. "I tried. I really did—to not be bothered by this twist-of-fate mumbo-jumbo, but can you seriously look me in the eyes and tell me it didn't happen to you, too?"

I stared in silence.

"I tried to deny it, but after I saw you again last night, I had to accept maybe something else is at work here."

It did sound crazy, but I had entertained the idea for days. To hear it from his lips, though? I couldn't believe it. I'd sworn never to allow myself to be swooped off my feet ever again. So how the hell did I permit myself to be drawn to this man?

The erratic thumps of my heart bruised the insides of my chest. If I could reach inside, I would have ripped its beating flesh right out of my body. The signs were there. It was happening again. I was losing control of my emotions and it made my gut twist and my stomach churn with acid.

"What are you thinking?" he asked, his eyes glowing with hope.

"Nothing," I blurted out, afraid to reveal the thoughts swirling inside my head, ripping my sanity apart.

He blinked at my response, then he leaned back on his chair and folded his arms across his chest.

Shit.

"I'm sorry. That came out wrong."

He clenched his jaw. "If this is too much, we can leave." His voice was gravel as he pushed off his seat and stood.

Without thought, I reached out and wrapped my hand around his wrist. "I don't want to go."

He stared at my quaking fingers as they pleaded with him to not give up on me yet. Then he found my misty gaze. "Sara?"

"Tom…" My voice choked as I tried to speak. I thought about urging him to leave me to my miserable self, but my eyes would not be able to hide the fear gripping my spirit. My soul was vulnerable and visible to him. I prayed he'd see something else, too—the hope of love I'd banished from my life.

His chest heaved as he sucked in a deep breath and sat back down. I unclenched my fingers from his wrist, but he reached over and took my hand and encased it in his, rubbing his thumb over my palm. Without saying a word, the gesture gave me the reassurance I needed.

After regarding the river through the windows for a brief moment, he turned to me, and with a deep gulp of air, he confessed, "It unnerves me, too."

My heart throbbed harder and I reached up to cup his cheek. I wanted to tell him I hadn't been able to stop thinking about him. At home, at work, in my sleep—he saturated my mind. I wanted him to know his scent enthralled me, his masculinity disarmed me, his lips enticed me, and his touch undid me to the core.

Most importantly, 1 wanted him to understand my body raked with agony at the thought of never seeing him again. My insides twisted and writhed when we were apart because my attraction to him went beyond the earthly world. It was monumentally seeded to his soul on an ethereal plane where I had no control.

I didn't need to utter a single word. He saw it all in my eyes—the feelings growing for this stranger I barely knew.

"Thank you for bringing me here." There was no need to say more.

He took my hand and kissed the center of my palm. "How about some food? I'm starving."

"I thought you'd never ask," I chimed in, relieved to end the melodrama of our temperamental hearts.

~

As promised, the food was exquisite, and during our wait, the fine Madeira wine betrayed me. I continued to fill my belly with our appetizer while my head spun warm and fuzzy.

Taking another morsel of my *foie gras*, I began my inquisition. "So...*Charming*, what do you do for a living?"

"I rescue princesses," he replied matter-of-factly as he sipped his water.

"Seriously, though," I countered, putting another chunk of food in my mouth.

He contemplated his answer. "I co-own a luxury real estate business with my best friend."

"That explains how you're driving around in a Range Rover and bringing girls here for dates."

His gaze narrowed as he gulped water from his goblet to wash his food down. "Range Rovers are nothing to fuss about, it's not as if I drive some obnoxious sports car." Then he pushed his empty plate away and wiped his mouth with a napkin. "You're the first woman I've brought here, by the way," he added with a smirk, satisfied with his reply.

I shrugged. "You have the perfect answers for everything, don't you?"

He took another sip of water. "Your turn. What do you do for a living?"

I tried not to grumble. "I work for a dance company in Midtown."

His eyes lit up with excitement. "You're a dancer?"

"No..." I groaned, more bitterly than I intended. "I'm the administrative assistant to the artistic director."

"Which dance company?"

"It's the Rebecca Fitzgerald Dance Company on Forty-Second Street."

His eyes twinkled as they lingered on me curiously. "Very interesting."

My response was quick to cloud any ounce of sparkling wonder about what I did for a living. "Actually, there's nothing particularly glamorous about what I do. In fact, it's a nightmare. I am convinced my boss is the Prince of Darkness in female form, no doubt about it. And our resident choreographer is a complete dickhead."

He chuckled as he shook his head in amusement.

"I'm not trying to be funny. I'm serious. I work inside Dante's Inferno."

"It can't be that bad."

"Oh, it is."

"So, quit and find something else."

Something else, he says. Because I haven't thought of that before. Because I wouldn't rather be dancing on that stage instead of filling it with dancers who aren't half as good as I once was.

Because, it's easy to forget your past, right?

"Sara?"

"Yeah?"

"You sort of spaced out for a moment there."

"I'm sorry."

"It's all right. You were talking about how terrible work is. Maybe it's time for a career change. Find something that makes you truly happy."

"It's...not that simple, Tom."

"Why not? You're young. There's plenty of time for you to pursue your dreams."

I fidgeted on my chair. Talking about work dug up memories of my past—ghosts I was not prepared to face. "It's complicated, Tom." My voice quavered as I tried to hold back the stampede of regret and sorrow pushing against the gates of my soul. My tearful gaze pleaded with him to drop the subject.

"How about we talk about something else?" he said, reading my thoughts.

~

As I finished my dessert, I set my utensil down and peered up at Tom. "Thank you for this evening. It really has been fantastic, the food phenomenal, and being with you…"

"You're very welcome. Come, let's take a walk."

As Tom stood from his chair, he reached for my hand, entwining his fingers through mine. His hand felt warm and strong. I relished the intimate moment as he led me to the outside terrace. The wind was chilly, but it offered relief against the rising heat from my skin. We walked over to the edge of the railing and gazed out at the East River. Tom snuggled behind me and put his arms on the railing, cocooning me between him and the wood planks.

"This night is so beautiful, Tom."

"Yes, it is, but it doesn't compare to you." He nuzzled my ear as he spoke, his breath raising the hairs on the back of my neck.

"You must say that to all the girls," I teased.

"All the time," he said, taking a tiny nip of my lobe.

I gave him a playful elbow jab, but he grabbed me and gently spun me around.

Wrapping his arms around me, we laughed as he placed my feet back on the ground. He brushed his knuckles against my cheek, pushing a runaway strand of hair behind my ear. My face flared at his touch, and I was thankful for the evening sky that he was not able to see the way my body divulged my secret thoughts.

Shivers ran down my spine, making me tremble. Looking at me

with his playful eyes, he took off his blazer and draped it over my shoulders. I smiled. Shamefully and against my better judgment, I'd fallen for his cheesiness.

"This is the second time you've given me one of your jackets," I said.

"I guess I like the way you look in my things."

"Is that so?"

"Yes."

He grabbed me by the lapels of his blazer, bringing me closer. I gazed up only to find myself bound by his olive eyes. My arms were trapped under his jacket, rendering me motionless. He'd snared me. "What would you do if I kissed you?" he asked in a whisper.

"Why don't you find out?" I replied with sweet command.

He pulled up on the blazer, drawing me into him. This time, I didn't blink and no iron wall came crashing down to shield me from his kiss. I closed my eyes as his lips touched mine. Our mouths parted, our tongues feeling each other for the first time. With tenderness, they tangled in each other, exploring their sensitive areas, sending electric currents down my back.

The kiss sparked flames at all my nerve endings. His tongue invaded me deeper. The hot-wire from my mouth to my groin flowed feverishly, igniting sensations I hadn't felt in a while. I sank deeper into his kiss, responding to his hunger. Our tongues swirled in harmony, hot and wet. He savored every bite he took of my mouth as I feasted on his succulent lips.

His hold on me loosened, but not for long. He reached under my hair, cupping my jaw and caressing my chin with his thumbs. My senses flooded with a myriad of feelings and tastes. My own hunger grew in beat with his heavy breaths. I knew it and he knew it—we couldn't continue the kiss. Fighting with all the will in my body, I broke from his hot breath. His eyes were drunk with lust, making my knees weak. I feared if we were completely alone, I would be consumed by his passion.

His lips curled, and in a husky voice, he said, "Perhaps, we should go."

I nodded in agreement. Taking me by the hand, we walked inside the restaurant where he settled the bill. I was woozy, not sure if from the wine or from his kiss, but I grabbed hold of his arm and melted into him as we walked out to the parking lot.

The evening couldn't have been more spectacular. I still wore his blazer, bathing in his scent. It was so masculine that memories of our kiss broke through my consciousness and I felt myself moisten at the center between my legs. I crossed them to keep from writhing on the seat.

"Everything okay?" he asked, eyeing my bare thighs.

"Never better," I uttered quickly, managing to hide my body's inner reaction to the remnants of his kiss.

He reached over and accidentally grazed my thigh before tenderly grabbing hold of my hand. My insides jumped at his touch. We held hands for the ride. His fingers were like small radiators emanating heat, making my body warm. I found myself caressing his knuckles and pulled on the small hairs on his hand and wrist.

The sexual tension built and I punched a hole to our silent bubble before it would burst on its own. "So, what else do you have on your playlist?" I asked.

"What do you want to listen to?"

"Surprise me."

He let go of my hand and rubbed his fingers through his hair twice before fumbling with the sound system. A local jazz singer piped through the speakers, singing the cover to an old favorite. What was usually a comfortable silence between us became unsettling. My lion was broody, and picking up on the subtle cues, I decided not to pester the beast. I left him to his troubling thoughts and dwelled on the imprint of his lips.

Fifteen minutes later, and much to my silent dismay, we arrived back at my apartment. Tom opened my door and ushered me out.

We walked up the stoop of the entrance, my hand longing for his. As we stopped at the door, I slid his blazer off my shoulders.

I handed him his jacket and he folded it over his arm. Our gazes locked, both of us waiting, but neither making a move. Finally, I looked at my fingertips; he stared at his feet, tapping them to and fro.

"So...I," we both said at the same time.

"You go first," I urged.

"No, you go first," he insisted.

"This night was amazing and memorable." I squeezed my palms together, trying to calm the tremors spurring at the thought of parting from him.

"Thank you for accepting my hasty invitation," he said, avoiding my gaze.

"When do I get to see you again?" I was hopeful I wouldn't have to wait too long.

He held me in his eyes. "I wish this night didn't have to end."

"It doesn't have to..."

"Oh, Sara. You do know how to temp a man, but I can't. I have a business trip and I'm leaving on a red-eye flight tonight."

My eyes widened. I had not expected that.

"We have a West Coast office, and I have some matters to attend to."

"Is that why you asked me out tonight?"

"I didn't want to leave without seeing you."

"Will I see you again soon?" I asked once more, not caring that I sounded desperate.

"I'll call you," he said, his voice staid, his eyes distant.

It was dismissive. I questioned if perhaps I'd done something wrong? Or maybe I had sound too desperate. He'd call me? Why not say he'd see me when he got back? His reply was short of the magic that bewitched me tonight. Maybe I was reading too deeply into things. Nevertheless, I stepped into defense mode, wanting to salvage my dignity. I pushed a strand of hair behind my ear then placed my hands on my hips and played it off as if it was a non-issue. "Sure, whatever."

He leaned in quickly for a chaste kiss on the lips. "Goodnight."

"Goodnight to you."

Something inside me ached as I watched him walk back down and into his car. He pulled away without the slightest wave goodbye, leaving me lingering on his kiss and wanting more of his taste. The evening could have ended perfectly, yet, after the lavish gift, the romantic setting, scrumptious meal, and divine embrace, I was left feeling ripped off and cheap.

Ten

TOM

I SHOULDN'T HAVE ENDED THE NIGHT LIKE THAT, BUT I panicked. I fucking panicked. If I'd lingered on that stoop I would have dragged her back to my car and to my apartment. I would've done every filthy thing to that body that my mind could conjure.

And I would've had my fill then sent her on her way.

At least that's what old me would've done. This new man I was becoming—this man I hardly recognized—wanted more. And that's the part that scared me shitless. The last time I'd wanted a woman like this, my world collapsed. I'd made a vow to myself then. A vow to never let another woman own my heart. And this woman—Sara—something about the way she looked at me had me believing she could be the type of woman who could wreck serious havoc through my heart.

It's why I didn't cancel this trip. I could've easily let Jake handle the West Coast deals, but the instant I spotted an escape, I took it.

83

Being far from Sara was the safest thing for both of us. I mean, for Christ's sake, especially after that kiss.

That fucking kiss...

I pressed my fingers to my lips, remembering the heat of her breath, the slippery savagery with which she tormented my senses, making me want more. I couldn't help but let a grin creep at the corners of my mouth.

God, that woman could drive me crazy.

Who was I kidding? She was already driving me crazy. Yet, everything seemed so easy with her. The way we talked as if we'd known each other forever. When I held her hand at the restaurant, it just felt natural. Like two puzzle pieces finally coming together.

Fuck. I ran a hand through my hair. This wasn't me. I didn't do this sort of thing any more. Catching feelings for a woman I barely knew? The instant I got back to my apartment, I stripped off my suit and changed into a pair jeans and T-shirt, though I didn't bother washing my hands. Her scent still lingered on my skin and a part of me couldn't let go—didn't want to let go.

I needed to stop overthinking my decision to leave for California or I would end up reaching for the bottle of Dalmore sitting on my bar—something that hadn't crossed my mind in years and that needed to stay dormant. After packing a small suitcase, I called my car service and gave Bax a couple of snuggles. I hated leaving him when I went on business trips, but at least my neighbor was a dog lover and she looked after Bax while I was gone.

"I'll miss ya, buddy. But I'll be back in a couple of days, okay?"

He offered me a few wet kisses and I gave him a bone to keep him happy until my neighbor arrived home from work.

The ride to Teterboro Airport seemed to take longer than it should've, and it only served to rattle my nerves even more. I hated flying. Even in the military, I was never able to shake the fear, not after countless flights or countless dives. I'd started booking private charters to and from L.A. to feel more in control, but it only helped to alleviate my anxiety somewhat. Knee bouncing, my hands trembled as I looked out the car window. We were nearing the exit to the airport, and as I watched a plane take off the runway, the only thought that eased the acid churning in my stomach was that of Sara.

It was as if she was the only thing that could ground me. I resisted the urge to call her for fear of sounding desperate. Or maybe for fear of sounding like a total psycho. I mean, one second, I was lavishing her with gifts and taking her to a fancy restaurant and kissing her like there was no tomorrow, and the next I was giving her a peck on the lips and leaving her on the stoop of her entrance like the asshole that I was. She was probably wondering why she'd even bothered to accept my invitation to dinner. Still, while I was able to resist the urge to call her, I wasn't able to resist the itch to text her, so I pulled out my phone and typed away before I could change my mind again. I needed her to know she hadn't done anything wrong. I was the shithead who needed to screw my head on straight.

Me: *Hey*

Coffee Girl: *Aren't you supposed to be on a red eye to sunny California?*

Me: *Arriving at Teterboro soon. Flight leaves in an hour.*

Coffee Girl: *Teterboro? You have a private jet too? Fancy schmancy.*

Me: *lol I don't own one. I'm not that schmancy, but yes, a chartered flight. Not a fan of flying and commercial planes give me too much anxiety. Did I wake you?*

Coffee Girl: *Getting ready for bed. Long day tomorrow.*

Me: *Didn't mean to disturb you.*

Coffee Girl: *You didn't disturb me*

Christ. I knew that comment was an invitation. I knew how these texts were supposed to go. I was supposed to say something flirty, and we'd have a bit of banter back and forth, then we'd get all caught up in the tingly bubbles circulating through out blood. Before we knew it, we'd be in too deep and I'd have to figure out another way to get out of taking things further because...

Because I didn't know how to do this real-dating thing. I didn't know how to have a meaningful relationship with a woman without getting my heart trampled on.

Because what I really wanted to tell her was that I couldn't stop thinking about her. That right now, I was nervous as hell and the only think keeping me from reaching into the limo's mini bar and downing a drink was texting her. That I was a total asshole before and I should've never left her feeling like I didn't want a second date. That I actually couldn't wait to hold her again. Kiss her again. That I was regretting not cancelling this trip, and if she told me not to get on that flight, I would tell my driver to turn around drive me straight to her place.

I should have told her exactly how I felt. Instead, I let the old me finish my text.

Me: *Well. Just wanted to tell you goodnight. Talk soon.*

Eleven

SARA

I ALMOST WISHED HE HADN'T TEXTED ME AFTER OUR DATE last Tuesday, because after the anticlimactic end to our magical evening, I went up to my room and iced my sadness with a hearty bowl of Rocky Road and accepted the fact that the fairytale had ended before it even started. A part of me was actually glad it had ended so sourly because it cemented the fact that love simply wasn't in my cards, and at least things went up in smoke before any true feelings formed.

He'd spared me of a potential heartache.

Then he sent me that text and while he didn't say much, it kinda sparked hope in me again—despite my better judgement—that he was actually still thinking about me and that I hadn't done anything wrong to turn him off. I knew it was stupid of me to think like that, to allow myself to imagine that he was still interested in me. Love had been the furthest thing from my mind in the last four years and I'd been okay with that until this man had butterflies fluttering around in my stomach.

And boy did those butterflies feel so so so good. I'd forgotten what it was like to be kissed like that—like he couldn't get enough of me. I'd forgotten what it felt like to have a man's hands on me or to be looked at like I was the most beautiful woman in the world. And that stupid text filled me with unnecessary and unwanted anticipation that I would get another chance to see him and to taste his lips again.

But after Wednesday, Thursday, and Friday went by without a single text or call from him, I slipped back into self-pity mode, completely doubting everything and hating the fact that I'd allowed myself to dream again.

Sure, I could've texted him or called him, but I guessed a part of me was still old-fashioned, believing that the man was supposed to do the chasing. Not to mention that Jen warned me against being the one to reach out. *That isn't how the game is played,* she'd said. I needed to play hard to get, apparently. According to her, all I needed to do was forget about him, immerse myself in other things, and convince myself I was the prize. If he was meant to be in my life, he'd find me. And if not, good ridden.

Forgetting about him was impossible, no matter how hard I tried. And I secretly hoped he wouldn't just disappear. I wanted him to text me. Wanted him to simply show up at my doorstep with flowers and a huge smile on his face, apologizing for making me feel like I'd been nothing but a Tuesday date.

I sounded so foolish.

By Saturday morning, he still hadn't made a peep and his silence mutated me from sad and lonely to gloomy and grouchy. It was actually Jen's birthday, and she'd planned a very packed day of festivities, but I couldn't find the energy to be happy. Remaining under my blankets, dressed in sweatpants, and sulking all day about Mr. Avoidance was more appealing than taking a shower and getting dolled up for a full day of drinking and potentially thinking even more about how *coffeeless* I was.

Men suck.

I rolled to my side and stared at the clock. The minutes seemed to tick by in slow motion, prolonging the misery of waiting for his call or text. My cellphone sat on the night table, quiet as ever. No blinking lights or notification beeps. A part of me hoped he'd messaged me sometime throughout the night. I was afraid to pick up the phone because it would confirm he hadn't texted me. At least if I didn't look at it, the possibility he messaged me still existed and somehow that made me feel better. Perhaps my phone was glitchy and the lack of the blinking blue light, which usually told me a message was pending, wasn't working. Maybe I had lost reception for no effing reason.

Maybe...

Maybe I've hit a completely new low level of sad, lonely person.

For a brief moment, the sunrays of reason broke through the doomsday clouds that smudged out my common sense. I managed to roll out from under my covers and sat up in bed. If I could only manage to go a day or at least a couple of hours without thinking about him, I might have the energy to go about my day without feeling so emotionally and psychologically exhausted.

Looking for some orange juice, I strolled into the kitchen and found Marco, Jen's boyfriend, whizzing around the stove. He drove down from Boston on Friday night to spend the weekend with us and now appeared to have transformed into our morning chef. There were broken egg shells on the counter and an open milk carton sat by the sink. Flour clouds hung in the air, some coated his favorite maroon Boston University T-shirt, and there was a pot or pan on all four stovetop burners.

Marco was a walking cliché—tall, dark, and handsome. He'd inherited most of his Cuban mother's features, but the emerald-colored eyes he got from his Irish father. His brown hair was shaggy in that on-purpose sexy way and his skin was flawless and olive toned. If he were any better looking, he probably wouldn't be from this world.

"Morning, Marco."

"Why are you up so early?" he asked, draping a kitchen towel over his muscled shoulder.

"It's seven in the morning. It's hardly early," I replied, taking a gulp of my pulpy OJ.

"It's Saturday," he reminded me as he flipped a flour patty over the griddle.

"It's Jen's birthday Saturday," I reminded *him*.

"Oh yes, you two are going out for birthday..."

"Manis and pedis. And yes, your girlfriend doesn't believe in sleeping in on her birthday."

"I'm making my famous pancakes, want some?" he asked, pointing the nonstick spatula toward a stack of perfectly round and fluffy cakes.

"Famous, huh?"

"Oh, you doubt me?" He plopped a freshly warm, cooked pancake on a dish, dabbed on some butter, and poured real Vermont maple syrup very gingerly. "Please, take a bite."

The gooey and sweet pancake hit the spot. The touch of vanilla and cinnamon played with my taste buds. He made a mean pancake. "Okay, you are going to make my friend a very happy wife one day. I'll place an order of your famous pancakes with scrambled eggs, bacon, and some fresh fruit."

"I didn't know this was full service."

"If you're going to offer breakfast, then you better be prepared to *serve* breakfast. Now, chop-chop, I'm starving."

"You're sure you're not the birthday queen this morning?"

"Speaking of birthday queens, where is my BFF?"

"Sleeping," he said as he continued to cook breakfast.

"Really? I hope she didn't make me get up while she sleeps and has pancakes in bed."

"It's her birthday," he said, laughing.

"And I'm going to give her a birthday wake-up."

Later that morning at the spa—my birthday gift to Jen—I failed to concentrate on my e-book. The pedicure was a much-needed small indulgence and the pedicurist was doing a fabulous job, but I couldn't relax.

Jen flipped through her latest gossip magazine. "Sara, can you believe it? Tanya Swimmer broke up with her boyfriend."

"This is a shocker to you, why? She changes boyfriends like I change underwear." I pretended to read my book and didn't even bother to look up.

"Why are you such a sourpuss today?"

Her words made me snap my gaze up at her. I guess I *was* being a bitch. "You're right, I'm sorry." Sucking in a deep breath, I said, "So, who else did you invite out with us tonight?"

"Promise you won't get upset?"

"Why would I get upset?"

"Lisa called me last week and told me she was going to be in town, so..."

My eyes bulged and my hands trembled, causing my e-reader to slip through my fingers, the loud thud cutting off Jen mid-sentence. The device missed landing inside my dirty pedicure water. "Lisa..." I whispered, hoping I'd simply misheard or perhaps Jen didn't mean Lisa Buckley, Josh's little sister.

Jen nodded, confirming my fear.

"Why the hell would you invite Josh's sister out with us?"

With a fidgety hand, Jen twirled one of her blonde curls around her finger. "We haven't seen her in a while and I thought...I thought it would be nice to catch up." The frown between her eyes told me she knew I was going to explode.

"I'm sorry. I know I should've told you sooner, I just didn't know how. But were such good friends with her and when she asked if we were busy tonight, I told her about the club."

"I don't know, Jen. After the way things ended with Josh..."

"Sara, she's not him."

"No. But she's his little sister," I continued, "and I'm sure she talks to him. I don't want her knowing my business. I don't want *him* knowing my business."

Jen crossed her arms, her magazine now discarded.

"When he left," I said, "Everyone thought I was going to jump off the Brooklyn Bridge. I was miserable and devastated. He left me right after my mom died to go chase his dream, and you know what? Last time I heard, he was still living his dream—photographing rhinos on the savannah or some crap, so excuse me if I'm not jumping at the opportunity to a) get reports on his adventures from his little sister, and b) let him know my life pretty much still sucks." I paused. "My dreams...my dreams never happened."

"I'm so sorry, hon."

"Why did you wait until now to tell me?"

"I wasn't thinking. I'll cancel."

"No, you are not cancelling anything," I told her. "I'm being a big baby about this, and it's your birthday. Since you want her there...I'll just suck it up."

"I should have known better."

"It's fine. Really." I turned from her and stared out the window, watching as the city went on with its life.

"What's really bothering you?" she asked.

I turned to her and showed her my phone. "No calls. No texts."

"Still thinking about that jerk?"

"Does this sort of thing really happen to people?"

"Love at first sight? Marco and I knew each other for a while before we started dating. I'm not the right person to ask."

"I wouldn't call it love. Love is...more. I barely know him. This feeling, though, it's unlike anything I've ever felt before and it's driving me crazy."

"I know I told you not to text him, but if it's really driving you that mad not knowing, then ask him."

"Ask him what exactly? Why he hasn't called or texted me?"

"Yeah..."

"He's going to think I'm desperate."

"And you're not?" she asked, but it felt more like an accusation, and her hiked up eyebrow didn't help.

"You're his defense attorney now?"

"I love you, hon, but honestly, I just don't want to see you miserable because of this guy. Seriously, just text him and get it over with. If he ghosts you after you text him, then you know it's definitely over and you can move on. You need to return to the world of the living." She stood up from her chair and waddled over to the manicure table with her toes spread. "Can we please stop talking about Mr. Ghost for a bit and focus on just having fun today? Where should we go for lunch? We need some afternoon margueritas."

A few hours later, I stood in front of my closet, staring blankly at my clothes. I couldn't decide what I was going to wear. I was still pissed at *anti-Charming* for not calling me since Tuesday night. I was left with little choice but to deal with my anger issues by wearing something slutty and perhaps tearing it up on the dance floor with a sweaty, hunky stranger. Problem was, I didn't really own anything slutty.

A shimmery black, loose fitting dress would have to do. It was off the shoulders and came up mid-thigh. I styled my hair into long wavy curls and dotted on some dark eye-shadow and red lipstick. After strapping on a pair of my highest heeled sandals, I looked at myself in my floor-length mirror and smiled. It wasn't as slutty as I'd hoped, but I looked cute and ready for a fun night in the city.

As I walked through a mist of perfume, the intercom in the living room buzzed, announcing the arrival of Jen's guests along with the moment I was dreading—seeing Lisa. I smeared a fake smile on my face and trotted out to greet them.

After so many years, seeing Josh's little sister felt awkward, especially when I tried to act like it wasn't. She hurried up to give me one of those overly affectionate fake hugs with double-cheek-kiss combos. "Sara, you look fabulous, girl. What have you been up to?"

I fought rolling my eyes. "Oh, you know, working...stuff."

"Can you believe it's been like, four years, right? You and my brother had just broken up."

"Yeah, I'm not really keeping count," I responded with a short smile that I was sure never reached my eyes.

I regretted not letting Jen cancel on her. Of course, she still looked gorgeous. She could be Josh's twin—big blue eyes, thick blonde hair, sun kissed skin, and a sprinkling of freckles adorning her cheekbones. She wore some hot, red skimpy dress that perfectly hugged her outrageous curves, making me feel less slutty and a little flatter and formal.

We did the pleasantries. She brought two friends with her, Derrick and Taylor. They looked like cutouts from a fashion catalogue. They barely talked and couldn't look more disinterested to be there if they tried. Jen's med school friends arrived also. They appeared tired and worn, but eager for a night out. We sang happy birthday and ate some of the *tres leches* cake Marco brought for Jen.

After I downed about four glasses of champagne, Jen brought me to her bedroom and showed me the beautiful charm bracelet

Marco bought her. She couldn't stop talking about all the charms and what each represented.

I tuned her out. She was so ecstatic and dripping with happiness, it only highlighted how miserable I felt. It wasn't her fault, and I was a shitty friend for feeling that way, but the happier she was, the sadder I felt. Marco and Jen were deeply in love, and tonight I couldn't stand it. On a different night, I'd be jumping up and down with her, but at the moment, I struggled not to throw up.

When the champagne hit me, my blood pulsed with tingly bubbles, the buzz reaching my brain. I thanked the heavens for the mental relief. My inner vixen slowly emerged, numbing me into the shadows of my subconscious. I even flirted with Taylor, giggling at everything he said. Well, my vixen did, the real me had no idea what was so funny.

At around eleven, we headed to the club in a couple of cabs. Jen, Marco, and I took off in one, the rest of the group tailed behind us. I stared out the window of our cab, watching the blur of city lights as we drove through Manhattan. My head spun. I'd definitely had too much champagne. As badly as I'd hoped flirting with Taylor would erase all thoughts of Tom, all it did was make me think of him harder.

All I could do was wish I could see him, that he'd come find me and rescue me from this nightmarish day. So, as we pulled up in front of BLISS, one of the trendiest nightclubs in the city, I finally relented and did the one thing only my intoxicated vixen could do. I pulled out my phone, and started typing away.

Me: *At BLISS. Wearing a short black dress. Nothing underneath.* (well, I was still wearing panties, but he didn't need to know that).

Anti-Charming: ...

He saw the text. He started typing, but then the dreadful dots disappeared. My heart sank. And at the same time, I felt relief weave through me. I'd taken the reigns and it felt damn good to finally take control of my own destiny. If he wanted me, he needed to come get me. And if not, I was determined to have the best night of my life either way.

Twelve

SARA

BLISS, ONE OF THE MOST EXCLUSIVE CLUBS IN THE Meatpacking District, was a little hard to get into—but Marco promised Jen a night out she wouldn't forget. Spewing Roman and Renaissance overindulgence, the club boasted from a very eccentric décor. The chandeliers, painted ceilings, and colorful lighting made it somewhat whimsical.

Our table was close to the dance floor, and bottle service began with two bottles of champagne and a top shelf bottle of tequila. We dove right into our glasses and toasted to a fantastic evening. After another four glasses of sparkling wine and a few shots of tequila, my vixen completely took over and thoughts of Tom became dormant. Taylor proved to be quite the distraction after all. I didn't know how liberating it would be to shed my anxious skin and finally let loose.

Electronic symphonies swam through my ears, and bass pounded through my chest. My body wanted to burn through the dance floor, yearning to absorb the sound—if only to silence the longing tearing at me to come out and be unleashed. I uncurled myself from under Taylor's arm and stood up, holding his hand.

"Come dance with me," I pleaded.

"Now?"

I tugged on him a bit impatiently. "Yes, now please. I want to dance," I implored.

He conceded and I dragged him to the dance floor, bobbing and weaving until we pushed to the center of the crowd. We began to sway and I let the music guide my muscles. I didn't care that Taylor looked like a discombobulated idiot while he danced. Didn't care that as hard as I tried willing a connection between us, we couldn't be more wrong for each other. We had zero chemistry, but it seemed we were both committed to the charade in an attempt to forget the real reason we were both there.

I needed to forget that Tom existed and that his absence was making me bitter about being at the club without him. I put one arm around Taylor's neck and guided his other arm right below my waist, trying to get him to match my moves. Slowly, I gyrated against him, inviting a reciprocating response. I needed the connection. *Look at me, Taylor,* I yelled in my mind. With my hand, I tilted his head down toward mine. My eyes searched his for that something, that familiar gaze, but I saw nothing.

I *felt* nothing.

While my vixen put on her best moves and felt victory slowly rising against her hip, my real self stared blankly out at my partner who seemed more concerned about his rising erection than trying to establish a meaningful moment with me. I'd really hoped I could lose myself entirely to this night, but I couldn't stop yearning for more than this. I wanted to give in to the music, yet I couldn't succumb. I was on autopilot until the song ended along with the lame dry hump.

As we broke from our hold, Taylor coldly turned around and

headed for our table. As I trailed after him, a strong hand entwined its fingers through mine, and I was slowly swallowed up again by the crowd.

I nearly tripped a couple of times as I was dragged across the dance floor, not being able to see who was in front of me pulling my arm. Seeing double, and deaf to human sound, my confusion intensified with the constant flash of strobe lights. Finally, synchronized with a break in the music, my kidnapper spun me around and pinned my back against a wall, caging me with their body.

His body.

My knight came to rescue me once more.

Was it the alcohol? The music? All the emotions consuming me since Tuesday night? I didn't know, but I wanted to collapse into him. I wanted to kiss him. I wanted to hug him. But I also wanted to scream at him, then maybe kiss him again. Most of all, I wanted to cry because even though I was so ravaged by emotions, the only true emotion I felt was happiness.

All night, I'd lied to myself, letting my vixen run crazy, believing all was right with the world, that I couldn't care less he wasn't there, or didn't need him to so I could be content and alive. I was terribly wrong. I needed him more than I could dare imagine.

One single thought ran wild in my mind—*he came for me.*

Paralyzed, we waited, our gazes anchored to one another. When the rumbling sound of a new song began to thrum, his palm slid up my thigh, stopping right below the hem of my dress. Brushing his stubble across my cheek, he whispered in my ear, "You wanted my attention. Now you have it."

As if on cue, when the song broke, he crashed his lips into mine without warning, his tongue keeping beat with the music. I surrendered to his touch and let him consume me. His familiar scent mixed with the heat of his body drugged me. With both my arms wrapped around his neck, I forced him to tilt his head down, to lock his gaze with mine.

Panting, we stared into each other. This was the moment I'd waited for—the connection, the rhythm of our bodies pulsating to the beats of the music.

"Fuck," he said, as if he too felt the electric wire vibrating between us.

I smiled. "You came."

His palm slid up my thigh even higher. "What did you expect after that text you sent me?" he said, nipping at my lips.

I nipped back, demanding he give me his tongue, but he held back.

"What I want to know," he said, denying me the kiss I was desperately seeking. "Is why you'd temp me to come find you, only to slather yourself all over *Fabio*."

Suddenly, my mind seemed to sober up really quick. That fire in his eyes wasn't lust...that was ...jealousy? I fought the wide smile that tugged on my lips. "You mean...Taylor?"

"I don't care what his name is," he growled.

"How long were you watching me?"

"Long enough."

His tone darkened, and it was enough to pull me out of the erotic tension building between us. I couldn't deny it made me glad that seeing me with Taylor made him jealous, but at the same time, the possessiveness in his voice wasn't warranted. He'd practically ignored me for the last four days. Who was he to come here demanding explanations?

Needing space, I slid away from the wall and the hand that was still resting on my thigh—a hand my thigh missed terribly the instant it lost contact with his skin.

"I think you should let me take you home." He grabbed me by the hand, but I yanked it back in protest.

"Excuse me," I said, feeling even more sober. "What makes you think you can waltz in here and drag me out like a teenager breaking curfew? You know what, after ghosting me for four days, you have some fucking nerve acting like I'm the one who did something wrong."

"This was a mistake." He turned to leave.

I grabbed his arm. "Wait. We're not finished, Tom. One moment you're hot for me, the next you're an icebox, then you text me goodnight only to go dark for four days. What gives?"

"It's complicated."

"There's somebody else?"

"I may be a lot of things, but I'm not that guy."

"Then what is it?"

Rubbing a palm down his face, he puffed out a breath before turning from me in silence.

I watched him weave through the crowd, disbelief curdling in my gut. Grumbling, I followed after him. This guy was so fucking infuriating, yet I couldn't stop myself from chasing after him. He wasn't going to just walk away from me without telling me what happened. Without telling me something that made sense. What we'd felt back at the restaurant—that kiss—it had been explosive. And the way he kissed me tonight, like he'd been jonesing for me, I wasn't ready to walk away from *that*, not yet.

As I slithered through the thick crowd, I spotted him standing by the bar. Hair mussed up and decked out in a fitted gray button down accompanied by faded jeans, he looked every bit as sexy as the day I first set eyes on him. My vision went in and out of focus, my mind spinning again from all the alcohol. I did my best to balance my weight and not fall.

I squeezed next to him. "If you don't want me, why did you come?"

He turned toward me, eyes narrowed.

I raised my voice. "Why else would you ghost me?"

Leaning down, he whispered in my ear, "If I didn't want you, do you think I'd kiss you the way I did? You think seeing you dancing with another man would make me so fucking jealous I want to rip his head off?"

For a brief moment, we just stared into each other's eyes. Seemed we were both scared of something, both of us holding something back. Words weren't coming out easy, especially in this loud and obnoxious club, but the silence between us was louder than the music blasting off the walls and it made my heart ache. I couldn't talk to him with words, so this time, taking his hand and entwining my fingers through his, I guided him where I could show him how I was feeling, the other way I knew best—on the dance floor.

He followed without resistance.

When we reached the dance floor, I turned my back to him and nestled close. He buried his face in my neck as he gently guided my hips with his hands. The sound fusion melded us together, the crowd ceasing to exist. My heart and soul were imprisoned by the music, every muscle now governed by him, and him alone.

We were encased in each other, dancing until we lost all sense of time.

When the alcohol won and my mind and body were no longer coordinated, I whispered in Tom's ear, "Take me home."

Hands entwined in each other, he guided my wobbling body to Jen's table. Her two med friends were nowhere to be found, Lisa and Derrick looked like they'd had a fight, and Taylor was nearby on the dance floor, awkwardly dry-humping some girl. I waved to Jen, trying to get her attention. Scooting over, she leaned her ear toward me. "Not feeling so hot. Tom's taking me home."

He waved at her and she gave me the eye. I knew exactly what she was thinking.

"I'll tell you everything tomorrow," I mouthed.

She reached for my neck and brought her lips to my ear. "Seize the day, baby."

"I'm sorry for leaving early on your birthday."

She pulled me close again. "No worries. Just get home safe or I'll have to kill him."

~

Outside the club, I stumbled on my feet, eyes at half-mast. Tom helped me inside his car. He leaned over to buckle my seatbelt, his chest lightly brushing against my breasts, sparking a tingle in my body.

Whoa.

He quickly popped into the driver seat and the Rover jumped to life. I wanted to reach out and touch him, to invite him to touch *me*. I wanted more of the hungry beast—the man who'd stormed into the club and claimed my lips on that dance floor. My drunken vixen was desperate to make one last appearance. She'd been listening to my very secret thoughts, and unlike me, had no inhibition.

"Pull over," I whispered.

He turned toward me, a puzzled look etched on his face. "Where?"

"I don't care."

"Are you sick?"

"Not planning on ruining your leather seats. Don't worry."

"That's not what I'm worried about."

"Just pull over."

He made a quick turn down a dark and lonely street then parked the car, the engine idling.

"What is it?" he asked.

"Why so serious, hmm? Don't you want to have some fun?" I raised an eyebrow, trying to hint at my intentions?

"Are you asking me to take advantage of you?"

"Wouldn't be a bad idea."

He leaned in closer, staring me down, lips twitching at the corners. "That would be a very bad idea."

I parted my legs as I unbuckled my seatbelt. "Don't you want to check if I was telling the truth about not wearing anything underneath this dress?" I couldn't believe I'd actually taken my thong off in the restroom prior to leaving the club—because I clearly couldn't stop making stupid ass decisions.

His eyes darkened and I knew I'd gotten his full attention now.

Leaning over the console, I toyed with the sound system and fiddled through different songs until I found what I'd hoped for— something deep and sexy. I closed my eyes and jived to the music, gyrating my hips on the seat. When I opened my eyes back up, I caught him staring, lips slightly flushed.

"Not such a bad idea after all huh?" I asked, but I didn't give him a chance to reply and literally crawled unto his lap, straddling him before I could change my mind, my mouth crashing into his, devouring his lips with hunger. He accepted with caution before fully succumbing to my trap. I pressed my body into him, running my fingers through his hair. He tensed underneath me as he wrapped his arms around my body. Drowning in his hot and heavy breath, I writhed on his lap, sensing his erection under the soft fabric of his jeans as it brushed against the moist center between my legs.

Oh God...

Slippery with desire, I was overwhelmed with need.

I'd wanted to be this close since I first met him. To know the feeling of being held in his arms, dominated by his hands. I tried to reach below his belt, but he took my chin in his fingers and forced me to look at him. The fire in those olive eyes finally spoke of pure lust, turning me to butter. His thumb caressed my bottom lip, slowly parting my mouth.

His chest heaved. "Fuck, Sara. What are you doing to me?"

My tongue touched the inside of his thumb, slowly guiding it inside my mouth, where I gave it a slow and wet suckle before releasing it with a sloppy kiss. His mouth opened wider with an aroused groan, demanding my submission to quench his greedy need for me.

His mouth dove for my neck, savoring me while one of his hands rode up my thigh and cupped my naked ass. His other hand forced me to tilt my head back then he slid it down my sternum. I glided my hips back and forth to the rhythm of the song, pushing myself further into ecstasy. My breasts tingled with eagerness, wanting to break free from the confines of my dress, my body aching for his touch, for the feel of him inside me. I reached for his belt buckle again and raced to release his erection, but he put his hand over mine, stopping me in my tracks.

I peered into his eyes, but couldn't read what he was thinking.

Doesn't he want me?

The short pause was all I needed to realize the mistake we were about to make. I dropped the net over my vixen and dragged her back to her cage as she clawed and screamed.

What the hell was I about to do?

I unclenched my thighs from his lap and sank back into my seat, pulling my dress down, heart beating fire through my veins.

Tom didn't say a word but I watched him tug at his groin as he breathed heavily.

There was no shying my gaze away from what I saw, and I had to swallow deeply. He was so hard the outline of his sizable cock through his jeans was unmistakable, making me salivate. I couldn't believe I actually salivated thinking about putting him in my mouth.

"Drive, please," I said breathless, needing him to save me from myself before I continued to make a mess of things.

Without hesitation, he pushed the car into drive, and we glided home through Manhattan.

Despite my embarrassment, I fell asleep, likely from all the alcohol. When we arrived at my apartment, an eternity seemed to have passed. I heard distant sounds, but could only see blurry figures through slitted eyes. My legs were unresponsive. Hard hands gripped my body and I felt weightless. My mind faded in and out of consciousness, and hushed voices made broken appearances. All I deciphered was Pedro telling Tom my apartment was on the fifth floor.

Still floating, I heard the obscure sounds of jiggling keys followed by a meow and a hiss. Then, soft pillows clashed against my body. It was heaven.

Until I realized why. "No. Don't go…" I clamored.

"I'm not leaving you."

"Lay with me."

"I can't."

His words pricked my heart. "You don't want me."

"Christ, Sara. I want you more than you know. But not like this. If I lay down with you I won't have the strength to restrain myself. Close your eyes. Sleep. I'm not going anywhere."

The soft touch of his fingers cascading down my hair calmed my anxiety. He caressed my forehead, my cheeks, and before I knew it, I slipped into a deep dream as a tender kiss descended on my lips.

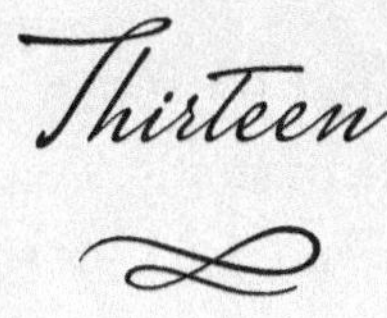

Thirteen

SARA

Five-thirty a.m.

An early dawn ray of light poked through the blinds, hitting me in the eyes. I was groggy, but tried to rise anyway, then it hit me—the throbbing pain in my head. It sent me crashing back onto my pillow. Tiny fragments of the previous night broke through.

What happened? What did I do?

I pushed the covers aside and attempted to roll out of bed, but my body felt like a ball of lead. Squinting toward the window, I noticed a figure lying on my chaise. Straining to focus, I rubbed my eyes until I was able to see clearly.

Tom?

He was sprawled on the chaise, passed out. One arm hung off the side, the other arm was folded, resting above his forehead. With jeans unbuckled and his shirt bunched up, his bare stomach was visible right above the waist. Even in my groggy state, I couldn't help but focus on his chiseled abs dusted in soft, dark hair. My eyes traveled down his happy trail to where the zipper ended and his dark briefs began.

My mind spun again. This guy gave me a serious case of panty-dropper syndrome.

As I regained my vision, I stared, trying to take in his calmness. No brooding, no tension, just my sleeping lion. A warm peace embraced me. Smiling, I laid back down and instantly faded to sleep.

~

Eleven a.m.

Ring! Ring! Ring! Ring!

At full volume, my phone roused me out of deep sleep. Stumbling out of bed, head pounding, I tried to locate the damn device so I could stomp on it and fling it out the window.

Shut up. Shut up.

By the time I reached the dresser, I'd missed the call. Still struggling to focus, I closed one eye and stared at the screen as a text came through.

Tom: *Get Ready. Picking you up at noon.*

As I grimaced at his insanity, my stomach turned, forcing me to the bathroom. Barely making it to the toilet, I heaved once before finally emptying what was left. I wiped my mouth and took one look in the mirror, almost fainting. My hair was curled into a bird's nest and my raccoon eyes did little to aid the situation. I'd slept in my clothes and my dress was a crumpled disaster. More importantly, the night washed over me in tidal waves of shame. I closed my eyes as I painfully remembered the ludicrous amounts of champagne and tequila I drank.

The club. Taylor. Arguing with Tom. Dancing. The car.
Oh, Christ. The car.

I palmed my face, regretting everything my debauched-self had done.

How the hell was I supposed to face Tom after what I did...well, tried to do?

Some hydrotherapy might help me figure this out.

I washed my teeth then jumped in the shower. While refreshing, the cold water did little to alleviate the nausea, nor did it help me conjure up an excuse for my less-than-honorable behavior. Not to mention the guy didn't give me much time to get ready. With my head still pounding, I rushed to put on a pair of white, skinny jeans and a turquoise blouse. I slid into a soft pair of silver flats, hoping Tom hadn't planned a fancy brunch.

It was a beautiful Sunday morning, bright sunshine streaked through a few scattered clouds. I stood on the stoop of the entrance, waiting for my looney date to arrive, but there was no sign of the Rover. As I scanned the streets for Tom, a guy sitting on a sports motorcycle parked in front of my building took off his biker helmet.

Yowza.

"Talk about dangerously sexy," I said as I walked up to the rider, eyeing the bike.

"Why thank you," Tom replied with a toothy smile.

I nodded toward his metal toy. "I was referring to the motorcycle."

Tom's happy expression morphed into a frown as he traced a finger from his right eye down his cheek. "Single tear," he said with a sarcastic pout.

I rolled my eyes. "Fine. You're sexy, too. Happy?"

He grinned.

"Where's the Rover?" I asked, shaking my head at his silliness.

He patted the back seat. "This is more fun."

While I was not typically fond of sports bikes, after what happened the night before, the forced silence was a welcomed opportunity. There was something incredibly hot and sexy about a guy on a motorcycle anyway.

His biker look—black jeans and boots with a white T-shirt and black leather jacket—was straight out of a wet dream. Yeah, my looney date was pretty damn smoking hot.

"Feeling hungover?" he teased, a playful smile making his lips twitch.

I lightly punched his arm. "You're lucky I like you. Giving me an hour to get ready after the night I had—not very gallant of you. I could have plans, you know."

"Do you?"

"That's not the point."

He crossed his arms over his chest. "What's the point, then?"

I crossed my arms also. "The point is..." I paused, realizing I'd never win this battle. "Never mind."

He dismounted his steel white horse, dug his hands into his back pockets, and looked at me. "I'm sorry." His sweet, sorrowful eyes were completely disarming.

"It's okay. I would have cancelled them anyway." I winked at him. "So where are we going?"

"Thought we'd grab a bite to eat. Talk."

My eyes widened. "About?" I hoped we wouldn't need to discuss what happened between us. I still didn't have an excuse for my behavior other than the old *alcohol made me do it* which would only make me sound like I was a pro at drunken expos. Clearly, I wasn't, but denying it would only sound worse.

He grabbed the extra helmet and slid it over my head, lifting the visor and ignoring my question. Then he handed me a matching women's jacket, and as he zipped me up, he eyed me from top to bottom. "Well, you look dangerously sexy yourself."

"I *do* enjoy you on me…I mean, your things on me." My cheeks flared as I realized my slip.

He cleared his throat. "Have you been on a motorcycle before?"

"Never," I replied, my knees trembling.

"Nervous?"

"Yeah, a bit."

"I would never put you in danger."

Images of horrific motorcycle accidents scanned through my mind.

"Some simple rules—keep your legs against the bike, feet on the footrests, and your arms wrapped tight around my body. Lean the side of your head against my back if you want. Got it?"

Wrap my arms tightly around you? Sure.

"Yes."

"Get on." He handed me a small knapsack. "Strap this on first."

"What's inside?"

"You'll see."

Securing myself behind his large frame, legs pressed tight and arms around his chest, we fit like a puzzle. Last time we were this close, we were famished animals feeding on each other's mouths. His body was broad and strong. I could feel his tone muscles through his clothes. Last night's memories of me writhing on his lap made my thighs tremble with unbidden want. Sweet warmth swirled its way down between my legs. Not being able to close them was silent torture.

I kept my eyes shut most of the ride, clinging onto Tom for dear life. His gloved hand rested over mine, trying to reassure me everything was okay. Once we jumped on the Henry Hudson heading north, although I didn't loosen my grip, my body relaxed. His driving was smooth and steady. Eventually, my fear dissipated and I was able to enjoy the freedom of the wind hitting against my body, and I reeled in the thrill of the danger. Anchored to this pillar, I couldn't feel any safer.

Once on the Jersey side, we made a short stop at a gas station, unsaddled, and stretched.

"The rest of the ride should be more pleasurable," he said. "Long though. Now would be the time to use the restroom."

"I'm okay."

"How's the ride?" He bounced on the balls of his feet.

"Terrifying. Amazing."

His left eyebrow hiked. "That awful, huh?"

"No, silly. It's like riding a crazy-fast, upside-down roller coaster. You know you're safe, yet you still get petrified while having tons of fun." I gave him a little nudge on his arm. "I did say amazing also. Relax. I'm thoroughly enjoying the ride. Really."

He beamed. "Let's get back on the road. First, since you're always asking about my playlist...I created one especially for this trip." Placing my helmet back over my head, he briefly touched the side of the helmet, and a beep sounded by my ears.

Before pulling down the visor, he said, "Enjoy it, baby." Then he hopped on the bike, patting the back seat. As I climbed on and he drove onto the road, a familiar song piped through the Bluetooth speakers inside the helmet. My cheeks flared—along with all other parts of my body. It was the song I played in his car the night before.

We hopped onto Route 9 West, heading to upstate New York. The scenic ride offered occasional views of the city and the Hudson River. I'd driven on this road before, but this was a whole new venture for me. With my arms wrapped snuggly against him, I couldn't believe only a week before he had been a complete stranger in a coffee shop. Now, I was a magnet strapped to his back, my life entrusted to him and his metal horse.

I held on tighter, fearful I was about to make the same mistakes all over again. The moment I dreaded for years had finally caught up with me and I was not sure I was ready to go diving for pieces of my broken heart.

Josh had been the love of my life. We'd known each other since grade school, but it wasn't until our senior year, when mutual friends and the convenience of sharing multiple classes brought us closer together. My teen heart swooned at his boyish good looks. Tall, muscular, blond, blue-eyed, and captain of the football team, he was every girl's dream.

I wasn't much of a looker. Even in my last year of high school, I still lacked the curves most boys craved. Plus, my life revolved around dance. It was all I breathed. You could say we were very much an unlikely match, and never in my wildest dreams would I have thought Josh Buckley would fall for a girl like me.

He was wild, exciting. For the first time in my life, dance wasn't the only thing that made me feel alive. I knew he was trouble, but I wasn't above the fatal female flaw of falling for the bad boy with the hopes of one day changing his ways and making him the perfect man. Swearing true love and that we would never be apart, I succumbed to his charms in the backseat of his cramped Camaro—mind, body, and soul—and gave myself to him on prom night.

No one thought it would last, but we vowed to prove them all wrong. We almost did. After graduation, we were inseparable. We fell madly, deeply in love. That love was our crystal ball. We thought we could conquer the world. After I finished dance school, we were going to get married. I'd work for a famous dance company, he'd manage his father's grocery market, and we'd travel the world. Eventually, we'd settle down in a nice suburban town, have two kids, and a dog named Charlie. We were so focused on the end product, we never bothered to think about the road there. I guess we never thought the magic could end.

For him, it did.

Shortly after my mother died, he packed up his bags and left. No goodbye. Not even a note. I'll never understand why he left without an explanation. With the loss of my mother, and me being laid up in bed for months while I healed from my spinal injuries, I needed him more than ever.

Whatever. Old news. What mattered was the present. I wanted to be with no one else but Tom, on his bike, destination anywhere, welded to my savior and perhaps my undoer as well.

We crossed the state border into New York, and the two-lane road transitioned into peaceful suburban surroundings. Traffic was sparse and we were able to glide up and around the winding road with ease. A dulcet serenade swam through my ears. Coupled with the fluid motion of the bike, and the serenity of the mountains, the music made my soul do pirouettes.

Our destination was a small-town pizza café, Thomasina's. The two-story building had a beige facade and dark-wood trim. Tom pulled over by the curve and parked the bike. He took off his helmet as he dismounted, releasing his unruly hair. We crossed the sidewalk to the café and Tom opened the door to usher me in. The tantalizing aromas of melted cheese, garlic, and basil in simmering tomatoes hit my nose with a vengeance. I hadn't realized how hungry I was until then.

Copper ceilings, checkered floors, and green-accented walls made it cozy and inviting. We were greeted by a friendly young girl who took us to our table. There weren't too many patrons, and I welcomed the added privacy.

"This place makes the best brick-oven pizza you have ever tasted," he boasted as if he owned the place.

I wouldn't have been surprised if he did.

"That's a pretty bold statement. You don't know what I've tasted."

"Sara, please. I'm telling you, once you have a slice, you will never want pizza elsewhere."

"You're saying, if I ever want to have pizza again, I'm gonna need to drive an hour and a half to get it?"

"Thomasina will ship it out to you."

I tilted my head, eyes slit in doubt. "They deliver to Manhattan?"

"No, they will ship you a frozen pie that you can stick in the oven."

"Best brick oven, you say?"

"I don't lie."

"Not going to take your word for it, so just order it and we'll see."

While we waited for our Margherita pie to arrive, our calamari and garlic knots appetizers were served along with my cherry cola and Tom's homemade, unsweetened iced tea.

As we ate, I decided it was time to breach the topic. "Tom, about last night—"

He stopped me before I could continue. "There's nothing for you to say."

"I'm not going to sit here and make excuses for my behavior; tell you it was the alcohol. The truth is...the truth is I'm glad you...well, I'm glad I didn't have any regrets this morning. Let's just put it like that. It's not to say I didn't want to...you know. Just not like that. You understand?"

"Of course," he replied quickly, but he didn't look me in the eyes.

I reached out and placed my hand over his. "Thanks for staying. Really."

His eyes met mine. "I wanted to make sure you were okay."

"What time did you leave?"

"I heard your friends stumbling in through the front door around six. I didn't want them to know I was there. Didn't want them to think I *dishonored* my maiden." He smiled playfully.

"Ha. Too late for dishonoring this maiden."

Our pizza arrived piping hot and oozing with bubbling melted cheese. I took my first slice in my fingers and worked on the stringy cheese. Tom planted his on a dish and used a fork and knife to cut a small bite then blew on it to cool it.

I burst into a laugh. "Who eats pizza with a fork and knife?"

"Making fun of me?" he asked with a hurt look.

"Tom, seriously, a fork and knife? You are disgracing this pizza."

"You eat it your way and I'll eat it my way."

I continued to laugh. "Your girly-ass way."

He arched an eyebrow and gave me a fake scowl.

We devoured our six-slice pie in no time. Taking a long gulp of my soda, I wiped my mouth with a napkin. "You were right. Amazing."

"Told you I don't lie," he said as he gestured for the waitress. "Dessert?"

"You have room for dessert?"

"You don't?"

"What do you recommend?"

"Zeppolis?"

"Fried dough? Bring it on."

Tom placed the order and looked at me with contemplative eyes. "I'm sorry, Sara," he uttered.

"For what?"

His steady expression didn't change. "For not calling."

His apology caught me off guard and washed me with a bit of embarrassment at my outburst at the club. "You don't have to apologize. I'm the one who's sorry for yelling at you last night."

"Sara, I'm sorry I didn't call you."

I blinked. "Why didn't you?"

"On my way to the airport from your apartment, I kept replaying our date and the things you said. You made me realize I'd come on too strong."

"Well, we'd just met the day before."

"I know, but since the first day I saw you, I hadn't been able to stop thinking about you, though. Then your car broke down and we ran into each other...I thought maybe it wasn't complete coincidence, you know? It's why I drove you home. Why I took you to my mechanic. I couldn't let you go. Didn't want to." He ran his hands through his hair, shaking his head.

"You left your scent embedded in my leather seats," he uttered as he smiled at himself. "I sound like a babbling idiot, I know. I'm not the soft and cuddly type, but you...you have my mind going in circles."

I should have told him he was right; it wasn't a coincidence. I followed him to the club because I couldn't stop thinking about him either. Everything about him had me so confused I didn't know what I was thinking or doing anymore.

The words were there, but I couldn't utter them.

He looked at me, waiting for me to say something.

"You think I wanted to leave you on the stoop of your entrance like that?" he said. "I would have kidnapped you back to my place if no ounce of decency still existed in my veins."

My heart raced at the sounds of his words.

He went on, "Then, I texted you but I didn't know what to say, or more like, I didn't know how to say how I felt."

I hung on every word he said, unable to tell him how hard I'd been aching for his touch, for his kiss.

Say something!

Tom was pouring out his heart and I remained mute. He was telling me everything I'd hoped to hear, my heart thawing at his words, but my lips would not unfreeze.

"Sara?"

My heart pound so rapidly, the blood in my veins thrummed. I wiped my clammy hands on my jeans. I wasn't ready for this. For him. "This is all happening so quickly," I blurted out.

His eyes flashed with worry, but there was understanding in them as well.

Our dessert arrived, but he pushed the plate away. "I want to show you something," he said as he signaled for the waitress to return.

The girl came back and handed him the bill. Tom pulled cash out of his wallet, and as we got up to leave, I waved toward the back of the restaurant, intending to use the restroom.

"I'll see you outside," he replied coolly.

Happy to escape from the heat of the ovens inside the dining area and away from the immense heaviness settling over us, I made it to the back in a flash. Pushing through the bathroom door, I gasped as I leaned my back against the door and stared at myself in the mirrors.

You can't keep doing this forever. Hiding. Sooner or later, you are going to have to tell him or let him go.

I gave myself a conferring look. A long time ago, I threw away the key to the towering prison housing my feelings, hoping no one would ever find it. Somehow, someone did, and he was outside on a proverbial white horse, waiting to whisk me away to freedom. If only I could tell him why I denied myself the liberty of being loved.

A single flower now fought to bloom through the forsaken, barren wasteland of my heart. He'd planted the seed the first day I saw him, and with a flaring blaze, his presence etched itself onto my soul. Why else would I have stalked him, kissed him, mounted his bike? Why else would I keep dreading being away from him?

Every waking moment I spent away from him was utter despair. Not knowing where he was, what he was doing, who he was with. I could have closed the book on that part of my life right then and forgotten I'd ever met him. Or I could let him unshackle my wrists and finally release me.

I splashed water on my face, trying to gather my senses, and regarded myself with determination. I exited the restaurant, the glaring rays of the afternoon sun beating down on my head. Tom was already saddled on the bike, waiting for me.

We hastened away toward the awe-inspiring vistas of West Point where we parked the bike and stripped off our gear, attaching the helmets to the frame. Tom threw the knapsack I had been carrying over his shoulder, and we began our stroll through the perfectly manicured lawns and picturesque landscapes. Hand in hand, we walked in silence for a few minutes. My thoughts had been percolating since we left the café. I knew he was waiting for me to say something. After his big confession, he left me weak at the knees. I understood we'd both been trying to placate our feelings for each other. Meanwhile, our insides churned with unease.

Spotting a bench nearby, I guided us to take a seat. It took me a minute to gather the courage to speak, but I finally let go. "I gave my heart to someone once. The kind of love you believe will last forever. The type that makes you dream of marriage and children. Of growing old and gray. Of being inseparable, even after death. That man was my happily ever after. I believed it wholeheartedly with my flesh and soul. Then, one day, my world was shredded to pieces." My chest heaved as I recalled the moment I found out my mom was dead. "I lost my mother in a car accident. I'd been the driver. I was strapped to a hospital bed, unable to move, barely able to breathe. My sister delivered the news."

Recalling the memory made my chest burn with sorrow, tears bubbling at the corners of my eyes. Tom swept a lose strand of hair behind my ear in a tender gesture, warming my heart. "I'm sorry," he said.

My voice shook. "After my mother died, my body lay broken, my soul shattered. I didn't think I could ever recover. At least not from the emotional agony of her death. Somehow, amidst the horror and pain, I held on to a shimmer of hope. Him. I'd lost everything, but at least I knew I had *him*.

"Except. I didn't. One day, I woke up and he was gone. No goodbye. No explanation."

Tom massaged my shoulder. "What happened?"

I chewed on my bottom lip, trying to hold back the deluge I knew was hiding behind my eyes. Tom attempted to reach for my hand, but I slid from his grasp and pushed up from the bench, digging my hands into my pockets. "Never heard from him again." My voice cracked as tears swelled in my eyes.

Dammit. I didn't want to cry.

Not again. Not for Josh.

I turned away from Tom, not wanting him to see my shell crack. "I never want to feel that kind of loss again."

Tom joined me, and I looked up at him. He tenderly wiped my tears with his thumbs and peered into me like no one else ever had, into the deepest shadows of my soul. "I know the pain of losing someone you love more than life itself." Taking my hand in his, he guided it to his heart, softly placing my palm against his chest. "Since the first day I met you, it's been pounding harder than ever." He paused, letting the silence bring forth the thundering beats. "Sara, what I'm feeling for you scares me shitless, but I'm tired of being afraid. I don't want you to be either."

Tears continued to pour more heavily down my face. He bent down and kissed me, his lips wet and salty, a soothing balm against my wounds. Tom's affection radiated throughout my body, the tingly sensation reaching every cell and fiber, reminding me love was the only way to heal a broken heart.

I caved into his chest, burying myself in his strength, wanting to feel protected. He wrapped an arm around my shoulders as I snaked mine around his waist, hooking a thumb into his back pocket. We continued to walk, embraced in beautiful silence and bathed in the beauty and magic of the valley.

Near Trophy Point was an overlook of the valley, and I understood why the majestic views from here had been the subject and inspiration for countless artists, each lured and captivated by the scenic charm and comeliness of the surroundings. I unhooked myself from under Tom's arm and walked over to the concrete ledge, trying to take it all in. Tom followed behind me, wrapping his arms around my shoulders, giving me a tender graze with his lips on the soft place below my ear.

"It's amazing, isn't it?" he asked.

"Breathtaking. I never want to forget it."

"And you won't." He released me and sat on the ledge, opening the mysterious knapsack and emptying it of its contents. Inside was a sketch pad and pencils.

"You're an artist?" I couldn't mask the tone of surprise in my voice.

"Sketch artist, and it's not something I normally advertise. I'm not that good."

"I'm sure you're being modest."

He didn't deny it. "How would you like to be the subject of my artistic endeavor this afternoon?"

"Oh, I don't know."

"Sketching portraits is a small passion for me, and yours is one I've wanted to capture ever since I saw your face. This is the perfect place, Sara. Please let me do this for you."

My face flushed. "Seriously?"

"I have to."

"Why?"

He stretched his arms out, inviting me toward him. Grabbing my wrists, he reeled me in closer, trapping me between his legs, our gaze eye level.

With his fingers, he traced the outlines of my facial features. "For me," he said smiling, "when I see someone who enthralls me as much as you, with these deep brown eyes and this cute little button nose..." He continued to trace until his thumb found my lips. "Not to mention, these soft, rosy lips..." Gently but briefly, he brushed his mouth against mine, his hot breath delicately sweeping over me.

"Keep going," I moaned.

He smiled, amusement reaching his eyes before he continued to trace my cheeks and jawline. He kept his lips close to my face, breathing the words onto me as he spoke. "Who can forget these tiny, half-moon dimples. I mean, my mind simply draws every line and curve, every crevice, shade and color to the smallest detail, over and over again, until your image is permanently etched into my memory. Only thing left is putting memory to paper."

By the time he finished pronouncing the last word, my skin was prickled with goose bumps. "Whoa," I said, releasing the breath trapped in my chest and surfacing from his drowning spell.

"Let me do this," he begged.

I sighed. "Okay…"

He helped me climb onto the ledge. "Sit here. Eyes on me."

"Is it gonna be long? How should I pose?"

"Relax. Just be you." Followed by his kiss, my anxiety faded.

I eased and burrowed my gaze into his. While holding onto the pad, he put a pencil between his lips and took another in his hand. With a scrunched-up brow, he got to work, his hand breezing through the pad. Shadows of half smiles poked through the corners of his lips.

While he drew, my mind wandered to the comment he made earlier about knowing loss.

"Tom, can I ask you something?"

"Sure."

"Earlier you said you knew about broken hearts?"

He looked up from his drawing and gave me a hesitant look before returning to the task. He took the pencil out of his mouth, and replied, "Love hasn't been kind to me either."

"You don't want to talk about it?"

"It's a nice day, I don't want to sour it with stories of my past. Perhaps another time."

Fourteen

SARA

WHILE HE FOCUSED ON HIS ARTISTIC ENDEAVOR, MY MIND wondered to more sensual places. Every fiber in my body craved him. My only desire was to ease the always-present tension, regardless of his mood. I ached to unsheathe him, to shred the fabric of his clothes with my fingers, and to caress all the stiff muscles of his body, gently massaging him into submission. My body temperature rose at the thought of owning his release and surrendering mine to him.

Loud thunder shook me out of my daydream. Out in the distance, the heavens darkened with the sudden creep of ashen clouds, the threat of rain looming in the horizon. A satisfied grunt from Tom drew my attention, and I was more than happy to stand up and stretch.

"Well, how does it look?" I asked.

"No artist could capture your full beauty, Sara."

I snickered at him. "Okay, you seriously have to stop talking like that."

"Like what?"

"Like you are from some other time, that's what."

He frowned.

My eyes widened. "C'mon, you know most guys don't say those kinds of things to women...at least not anymore. Unless, they think that shit will get them laid, I guess."

His lips thinned into a tight line. "I'm not most guys." He threw his sketch pad into the backpack followed by the pencils.

"Wait, what are you doing? Aren't you going to show me?"

He zipped up the bag, ignoring my question. "Is that what you think I'm doing? Trying to get you into bed?"

I finally realized why he was mad. "I didn't mean to imply—"

"Look, I brought you here because this place means something special to me, and I wanted you to know what's been happening to me since I met you."

I lowered my chin. "I'm sorry. I wasn't thinking when I made the comment."

"It's not like that."

Abashed, I looked back up.

"If...if getting you in bed was all I wanted..." He looked away before continuing. "Last night—"

"You didn't," I said, cutting him off. "I was a wreck. You could have taken advantage of me and you didn't." I walked up to him and put my arms around his neck. "I'm sorry for making you feel like a jerk."

After a brief moment, we released each other and he walked over to the ledge where he stared out at the endless view of the Hudson River cutting through the valley. "I *am* a jerk," he admitted. "Relationships with women...they haven't gone past the bedroom. I'm not proud of it, but it's been safer for everyone." He turned toward me, the torment in his eyes matched the stormy clouds in the sky. "With you, I need things to be different. I don't want to mess it up."

Thunder broke again, shifting our attention to the impending rain.

"We should get going, looks like it's gonna pour soon," he said, following the cue from the sky.

"Don't I get to see my portrait first?"

"You're sure you want to see it?"

"Are you kidding? I didn't sit on hard rock for twenty minutes for nothing. Hand over the bag, mister."

He held on with an iron fist. Then, with terrified eyes, handed it to me.

"Oh, c'mon," I said, "it can't possibly be that bad." I unzipped the bag and slid the pad out.

Oh, God.

While I held the drawing in my hand, my heart free fell into the pit of my stomach, causing me to drop the bag.

"It's horrible, isn't it?" He tried to grab it away from my hands, but I was able to steer away.

Moved to tears, I pressed a hand to my heart.

"Sara, enough with the theatrics. You don't have to patronize me. See, this is why I don't tell people. Why I never let anyone see my drawings. I shouldn't have done this."

"Would you shut up? Tom, it's gorgeous."

He rolled his eyes. "It's just a sketch."

"Stop it. It's positively the most beautiful thing anyone has ever done for me." Looking at it more closely, I absorbed every pencil stroke. It was more than a portrait of me—hair wild in the wind, the landscape sweeping behind me. It was a snapshot of my raw spirit and my eyes. He reached into the depths of my abyss and pulled out all my secrets, putting them on display for all to see, every detail intricately drawn to perfection. I couldn't stop gawking. A warm breath by my ear startled me, sending chills down my spine.

"What were you thinking as I drew?"

I looked away from him, trying to disguise my blush. "Like the Mona Lisa, you'll never know, and I'm never telling."

"I can live with that."

Tom put the sketch between the pages of his pad then stuck it in the knapsack. We hightailed it back to the parking lot, hoping to outrun the rain, but the water fell by the buckets moments later. By the time we arrived at the visitor center seeking shelter, we were drenched. Dripping wet, our shirts clung to every nook and cranny of our bodies. Tom's rippled chest and stomach were visible through his white T-shirt and my light cottony turquoise blouse seemed to have been washed completely of color, melting into my skin and revealing my pale-white, lacy bra.

"I didn't know it was supposed to rain today," I said, trying to divert the attention from our almost-naked bodies. Tom realized the same and attempted a distracted look away from my breasts, where my nipples had decided to perk up in salutation.

"Weather guy said scattered showers. Thought we'd get lucky. Can't ride out until the rain stops."

A few minutes later, the downpour became a short drizzle before turning into a light mist. Tom opened the door and urged me out. We sprinted to the bike and took our jackets out from the top-box and unlocked our helmets from the frame. After gearing up, and despite wearing the jacket, my body shivered. Tom noticed me trembling and rubbed his hands up and down my arms. "Gonna take the highway to make it home quicker. It'll be cold since we're wet. I'm sorry. I should have planned better."

"Don't worry, just get me some place warm," I stuttered out.

"We should probably stop at my place to dry up before I drive you back to the city."

"Sure. Let's get moving."

～

Malcolm Place, Tom's apartment complex, located near Sinatra Drive in Hoboken, was a high-rise luxury residence sitting on the Hudson River waterfront with views of the Manhattan skyline. We pulled into the garage and parked next to the Rover then took the elevators to the ninth floor.

It was a long walk to his unit, and Tom fumbled with his keys as we approached. The idea of being alone made my insides churn. In public, I was safe from the clawing feline I put away in her cage the night before.

In private, there was no predicting what could happen.

Tom opened the door to his home and I gasped as I slowly stepped through, peeking around at the surroundings. The far wall of the living room and dining area was a splay of floor-to-ceiling windows facing the river. It was a corner apartment with a southern exposure, capturing a full-blown panorama of Midtown Manhattan, the Empire State Building dominating the view. And he thought my East Side apartment was something to brag about?

Before I was fully inside, soft taps padding against the hard wood floors thumped from inside one of the rooms. A large, bouncy chocolate lab poked from around a corner then made a beeline toward us. He huffed at my sight, but quickly saw Tom, and with recognition flooding his senses, he ignored my presence. The dog jumped up to greet him, licking Tom's face with excitement, tail wagging like a propeller.

"Hey, buddy. Good to see you, too." He patted the dog and gave him a scratch under his neck. The canine sat by his master's feet, head tilted back, enjoying his rub, tongue drooping to the side, panting in utter glee.

"You didn't tell me you had a dog."

"You didn't tell me you had a cat."

"You met Skiddles?"

"Skiddles? Yes, I met your angry cat. It wasn't very fond of me last night. I had to shoo her off your bed. She nearly attacked me before scurrying away in a never-ending hiss."

"Skiddles is harmless," I said, shaking my head. I nodded toward his furry companion. "He's gorgeous."

"This is Bax. Bax, say hi to our guest."

I let him sniff my hand and he stopped panting, intrigued by the new scent. He licked my hand and walked over, circling and smelling around my feet and crotch before stopping in front of me, waiting.

Tom whispered in my ear, "Extend your hand and ask for his paw."

Curiously, I looked at Bax then put my hand out to him. "Paw."

His eyes lit up and he gently gave me his paw. "Nice to meet you, Bax," I said with a gentle handshake.

Satisfied with our greeting, he pulled away and walked toward the front door and sat.

"He needs a bathroom break. Gonna take him for a short walk. Shouldn't be more than fifteen minutes. Make yourself at home." He clipped the leather lead hanging by the entrance to Bax's collar then headed out, shutting the door and leaving me alone in his apartment.

Well, this was unexpected. Looking around the apartment, I couldn't believe I was actually inside Tom's place. Mr. Wright. Mr. Iced Double. The guy who'd caught my clumsy ass when I tripped over my shoe. The man I'd fantasized about for days, wondering exactly where he went to sleep at night, and now, here I was.

Taking a gentle stroll through the open area, I took in every detail. Cherry cabinets lined the modern kitchen. It was well equipped with top of the line appliances and granite countertops. The rest of the living area was furnished with a more contemporary flare: straight lines, glass, and dark woods. By the windows, a massive, black leather sectional completed his living area. A large flat screen was mounted on the wall above a gas fireplace, and the console was packed with high-tech, big-boy toys. Plush white area rugs softened the room. The only touches of color came from abstract paintings scattered across the walls.

Seemed he owned an expansive collection of movies—mostly war dramas, epics, and psychological thrillers. Near the southern-most windows sat a massive telescope aimed at the heavens. Nearby, a long accent table was topped with an array of old, worn books. They tempted me to skim through their titles, but the covers and bindings were extremely faded and probably very fragile.

There were a few personal black and white framed photos on a wall. A picture of Tom and Bax on a hiking trail hung to the right of the wall collage. Another frame held the face of a young, beautiful woman. Her long, light hair was styled straight, but in a vintage style. She was laughing at something behind the field of view. The slight resemblance to Tom was uncanny.

In another picture, Tom wrapped an arm around another man's shoulder. They looked to be the same age, enjoying each other's company over drinks at a party. This guy also shared a slight resemblance to Tom. Finally, in the middle of this collage was a picture of a group of three men decked out in military combat gear and equipped with rifles. It was apparent from the background they were somewhere in the desert. The picture was taken at a distance, so leaning in for a closer look, I was floored when I noticed who was in the picture. To my amazement, in the center of the photo and flanked by two soldiers wearing the familiar Marine pattern fatigues, was a young unmistakable face.

"Holy shit, Tom's a Marine."

"Surprised?" Tom rasped behind me.

I jumped at the sound of his voice, my hand automatically leaping to my heart. "Christ. You scared me," I said as I turned to face him. "I didn't mean to...I was simply looking around."

"There's nothing to be sorry about," he said as he walked back toward the kitchen.

"You didn't tell me you were a Marine."

He reached into a cookie jar and pulled out a doggie treat that he fed to Bax. "That picture was taken a long time ago."

"How long?"

He breathed deeply, a hand pressed to his nape, as if mentioning his past was a heavy weight on his neck. "I was nineteen when I was first deployed to the Middle East."

My eyes narrowed, intrigued yet cautious of this side of him I didn't know. "Still in the military?"

He paused before he answered, a dark cloud hovering over his eyes. "My last tour was a couple of years ago."

"My father was also a Marine," I said. "A soldier in Vietnam and the Korean War. Never liked talking about it much."

Looking away, he said in a somber voice, "War is never an easy topic."

"I'm sorry, I didn't mean to—"

"Hey, you hungry?" he interrupted promptly, changing the subject. "I'm famished. I can whip up a quick meal."

Tom didn't want to talk about his time in the military. That was obvious. As civilians, one could never know the true demons soldiers combat in the face of war. The damage is at times irreparable, as I learned for so many years with my father. I didn't want to press Tom, but a part of me remained confused.

Being a Marine is such a big part of a soldier's life, and even though I understood why he didn't want to talk about it, what I didn't get was why he hadn't mentioned it before. Perhaps I was beginning to comprehend the cloud that seemed to hover over him at times.

Already picking things out of the fridge, he fired up the range, engrossed and happy to be cooking—a completely different man than two minutes prior. He was the opposite of my father. You wouldn't know by looking at him that he once wielded an assault rifle or witnessed more horrors and death than any one person could ever imagine.

"What are you making us?" I asked as I walked toward the kitchen.

Tom held a package of chicken tenders in one hand and a bag of lettuce in the other. "Given we kind of pigged out this afternoon, I was thinking...herb-rubbed grilled chicken tossed over fresh greens?"

"How can I help?"

"You can relax and keep me company." He poured me a glass of chilled wine as I sat on the island barstool.

Smiling, I sipped my crisp wine then I caught a glimpse of my reflection on the wall mirror near the foyer and nearly spit out my wine. My hair was twisted into a fuzz-ball, mascara was smeared across my eyes, and my damp clothes were wrinkly and unflattering. Completely self-conscious and utterly mortified, I jumped off my stool. "Um, actually, would it be okay if I freshen up?"

A smirk ghosted across his lips. "Ah...sure. There should be fresh towels in the bathrooms. You can use the one in my room down and to the left or if you prefer, the guest room is down to the far right."

"Okay, thanks."

"You can throw your clothes in the dryer if you want. I have robes in the linen closet."

The guest room was the more appropriate choice for my shower, but somehow, I ended up in Tom's room. Bax turned into my shadow and followed me into his master's chamber.

"What is it, Bax? You don't trust me in here?"

He sat down, looking at me, and tilted his head to the left.

"Yeah, I don't know what I'm doing in here either. Curious, I guess."

Tom's room was spacious, boasting of the same floor to ceiling windows and views of the city. Center stage belonged to the king size, four-poster bed. I ran my hand over the soft, dark-burgundy duvet folded at the foot of the bed and pressed my palm on the plush mattress, loving the cool feel of his white, cotton sheets. Unbidden images of bare skin tangled in those sheets flooded my mind. I shook the thoughts out of my head before those thoughts could get me in trouble.

Tiled in natural stone and equipped with double sinks and vanities, the master bathroom was straight out of a home design magazine. It was adorned with a massive soaking tub and a double shower. Literally, Heaven. I stripped off my sodden clothes and dumped them on the floor. After a quick ten-minute rinse, I wrapped myself in a towel and walked out into the coolness of his room.

Not wanting to be intrusive, but curious to find that robe, I slowly pried open the doors to his walk-in closet. If the manner in which he organized it wasn't a clue about his military background, I didn't know what else could be. Everything was neatly folded and stacked. His tailored suits and shirts were arranged by color and type. Shoes were shiny and placed in cubbies.

Still, no robe.

"Ahem." A cough at the door turned my attention.

Busted.

Tom stood at the entrance, holding the eluding white robe.

I shrugged, shamefully. "Oh, hey. Didn't mean to be looking through your closet."

"Don't worry about it...here." He stepped into the room and handed me the robe. "It was in the guest room." His eyes failed to cover the hungry look skimming up and down my-barely-covered-in-his-towel body. The realization of my nakedness in his room and the proximity to him and his bed made the wet beads on my skin evaporate. Tom noticed my flush and dropped his gaze. Seeing my clothes on the floor, he offered to take them to the dryer and was off before I could refuse.

Just perfect. My undergarments were in that pile.

Wrapped warmly in the soft cotton robe, I padded out barefoot into the living room. The moon was now in her glory, and the evening sparkled across the river. Tom was finishing up in the kitchen and waved me over.

"Hey," I whispered, plopping my ass on one of the barstools in front of the kitchen island.

"Good shower?"

"That bathroom is amazing. Can I move in?"

"Tomorrow good for ya?"

"I'm being serious. I could live in there."

He smiled. "Ready to eat?"

"Yes. I'm starving."

He served me a large plate of tossed lettuce, fresh herbs, and grape tomatoes, mixed with grilled chicken chunks and sprinkled parmesan cheese, all drizzled with a zesty lemon dressing. Tom also brought out a steaming loaf of garlic bread straight from the oven. I drooled. He then sat next to me and poured me another glass of wine. "Hope you like it. It's all I could whip up in short notice."

I shoveled in a mouthful, savoring the juiciness of the chicken. "It's delicious."

His chest puffed and his triumphant smile spilled into his eyes.

"Where did Mr. Iced Double learn how to cook?"

He squinted in bewilderment. "Mr. Iced what?"

Crap.

"Uh, never mind. When'd you become a chef?"

"I just like to cook. Growing up, my mom always made sure there was something good in her kitchen."

"She taught you?"

"I watched."

"Just watched?"

He reached for the Pinot Grigio. "More wine?"

I slit my eyes. "I know what you're doing. Don't change the subject."

"I'm not."

"My glass is still full, so no need to fill it. It's okay if you don't like to talk about your personal life."

"Why do you assume that?"

"You never told me you were a Marine."

"I didn't think it was important."

"You don't really believe that."

He pushed his plate away, the meal only partially finished. Then he crossed his arms. "It makes me a bit uncomfortable...to talk about it."

I reached out for his arm and squeezed, offering reassurance. "I'm sorry. I didn't mean to press the issue. If you ever do want to talk about it..."

He hooded his eyes then turned to look at me. "I know. Thanks."

I didn't know what else to say after that. I turned to the rest of my meal and neither one of us said anything while I continued to munch on my salad.

Tom simply watched me eat. Eventually, an awkward silence settled over us. Finishing the last chicken morsel, I sighed and rubbed my belly. "Well, that was good."

"Was it?"

"Yeah."

"Now what?" he asked, a playful smirk emerging from his lips.

"You tell me."

"Well, how about we put you on the hot seat now?"

"On the hot seat?"

"You asked me questions."

"Barely."

"It's your turn."

"What do you want to know?"

"You haven't said much about how you feel...about this." He waved a finger between us.

I dropped my gaze. This was the part that always got me, the part I wanted to avoid. He was coming on a bit strong, but at the same time, I wasn't saying no. I wasn't pulling away. I wasn't looking for my clothes rushing to leave his apartment.

Quite the opposite. My knees turned to gelatin every time he came near. And that's probably what he wanted me to say. That no matter how hard I tried to stay away, I would always end up here, wanting to be with him.

Fuck. Why couldn't I just open up?

"Tom, what do you want me to say? We just met. This is happening crazy fast and..."

"You think I don't know that?" His hot gaze buried into mine. "Sara, you think it doesn't cross my mind too, how crazy this shit is? You stumbling into my life only one week ago and not being able to rip you out of my head, no matter how hard I try? You're like a drug I can't get enough of—the heroin that's about to turn me into some type of fucking addict."

All I could do was stare.

"I'm scared too," he continued, his eyes still seated in mine with a fire he could barely contain. "Scared of what might happen if I reach over and take you into my arms." Then he lowered his gaze. "Mostly. Scared of what might happen if I don't." He looked back up and a shadow of doubt clouded his eyes. "Baby, you've got me so fucked in the head, I don't know what I'm doing anymore."

Thunderstruck, I chugged the rest of my wine in one swig. How was I supposed to follow all that? I couldn't deal with so much intensity. It was one thing to feel these things, another to have someone recite back exactly how you felt, as if they'd dug deep into your chest cavity and excavated your soul. He terrified me in the sweetest most surreal sense of the word. Not knowing how to react, I stood up to pick up the dishes, but Tom grabbed hold of my waist and pulled me in between his indecently spread legs. Unintentionally, I rested my hands on his thighs, feeling the strength and power of the muscles beneath his pants, too aware of the level of intimacy, but not backing away from the intrusion.

"Leave that," he said firmly, then breathily added, "I know what I want, Sara. As much as you want to deny it, you feel it, too—this electricity that singes us both when we touch. I might have denied myself your taste last night, but I'll be dammed if I'm going to let you slip through my fingers again." He took a loose strand of damp hair from my face and tucked it behind my ear, slowly caressing my cheek with his long finger and tracing my jaw.

Succumbing to his touch, I closed my eyes and felt the soft press of his lips on mine. He nibbled, the sensation of his hot tongue slowly parting my mouth and tasting me with his wetness sent shivers down my spine, desire coiling in my center. Tom held my face in his hands, and as he kissed me, he whispered through heated breaths, "Stay with me tonight."

I tried to resist his invitation.

Really, I did, but it was a losing battle. Everything he'd professed spun in my mind. I knew it since the first moment I laid eyes on him. I knew this man was meant to be in my life. Denial was not serving me any purpose. I wanted to be cradled in his arms and be absorbed into him like never before. Every ounce of my being raged with need.

I need this.

I need him.

And not wanting to separate from his mouth, I nodded in agreement, sealing my fate.

Fifteen

TOM

The instant she accepted my proposition, I hoisted her up into my arms. Wrapping her legs around my waist, she held on tight as I carried her to my leather couch, her body straddling mine as I sat us down. Taking a second to admire the blush rising up her neck and warming her cheeks, I gently uncoiled the robe's fabric belt, letting the robe fall off her shoulders and pool at my feet.

I took in a sharp inhale at the sight of her perfect breasts. Fuck. I'd imagined her like this since last night. I had no clue how I was able to resist her when she crawled onto me in my car. They way she'd moved her hips...the way she'd crashed her mouth into mine—it had made my mind spin out of control. And when my hand slipped under her dress and found nothing but bare flesh, I nearly lost it. I was seconds from ripping my jeans open and burying myself inside her.

It would've been so easy, so fucking hot, but so fucking wrong.

Taking her last night would've been a mistake I could've never taken back. The first time I claimed her, I wanted her one-hundred percent conscious and aware of everything I was doing to her body. I needed her to give me her true consent, but I also wanted her to remember the way I fucked her and tasted every part of her.

Sara really had no idea how madly infatuated I was with her—since the first moment I spotted her at the coffee shop. And I tried—I fucking *tried*—to do the noble thing and stay away. The distance had helped, plus burying myself in work. I didn't know how I'd done it, but I'd managed not to call or text her for four days, and up until she texted me that she was at the club, I thought I'd escaped my fate. But I hadn't done it just for me. I'd tried to spare her the heartache too, because at the speed we were going, we were destined to crash.

But that text...I'd not even stopped to think if what I was doing was right. I didn't bother to consider what would happen once I saw her. I simply grabbed my car keys and raced to the city, storming into the club like some crazed boyfriend. *Boyfriend*...the word sounded odd inside my head at the time, but when I finally spotted her on the dance floor dancing with that other man, something inside of me went feral.

The sheer possessiveness that raked my body was borderline criminal. How could I feel this way about this girl when we weren't anything? And, well, that was the goddamn problem, wasn't it? I *didn't* own her. And the thought of not being the one to own her smiles... Or own her kisses... own her touch—that thought mauled my mind like a grizzly bear tearing up its prey. In that exact moment when I saw her pressed up against that long-haired asshole, only one thought rang inside my head—mine.

It was illogical. Barbaric. But I didn't care if it made me look like a Neanderthal.

I'd known then there was no other option. She was going to be mine. I just needed her to know it too.

Right now, though, I couldn't even touch her. I just wanted to look at her like this forever, sitting on top of me, her nude body exposed to me—a goddess upon her throne. There was a bold yet vulnerable aura about her that stirred up my need to protect her, to want to keep her safe, including her heart—*especially* her heart.

Did I want to own every inch of her body? My cock could attest to that—prick was growing impatient with me. What, with her skin still damp from the shower, she looked dewy and delicious, beckoning me to touch her soft skin. But I kept resisting her as bad as it hurt to not run my fingers across her jawline. To not caress the perfect mounds of her breasts. To not slide my fingers between her thighs and feel the wetness pooling at her core.

Because tonight wasn't just about exploring all the different ways I could make her come. It was about letting her know that with her, things were going to be different. I wanted more than her body. I wanted all of her or nothing.

She undulated her hips over my thighs, pressing her center hard over my jeans. Her soft moans made my entire body vibrate. She was seeking pleasure and denying her that right now lit up a spark of satisfaction inside my chest. Maybe a dark side of me wanted to punish her just a little for making me murderously jealous at the club.

Sara licked her lips as she moved faster, her movements fluid. A smile carved across my face. "You might kill me if you keep doing that."

Biting her bottom lip, she said, "Why aren't you touching me?"

I closed my eyes and clenched my jaw. "You have no idea how much I want to."

She leaned into me, her dark silky hair cascading over both of us. "What's stopping you?"

Cupping her jaw, I drew her in closer. "What you did to me last night...letting me see you dance with..."

"Taylor," she said with a smirk.

"Whatever the fuck his name is, don't ever do that to me again."

Her eyes flashed with worry. "Tom...I'm sorry. I—"

Claiming her lips, I swallowed her words. I didn't need an apology. All I wanted was for her to know that there was no turning back now. She was mine, and to prove it, I branded her with my kiss until she moaned my name into my mouth.

Fuck, she felt so good sitting naked on top of me, my arms wrapping tight around her body. I could do this all night, just kiss her and have her moan my name over and over again. She reached for my belt buckle, but I put my hand over hers. "First, I want to feel your body, then, you can play with mine."

Cupping each breast, I softly rubbed my thumbs across her dark nipples, turning them into hard buds. She arched her back, and I took the opportunity to take each nipple into my mouth. She writhed, her body clamoring for me to touch her lower and lower.

Sliding my fingers down her sternum, I drew a path down her chest to her navel, then lower until I reached the spot right above her completely bare center, exactly where her body was begging me to touch her. Her skin was silky smooth, and I could see the pale pinkish color of her pussy already glistening with arousal. Devil have mercy on my soul. I couldn't wait to slide my finger...my tongue...my cock...inside her.

"I've wanted you like this since last night," I said. "Sitting on me, completely naked. Completely under my control." I swirled my thumb right above her slit, inching it closer to her clit with each revolution. She parted her legs wide and I could see even more of her.

"Touch me, please," she begged in a soft whisper.

I smirked. "I like the way you sound when you ask for it."

"I need you," she implored more forcefully.

"Tell me where you want me to touch you."

She took my hand and brought it to her center, but I refused to touch her. "I want to hear you say it."

Sara bit her bottom lip again, cheeks reddening.

"You haven't talked dirty before, have you?"

Swallowing hard, she gently shook her head *no.* I brushed my knuckles across her warm cheeks. God she was beautiful, and her bashfulness only made me want her more. "You want me to touch your pussy? To play with your clit and make you come on my fingers?"

A seductive smile danced on her lips. Maybe she wasn't so innocent after all.

Licking my thumb, I reached between her legs and softly rubbed around her clit until I felt her wetness coat my finger. "Ah, fuck, baby girl. You feel so goddamn good." I kept rubbing in small circles until I knew her clit was engorged, then I touched her right where I knew she needed.

"Oh, my God. Yeah...just like that. Don't stop." Panting, she kept her legs spread as wide as she could, hips moving in tune to my touch.

I knew what she craved, so I gave her a small taste and pushed one finger inside her. "Shit, you are so wet." Massaging the inside of her walls, I pressed on her G-spot until I felt her body shiver. She hung her head back, riding the pleasure wave.

But I wasn't about to let her off that easy. After all, she wasn't off the hook yet for what she'd done at the club. "You come when I say you can come. Understood?"

She groaned, disappointed. Such a little brat. Sliding my hand up her neck until I cupped the back of her head, I brought her face closer to mine, our lips brushing against each other. "Coming is the finish line. Getting there is the fun part."

"You're torturing me," she said with a pout.

I licked my slick finger. "Torture is craving your taste for days and forcing myself not to go looking for you because I knew once I found you, I'd become a fucking addict."

"Well, you've found me. What do you want to do to me now?"

"What I want is my tongue sliding up and down that pussy. Get on the couch and spread those legs for me."

Once she was flat on her back, she parted her legs, her fingers lazily skimming over her sex. I stripped off my clothes and wrapped a hand around my rock-hard erection. Sara's eyes widened, watching me intently as I stroked myself. She licked her lips, practically begging me to fill her mouth. "Not yet," I told her as I brought my tongue to her slit, diving deep inside of her before flicking her little bundle of nerves.

I repeated the motion, lapping up and down her entire slit before diving my tongue deep again. Her body tightened as she neared climax, so I penetrated her with my middle finger while my tongue continued to lick.

Sara raised her head off the couch and gorged on the sight of me devouring her pussy. "I'm so close, I can't hold it anymore."

I licked stronger, flicking her clit with the tip of my tongue, thrusting faster and deeper with my finger. "Come for me, baby."

Her hips bucked as she came, and our gazes met as I lapped off every drop of her arousal. She couldn't even blink as she watched me slowly brush my tongue over her still-swollen clit, her legs quivering.

Yeah. I definitely own you now.

My raging male instincts begged me to fuck her. I was so mad with lust, the tip of my cock dripped with precum. But I knew once I went inside of her, I'd lose all self-control, and right now, I wanted to prolong the pleasure for as long as I could. I wanted those fucking pretty lips of hers wrapped around me, sucking on my dick like she couldn't get enough.

When I approached her mouth, she greedily took me in her hand and guided me through her parted lips. Fucking hell. That wet and warm tongue licked off all the precum in slow, sensual movements, and I thought my body would combust. She sent a rippling shockwave of erotic pleasure up my spine. Tangling my fingers in her hair, I pumped faster, harder, unable to take my gaze off her mouth as she struggled to take me all in. She focused on my head instead, lavishing it with her tongue, sucking on it like the good girl she was.

Fuck. This was the woman I hadn't been able to stop thinking about since that day at the café. And shit, remembering the way she was dressed that day in the white silk blouse and black pencil skirt, and knowing that I now had her before me completely naked and sucking on my cock...I almost lost control, and almost came in her mouth.

I pulled out just in time, and again she pouted. Fuck. She didn't know it yet, but she already owned *me*. "You think I'd deny myself your body one more night? I want to bury myself so deep inside you, baby, you're gonna scream my name."

Reaching down for my jeans laying crumpled on the floor, I pulled out a condom from one of the front pockets, and quickly slid it on. Then I took her by the hand and guided her to her feet before picking her up. She roped her arms around my neck and wrapped her legs around my waist as I slowly buried myself inside her warmth.

We kissed, our tongues flicking as I grabbed her hips and guided her down into my thrusts, teasing her with just half the length of my cock. Her moans reverberated through the room, prickling the hairs on my skin. Fuck. She felt so good and I hadn't even pushed myself all the way in. "I can lose myself in you tonight," I whispered into the crook of her neck.

"Deeper," she urged.

I wanted to oblige her, but I needed to ease myself in or I'd cause pain. Laying her down on the couch, I spread her legs wider, slowly burying myself as deep as I could go without hurting her. My size wasn't something everyone could take, and she was so tight, I wanted to make sure she wasn't in any discomfort.

She winced as I filled her and stretched her walls to the max, but she nodded, wanting me to go all the way. I leveled my breaths, trying to control the beast inside me, the one demanding for me to fuck her mindless. *Not yet*, I told myself. There would be time for that. Right now, I needed her to get used to my nine-inch length and considerable thickness. Once we found an easy pace, I reached for her neck, gently wrapping a hand around the long, silky column.

Confident now that she could handle me, I pumped faster and faster while she moaned my name. "That's it, baby, I want you to come for me again."

Her back arched and I knew she was close. Licking my fingers, I brushed them over her clit as I slid in and out of her tightness.

She squeezed her legs together, muscles trembling. "Fuck, Tom... I'm almost there."

"Spread those fucking legs, baby girl. I want to see your slick pussy as you come all over my cock."

Her breaths grew heavier until she reached her orgasm and she screamed my name, just like I told her she would. Watching her skin flush, eyes rolling to the back of her head in pure abandon, triggered my animal instincts to claim her, to finally come inside her. Lowering my body over hers, I took her lips in mine as I ground my pelvis, seeking my own release.

Our breathes danced with each other as she wrapped her legs tight around my waist. My balls tightened and my cock grew even harder as my orgasm peaked and peaked and, ah fuck...

Unable to hold it any longer, I came inside her—in the goddamn condom—in wave after wave of mind-blowing ecstasy. Grabbing her chin, I brought my lips to her, delivering a heated kiss. Her mouth was the ripest of forbidden fruit, tart, yet sweet. She didn't know it yet, but this was only round one. I planned to feast on those goddamn lips all fucking night.

Sixteen

SARA

My eyelids fluttered open as the bright rays of the morning sun hit my face. Rubbing my eyes, I sat up in bed and looked around, taking in the strange surroundings, memories of my night with Tom rushing back.

I was still in his beautiful four-poster bed, his sheets draped over my waist, the light from the sun splaying on my naked breasts, warming my skin. I rushed to cover myself then smiled, realizing it was a little too late for modesty. Craning my neck to my left, a disappointed sigh bubbled from my lungs. Tom was gone, but a neatly folded note sat on the feathery bulk of his pillow.

Seriously?

I stretched my arms as I took a deep breath, feeling sore, yet refreshed, but the smile that had begun to pull at the corners of my mouth quickly faded as the sad realization the weekend was over washed over me.

There was no way I'd make it to work on time. I jumped out of the lofty comforts of his mattress and scanned the room for my clothes. They were nowhere to be found. The place seemed eerily silent, and cloaked in his thick cotton sheets, I walked over to Tom's side of the bed and retrieved his note, flipping it open:

Sara,

Had to go early into work. You looked so peaceful wrapped in my things, I didn't want to wake you. Please, make yourself at home. There are muffins on the kitchen counter, coffee in the pot. Fresh fruit and juice in the fridge. I'd love to find you still naked in my bed when I return from work, but I know you have a life of your own and it doesn't revolve around me...not yet at least ;-). I left you the keys to the Rover in case you absolutely have to leave. Call you later.

I read the note a million times, my face hurting from how big I was smiling.

His proposal was tempting. Staying in his posh apartment, gazing at the city from the feathery softness of his bed, my naked skin reeling in the cool caress of his sheets? Who wouldn't want to stay?

But reality hit hard and fast. I did have a life of my own and right now I was running late for my job.

Losing the sheets, I walked over to an armchair where his bunched-up shirt from last night rested. The smell of him lingered on the fabric, and I inhaled him deeply as I pulled the shirt on. It was huge for my frame, but who cared.

Me in his things...

Still, I needed to find my clothes. ASAP.

The washer and dryer were behind a set of double doors in the kitchen. A laundry basket sat on top of the dryer, my clothes neatly folded, including my bra and panties.

After getting dressed, I rummaged through my purse, looking for my cell. As I retrieved it, the missed-calls notification flashed at me. Ten calls. All from Jen.

I was supposed to call her the day before. Dammit.

As I headed out the door, I grabbed a banana and muffin off the counter, and actually contemplated taking the keys to the Rover. However, as much as I would've loved to drive into the city in pure luxury, the PATH train was a more efficient way back home.

Once I made it to my apartment, I skipped the shower and threw on the first pencil skirt I found along with a cream-colored, silk camisole and matching cardigan, then slipped into a pair of black pumps. After brushing my hair really quick and dotting on some light makeup, I shot back out the door in less than fifteen minutes. As I ran down the hall, Jen came out of the elevators, her eyes blood-shot from working an overnight double.

"Jen."

She barely looked at me. "Hey."

I grabbed her elbow. "You okay?"

She turned around, her face grim. "Just a long night. These double shifts are killing me. How did your date go? You didn't come home last night, so it must've been good?" She mustered a meek smile, her eyes practically closing as she spoke.

"I'm running late for work and you look like the walking dead. I'll catch you up tonight. Sounds good?"

She nodded half-heartily then turned toward the apartment and continued to walk, looking exactly like a zombie. My heart ached for her and the number of hours she put into her work and studies. It was who she'd always been, a bit of an over achiever. I'd known her all of her life, and she'd always been top of the class. The best at every-thing she did. But I knew she did it all for her parents—for their approval.

Sometimes I simply worried she pushed herself too hard. One of these days it was going to take a serious toll on her.

The elevator doors opened, and even though I wanted to run to her and make sure she went to bed to grab some shuteye instead of drinking coffee to keep herself going, I jumped in the elevator. I growled out a curse. I'd have to find a way to make it up to her for being so caught up in Tom the last few days and neglecting our friendship.

I arrived at work by eight thirty, and thankfully, Rebecca was running late as well. It was shaping out to be a slow day, which sucked because I couldn't keep Tom out of my mind. The whole weekend had been a whirlwind, then he kind of just up and left me that morning, naked on his bed.

Were we dating? Were we exclusive?

Not being able to focus on much, I snuck into the studio to watch the dancers rehearse for the big show. It was my secret indulgence, stolen moments where I dared dream of the life I wish I'd had. I always left feeling sorrier for myself. Sitting in the back of the room, I watched as Alexei worked his magic. Having trained in one of Russia's most prominent contemporary dance companies, Alexei's style of dance was nothing the company had ever seen. He challenged the dancers to their max. While his pieces were works of art, they came at the expense of their morale.

As I watched them dance for their lives, that burning desire to join them sparked deep inside. The music licked my muscles. I swayed, living through their practiced moves. Up and down with each lift, spinning with them on their pirouettes, flying through the air with their leaps and arabesques. Before I knew it, I'd shed my shoes and was flexing my feet, pointing my toes. No matter how hard I tried, purging my blood completely of dance was an impossibility I hated to entertain.

"Stop the music," Alexei shouted in his heavy Russian accent as he approached the lead pair of dancers who had just finished the lift. "God dammit, Estella. How many times do I have to tell you to keep your fucking toes pointed? Your feet are hideous. You are ruining my piece. And you..." He pointed to her partner. "You are going to drop her. How can she perform if she has an imbecile underneath her? She needs a man holding her, not a pussy. Again. From the top!"

Alexei counted off beats, his hand snapping in the air. "Four.

Six...seven, eight...and lift...hold...hold...point your toes. Bring her down gently; slide her off your arms. Now look at her eyes. She is the ghost of your beloved and the last time you will ever see her. One...two...beautiful. Yes. Yes."

He was a hard ass, but when you watched his art take form, it was a painting coming to life. Magnificent. What I would have given to be one of them, to be up on that dance floor dancing for my life...

"Take five, everyone," Alexei bellowed.

Estella exited out one of the back doors. Moments later, Alexei looked around the studio making sure no one noticed as he followed behind her. He didn't see me sitting in the far back. A bad feeling burned in my chest. I remembered the rumors about him harassing the girls.

I headed down the same exit, which opened into an empty corridor, not sure what I was planning to do. As I walked down the hall, I heard strained voices coming from Alexei's office. The closer I approached, the louder the muffled sounds grew. When I reached his office, his door was ajar. The sounds were more urgent—an unmistakable panting noise vibrating through the door.

The worst thoughts ran through my mind. Part of me wanted to take off running, but another part of me felt an eerie feeling creeping up my spine. Something was not right.

What if he is forcing himself on her?

I peeked through the open crack.

My eyes widened at the sight. He had Estella bent over his desk with her legs spread open and her dance shorts by her ankles. Alexei's naked ass faced me as he violently thrust into her, muttering what I could only imagine were profanities in his native tongue. When he was done, he grabbed her by the long pony tail and pulled her head back. "Next time, don't make me have to tell you twice to keep your toes fucking pointed. Now, get your cunt out of my office."

I covered my mouth with my hand, trying to not make any noise as I leaned my back against the wall. Estella burst out of the office, not giving me time to disguise my presence. Startled to see me standing by the wall, she turned to close the door, tears streaming down her face. She paused for a brief moment to look at me, then ran off down the hall back to the studio.

As I tried to make sense of what I'd witnessed, my cellphone buzzed inside my skirt pocket. "Hello?"

"Girl, I've been texting you for the past fifteen minutes."

"I'm sorry, Martha. Had my phone on vibrate and I must have not felt it."

"Thought you might have been busy with the witch so I didn't want to bother you. You have a gentleman at the front desk waiting to see you."

"I don't have any dancers scheduled for interviews today. Who is he?"

"Don't know, but he looks important. Good looking. Very. Is this your mystery guy, hmm?"

"There's no mystery guy. What's his name?" I asked her abruptly as I reached my office, opened the door, and hid inside, needing to catch my breath after the atrocity I'd just witnessed.

"Um, sir, I have Ms. Hart on the line. What did you say your name was, again?" After a brief pause, she said, "Sara, he says his name is Mr. Charming. Is this guy for real?"

I shook my head as I tried to hold back my chuckle. Such impeccable timing. "Mr. Charming? Well, tell Mr. Charming he's going to have to give me a few more minutes to clear my schedule." Flutters sprung up in my stomach as I headed over to the reception area. When I spotted him, the oxygen was sucked out of the room.

Dressed in another perfectly tailored gray suit, he sat at one of our waiting area's modern chairs. His right ankle rested on his left knee while his right arm leaned on the armrest and those expert fingers supported his chin. He scrolled through his phone, looking very nonchalant.

I cleared my throat as I approached. "Ahem. Mr. Charming?"

Turning around, his eyes widened. "Miss Hart. You always keep your guests waiting this long?" he asked with a smirk.

I crossed my arms and raised an eyebrow. "Well, I wasn't expecting any guests, *Mr. Charming*," I replied pointedly. "If you would be so kind and accompany me to my office," I said turning around, my lips twitching, trying to suppress a laugh.

"Certainly, Miss Hart."

As we walked past Martha's desk, I whispered to her, "No interruptions, please." To Charming, I said, "Follow me. My office is right through here."

As we entered the long hallway, Tom moved up next to me, and I gave him a playful elbow jab. "So, *Mr. Charming*, nice of you to call me and let me know you were stopping by my office."

"And ruin the surprise? Unless you don't like surprises?"

I paused to look at him. "Oh, I love surprises. But did you forget my boss is a witch? She'll kill me if she finds out I'm hanging out with my...um...with you, instead of running her errands."

He kissed my pursed lips. "You look cute when you're mad. Did you know that?"

The soft touch of his lips was magic. Instantly, I forgot I was trying to be upset. Once inside my office, I offered him a chair in front of my small desk before closing the door. Tom removed his suit jacket, revealing the sculpted slabs of muscle covered by a matching suit vest and a black button-down shirt opened at the collar.

The coziness of my office made his large frame even more impressive. Guy was cut like a freaking Tight end in a pro-football team. He laid his jacket on top of the twin chair next to his. My heart drummed as I scurried over to my desk. The partially closed blinds to the picture window behind me muted the view of the noon chaos of Midtown Manhattan.

"So, what's up, *Charming*?"

He leaned back in his chair, slouching to one side as he crossed his ankle over a knee, regarding me intently, perhaps considering his answer. "What's the matter?"

"What do you mean?"

"Something's got you troubled. I can see it in your eyes. This isn't about me showing up here unannounced."

"You simply caught me at a bad moment."

"Boss giving you a hard time?"

"Not exactly."

"Then what is it?"

"Really want to know?"

"If it's bothering you, I want to hear about it."

Hands shaking, I told him every detail of my encounter with Estella and Alexei. I was so troubled by what I saw, I didn't think I could focus on anything else.

"You're sure about what you saw? He was forcing himself on her?" he asked.

"It's not entirely uncommon to have a relationship with your instructor. Dancing can be very intimate. You have to get very close to your partners. But, I don't know if this is that type of relationship. She came out of the office crying."

"They saw you?"

"Only Estella, but she bolted back to the studio when she realized what I'd seen."

"This Alexie sounds like a complete dick."

"Yeah, but he is one of the best in his field. This sort of shit could get someone fired and I'm afraid it wouldn't be him. The company needs him."

"Nobody needs a scumbag like him, I don't care how great a choreographer he is."

"These girls...people have no clue how hard it is to be a female dancer in this business. They are at the mercy of these sleazy men in power. It doesn't matter how well you dance, it's how pretty you are and how wide you are willing to spread your legs to get ahead. He probably promised her the lead."

"I'm sorry you had to witness that."

"It's not just what he did to Estella. I hate the way he treats all of the dancers. He's so fucking toxic and Rebecca just keeps kissing his ass."

Tom rose from his chair and walked over to me, kneeling down so we were face to face. "I don't like seeing you upset." He cupped my cheek in his broad hand. "He's an asshole that needs to be reported. Or I can simply kick the shit out of him and put him in his place."

I pulled away from his hand. "You're not serious."

"I am. Guys like that deserve to get their asses kicked. I'll be happy to do the honors."

"No. You don't need to get arrested. Not for him. I just need to figure out how to encourage Estella to open up about the abuse so we can report his ass."

He leaned in and kissed me. "You can try it your way, but if he lays a hand on *you*, trust me, he'll wish he were dead."

Shit. The cold, stern look in his eyes sent an arctic shiver down my spine. He was serious, and I didn't know how to feel about it. A part of me had warmed at his protectiveness. It made me feel safe, but another part of me felt a little sliver of dread coil in my gut. He talked about beating the shit out of Alexie a little too easily. Made me wonder about how many people had been at the receiving end of his fists.

"So, tell me..." I said, changing the subject, needing to get Alexei and his disgusting behavior out of my mind. "Why are you here? Did you come to save me again from my troubles?"

"Actually, I was hoping to take you to lunch. But now that I'm this close to you, I think I want to jump straight to dessert." He reached in for an even deeper kiss and I surrendered. He parted my legs with his hands, causing my skirt to ride up past my thighs. He pulled my chair closer to him, exposing my black, silk panties.

"How did you know I didn't stay in your apartment?"

"I asked the front desk to tell me if they saw you leave."

"You have people watching me?"

He narrowed his eyes. "Well, when you say it like that it sounds kinda creepy."

"That's okay. I like your kind of creepy."

He smiled. "Christ, Sara. I haven't been able to stop thinking about you. I couldn't focus on my morning meetings, my mind invaded by thoughts of you in my bed last night."

The warmth of his breath over my lips radiated throughout my body, plunging straight for my center. The temperature in my office seemed to have risen by ten degrees. Playful, but in that raspy sultry voice of his, he said, "You know, this is one of my fantasies."

"What is?"

"You and me. On this desk."

"Since when?"

"Since I walked through that door." Releasing me from his arms, he stood up and walked over to my blinds, then closed them completely.

"May I ask what it is you think you are doing?"

"What does it look like?" His gaze darkened, his intentions clearly broadcasting through the airwaves, loud and crystal clear.

"Tom. No. I can't. *We* can't." I pulled my skirt back down and crossed my legs. Yet, as I looked at him, I couldn't fathom how I would resist this man. His golden-brown hair was perfectly styled in that yeah-it's-messy-on-purpose look and his smooth, clenched jaw was still freshly scented with the mountain rain aroma of his after shave. With so much manliness wanting to explode out of those formal clothes, my mind went bonkers. Those deep predatory gold and olive eyes said so much without having to utter a single word, and right then they were telling me he was famished.

"You need to stop looking at me like I'm a juicy steak," I said.

Thrill crossed his eyes and his lips curled to the side. "I can't hide what I'm feeling for you, Sara."

"That was not an invitation to unleash all your artillery on me, you know," I continued.

In two long strides, he stood in front of me, looking down at my frazzled face. I eyed his crotch, unable to ignore the proximity of my face to the massive ridge rising under his gray pants.

"What's that you said about artillery?" he asked with a smile. He was just bluffing. He had to be. I was sure of it. There was no way he was really thinking we were going to have sex in my office—in the middle of the day.

That was ludicrous.

And fucking hot.

"Two can play this game, you know," I told him.

"Is that so, Miss Hart?"

My hand made its way up his thigh before taking a turn into his groin, but right when I was about to glide my hand up his beckoning erection, he took my hand in his and motioned for me to stand. He held me in his gaze for a lengthy moment. "I said *my* dessert. Never mentioned anything about yours." He gestured toward the door. "Is it locked?"

Speechless, I nodded yes.

Sliding his hand down my thighs, he brushed his hot lips over my ear. "This skirt is awfully sexy, but right now, I think I'd rather it like this." Grasping the hem, he hiked up the fabric until it was sitting scrunched up on my waist. "That's better."

He cupped my ass cheeks and electricity sparked on my skin as his eager mouth nibbled on my neck and jaw, culminating at my parched lips. When he kissed me, the whole world melted away. I was no longer in my office, two doors down from my boss. Nope. I was in my own little private fantasy about to have sex on my desk.

In one swift move, my papers were lying scattered on the floor and my almost-naked ass sat atop of my cold, cherry wood desk. The hum of my desktop's dying fan behind me suddenly made me aware of how crazy this was.

Tom was in his element. I was a hot mess, heaving and panting.

"Relax, baby."

"What if someone—"

A finger to my lips silenced me.

He scooted me closer to the edge of the desk, then he took a seat in front of me on my chair, gingerly parting my legs, exposing my silk panties. Circling my clit with his thumb over the material, he expertly awakened all of my nerve endings.

The tingly sensation reached every muscle. The pleasure was so heavenly, I arched my head back, succumbing to his hand. And right when I thought it couldn't get any better, he pulled my panties to the side, putting my pussy on full display for his eyes to feast.

"There's my dessert," he whispered as he parted me with his fingers to fully expose my clit. "How badly do you want me to lick you?"

"Very..." I said breathless.

He wasted no time getting to work, his tongue flicking me in just the right place, making me so wet, all I wanted was to spread my legs and be filled by him. As if hearing my thoughts, he pumped his thick middle finger inside me.

"Oh fuck..." I hissed as he hooked his finger and hit my G spot. "Yeah, yeah. Just like that," I urged him.

He smiled as he fucked me with both his tongue and finger.

Reaching for his shirt collar, I said. "I want you to make me come with your cock."

"I didn't bring a condom."

"Shit."

"Tell me about it. But don't worry. I promise my tongue can make you curl your toes, too."

Nodding at him to keep going, he closed his eyes as he devoured me, but I also noticed he'd unzipped his pants and was stroking his cock. My mouth salivated, and I wasn't able to hold on any longer, coming on his tongue in wave after wave of mind-blowing pleasure. I muffled my cries as best as I could and prayed Rebecca hadn't been in her office.

He helped me off my desk, guiding my hand to his cock so I could feel how hard he was for me. "See what you do to me?"

I slid a finger over the dewy tip, loving the silky feeling of his precum.

"I want you on your knees. But keep your skirt hiked up. I've had visions of you in that skirt and heels for too long. It's time I make those visions real." He lowered my camisole and bra, making sure my tits were out and ready for him to play with if he chose to. Right now, it seemed he just wanted to look at me like this, though. Like I was his little erotic play thing.

Doing as he instructed, I got on my knees and drew him into my mouth, practically gagging on his length, and he wasn't even fully inside. Oh, but the feel of his thickness made me wet all over again, and I sucked and sucked like I was famished and only his cock could fill me.

Tom threaded his fingers through my hair, loosening up my pony tail, making messy strands fall over my face. "Fuck, baby girl. You do that so well." He pumped his pelvis, and I swore he hit the back of my throat.

Then a knock sounded at the door. "Sara, you in there?"

Shit. Shit. Shit. I went to pull away from him, but he held me in place. "Not yet," he whispered.

My eyes widened. His smile curled.

"Sara, I need to speak with you!"

"She's currently occupied," Tom responded for me, his cock growing harder. He took it out slowly, letting the head brush my lips, signaling for me to reply.

"I'm..." I said, as he slipped his cock inside then back out.

"With..." He repeated the motion. "A client." This time he went deep, leaving it there, my lips stretching around his girth.

"Sara, answer the door this instant."

Using my hands, I pumped him fast making sure to suck on his head until I knew he was ready to explode.

"Swallow," he said before spilling his load down my throat, not giving me a second to process what was happening. Still, something primal came over me, and I drank it all like it was the most delicious filth I had ever tasted, licking up every drop off his dick.

He ran his thumb over my lips. "So fucking beautiful."

Rebecca knocked on the door even harder, jiggling the knob and sending my heart galloping out of my chest.

In less than a minute, Tom and I re-clothed ourselves and fixed my desk as best we could. Tom put on his suit jacket and sat down, looking like a typical business man at a meeting. I wiped my mouth, adjusted my skirt, then as nonchalantly as possible, opened the door.

Rebecca's complexion matched the fiery red mop atop her head. Ms. Fitzgerald did not like to be kept waiting. Arms locked across her bosom, she sneered at me as she peeked inside my office, trying to figure out why I hadn't jumped at her beck and call the instant she knocked at my door. "What the hell took you so long?"

I sucked in a shaky breath. "I was busy."

"You didn't have any interviews scheduled for today."

Tom stepped up from his chair and walked over to the door, extending his hand, a warm sensual smile coating his lips. "Ms. Fitzgerald, pleasure to meet you."

Rebecca's expression immediately softened at the sight of him. She was easily twice his age, but the look that crossed in every woman's eyes the moment they realized they were standing in front of pure manly gorgeousness hit her out of nowhere. And like the rest of us—whose drenched panties dropped to the floor whenever Tom entered our field of vision—she was instantly enchanted by his looks and charm.

She extended her hand to shake his, but Tom took her slim fingers in his and pressed a soft kiss on top of her hand. She blinked repeatedly at his gesture as her blood saturated her skin to a fire-engine red.

"Ms. Fitzgerald," Tom acknowledged, "Sara was telling me all about your wonderful work here. Seems your new Russian Choreographer, Alexei..."

"Vonorov. Alexei Vonorov," she replied quickly, her hand still in his.

"Sara tells me he is carving out a new dance masterpiece?" Tom finally let go of her hand.

"We are all very excited about the experience he brings to our company. Alexei is extremely talented and is an exceptional addition to our dance family. His professionalism is unmatched," she added proudly.

Tom looked at me, his eyes assuring me he knew I was figuratively gagging at Rebecca's praise for Alexei.

"So...mister?" Rebecca waited for his name.

"I'm sorry. How rude of me. Thomas Wright, but please, call me Tom."

"Well, Tom, what brings you to our doorstep?"

"My company handles real estate business for extremely high-profile clients. I have a couple flying in from Milan for a few days at the end of the month and I was hoping to snatch some tickets for your opening show. A gesture of appreciation for their loyalty."

Rebecca's eyes widened along with the smile tracing across her lips. "Really?"

Tom winked at her. "What better way to show them a good time in our city than by treating them to a spectacular dance performance. Europeans aren't the only ones with culture, after all."

Rebecca closed her eyes and shrugged with accord. "Isn't that the truth." She winked at Tom as she placed her hand on his forearm. "I like you." Then she turned to me, her charming smile now frosted with ice. "Please, ensure Tom gets the best seats in the house, compliments of the company."

"Of course," I replied with a tight smile.

She turned back to Tom and offered him her hand. "Delighted to have made your acquaintance."

"The pleasure was mine, Rebecca."

I dropped my chin to my chest and pinched the bridge of my nose, trying to avoid rolling my eyes at the awkward exchange between these two.

"Do you plan on staying long, perhaps you want a tour? I'll be happy to show you around," she asked, her chest puffed.

I don't think so, lady.

"Mr. Wright was actually just leaving."

She wasn't able to wipe off the disappointment from her face. "Oh? Well, I hope you enjoyed your visit. Sara will see you out." As she headed down the corridor, she turned back, and added, "Oh, Sara, come to my office when you are done, and please fetch me some coffee. I'm due for my afternoon caffeine break."

"Of course, Rebecca, right away," I called back with a mirthless smile as she trotted away. When I was sure she was out of earshot I turned to Tom. "Oh, my God, that was close. I can't believe I let you do that."

"Do what?"

"My boss almost caught me sucking on your dick."

"Don't tell me that wasn't hot."

I couldn't—because it was more than hot. It was the single most erotic thing I had ever done in my entire life and I was already craving more. My phone chirped with a text, the theme from a popular Halloween flick announcing the sender.

"Should I even bother to guess who is texting you?"

I separated from him to retrieve my phone from my skirt pocket, then looked at him and raised an eyebrow as I laughed. "Is it that obvious?" Rebecca sent me several coffee icons followed by a myriad of exclamation points. "Well, I guess that means she wants her coffee. I'm sorry. I have to go."

"It's okay, beautiful," he muttered with a sigh. "I can walk myself out."

"I thoroughly enjoyed your visit. Call me later?"

Tom reached across and rubbed his knuckles across my cheek before planting a kiss on my lips. "Of course." He turned to leave but stopped and looked back at me. "By the way. Do me a favor and stay away from that creep."

"Alexei? I can take care of myself. Don't worry."

"Sara. I mean it. Promise me. I don't trust that guy."

"I promise. Just go, before Rebecca comes looking for me again."

Seventeen

SARA

As the day neared its end, exhaustion knock me to my knees. Rebecca barked out orders all afternoon. Before heading home, I pushed through the red door to the bathroom and lurched back when I ran into Estella. She stood by the sink, applying makeup. Tall and slender, she was absolutely stunning. Her long, dark locks were pulled up on a high pony tail. She paused when she heard me enter, and looked at me from the corner of her eyes before returning to her task. The room vibrated with an uncomfortable energy. My gut twisted. I knew I couldn't remain silent anymore.

"Estella, I think we need to talk."

Without looking at me, she muttered, "I don't know what you mean."

"What I saw this morning."

Through the bathroom mirror, she glared at me with contempt.

"I'm just worried about you," I continued.

She finished her makeup routine with a touch of red lipstick. After smacking her lips together, she put her makeup back in her bag, then turned to look at me. "Honestly, I don't know how any of this is your business."

"I understand what you are struggling through and—"

She stepped closer, her face inches from mine. "No. You don't. You should stick to being Rebecca's little puppet. Leave the dancing to us."

My breath caught for a brief moment as I took a mental step back. "Dancing? You think I'm worried about your dancing? I'm concerned about what Alexei is doing to you. What he's doing to all of the girls. He not only humiliated you in front of everyone, he is using you until the next pretty girl comes around that he can fuck. He'll give her the lead and dump you on your ass. Can't you see that?"

Fury sparking in her eyes, she grabbed her bag from the bathroom sink and sneered at me. "All I see is a has-been. I know your little secret. Why you sneak into the back of the studio to watch us rehearse. Your dreams died already, Sara. Let me enjoy mine." Then she stormed out of the bathroom.

I stared after her, watching as the door to the bathroom slowly closed. Then I turned to my reflection in the mirror, my eyes crackling with anger and pain.

All I wanted was to protect her and she called me a has-been? My hands gripped the edge of the sink with an iron grasp. I'd been amazing once. Better than all of them put together. Now, I was nothing but a joke.

The Juilliard promise was a pathetic pencil pusher. The truth of my failure was smeared on my face. I was miserable and everybody knew it. Why had I chosen to work at a dance company after everything that happened? Why did I punish myself with the constant reminder of the person I'd never be? The torment of all the years living in denial hit my chest harder than a bolt of lightning.

Sara Hart is a has-been.

Tears pooled at the corners of my eyes and I sank to the floor. I had worked so hard to convince myself I was okay with lurking in the shadows of these dancers, secretly pretending to be one of them. Meanwhile, they'd known. And they'd been laughing at me.

God, I wanted to run out of there and never return. This whole thing was a nightmare I didn't know how to escape.

As I sat there on the cold floor, feeling sorry for myself, my phone rang.

Wiping the tears, I smiled as I saw who was calling. Of course. My Knight in Shining Armor. "Tom?"

"Hey, beautiful. Just checking in on you. How was the rest of your day?"

"Um...I ah..." but I wasn't able to finish my sentence because I started crying again. I hated that I felt so fragile. That I was sobbing like a goddamn baby even after all these years since the accident, but Estella really opened up my wounds and now I felt raw and completely broken.

"Sara, what happened? Did that asshole hurt you? Because I swear I'll come down there right now and smash his face in."

"It wasn't Alexei..."

"Then who?" he demanded. "I'm on my way over."

"It's okay. You don't have to come get me. I tried speaking to Estella, but it didn't go as I'd hoped and we just exchanged words."

"What did she say to upset you?"

"Honestly, I'd rather not talk about it right now. Maybe later?"

"You want to come over my place?"

"How about mine? That way you can meet Jen, too."

"Sounds good. I'll bring the wine."

Hearing his voice helped sap up my tears, and after hanging up, I rose up off the floor, and looked in the mirror again. I couldn't recognize the woman staring back at me. She stood defeated, helpless. A ghost determined to haunt me till the day I died. Taking a deep breath, I desperately wiped away my tears and smudged mascara. I felt stupid for breaking down on the phone with Tom. What was I going to tell him?

Well, seemed I had to figure it out soon because I had just invited him over for dinner and I hadn't even dropped the bomb on Jen yet. It was lasagna night at least, so I knew she'd cook enough for a family of six.

~

I called her on my way home and she screeched in my ear when I told her Tom was coming to dinner. "Are you freaking kidding me right now? The apartment is a mess, Sara. *I'm* a mess. And now, I need to make sure my lasagna is perfect. And I gotta run to the store to grab Italian bread…"

"Take a breath, Jen. Tom's easy going. Plus, your lasagna is delicious. Trust me. You don't need to go crazy."

"Easy for you to say. You're not the one cooking last minute for a billionaire. Gotta run. Donelli's might still have some fresh loaves. Bye."

Twenty minutes later, I arrived at my apartment only to find Tom already waiting inside, chatting it up with Pedro. "There she is," he said, turning around as I walked into the lobby, his broad smile stretching ear to ear, quite literally obliterating the cloud hovering over my head.

"How did you beat me to my own place?"

"I was already in my car when I called you." He showed me the bottle of wine he'd brought. "Hope Jen likes red. I told the guy to give me his best bottle."

"She'd be fine with a twenty-dollar bottle of cabernet. You didn't have to go get all fancy."

We headed toward the elevators and hit the call button. "Sara, I'm meeting your best friend. You understand how nerve-racking that is? If she doesn't like me, she'll convince you to dump my ass."

I knew he was trying to sound ridiculous to get me to forget about my awful afternoon.

It was working. The doors opened and we scurried in. When we arrived on my floor, he ran his fingers through his hair. I grabbed his hand and guided him out. "You don't need to be nervous about meeting Jen."

"You have no idea how badly I don't want to screw this up."

"You'll be fine."

As I unlocked and pushed the door open, Skiddles snaked out. She rubbed her body against my legs. "Hi, girl, mama's home." I scooped her up in my arms and nudged her nose as I walked through the foyer. I peered back over my shoulder. Tom stood outside the doorway, his face taut with unease.

"Are you a vampire?" I asked with a smirk.

His eyebrows quirked. "Huh?"

I rolled my eyes. "Are you waiting for an invitation? Come on in."

Jen's cooking saturated the air with the scent of herbs, sausage, garlic, and basil.

"Smells delicious in here," he said as he shortened his strides, making sure to stay behind me.

"You should wait to say that in front of Jen. She loves it when people compliment her cooking." I took him by the hand and pulled him over to the kitchen. "Hey, Jen..." I intoned softly, not sure how to gage her mood.

"Oh, hey. Just finishing up," she chirped as she tossed a green salad.

I blew a silent sigh of relief. She was livelier than I expected. "Jen, this is Tom. Tom, this is Jen, the best friend I've told you about."

Tom reached over to shake Jen's hand.

"All good things, I hope," she joked as she wiped her hand on her apron and accepted Tom's friendly gesture. I noticed her hard squeeze as she turned to me, her eyes sparkling with acknowledgement.

Yes, I know he's hot. We've said this. Can we move on, please?

"Pleasure to meet you, Jen," Tom uttered, calling back her attention.

"Pleasure is all mine." She removed her hand from his and tucked a loose curl behind her ear, a coy smile pulling at the corner of her lips. Jen was never shy, but then again, last time she'd seen him was briefly at the club. She hadn't had the full effect of meeting Mr. Panty-Dropper.

"Lasagna will be ready in a few minutes. Make yourself at home, Tom." She waved us away to the dining table as she turned back to the counter to finish cooking.

"Actually, we're gonna go freshen up first. Be right back."

In my room, Tom fidgeted with his suit jacket, not knowing where to sit or stand. Sensing the awkwardness, I guided him toward my bed and asked him to take a seat. He seemed so out of place in my tiny room. His master bedroom dwarfed the twelve-by-twelve walls that made up my sleeping quarters. Not to mention, I slept on a full-sized bed covered in a paisley duvet, while he slumbered on a four-poster California king made for royalty.

I sighed. I thought back to the moment I locked eyes with him at the coffee shop. The twinkling eyes, the playful smile, the gallant strut. He'd seemed so out of my league. The high-powered exec who drove fancy cars and took girls out on expensive dinners was seated on my bed, waiting for me to freshen up so we could have homemade lasagna made by my overprotective friend who was probably getting ready to grill his ass.

What the hell did I get myself into?

I asked Tom to chill for a bit in my room and hurried back out to the kitchen, where Jen was already arranging our place settings on the dining table.

"Jen."

"Yeah…"

I reached for the plates and utensils and finished setting the table. "I'm sorry."

She turned and crossed her arms. "For what?"

As I put the last fork down, I ruefully peered up to meet her stare. "For not calling you yesterday. For not being myself these last few days." It was a sincere apology. I hated I'd completely disregarded everything she'd done to protect me from myself. She deserved better.

She briefly closed her eyes and let out a short sigh before dropping her arms and reaching for the empty wine glasses on the counter. "You know, I'm not your mother," she said as she handed me the glasses, the chiding tone of her voice dissipating. "I don't have any right to be upset about you not calling or not coming home to sleep. But, the truth is…I care about you. You are like a sister to me and well, I guess…I'm just worried."

My eyes narrowed. "Worried?"

She placed her hands on her hips. "Yes, hon. Worried. This is not you. You don't get into cars with strangers, or get plastered to the point you barely remember the night, or run away to God knows where without telling me where you're going and then not come home. You don't bring guys over for dinner. You swore off men recently, remember? Now, all of a sudden there's this man in your room. I saw the way you two looked at each other. You haven't looked at anybody like that since…well…since Josh."

"What are you trying to say, that I shouldn't be in a relationship?"

"Is that what this is, then?"

"I'm still trying to figure it out."

"You just met this guy, Sara."

"I know. But he's sweet and funny and the kind of man I might need right now, Jen.

"Did you sleep with him?"

I blinked hard. "What?"

"Did you sleep with him?" she pressed.

The question startled me. I was accustomed to talking to Jen about my intimacy, but perhaps it was the realization that maybe I had moved too fast that had me acting all shocked? Instinctively, I shrugged and diverted my eyes.

"You little slut," she whispered with a laugh.

"Shut up. He'll hear you," I whispered back.

"When?"

"Last night."

"I can't believe you."

"You told me to seize the day."

"What? When?"

"At the club Saturday night, when Tom was bringing me home."

"I was drunk."

"Yeah, well. I slept with him and it was amazing."

She smirked as she poured me a glass of the red wine Tom had brought. "That good, hmm?" she asked, her eyes shiny with playful curiosity.

I took a long gulp. The thick liquid left a warm coat on my throat. "You. Have. No. Idea." Then we both broke out in girlish giggles.

A moment later, I brought Tom back out and we all sat ready to eat. In her best motherly impersonation, Jen placed the hot casserole dish on the table, and said, "Dig in."

During dinner, Tom and Jen volleyed questions about their backgrounds. Jen's eyes flashed toward me at Tom's mention of his military past. I knew she'd grill me about it later, especially since she knew about my dad's struggle with PTSD. Tom entertained her curiosity about his business but offered limited details about his more personal life. Overall, they seemed pleased with themselves. I'd been bored to death listening to them scrutinize each other.

When we were done eating, Jen and I stepped up from our chairs and gathered the dirty dishes. Tom tried to assist, but Jen ordered him to stop and sent him to the living area.

In the kitchen, amidst putting the dishes in the dishwasher and cleaning the counters, Jen grabbed me by the elbow and guided me to the side. I interrupted her before she could scold me. "Jen, I know what you're going to say."

"And what's that?"

"I need to be careful."

"The military? You know what happened with your dad. I know this guy seems like his head is on straight, but you know the kind of turbulent waters running underneath the calm current on the surface."

"Jen, I can handle this."

"Can you?"

"Just say what's really on your mind."

"I'm worried you're moving too fast."

"I'm not a child, Jen. I don't need a lecture on sex and dating."

"Sex can complicate things. I'm just telling you to take it slow."

She meant well, I knew that. I also knew I didn't want to screw things up with Tom. Sex *could* muddy things up and I could already see myself plummeting into a complete sexual relationship with this man.

This time, I needed to do things right.

She must have noticed my inner struggle and reached for my hand, offering some reassurance. "Hey, listen, all that aside, I like him. He really does seem nice. And the way he looks at you...every girl deserves a man that worships the ground she walks on."

The tension in my body dissipated and my lips stretched into a wide grin. "You really think he's nice?"

She nodded. "I'm happy for you, hon." She grabbed me by the

shoulders and spun me out of the kitchen and toward the living room. "Go keep him company while I finish up in here."

Tom stood over by the large windows facing Central Park, hands in his pockets, his broody eyes probably lost in thought.

"Hey," I said, startling him from behind.

He stiffened then pivoted around, flashing me his gorgeous smile. "Oh, hey back."

I tucked loose strands of hair behind my ears. "So...that was interesting."

He laughed. "Interrogations don't frighten me."

"No? Then what does, mister tough guy?"

He reached over and gently grabbed my chin. "You."

I knew he was teasing, but his gaze was unmoving and serious. "Is that so?"

Inhaling deep, he said, "I have to leave for L.A. tomorrow night."

"Oh...again?" The thought of him leaving caused an unexpected chill in my chest, and as if he'd sensed the coldness, he cupped my cheek.

"I don't want to go," he said. "But the constant travel is part of running my company."

The electricity between us was palpable, crackling around us, the warmth from his hand reaching every sensory nerve on my body. "Take the late-night flight again. You can sleep and not think about flying."

He chuckled nervously, holding my face with both hands, pinning our eyes to each other. "Silly girl. You know that's not why I don't want to go. I don't want to leave *you.*"

Why does he have to say things that hold promise and make my heart ache with longing for more of this—more of him?

Keys and purse in her hands, Jen called from the kitchen. "Can you believe I forgot dessert? Gonna run to the store really quick. You kids behave, okay?" Then she rushed out the door.

Tom tucked his hands in his pants while he rocked back and forth on his heels. "She's a good friend, Sara."

My eyes rolled to the back of my head. "I know..."

"Come with me to California," he blurted out of nowhere.

I blinked. "Wait...what?"

"I have some things to take care of in L.A., but I have a small place in Santa Monica. We can stay there for the rest of the week."

In my mind, my bags were packed at my feet and I was ready to follow him to the ends of the world if he asked me to. But another part of me shuddered at the thought of traveling across the country to stay with a man I'd known for only a few days. "Oh wow. You're asking me to come stay with you in Santa Monica? I mean, I would love to, but don't you think we might be moving too fast?"

Cupping his neck with his large palm, he turned from me and paced. "Christ. Sara, since I met you I've been stuck in the middle of an avalanche. It certainly is happening too quickly, but don't you want to figure out what's really happening between us?" He brushed his nervous hands through his hair so many times, the strands stood up in all different directions.

I stared at him blankly.

"Say something, Sara."

"I...don't know. I mean, yes, I want to figure out if this is all lust or something more, but I don't know. I have a job, I can't just take off on a whim."

"I'm sorry. You're right. I'm coming off strong again, demanding you give me your time. How about you think about it, yeah? You don't have to give me an answer right now."

"Thank you. I will definitely think about it."

After dessert, Tom bid me good night and I promised to give him an answer by morning. Though, deep down I already knew what I was going to say. After what happened with Estella, a short getaway was probably exactly what I needed.

Eighteen

SARA

Going to Santa Monica proved easier said than done. Unless you are your own boss and have enough money to burn, last-minute vacations are not the norm. The next morning, Rebecca nearly ripped off my head when I asked her for the rest of the week off. She profusely expressed how highly unprofessional I was to expect her to grant me a leave on such short notice. And perhaps it was a bit unfair, but I hardly ever called out sick or even took all my vacation days.

Did I mention my boss was a heartless, illogical harpy of a witch?

My real foolishness was expecting anything short of her insults and irrational explanations as to why I couldn't take a few days off. I'd practically busted my ass the last few weeks making sure every detail pertaining to the show was completed. Plus, it wasn't like I'd leave without first ensuring things would be under control while I was away.

I nearly fell backward when, after groveling at her feet, she at least let me take off that Friday. It wasn't what I'd wanted, but it was better than nothing. I strolled back into my office, dreading the call I was going to make to Tom. I knew how disappointed he was going to be, and so was I, quite frankly.

"You're absolutely sure there is nothing you can do?" he asked as soon as I told him about Rebecca's quasi-approval, the tone in his voice was absent the joyous bounce I'd grown accustomed to.

"I tried, but this woman is impossible."

"Quit and come work for me instead. You could have all the vacations you want."

"Really? And exactly what kind of work would I do? I know nothing about real estate."

"You'd be my personal assistant."

"I'm sure you already have one of those."

"I'll fire her."

"Tom, I'm not quitting my job and I'm not coming to work for you. We'll just have to make the best out of the long weekend."

"I haven't left and I already miss you."

"Stop it. No, you don't. It's only going to be a few days and then I'll be up there on Friday and we can do all of the things..."

"All of the things, huh? Great minds think alike."

I laughed. "I meant exploring Santa Monica, not sex. I've never been to California before. I'm not spending all my time tangled in sheets with you."

"Ha. That's what you say now. Wait until I have you on your back, legs spread, and my tongue sliding up that pussy."

Shit. The way he said that, like he already knew how helpless I was against his oral talents, made my girl parts clench, proving his point.

"Cocky much?"

"Very much. And if my flight wasn't leaving in two hours, I'd come to your place and show you exactly how cocky I am."

"You're insane. Go, finish getting ready for your flight. And call me before liftoff."

~

Although I'd known on Tuesday that I was leaving for Cali that Friday, I waited until Thursday to break the news to Jen. I knew she was going to give me a speech about how it was too soon to go away with a guy I'd only recently met. Perhaps it was, but that didn't mean I couldn't take risks. I'd been protecting my heart for four years, and probably would've continued on that path if I hadn't met Tom. And I'd still be sad lonely girl spending Friday nights with her cat.

And while not all women needed a man in their life to feel happy, I recently rediscovered that I *was* the kind of girl who needed love in her life. I'd been miserable the last four years not only because I'd given up on my dream to be a contemporary dancer, but because I'd denied myself the opportunity to find love again. And now that I'd had a taste of what that was like...of the butterflies in my stomach, of my heart fluttering when he called, of the way my nether regions tingled at the mere sound of his voice...I didn't want it to end. I wanted more and more of him and if that meant I needed to follow him to California and spend a long a weekend at his Santa Monica beach house, I was gonna pack my bags and get on that plane no matter how Jen felt about it.

I decided to soften the blow by offering to buy her favorite takeout so she didn't have to cook. After dinner, we sat on the couch and I finally told her I was leaving for the weekend to meet Tom in California.

"California?" Jen jumped off the couch and paced. "You're not serious."

"Jen, I don't know what the problem is."

"I thought you guys were going to take it slow. Going away on a weekend trip is not taking it slow."

"First of all, you were the one who told me I needed to start dating. That I needed love in my life."

"I also said you needed to take a breath and slow it down."

"Look, everyone's relationship is different. Not everyone works on the same time line. Tom and I...the connection we feel is more than visceral, more than the sexual chemistry we possess. I can't explain it, but the mere thought of not being with him hurts."

"That's what scares me. Relationships like these are so hot, they tend to burn up quick. I wanted you to date, but I don't want you going through heartache. I just wanted you to have fun."

I turned from her, unable to meet her eyes. "I know I made mistakes with Josh, but that life is over. Tom and I... this is different than what Josh and I had. I was a kid back then. We both were. We weren't ready for a future. Now, I feel freer to explore what might be, and I want to do it with Tom. So, can you *please* have some faith in me? I know what I'm doing."

She sat next to me and I took her hand in mine. "Jen, ever since my mother died, you've taken on the role of protecting me, of sheltering me from the pain of the world. I couldn't be more grateful for having someone like you in my life. You were the only one left when everyone else took off. I didn't just lose the most important woman in my life. My father, the man I had grown to admire as my hero, also died in my heart when he married the woman he was having an affair with. I lost both my parents, and you adopted me. You weren't only my best friend, you were there for me even more than my own sister. I can never forget what you did for me then and what you've done for me always."

She lowered her gaze. "Sara, I don't know what to say."

"You don't have to say anything. I know you mean well and you're simply looking out for me."

She smiled, tucking a loose strand of hair behind my ear. "Okay. Fine. But I'll help you pack. If you're gonna spend a long weekend with a hunky billionaire in his beach house mansion, then you need to dress the part."

"Are you saying I don't know how to dress?"

"Your wardrobe is a bit frumpy..."

"Frumpy? Oh my God. I don't have time to go clothes shopping."

She gave me a warm smile, "Don't worry. We'll go shopping in my closet."

I threw my arms around her, smothering her in a hug. "Thank you, babe."

"As much as you like to think I shelter you like a daughter, I know I'm not your mother. I could never fill those shoes. You don't need my permission to go after your prince."

Nineteen

SARA

At four-thirty in the morning, my limo arrived. It glided through the city, easily navigating at the early hour. The sky was a hazy, navy blue that slowly paled as it prepared to welcome the warming rays of the June sun. Looking around at the interior, I shook my head in disbelief. I could've taken an Uber, but Tom was determined to shower me with luxury. I'd never even been to Teterboro Airport, and the thought of flying on a private jet had me pinching myself to see if I was dreaming. I'd told Tom I was perfectly okay flying coach on a commercial flight, but of course he refused.

I guess what was the point of having a filthy rich boyfriend if you couldn't be chauffeured around in fancy cars and be flown on private jets, right?

Boyfriend... I didn't know why I called him that. We hadn't talked about making our relationship official. All I knew was that we were infatuated with each other, wanting—needing to spend every

181

single second of the day together or talking or texting or daydreaming about being naked and Tom doing all sorts of filthy things to my body. At least he'd promised as much.

Stars. Felt like we were free-falling off the Empire State building.

The limo drove me up to the hanger where a full flight crew greeted me like I was a celebrity. I was the only passenger on board the twelve-passenger charter, which felt like a total waste. Once in my seat, I was told we'd be taking off shortly, so I took the opportunity to give Tom a brief call, though I knew he was likely still asleep on the West Coast.

A groggy and crackly voice answered on the other end. "Hey, baby."

"Did I wake you?"

"Nah."

"You're a terrible liar."

He chuckled. "I tried to stay up, but sleep beat me. I'm sorry."

"You didn't have to wait up for my call. I was going to just leave you a message."

"I needed to make sure you made it okay to the airport."

"You know, between you and Jen, you guys should be my parents. I'm a big girl. I think I can figure out how to board a plane."

"I'm sure you can, baby, but I also wanted to hear your voice. I'm lonely here. I miss you."

I smirked. "It hasn't been that long."

"I guess that means you haven't missed me."

"You know that's not what I meant."

"What's the matter, you sound edgy. Are you nervous?"

Tom was either supernaturally attuned to me or I was terrible at hiding my emotions.

"A bit," I said.

"About flying?"

"About everything. This trip...us."

There was some silence, before he said, "There's still time to turn around."

"No. I want to come see you. I *need* to see you."

"It's only six hours, Sara. You'll be here in my arms before you know it."

"By the way. Thank you for the private charter, though you know it wasn't necessary. I would have been fine in coach."

He laughed. "You've told me. But why would I put you in coach when I can fly you in absolute comfort? Relax, would you? Enjoy it."

I took a deep breath and tried to relieve the tension crawling up my spine. "Six hours?"

"Yes, baby. I will be waiting for you. Call me as soon as you land."

"Okay. We're starting to taxi. I...ah..."

"I can't wait to see you," he said, taking the words from my mouth.

"Me too."

Six hours later, my flight began to descend. I couldn't wait to get off the metal bird. As amazing as it felt to be catered to like I was some famous person or the one with the millions, I'd had enough of being enclosed inside a tube. Needing to hear Tom's voice, as soon as we landed, I turned on my cell and called him.

He picked up after two rings. "Hi, baby," he chirped.

"Just landed."

"I know. I've been here for like...forty minutes, watching the monitors."

"Can't wait to see you."

"Me, too. You have no idea! I'll be waiting for you by the hangar."

"Okay, see you in a few."

When we were done taxing to the hanger, I jumped out of my

seat and reached for my carryon, though my flight attendant made sure I wouldn't carry anything down. My knees trembled as we disembarked. Standing at the bottom of the stairs, Tom stood with a huge grin carving across his cheeks.

I drank in the sight of his body and almost couldn't believe this was the same guy I'd fallen for in New York. Back in Manhattan, he was always dressed to impress. Here? He was dressed like a surfer about to hit the beach. A blue tank top stretched across his torso, showing off his tan muscles. A pair of red, board shorts rested right at his narrow hips, and a pair of brown leather slip-on sandals completed his ensemble.

After the drought of not seeing him for days, the sight of him was like pouring iced cold water on my face after spending a day in the Mojave Desert.

I sprint-walked down the stairs and threw my arms around his neck. The fresh, salty scent of the ocean on his skin conjured images of paradise. He set me down, and pressing his lips to mine, he dried up any lingering doubt I had about coming to see him. This felt right.

He felt right.

I'd not told him, but as much as I wanted to rip off his clothes already, I'd come prepared to spend less time tangled in his sheets and more time actually getting to know him—his past, his family, his hobbies. Everything. But when his tongue parted my lips and I felt that electric wire that ran the length of my spine vibrate with erotic promise, I realized that resisting this man for the next three days would be completely futile and potentially one of the inanest ideas I could have ever had.

Separating from our kiss, Tom tucked a loose strand of hair behind my ears then caressed my jaw with his fingers. "Christ. Sara, I've missed you so much. Here, let me take that." Tom grabbed my carryon with one hand and entwined his fingers in mine with his other. "This is all the luggage you have?"

"Why is that so surprising?"

"Don't women usually pack a ton of stuff?"

"I'm not that kind of woman."

He smirked. "They feed you on the plane?"

"The service was amazing, but I was too nervous to really stomach anything. I can certainly eat now."

"I can take you to a restaurant nearby, or we can drive back to my place and I can cook you breakfast?"

"Your place sounds fantastic. I'd also love a shower."

He raised an eyebrow, mischief dancing in his eyes. "Shower, huh?"

I pinched his side. "Stop it. I know what you're thinking."

He chortled. "I'm not thinking anything."

"Yeah…" I hadn't been able to stop thinking about it either, though—our bodies naked and writhing to our own rhythm, us heated and washed in sweat. I shook my head at my thoughts. This was not going to be easy.

The sun was bright and hot, casting beautiful highlights off Tom's tousled golden-brown hair. He was a creature to behold. Tall and masculine, Tom looked divine in that tank top that clung to his torso in all the right places, accentuating all his lean muscles and tone physique. His sun-kissed skin glowed, making him look youthful and less stressed. It was as if here, he could strip off the suit and just be Tom.

This was the man I wanted to get to know.

In the parking lot, we stopped as we approached a red Mercedes-Benz boxy SUV waiting for us, all the windows rolled down. "Well, this is an interesting car. For some reason, I pictured you driving a fancy sports car through the streets of Los Angeles."

His brow creased. "Me? In a fancy sports car?"

"Isn't that what you L.A. people drive around here?"

"You L.A. people?" he asked as he threw my carryon onto the back seat, then he held the passenger door open for me and helped me up. "I was born and raised upstate New York. I'm one-hundred percent not L.A. people."

"You know what I mean. Successful, young guys on the prowl."

When he jumped into the driver seat, he looked at me with those sparkling golden-olive eyes I had been missing so much. "First, why would I be on the prowl when I've got you?" he asked with a wink. "And second, just because I can, it doesn't mean I always have to drive some fancy sports car. Plus, when I'm out here, I try to spend as little time as possible in the city. I prefer being near the water surfing or in the mountains hiking. The AMG makes more sense for me."

"AMG?

"It's the SUV model."

I took in the cool and sleek interior with all the high-tech mixed with luxury design and rolled my eyes. My Jeep was prehistoric compared to this. I couldn't even fathom how to use this car. Shifting the SUV into drive, we took off toward Santa Monica.

"I didn't know you surfed," I said as I tied my hair back so it wouldn't whip against my face.

"I can take you with me tomorrow, if you like?"

"I don't have the slightest clue how to surf."

"I can teach you. We'll have a blast. And I get to see you in a bikini."

"I didn't bring a bikini."

"Even better." He tried to hold back a devilish grin.

I simply shook my head. "How long does it take to get to Santa Monica?"

"Depends on what route you take, but no more than thirty minutes, maybe less, depending on the traffic."

I glanced over at Tom and he couldn't have looked more perfect. "You know, this suits you," I said.

"What do you mean?"

"California. The beach."

"How's that?"

"Golden tan and your hair wild in the wind. Carefree. A total surfer. Not the business man in a suit I met a couple of weeks ago."

"Is that a bad thing?"

"No. You're just...even more beautiful like this. Women must tell you that all the time."

He reached over and grabbed my hand, lacing his fingers through mine and bringing them up to his lips where he planted a soft kiss. "There's only one woman I wish to impress, and that woman is you. And I can't wait to spend the next few days alone with you. No distractions."

"You're done with work?"

"We had a few multimillion-dollar properties that were sold and bought. Projects our agents had been working on for several months. Jake's in town also. He can handle anything else that comes up."

"I didn't know Jake was here."

"When we're dealing with huge sales, Jake and I like to be in the area. It's tricky when you deal with these high-profile clients. At times, you don't even work directly with them. Everything is done through the agents or reps. Makes the back and forth that much harder. Plus, even though our company name precedes us, and we have extremely talented and successful agents, some clients prefer to work directly with me and Jake. I'm not exactly crazy about working that side of the business anymore, but sometimes it's necessary if you want to keep this type of clientele happy and coming back."

"Sounds like you've been pretty busy."

"Yeah, well, for the next couple of days, I'll be busy with *you*." He kissed my hand and with his fingers still tangled with mine, he gently placed it back on my lap. The subtle intimacy made my heart swell and I couldn't wait until my entire body, and not just my fingers, were encased in him.

As we entered Santa Monica, the road snaked alongside the ocean. The smell of the salty air swam through the warm breeze flowing freely through the SUV. The Pacific Ocean gleamed under the morning sun, sparkling and inviting. My feet were anxious to sink into the soft sand while I sipped wine and watched the sunset.

We merged onto the narrower Pacific Coast Highway. A long row of houses lined the beach. Tom turned us around and pulled the SUV alongside a row of about ten three-story oceanfront homes. My eyes widened. "No. Way. You can't be serious."

"What?"

"You live here?"

"Home away from home."

We pulled up to a bluish-gray house with a driveway big enough for at least three or four cars. "Trust me," he continued, noticing my awestruck expression. "This place is hardly spectacular compared to the real mansions lining the beach farther north. Personally, I'm not a big fan of monstrous-sized homes. I grew up humble and near water, so for me, all I need is a cozy place with an oceanfront view and a private beach, and I'm good. Can't wait to show you inside, though. It's really quaint. Come on." Tom took my suitcase from the backseat. We walked up a few steps to a slim entryway. He fumbled a little with his keys before finally opening the red, wooden front door. "Welcome home."

Of course, nothing short of amazing awaited inside. Similar to his Hoboken apartment, the far back wall of the house was a splay of windows, except these faced the beautiful dark-blue waters of the Pacific. The rich espresso wood floors were a stunning contrast to the light sandy beach visible through the glass walls. The home was narrow but very long. The foyer led to an impressive contemporary new kitchen, which was laden with granite counter tops, stainless steel appliances, and dark wood cabinets. Further along, and carved out of the right wall of the house, the kitchen and living/dining area were separated by a massive, wood-trimmed staircase that led both down to a ground floor and up to a third floor.

"Jesus, Tom, this place is sick."

"You haven't seen the rest."

Dropping my handbag on the kitchen counter, I continued the tour into the living room. I abandoned my sandals by the entrance, my feet padding along on the soft Asian area rugs; the once deep burgundy rich colored fabrics were faded but still looked and felt opulent. The living-room was furnished with an eclectic collection of antique furniture comprised of a distressed, natural-wood armoire, double bookcase, and small desk. A large brown leather sofa and two darker brown, leather arm chairs surrounded a matching coffee table to the armoire.

What was more impressive about the room was the art on the wall. Framed sketch drawings, portraits, and landscapes adorned the north wall behind the couch.

"Did you do these?" I asked.

"Only a handful of people have ever seen those. I don't get many visitors."

A familiar face stared back at me from those sketches. "I've seen her before...back at your apartment. She is beautiful."

"That's my mother, Adeline. And yes, she is a breathtaking woman."

I pointed to a sketch portrait of the same young man I had also seen at his apartment.

"That's my twin brother, James."

I spun my head toward him. "What? You have a twin and you never told me?"

"I didn't see a pressing need to talk to you about my family. Not yet, at least."

"For not being identical, you seriously resemble each other."

From behind, Tom wrapped his arms around me and nuzzled my neck. "Yeah, but I'm the better looking one," he chuckled, nibbling and tickling my ear with his lips and hot breath. That was all it took to plunge me into a heated pool of desire. My skin prickled with sensation as he swept my hair to the side and kissed my neck. Feathery kisses trailed to my bare shoulder where he nipped the spaghetti strap of my dress and effortlessly rolled it off the rounded edge of my arm.

His fingers traced gentle steps up my arms, lighting me up as they slowly reached the heated skin of my shoulders and neck. Finally, with a slight touch to my chin, he turned my mouth toward his, and when our lips met, a volcano erupted.

I turned around and we were lost in a feverish embrace, tasting each other like it was our first time. His tongue licked the cleft of my lips, teasing and inviting, making me crave the same touch elsewhere. Before we knew it, we were laying down on his couch, the weight of his body pinning me onto the cool leather; his hands hot and demanding.

I'd longed for the feel of his body on mine, the hardness of his length pressing against me. Between whispered breaths, I tried to speak, my uttered words a jumbled mess. My mind knew my body was surrendering and about to give into the pleasure, but it was Tom who pulled away, his chest heaving as he sat at the other end of the couch. "I'm so sorry. I promised you this trip was not going to be all about sex and here I am, ready to rip your clothes off."

I sat next to him, my pulse still beating with the hum of my blood as it burned through my veins. "There's nothing to be sorry about."

"You're like a magnet...and this is going to take a whole new level of self-control." Turning toward me, his brows dipped. "I don't know if I have it."

Staring at him, I couldn't remember why I even wanted to resist the attraction between us. I inched toward him and cradled his cheek in my palm. "Hey, I chose to kiss you, too. Perhaps it was a bad idea anyway."

His eyes stilled over me and his jaw clenched as he took my hand from his cheek. "Coming here?"

I shook my head and moved in closer, bringing my mouth to his. "No. Pretending I could be in the same room with you and resist these lips." I buried my hands in his hair and drew in for a kiss, but he turned away, wounding me more than I cared to admit.

"Sara, I don't want to pressure you into doing anything you don't want to."

"Believe me. I want this."

He stood. "I made you a promise."

I stood up as well, looking up into his eyes. "Forget the promise."

Taking my chin in his fingers, he fixed his devilish eyes into mine. "I want you. Trust me. I could strap you across my shoulder right now and carry you upstairs to my bed. I want to defile your body. In. Every. Way. Possible."

He wasn't finished.

"Christ, Sara. You make me want to do things to you I've never done to a woman." His eyes filled with feral lust as his gaze drifted from my lips to the soft mounds of my breasts. "Hell, it's taking every ounce of will power not to rip off your dress right now, but…"

"So, do it.

"Baby, you wanted to take it slow."

I rolled my eyes. He wasn't going to let it go. "I know what I said, but when I made you make that promise I was across a freaking telephone line. Now, being next to you, I don't know what the hell I was thinking."

He smiled, pulling hair from my eyes. "I love it when you get fired up. But, at minimum, I think I should cook for you first before I fuck you, what do you think?"

I returned his playful smile. "You do have a point there."

Walking toward the kitchen, he began searching through his cupboards.

"So where am I sleeping?" I asked. "I'd like to freshen up a bit."

"You're sleeping in my bedroom on the top floor," he called over the fridge door.

"So, we're sharing a bed?"

His eyes met mine, an eyebrow hiked. "Unless you prefer not to. I can always sleep in the guest room."

"That won't be necessary. I'm happy to room with you."

His wide grin made my knees weaken. "Make yourself at home," he said. "Breakfast should be ready in twenty minutes."

When I walked upstairs and saw his bedroom, my jaw dropped. Facing the ocean, the master bedroom was as grand as a honeymoon suite. The top floor was completely carpeted in soft, sandy-colored fabric, and similar to his apartment back home, the furnishings were dark and modern. The large headboard of the wrought-iron California king canopy bed was flush against the east wall. The tall mattress was draped in a white, plush, cotton comforter; the matching canopy panels were drawn back and tied at each corner. A black, five-drawer dresser and matching night tables completed the look.

The balcony was equally amazing. A beautiful claw-foot tub and a canopied daybed were secluded from the neighbors by frosted glass on each side. It was perfect for a late-night soak under the moon and stars.

Tom called from downstairs, interrupting my self-guided tour. "Breakfast is about ready!"

I changed into a pair of denim shorts and white tank top before rushing back to the kitchen.

The air smelled of cinnamon and vanilla, mixed with the smoky aromas of maple-flavored sausage and bacon. My mouth watered the minute my eyes took in the sight of the breakfast feast sprawled on the kitchen counter. French toast, eggs, fresh strawberries, and bananas accompanied the perfectly crisp bacon, ham, and sausage.

"Wow, this looks amazing. Everything smells fantastic."

"I hope you're hungry," he said as he handed me the dish of stacked French toast. "Bring these to the deck, we'll eat outside."

Minutes later, I was pouring extra syrup on my toast as I finished my fourth slice. It was buttery and gooey. All the flavors danced in my mouth. My stomach protested, but everything was so scrumptious, I couldn't help but continue to stuff my face as I washed it all down with a tall glass of orange juice.

"I like watching you eat," he said, amused and finally breaking the silence.

"Oh yeah, and why is that?'

"Because you don't seem to care about counting calories."

"You're calling me a pig?"

He laughed. "No. I simply enjoy cooking for someone who likes to eat."

"I only eat like this when I'm around you. Or when Jen has time to cook. Otherwise, I'm always eating girl-lunches or girl-dinners."

"And what exactly are those?"

"Meals comprised of snacks. I'm a terrible cook, so I don't even bother. Though my mom at least taught me and my sister how to make scrambled eggs and toast. It's a survival skill."

"Tell me about your sister."

I set my fork down and took a deep breath. I wasn't ready to rustle the leaves of my family tree. Still, I couldn't keep Tom in the dark forever. "Megan? She lives up in Seattle. She moved there after our mom died."

"That must've been hard for you...to lose your mom then your sister moving away?"

"It was very hard, but thankfully, Jen was there for me." The smile accompanying my words wasn't wide. Jen helped me heal, but the scars would always be there.

"You guys seem very close. I admire your friendship."

"Is it just you and your brother?" I asked, pivoting the attention toward him.

"James was enough. Trust me," he laughed.

"Must be interesting being a twin."

"We are not identical, so we don't share any of the identical twin phenomena, but we were very close."

"Were?"

Tom was about to take a sip from his OJ but stopped and thought for a moment. "I haven't been home in a while." Then he took a deep gulp of juice. All amusement was gone from his voice. I could have pressed further, but it wasn't the time to delve into those murky waters. At least not yet.

"Your mom is beautiful. Now I know where you get your looks from."

Warmth filled his eyes as he thought about his mother. It was obvious he loved her deeply.

"What about your father?" I asked.

"My father died from a heart attack," he replied coolly. "I was stationed in Afghanistan when it happened."

"Oh, God. I'm so sorry."

"Don't be. There was nothing I could do about it. Plus…" He paused and stared out across the sand."

"It's okay if you don't want to talk about it."

He looked back at me, subtle fury hiding behind his green eyes. "My father was a terrible man, Sara. He wasn't a good husband, and he was an even worse father. I can't say I was especially moved when I heard he passed."

My mouth dried. I didn't even know what to say.

"I've moved on," he said, saving me from my awkward silence.

"Yeah, but moving on is not easy," I said.

"There are things that still haunt me about my past. God knows there's so much I would have done differently. But when it comes to the man who fathered me, I've made peace with it."

We looked at each other for a long moment. Neither one of us knew exactly what to say after that. Our sunny day was clouded by memories of troubled pasts, but I wasn't about to let our day get ruined. "So, what do you want to do today?" I asked.

"Well, there's a bike trail nearby that runs right along the beach."

"Perfect."

He mounted the bikes onto the AMG and we took off around noon. After a couple of hours, we ventured away from the beach and into town, stopping at a café nearby for a late lunch. We sat on one of their outside tables and lazily ate our food while enjoying the afternoon sun and ocean air.

"So, Jake is having this party tonight," Tom said in between mouthfuls. "It's a penthouse party at his Hollywood apartment."

"What's the celebration?"

"The recent sales, and truthfully, he likes throwing a party for no reason at all," he scoffed. "I'm not crazy about going, but he is my partner and some of our clients might be there."

"Will you be gone late?"

"I was hoping you'd want to join me. You could meet Jake."

"I didn't bring any fancy dresses."

A self-assured look crossed his eyes. "I've already taken care of that. You're going to like what I had my assistant bring."

"Oh? Who's this mystery shopper?"

"Tiffany."

"Hmm, so is purchasing dresses for me part of Tiffany's job description?"

"She's also a close friend of mine and offered to help."

"Was she the one who bought the Geena Salvatore dress?"

His eyes narrowed over me in a swift look of seduction. "That one was all me."

"So, she knows about us?"

"Yes. Why so many questions?"

"So, you two are very close?"

"She works for me. We're friends."

He didn't seem very eager to offer more on this Tiffany, but I wasn't going to easily forget about her either. Close female friends weren't always just friends. I would need to let that simmer for a while.

"We don't have to stay long tonight," he continued. "I need to make an appearance, say hi to a few people, shake a few hands then we can leave."

"I'm here with you, so I go where you go."

I tried to play it cool, but the thought of going to some Hollywood party terrified me. I wasn't the type to mingle with fancy socialites. I already felt out of place traveling around in luxury cars and private jets, now I had to play the part of pretty arm candy.

We made it back to the house around three p.m. My legs were sore, but the small workout felt great. Tom dropped his keys on the kitchen counter then reached inside the fridge for a bottle of water and offered me one. I took it and stared as he downed his in less than twenty seconds. I admired his physique as he drank.

Sticky and drenched in sweat from being in the sun all afternoon, he looked so smoking hot I couldn't stop my mind from summoning lewd thoughts of his naked body grinding into me. I pressed the cold bottle against my forehead, trying to freeze frame those images or I may have lost all self-control.

"Shower," I said, taking a gulp of my water and nodding up toward the third floor.

He raised a brow, a smile curling at the corner of his lips.

"Not with me, buster." I winked at him, stopping him before he had a chance to finish his thought. "Nice try, though. You had your chance to fuck this body earlier, remember? Now you wait until I'm ready."

He laughed. "Touché, my lady. But you insult my honor."

"Honor my ass!" We both laughed, but his chuckle carried a sensual guttural sound that made me crave more of his playful nature, but also made me regret my idiotic idea. No sex with this man? Yeah, moronic to the umpteenth power.

"What time's the party?" I asked.

"Eleven."

"After the shower, can I take a short nap? Otherwise, I won't make the party."

"Yeah of course, you should definitely rest. I know jet lag can be hard on your body."

That. And wanting him so badly and not being able to do anything about it because I was ridiculously delusional also made it hard on my body.

I left him in the kitchen with his water.

Upstairs, I daydreamed about him walking into the bathroom and joining me under the warm water that flowed like rain in the large shower. My skin vibrated with desire, aching for the feel of his hands. Recalling our last intimate encounter—his body on top of mine, his naked chest, his long muscular limbs, his iron-hard erection, and the heat in which he beat into me—made me lightheaded. I throbbed with the need to orgasm and almost reached between my legs, but thought better of it. The sweet torture was keeping me on edge and the anticipation of having him own my release was worth the wait. I wanted it to be his and his alone.

I slipped into a comfortable pair of cotton shorts and a camisole, then sank into his bed and mercifully faded to sleep before being assaulted by more images of Tom and his glorious nakedness.

Twenty

TOM

I brushed my knuckles softly over Sara's cheek. "Hey, sleepyhead, open your eyes. You're gonna miss the best part."

"Huh?" she mumbled, rousing from her drowsy state, seemingly annoyed at being awakened. She sat up, her eyes still at half-mast. "Miss what?"

"The most beautiful sunset you've ever seen. Come on. You said you wanted to sink your toes in the sand while sipping wine and watching the sunset."

"Do I need to get dressed?"

"I mean, I don't mind you in those tiny shorts, but you might get cold near the water."

Clumsily, she dragged herself out of bed and pulled out a pair of sweat pants from her luggage. Tugging them on, she fell back onto the bed, body slamming down on the mattress—face first.

I stifled a laugh.

Christ. She was so fucking adorable.

"Let's go, get up." I took her by the arms and helped her up, hauling her over my shoulder and carrying her down the two flights of stairs to my ground floor. Once there, I placed her back down on her feet. She was still pouty, but at least she could stand. She hadn't bothered to fix her hair, but I didn't say anything because the woman had the sexy messy bun thing down to a science.

I handed her one of my oversized hooded sweatshirts. "You may need this." She took it, her face still scrunched in a grimace as she slid it on. Seemed sleep deprivation turned her into a bit of a grouch, which I found endearing because she was the cutest grouch I'd ever seen. Grabbing a bottle of champagne, two flutes, and hooking two beach chairs under my arms, I gestured for her to join me. "Let's go, grumpy pants. I don't want you to miss this."

Still in half a daze, she grunted behind me as she skipped out onto the sand through the French doors.

"We only have a few more minutes before the sun sets," I hollered over my shouldered as I settled us near the water's edge, close enough for the waves to splash at our feet.

A brisk breeze brushed against our skin and the powdery grains felt cool under our toes. Sara's body was swallowed up in my sweatshirt which fit her more like a dress. She pulled the hood over her head as she plopped down on one of the beach chairs.

I popped the cork to our champagne bottle and poured us each a glass while we sat in silence waiting for the quiet spectacle. The ping of our flutes coming together signaled the beginning of a memorable evening.

After a few sips of champagne, Sara came back to life like a butterfly emerging from a cocoon. "There's the girl I know..." I said as she offered me one of her heart-melting smiles.

"I'm sorry. Didn't mean to be such a downer. I was just exhausted from the flight."

"No worries. Everyone's entitled to be a little grouchy sometimes. What matters is that you're here with me now about to enjoy one of the most beautiful sunsets you'll ever see."

Thankfully, the California sun didn't disappoint. The hot fiery sphere looked immense as it fell beneath the horizon, leaving a trail of burnt yellows, purples, and reds that sailed over a sea of blue sky. Sara sat speechless as her eyes lingered on the departing sun and the endless beauty left at its wake.

After a few silent moments, she said, "Thanks for forcing me to get up. I've never seen a sunset like this."

"I'm happy you had a chance to see it," I said with a toothy smile. Sara lowered the hood from her head and the wind swirled strands of her hair loose, the soft fading rays giving her skin a rosy glow. She smiled back, and my heart clenched.

God, this girl had no clue what she was doing to me. These feelings that had begun to brew, they were the dangerous type. I'd been here before. I'd fallen hard for a woman once and the heartache cracked my foundation. I wasn't sure I wanted to go through that again and a part of me wanted to bolt, to hide from what I was feeling. But another part kept me here, glued to my seat, my gaze swimming in hers, unable to fight the pull because being near her felt too goddamn good.

Leaning closer, I tipped her chin up and kissed her soft lips, gently and unrushed. I wanted to savor this moment, to make it last forever. Her fingers buried themselves in my hair and a sweet moan escaped through a shallow breath. Fuck. I wanted this to be an innocent kiss, but hearing that moan stirred the beast inside of me, awakening my dark thoughts.

I swept the inside of her mouth with my tongue and stroked in fluid motion, imagining all the different places on her body I wanted to explore with my lips. It had only been a week since I'd had sex with her, but it felt like a lifetime. My blood raged with need and I couldn't wait to get her naked and in my bed.

The cold water hit our feet and the chilly wind cooled my skin, calming the beast a little. "I think," I said hoarsely, "we should head inside and get ready for the party."

The disappointment that flashed in her eyes made me realize she'd likely been thinking the same thing—we were going to spontaneously combust soon if we didn't address the searing sexual energy threatening to scorch us from the inside out.

Unfortunately, I'd promised Jake I'd be at his party, and I was more than certain that once I got Sara down to her birthday suit, there was no way we were going to leave my room tonight.

I chose to dress in the downstairs guest room and gave Sara the privacy and comfort of getting dressed and dolled up in my master. I'd told Tiffany to spare no expense and had her purchase several designer gowns for Sara. I had no idea which one she was going to choose, but it didn't really matter. She'd look spectacular in anything she put on that gorgeous body of hers.

Pacing down by the staircase, I anxiously waited for her to come down so I could give her my other surprise. I sure hoped she wouldn't think I'd gone a bit over the top—though I probably had—but for some reason, I wanted to shower her with all of the gifts. If it made her smile, I wanted to give it to her. I didn't care what it was. If she wanted to own a million kittens, I'd have a truckload of them delivered to her apartment by Monday.

I sounded crazy. But that's what she'd done to me.

When the door to my bedroom finally opened, I adjusted the cufflinks on my tux and stared up, waiting to see her. You could have probably picked my jaw off the ground the moment she came into view. The woman looked like a movie star. She'd opted for a floor length, white, form-fitting silk dress with a plunging neckline. Silver stiletto heels and a matching clutch finished off the outfit. The gown accentuated her body like it was made for her. She'd styled her gleaming dark hair into loose curls that made her look like a 1940's Hollywood starlet.

She descended the staircase, and I couldn't keep my gaze off the way the fabric hugged every female groove of her body. "Baby...you look...wow. I can't even speak."

She winked at me. "You look *wow* yourself."

After a brief moment of simply staring at each other, I finally mustered the courage to hand her the small square box I'd been holding. "Here, I bought you these to wear for tonight."

Her eyes widened, skin flushing as she took the box from me with caution. "Tom...you've already given me this gown, which by the way, your assistant forgot to remove the tag. I saw how much this cost and it's like more than I make a month...so—"

I placed a finger over her red lips. "Baby, open the box."

Nodding, she finally uncoiled the ribbon and opened the black, velvety container. "Christ," she said, putting a hand to her heart. "They are gorgeous. I mean, these can't be real?"

"You think I'd give you fake diamond earrings?"

She shot her gaze up to meet mine. "Tom, these are easily more than a carat each. I can't possibly accept them."

Shaken, she tried to hand the box back to me, but I closed my palm around hers. "Sara, all I want is to see you smile. So, if you don't want them, that's fine, but I hope you'll accept them. I wanted you to feel as beautiful as you look."

With a trembling smile, she took the earrings from the box and put them on, looking at herself in the foyer mirror. "They *are* gorgeous."

I snaked my arms around her waist and looked into her eyes through the mirror. "*You're* gorgeous. And tonight, everyone is gonna think I'm the luckiest motherfucker on the face of the planet."

"I feel like Cinderella on my way to the ball."

"Are you saying I'm your Fairy Godmother?"

She spun around in my arms, her brown eyes twinkling. With a gentle kiss on my lips she said, "No baby. You're the fucking prince."

Twenty-One

SARA

Tom tried to go in for a deeper kiss, but I swatted him away. My makeup looked flawless and I didn't want him smudging my lipstick. I needed to look the part of Tom's perfect arm candy. I could only imagine the scores of pretty women looking to snatch a handsome billionaire tonight, and even though Tom had gone out of his way to make me feel beautiful, my confidence was still shaky. After the accident, I wasn't the same. Though subtle, there were things I noticed, even if others didn't. My gait was slightly off balance, which was why I was clumsy on my feet. My muscles were stiff in certain areas, and there was a scar near the top of my hairline that I always managed to hide with hair or coverup. I doubted Tom had even noticed.

But it didn't matter if he never took note of these little imperfections. I knew they were there, and they always fucked with my head.

"Let's hit the road," he said, taking my hand in his.

He took me through the garage, and when he flicked the lights on, my eyes widened at the sight. A Maserati Gran Cabrio convertible sat parked inside, the metallic, ocean-blue exterior glimmering under the fluorescent lights.

I stood speechless at the entrance of the garage.

Tom gingerly opened the passenger door, waiting for me to enter. "Sara?"

"I thought you told me you didn't own a sports car?" I said as I walked toward him.

"Um, not entirely. What I said was I didn't have to always drive one just because I could. That didn't mean I didn't own one. Plus, you didn't really think I'd take my girlfriend anywhere—looking like a million bucks—in anything other than a sexy sports car, now did you?"

When he popped into the driver seat, I turned to him. "Girlfriend?"

"Well, that is, if you say *yes*?"

"You mean exclusively?"

"What other kind is there?"

"You're sure this is what you want?"

"I wouldn't have asked you if I wasn't."

I wanted to shout yes at the top of my lungs, but I turned into an ice cube. Tom stared at me for a long minute before venting his frustration in one solid breath. He ran his hands through his hair. "Listen, I know I kind of sprang this on you, so you don't have to answer me right now. Just think about it, okay?"

I nodded. "Tom, it's not that I don't want to...I just...it's so sudden..."

He brushed his knuckles across my cheek. "It's okay. I understand."

"No. You don't. What I mean to say is...it's so sudden and so soon, but it couldn't feel more perfect."

He took my hand in his and kissed me, and with his hot breath still on my lips, he uttered, "So, how 'bout we go for that ride, baby?"

The car sprung to life as the engine purred beneath the hood. The garage door opened and we spilled out onto the pavement. That morning, I'd thought Tom fit perfectly into the surfer mold, but watching him handle the wheel of the Maserati had me second guessing myself. Sexy was an understatement. The speed and sensuality of the car's roar when Tom sped us down the highway made me blush. Shit. This man was too fucking hot. And apparently, he was now my boyfriend.

Had I bagged Mr. Iced Double? How did this even happen?

I said yes without giving it too much thought. Had he really swept me up with his dashing good looks, lavish gifts, and his fancy sports car?

No. What I was feeling for Tom was real and went beyond any of the superficial or material things. It was his thoughtfulness and tenderness. It was the gentleness of his touch and the hidden desire behind each kiss. It was the way he looked at me with such adoration. Like I was the only woman for him, and he would move mountains to make me happy.

No one had ever made me feel this way, and I was drunk on it, ready for another shot.

The heat on my face was an indicator of my fevered thoughts and I couldn't wait to be done with this dumb party we were going to and be back at his house instead, ripping each other's clothes off and pretty much fucking all night long until my pussy hurt and my legs gave out.

We arrived at Jake's party a little after eleven. The place pumped to the sounds of a club remix. I didn't see anybody I particularly recognized, but it was pretty obvious the prerequisites to attend this party included: a) having a lot of money, and b) being inhumanly good looking, just as I'd expected. Bobbing and weaving through the sea of gyrating torsos, Tom led me to the VIP lounge area where he expected to find Jake. As we approached, heads pivoted in our direction. Women lit up and tucked their hair behind their ears as their gazes lingered on Tom, completely ignoring the fact he was with me. I should have walked prouder, but my confidence wavered a wee bit. Standing in a room full of supermodels was downright intimidating.

As we neared a large white leather sectional, a man sitting in between two gorgeous Eurasian looking women waved us over. He immediately rose to greet us, leaving the two women under his arms on the couch. "Bruh, you made it!" he said to Tom as they shared a man-hug.

He was a little shorter than Tom, and had a thick mop of curly, dark brown hair. His blue eyes twinkled brightly underneath beautifully sculpted dark eyebrows. His blue, silk suit did little to hide his muscled body. Jake was exceptionally good looking, but he gave off a sinister vibe that rolled off his shoulders, like a menacing energy that lurked behind his easy smile. My body shuddered when he shook my hand.

"Jake," Tom said, "this is Sara...Sara, Jake."

He smiled crookedly. "This is the famous Sara?" He eyed me head to toe, the cold gaze of his blue eyes leaving icicles on my skin.

"It's nice to finally meet you, Jake," I replied.

"Likewise. I've heard so much about you. You are as beautiful as Tom described." His sly smile made me cringe.

"It's a great party," I said, shifting the attention.

"Please, make yourselves at home. Let me get you something to drink."

Tom grabbed Jake by the arm. "I'll take care of it. You guys get to know each other."

When Tom left to get my drink, both Jake and I noted the awkward space between us.

He turned to face me. "So, Sara. What hotel are you staying at?"

"Actually, I'm staying with Tom."

"In L.A.?" he asked, his brows knitting to a tight pinch.

"Santa Monica."

"You mean the beach house?" he asked, incredulous.

I couldn't understand his confusion. "You seem surprised."

"I was simply not expecting that," he chuckled with little amusement.

"Expecting what, exactly?"

He took a couple of steps closer and leaned in toward my ear. "The thing is, sweetheart, Tom never brings *girls* he's fucking home. Guess you must be more than his typical hook-up. Consider yourself special."

My bones splintered. Was he fucking kidding me?

Embarrassed, I felt heat rise to my cheeks. Is that what I was? A *girl* he was fucking? Is that what he'd told Jake about me? I didn't know what to say to this guy. Any other day I would've had something witty to say. I would've put the damn asshole in his place for disrespecting me like that, but I simply froze. It wasn't so much that I couldn't stand up to the prick, but the fact he made me feel like I wasn't special at all. I was just another girl in Tom's collection of girls he fucked.

My heart cracked and I hated myself in that instant for allowing myself to dream. For allowing myself to believe that true love existed. That perhaps I could live in a fairytale and have my prince. I was such an idiot. And the fact I permitted myself to be duped by all the magic of Tom's bullshit, infuriated me as much as it hurt me.

I turned from Jake without bothering to say excuse me, and pushed through the thick crowd of impossibly beautiful people. My body turned to stone when I caught sight of Tom standing by the bar.

He wasn't alone.

Perched on six-inch stilettos, next to him stood a gorgeous

redhead. Her fiery, silky curls cascaded down to her lower back. Dressed in a form-fitting, black cocktail dress, her outrageous curves screamed *sex goddess*. She was practically draped over Tom and I was about ready to go punch a hole through her face. The closer I neared, the hotter my blood raged. I hadn't felt this kind of jealousy in a long time, and I was about to lose it.

The intense possessiveness inside me was unnerving. It wasn't just that this other woman was flirting with him, it was the way she looked at him. I knew that look because that's how *I* looked at him—in awe and total fascination. The woman was clearly head over heels in love with him.

They shared an intimate laugh and their proximity to each other brought me close to an eruption. What enraged me even more was Tom's nonchalance about the whole thing. He was so comfortable with her. Were they close friends or perhaps, something more?

I was ready to interrupt their private conversation, but I lost my nerve. Who was I? What right did I have to demand explanations? Watching their intimate conversation with each other, made me feel insignificant. They looked perfect together. She resembled a celebrity standing on top of the world, and I was an ex-contemporary dancer with broken dreams, dressed in a designer gown I could never afford.

I was a phony. How could I've ever believed a man like him could ever want a girl like me? Oh God. I sounded so pathetic. I felt ashamed and foolish. I didn't belong in some high-rise, Hollywood party with a man clearly out of my league. As I started to turn back around to walk away, Tom caught me in his gaze.

Stars. The way he lit up when he saw me stopped me dead in my tracks. I could never escape him, not when he looked at me like I was the only woman in the world. Why did he have to be so good at his game? Why did he have to make me believe that this could all be real and that we could be together? He reached out with his hand and gestured for me to join them.

Powerless against his charm, I obliged. He grabbed me by the wrist and drew me in close, wrapping his arm around my waist and planting a soft kiss on my neck. "Here she is. Tiff, this is Sara."

Tiff? As in Tiffany? The personal assistant aka close friend?

Gravity pulled the blood from my head straight to my feet.

"Sara, meet Tiffany, my personal assistant," he said while wrapping his arms tighter around my waist. I stretched out my hand to greet this woman, but all I really wanted to do was run. Tom may have been oblivious to it, but I sure as hell wasn't. Women can sense when another woman is trotting on our territory, and this one was stepping a bit too close for comfort.

"Nice to meet you, Tiffany."

"Same," she replied coolly, but I knew it was a lie. She probably guessed the identical sentiment from me. Our grip tightened, both of us wanting to stake our ground.

"Where's Jake?" Tom asked.

I shrugged, not interested in talking about that dickhead. "Where's my drink?" I asked, needing something strong to take off the edge.

"Oh, right. Sorry. Got sidetracked. Tiff was telling me about one of our clients who apparently has been trying to hunt me down. Mrs. Westinghouse seems determined to meet me in person. It's why I try to avoid these social events."

"Mrs. Westinghouse," Tiffany added, "is a well-respected philanthropist. She's been looking to move to Malibu for years, but could never find the right home. She's a very eccentric woman with distinct tastes. One of our agents found her the perfect home, but the clients couldn't agree on a price. Mrs. Westinghouse wasn't about to walk away without this historic mansion, but she wasn't willing to pay a single penny more than she had already offered. It was a tough deal, but Tom worked his magic and closed the sale in thirty days and even managed to save her a few million. This would never be her type of venue, but she was adamant to meet our Tom, the man who got her the home of her dreams." She flashed Tom a crooked grin accompanied by a light squeeze to his arm.

"Of course, who wouldn't want to meet *our* Tom," I replied, smiling and looking at Tom. "So how about that drink, baby?" I reminded him.

Tom released his arm from around my waist and turned to find the dancing bartender behind the bar who was expertly flipping bottles to impress the hordes of women spilling over the counter trying to catch a glimpse of his show.

Tiffany wasted no time dropping the nice act. "You chose the white one."

My brow creased with confusion. "Excuse me?"

"The dress. Safe choice."

"Safe choice?"

"A bit muted. Not too flashy or overly sexy. Fits you, I guess."

"Well, you know Tom. He prefers classy over slutty," I said, eyeing her dress. I had no clue if that was even true, but who cared? The viper wanted to show me her fangs? I could show her mine.

She pressed her lips into a tight line and gave me a murderous look. Victory flamed in my veins, and before she could reply, Tom returned with my drink.

"Any sign of Mrs. Westinghouse?" Tom asked Tiffany.

"Haven't seen her," she replied dryly.

"Well, I'm not sticking around here long. We'll probably be heading out in a bit, so if you see her, tell her I'll give her a call first thing tomorrow morning."

Tiffany stood stiff as a board with her arms crossed over her chest, plumping her already generous bosom. I gently whispered in Tom's ear about wanting to dance. Happy to leave her presence, as Tom led me to the dance floor, I glanced back over my shoulder, smiling with triumph, a glint of dark glee in my eyes. Tiffany's flaming face assured me she was ready to jump out of her own skin with anger. Good. Welcome to the club.

Trying to forget everything Tom's tactless friend had said, I gyrated against Tom's hot body, deliberately showing off my best moves in a juvenile attempt to make Ms. Flaming Face a bit more jealous. The problem was, I couldn't pull Jake's words out of my head. How many girls did Tom bring to Los Angeles? And how many did he set up in hotels? The thought made my head spin. Not to mention my interaction with Tiffany left me uneasy.

I couldn't concentrate on the music or dance steps. My body felt stiff as a board and I pulled away, walking toward the exit. Tom followed after me until we reached the elevators. "What's the matter, Sara?" he asked, grabbing my wrist.

Not meeting his eyes, I kept my gaze trained on the floor. He tipped my chin up. "Hey, what's wrong?"

Despite all the nonsense around us, he was still so attuned to me. It filled me with hope. Perhaps what we had *was* real. There was only one way to find out. "Can we get out of here?"

"Are you not feeling well?"

"I don't know. I'm not feeling the vibe. If you want to stay I can take a cab back to your house."

"Don't be ridiculous. I'm not staying here without you." When the elevator doors opened, we hurried inside and rode it down in pure silence. Once in the garage, we waited for the valet.

As we drove through the late-night traffic of Hollywood's streets, I turned to him. "We were barely there for an hour. You didn't even say goodbye to Jake."

"He'll survive. I don't like those parties anyway, so I'm happy we left. Right now, I'm concerned about you." He waited for a reply, but I struggled for the right words.

"Sara, are you going to tell me what happened back there?"

"Tom, why did you invite me here?"

"To the party?"

"No. California."

"What do you mean? Aren't we trying to get to know each other better?"

"Tom," I said more firmly, "why did you ask me to stay with you at your house?"

He let go of my hand. "I was clear about how I felt. I asked you to be my girlfriend tonight."

"Jake told me."

"Told you what?"

"About the hotels...the girls...he thought I was one of *them*."

He didn't take his eyes off the road and I sensed the increased tension as he gripped the steering wheel and the car sped faster.

"Apparently, he was shocked I was staying with you at your house since you never bring the girls you're fucking home. He said I should feel special. So, am I?"

"Are you ...?

"Special or as Jake said, just another girl you're fucking."

"From the tone in your voice, you seem to have your mind already made up."

"I want to know the truth because I didn't fly all the way out here to just be another notch on your headboard.

He snapped his head toward me, swerving as he took his eyes off the road. "A notch on my headboard? After opening my heart up to you?"

"I want to believe that what's happening between is real but after what he said, after how he made me feel..."

"What about how *I've* made you feel? Does that mean nothing? You meet Jake once and all of a sudden his words have more validity than mine?"

"He's your best friend. He knows you better than I do. Why would he say those things to me if he thought we were ... more?"

"Jake's an asshole. Regardless, the fact that after everything we've talked about, after I literally asked you to be my girlfriend, you still doubt my intentions...I don't know. Maybe this whole thing *is* a big fucking mistake."

Neither one of us uttered another word for the rest of the ride. For the first time since I met him, I thought I was sitting next to a stranger. When we arrived back at his house, he jumped out and rushed to open my door. He didn't look at me as we walked back into his house. He thrust the door open and stormed in. He flicked the lights on and flung his keys onto the kitchen counter, and with his back to me, dropped his chin to his chest and placed his hands on his waist.

I approached him slowly. "All I did was ask a simple question. I felt like shit when your friend said those things to me. My blood literally drained from my head."

"It wasn't his place to speak to you like that, but that doesn't give you the right to act like you have me all figured out. We barely know each other. Fuck. I only met you two weeks ago."

I blinked several times "Wow. So, now I'm just some girl you met two weeks ago? Maybe Jake wasn't so far off with his comments." I clenched my jaw. "I should've never come here."

"Sara."

"I'm gonna grab my things. I'd rather stay at a hotel tonight than here with you."

"Stay," he said in his deep voice.

The word planted me where I stood, but I didn't turn around. My eyes filled with tears, a river ready to crest. I couldn't let him see what his words had done to me.

"I'm sorry. I didn't mean it. Any of it."

With my back still to him, I stood in silence.

"Sara, please turn around," he implored.

My mind begged me to run up the stairs to his room, pack my bags, and leave. But I was weak. Too goddamn weak. And my body refused to comply. The power of his voice disarmed me. "What is it?"

I asked, turning around. "You've already made it perfectly clear you think this is all one big mistake."

"That's not true."

"That's what you said."

"I was mad and I was an asshole for saying it. I didn't mean it… you have to believe that."

"I don't know what to believe. One minute you are the most charming man in the world, the next you are speeding down the freaking highway and talking to me like I'm some chick you picked up off the street."

"You have every right to be pissed at me."

"I'm hurt, Tom."

"Let me explain."

"Explain what? I don't even know if I care anymore. Right now, I want to get my things and go."

"I'm not about to let you walk out of my life that easily. Not without you knowing the truth."

"And what exactly is the truth?"

"Sara, up until two weeks ago, I was a different guy. I worked and then…I liked to have fun. I wasn't interested in relationships. I wanted to have a good time and then come back to my place alone, where I'm able to unwind and just be me. Things were simple and uncomplicated and that's the way I wanted it."

"And now?"

"And now my world is all shades of fucked up, but I can't imagine a world where you're not in it."

"And all of a sudden you are a changed man? You go from only being interested in hook ups to now you want to be in a relationship with a girl you only met two weeks ago?" I scoffed at him in disbelief.

"You're gonna keep throwing my words back in my face? I told you I didn't mean that."

"Well, I guess words are hard to forget, especially when they jab you right in the chest."

"I'm sorry. I was an asshole and I deserve that, but it doesn't mean that what I'm telling you now is not true. Sara, you're here. In my house. You are the first woman I've ever invited over. Christ, for the past two weeks, I've done things with you I haven't done with anyone. I can't imagine myself without you and that's the fucking truth, whether you want to believe me or not."

"And Tiffany, how does she fit into all of this?"

He shifted uncomfortably on his feet. "What does she have to do with anything?"

"I saw the way you two were with each other."

Tom's brow pinched. "What are you talking about?"

"She cares about you."

"We're friends. We've known each other for years and she's my assistant."

"I mean she *really* cares about you."

"You're threatened by her?"

I said nothing. There was no way I would admit that to him.

"She is just a friend who also happens to be my assistant. Nothing more," he reaffirmed, as if he read the doubt circulating in my mind.

Did he really think I was that naive? "Two people like you can't be just friends. You said you have never lied to me, so tell me, have you ever been more than just friends?"

He looked away from me. I knew it, but I needed to hear it from his lips. "Tom? Were you ever more than friends?"

"It was a long time ago, Sara. I don't see her that way anymore."

My heart stopped. I should have ended my questions there, but I couldn't help myself. "What happened between you two?"

"Nothing happened. That's the point. She wanted something I couldn't give her. I could never be that guy for her."

"So, you broke it off?"

"We were never really together, Sara."

"Friends with benefits?"

"Why are you asking me these questions?"

"Well?"

"Fine. We fucked. Happy?"

Christ. I knew it'd sting, just not how badly. My blood sizzled at the thought of them together. Strong heavy breaths pushed in and out of my chest. I had asked the question. I had pushed him. Now I needed to deal with the aftermath.

He took a few steps toward me. "I know that's not what you wanted to hear, but I told you I wouldn't lie to you. Tiffany is a great girl, but we would never last. She wasn't the woman for me, and I certainly wasn't good for her."

I put a palm out to keep him from coming closer. "So, why did you stay friends?"

He stiffened at my gesture, but respected the silent request. "We are better at being friends. She is a great assistant and I know she needs the job. She was getting attached and if we continued messing around, she was only going to end up hurt. Eventually, we wouldn't be able to work together and neither one of us wanted that. It was better that way."

I couldn't really process anything I was hearing. All I kept seeing in my head was the both of them tangled in sheets, naked. It was infuriating. My body could not handle all that emotion. My hands trembled. I knew there was no way Tiffany was ever going to be out of the picture. "I...don't think I can share you with her."

Before I had a chance to stop him, Tom walked over to me and took my face in his hands. He speared me with his gaze, and all I could see was a love and a devotion to me I could not explain. "Share me? Baby, look at me. I'm totally yours. *Only* yours. You aren't sharing me with anybody."

He crashed his lips into mine and instantly all my fears faded. I melted into his lips, welcoming his wet tongue into my mouth. He made me believe in him with every inch of my body. His love was fire and ice. We consumed each other's breath until nothing was left.

Anger, pain, frustration, lust, love—all melded together into pure heat. He was hard and panting, and I wanted him with such madness my heart ached.

Still, I wasn't ready. I had so much to process, and Tiffany's face was still too vibrant in my mind. The thought of them together haunted me. I needed to be alone to figure out what I wanted. Being so close to him clouded my mind. It took every ounce of my will to separate from his mouth. He held on to me; the fire inside him molten iron.

Eyes aflame with longing, he whispered, "I need you, baby." He nibbled on my bottom lip as he kissed me again. He cradled my face in his hands as his tongue gently parted my lips. He took a few steps forward, forcing me to step back until I felt my spine press against a cold wall. Tom placed his hands on the wall, caging me with his arms. With gentle kisses, he began a slow and torturous downward trail down my neck. He kissed every inch of my skin until his lips met my collarbone and shoulders. My body was boneless. The muscled planes of his chest vibrated with carnal need. It was intoxicating. My body craved him like a flower hungering for the sun.

His hand crept up my thigh and dress. The heat of his skin caught me off guard, but it sent a jolt of pleasure to my core. Our lips found each other once more, and I knew it would lead me to an undeniable defeat. The thin fabric of my underwear was drenched by the time his hand found the center between my legs. When his breathing stopped, replaced by a moan, I knew he felt it too, how wet he made me. His deep growl rumbled in my chest, and it was all it took to undo me.

"Christ, baby," he panted. "I want you so bad. I can take you right now. Just ask me to." He rubbed and pressed on my mound so expertly with his hand, I was about to erupt. "Tell me you want it," he pleaded as he spun me around, lifting my dress and sliding my thong down my legs.

My mind was lost.

He splayed his large hand on my back, making me arch as he bunched the dress up on my waist. Brushing his lips across my ear, he said, "Spread your legs. Tell me to fuck you, Sara. Tell me you want my cock inside you." He slid his fingers between my pussy, and I couldn't help arching more steeply, pushing my ass against his pelvis. He was still dressed, but I felt the hard ridge of this erection pressing on my backside.

All I desired in that moment was for him to make me his again, to feel his hardness sliding in and out of me, to feel him filling me and stretching me until it hurt.

Determined to get me to beg for his cock, he inserted his middle finger, finger-fucking me so good, I didn't think I could spread my legs in this position any further. I gasped as he pressed on my G-spot. The touch almost incinerated me. I would have given myself wholly to him. There would have been no turning back.

While my body screamed at me to surrender, my mind refused to succumb. God, I wanted this man so bad it made me dizzy. But my heart wasn't ready for what came next. For the fact that if I gave myself to him right now, it would mean I accepted his apology. That I accepted a relationship where his best friend thought I was just another fuck-girl, and his assistant who'd he'd been fuck buddies with still pined after him.

No. I needed time to think. To get my head on straight. To ensure my heart would be protected.

"Stop," I said, the word tasting of ash on my tongue. I didn't want him to stop, but I knew it was what we both needed. I wanted more than for him to fuck me. I wanted his heart. And I wanted him to be one million percent certain there was only room for me in his life.

He withdrew immediately. I turned around, lowering my dress.

"Sara, did I do something wrong?"

"Tom, I...can't."

"Can't or won't?"

"After all that happened tonight, I'm not ready to be with you. I need time."

He brushed his hands through his hair. "You're right. This would have been a mistake. I'm sorry. I really am." He walked back to the kitchen counter, took his keys, and stormed out of the house. A minute later, the Maserati purred to life. I ran after him, but by the time I made it to the front door, the car had peeled away and Tom was gone.

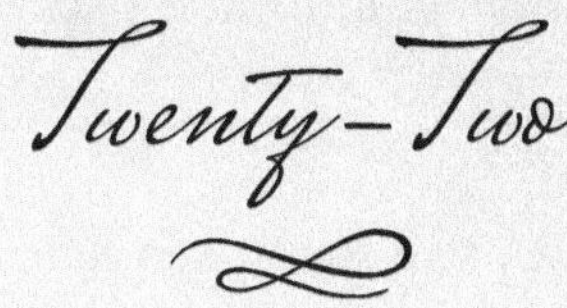

Twenty-Two

TOM

THERE WAS NO DESTINATION. I SIMPLY DROVE FOR HOURS, aimlessly and hopelessly trying to get her out of my system.

What the fuck happened back there?

None of it made sense. No matter how hard I tried, I could not stave off the hunger—my need for this woman.

As far as I wanted to get away from her, every turn I made seemed to lead back to my place. Where I'd left her. And she was probably confused and wondering what type of asshole she'd gotten messed up with.

I wanted to end it. To walk away before things got really ugly.

Shit.

I knew it the first time I kissed her. My cock was harder than a fucking lead pole, but it was more than physical, what she did to me. She brought something back. Something I thought was long dead and buried six feet below the ground. What a fool. To think my past wouldn't be unearthed one day.

Pulling into my driveway hours later, I couldn't remember how far or for how long I had driven, but it hadn't been long enough. My body still raged with some kind of fire. I stared up at my third-floor window.

Could she still be here?

If she had any sense at all she would have packed her things and left my sorry ass behind. Alone was better, safer for both of us. Hell, I knew it but I didn't want to accept it. The thought of losing her now made my body tremble.

Forcing myself on her?

Fucking asshole.

But I hadn't been able to resist her. Not by a long shot.

I'd been there before and lost, badly—barely even made it out alive. Literally.

So why the fuck am I doing this again?

I thought I was stronger than this. Stronger than my need to possess her and make her mine. But the scent of her sweet perfume still lingering on my shirt and hands...*shit*. She was gonna be my downfall. No other woman had been able to resist me. None had made me throb with desire like this, either. Perhaps it was because there was an innocence about her. She wasn't trying to impress me. She wasn't trying to be sexy or alluring or interesting. She simply *was* all of those things without even knowing it. And it was effortless. It was that genuineness that attracted me to her. That snared me and wasn't letting me go.

Or maybe it was because my charms, my money, and my good looks—none of it mattered to her.

"God dammit, Sara. What the hell did you do to me?"

I pulled the car inside the garage, and in the dark, walked up to the kitchen. Place was silent except for the sound of the crashing waves of the ocean echoing through the house.

It was why I'd bought this property. I'd grown up near water, but Lake George was a place I didn't care to return to, too many bad memories. Too much baggage.

The ocean gave me a sense of freedom and peace while washing away the darkness and pain that lingered with the lake.

After dropping my keys on the counter, I took off my blazer and walked over to the bar. Instinctively, I reached for the old bottle of scotch. I'd kept the bottle unopened—a personal reminder of the battle that almost claimed my life once. Staring hard at it as I had so many other times, I contemplated the possibilities.

I could drown it all out again.

Without hesitation, I broke the seal and poured myself a glass.

Tightly gripping it, the damn need to numb the burn slowly consumed me. It crept from the tips of my fingers, up my arms, to the thirsty dry desert of my mouth and finally down to the cramp in my gut.

It could be so easy.

One sip would end it. It was so tempting, almost too much.

I let the tumbler hover over the sink.

I've already broken one rule, what's one more?

My mind and body were at odds. One drink would end the ache building in my chest, but it would also plunge me into an abyss from which there might be no return. Tipping the glass, I watched intently as the alcohol slowly poured out and disappeared down the drain.

It will not beat me. Not tonight.

I walked over by the stairs and stared up. She didn't leave. Her scent was as real and vivid as it had been when I'd held her in my arms. Once, I might have gone up the stairs and tried to finish what I'd started, but that was not tonight. Sara was home. My home. And now it would never be the same.

Plopping on the couch, I stared out the double doors and into the darkness of the night, waiting for the sleep that never came.

Twenty-Three

SARA

I SHOULD HAVE BEEN MILES AWAY FROM THIS PLACE, BUT I chose to stay. When he'd left earlier, my heart shattered. It was pain I swore I would never feel again. I was angry and wounded, but most of all, I was terror-stricken that no matter what happened, I would not be able to walk away from him. I probably should have left. God knew it would have been the best decision I should have made, but as much as my heart anguished, I couldn't leave Tom—*wouldn't* leave him.

After the way the night ended, there was zero chance of getting any sleep, so I sat outside on the balcony of his master bedroom, gazing up at the starry sky, sipping on a glass of wine that I nursed for what seemed like hours. Eventually, I actually dose off for a little bit until I heard him pull into the driveway sometime during the night, the rumble of the Maserati's engine stirring me awake.

The sound sent a jolt through my spine. I didn't know if it was the shock of being awakened so abruptly, or if knowing he was home just made my heart pound like it was going to race out of my chest. I may have held my breath for five minutes—well, it felt like it at least—waiting to see what he would do.

Would he come upstairs and try to talk? Would he even want to talk to me after I'd refused him downstairs? I'd allowed him to get me to the point where I wanted him to fuck me like his life depended on it only to shut him down. Still, I didn't regret my decision. He would have fulfilled my need for his cock, but my heart would've felt empty.

I pressed the side of my head against the door and tried to listen to what he was doing downstairs. The only sound I heard was his keys landing on the kitchen counter, and minutes later, he turned on the faucet, then nothing.

What the hell?

Pacing, I contemplated going downstairs to look for him. But what could I possibly say? This was so fucking awkward I wanted to just disappear and reappear back in New York in my apartment, on my bed with Skiddles, with a bowl of ice-cream while watching re-runs of Friends.

As badly as I'd not wanted to screw things up with Tom, this was possibly one of the worst screw ups ever. Maybe I had overreacted about the whole thing with Jake. Guy was clearly an asshole. I'd figured that one out before he ever uttered a single word. It irked me to know that said asshole was Tom's best friend, though. Perhaps the dude had some redeeming qualities I wasn't aware of?

Then there was the whole thing with Tiffany. I turned into the jealous girlfriend in a Nano second, which was so not attractive and so not like me. Sure, I had confidence issues, but I still had my brains. Tom had been nothing but gentlemanly with me. He'd showered me with so much attention, and I'd reacted like a toddler. God, he must've thought I was such a brat. I'd been irrational and childish.

But that's what this fucking man did to me. I couldn't think straight when he was around.

I paced so hard I thought I was going to trace a hole into his carpet. What was the point in staying silent? I hated unresolved issues. If he wasn't going to come to me, then I was going to go to him and figure this shit out tonight because I refused to lose sleep over this nonsense.

Marching up to the door, I turned the knob and yanked the door open only to find Tom standing right outside. He stood shirtless, hands stuck in his tux pants, eyebrows quirked in surprise.

Holy mother of God. The man was so fucking gorgeous, he could set me ablaze.

A small smile twitched on my lips. "Hi."

"Hey," he crooned back with a half-crooked grin that almost seemed apologetic. "Didn't mean to bother you. I was just coming to see if I could get my ... toothbrush."

His toothbrush? Talk about having the lamest excuse of all time.

"It's fine," I said. "I wasn't sleeping."

Staring into each other's eyes, a deep silence stretched between us. There were too many unanswered questions. I knew he hadn't come for his stupid toothbrush, so I manned up and spoke first. "Tom, I'm sorry about earlier tonight. It wasn't my place to say all of those things or to judge you or to—"

"Sara, please, you have nothing to be sorry about. I was a complete jackass. Leaving you here by yourself was cowardly and stupid and—"

"Stop. We both screwed up."

He dropped his chin, hands still stuck in his pants.

"What's the matter, Tom? What aren't you telling me?"

"I never meant for any of this to happen, Sara."

"What do you mean?"

Sucking in a deep breath, he looked back up, his eyes misted over and red. "Baby, I'm fucked up, and I don't want to drag you down with me."

"Fucked up doesn't scare me." I reached for his wrist and pulled him inside the bedroom. Closing the door, I said, "What scares me is leaving you and wondering for the rest of my life what could've been. But if we can't survive a stupid fight, then we might as well say our goodbyes now."

"So, what happens next?"

"We do what we said we planned to do this weekend. Get to know each other."

Running a hand through his hair, he walked over to the balcony doors and stared out to sea, hands back in his pockets. The wind swirled his hair and the platinum light of the moon gleamed off his bare shoulders. "I wouldn't even know where to begin."

I joined him at the balcony, wrapping my arms around his waist and leaning my head against his back. "How about with her name?"

"Her name?" he asked, bringing me around to face him.

"The woman who broke your heart. It's the reason you closed yourself off to love. Trust me. I know. I've been there."

"My closed-up heart is a product of a lot of things, Sara. My past, my present...all of my fears."

I looked deep in his eyes, trying to find the man I met two weeks ago—the confident business tycoon who owned the world around him, but he wasn't there. All I saw was the raw spirit of a tortured soul. This was a Tom I didn't know, perhaps the Tom I needed to know. "You can trust me," I said.

"If you didn't run before you sure as hell will run now," he chuckled.

"It can't be that bad."

"It is."

"What was her name? Who was the woman who screwed you up for the rest of us?"

"You really want to go there?"

"The whole point of me coming out here was to get to know you better. So, let's have it."

"I haven't talked about it...her...for years. It's not easy."

"It's never easy to talk about your ghosts. I get it, but we have to do it sometime."

He guided us toward the lounge couch on the balcony. With silent resignation, he leaned back on his seat and closed his eyes. "Shayna." His hands shook and he chewed on his bottom lip as he tried to put together his thoughts. The memory seemed to shadow over him like a dark cloud about to break.

The ocean breeze felt cool, it's salty smell refreshing. Dressed only in my white nightgown, I shivered as I sat beside him, resting my head on his shoulder, seeking his warmth.

"I loved her like I'd never loved a woman..." His voice trailed off with a din of regret.

I didn't know how to respond. A part of me was scared of what secrets laid buried inside that trove, but I needed to be strong for him. Reopening old wounds required careful fingers and a loving heart. I reached for his trembling hands and gave them a light squeeze. He turned to me, and with unspoken words, I reassured him his secrets would be safe with me.

He smiled and nodded in appreciation. "My father," he began, "was a terrible man. Possessive, abusive. He nearly killed my mother in front of me in a fit of rage. My brother and I tried to protect her, but we were no match for him. My mother..." he paused. "It used to piss me off that she wouldn't simply leave him. But I was just a kid. I didn't understand the true dynamics of her situation. It wasn't that she didn't want to leave him. She felt she wouldn't know how to support two children on her own when she'd never earned her own money. Well, eventually I got tired of the constant fighting. I didn't want to leave her—it hurt me beyond words— but I had no choice. I would have killed my father with my own two hands if I'd stayed. When I turned eighteen, I enlisted in the military and I left. I should have never abandoned my mother and brother, but like a fucking coward, I ran."

"You were just a kid, Tom."

"It was no excuse. James never left. And a year later, I received the news my father had passed from a heart attack. I felt nothing. I was numb. As far as I knew, I never had a father to begin with. I came home for the funeral. My mother begged me to come home. She needed me there. It was the only reason I came back, to be there for her. I was guilt ridden for abandoning her. It was the least I could do. And it was during the funeral that she told me why she had never left him. She'd done it to protect us. He'd promised he'd kill us if she ever left him."

As Tom told his story, his eyes flashed with the terror and innocence of a young boy. He said he'd been numb when he heard his father died, but I found it hard to believe. Tom did mourn his father, the father he never had and never would. I didn't want to tell him what I saw written on his face. He had to protect the little boy still living inside.

"Nice father figure, eh?"

"Can't imagine how terrible it was to hear that about him."

He pivoted on toward me, eyes arrowing deep into mine. "You want to know the honest truth? It didn't entirely shock me. He was a monster. But at least I knew my mother didn't stay with him because she loved him. She did it to protect us. I only wished she'd told us sooner." Tom's jaw muscles twitched and his fists clenched.

"Tom, if it's too difficult to talk about, I understand."

"It's fine," he said, but it took him a few moments to gather his thoughts and continue with his story. "After the funeral, late that night, a bunch of us got together. My friend asked us to come over his house, drink, and maybe help clear my head. I needed to get out of the house. After a year, the place hadn't changed much and I couldn't stand being inside. I got pretty wasted. I was a fucking mess. My brother left early. Apparently, he'd tried to get me to go back home with him, but I violently refused. Somewhere between my last beer and by the time I made it home that night, I blacked out. However, there was always something I did remember. Her face. I knew someone had driven me home that night, and the next morning, when everything else was a fog, the only thing—the only person I could remember— was her, Shayna."

"That's when you met her?"

"She was the sister of someone at the party who ended up at my friend's house. Apparently, in an alcohol stupor, I opened up to her and told her all about my messed-up family and about my dad. If it hadn't been for her, I probably would have drunk myself to death."

"She saved you."

"In more ways than one. She was the one who drove me home. I thought I'd never see her again, but I ran into her at a local joint a few days later. We clicked. The rest is history. I was a hot head with a drinking problem, Sara. I was on the verge of being kicked out of the military for disciplinary issues, but she straightened me out."

"Is that why you fell in love with her?"

"I fell in love with her because she gave me what no one else had. I felt safe and loved. She tamed my hot temper and made sure I got the help I needed so I wouldn't become some deadbeat drunk. She was all I had, and I latched on to her too tight. I would have left the military for her. I would have left everything for her, but she kept me in line and helped me remember what was important. I stayed in the military and came back home to her at the end of my first two tours. Her face, the promise of her love for me, was all that kept me sane. Knowing I could come home to her gave me something to live for."

"So, what happened?"

"We'd spoken about marriage, and I promised her after my final tour I was going to leave and come home to marry her. I proposed one evening. The big day was set for the end of my tour. That last year, though, was different. I sensed a change in Shayna. She wasn't the same woman I fell in love with. I couldn't put my finger on it, but she seemed distant, withdrawn from me. I thought I was losing her."

"That must've been difficult, especially being so far away."

"It killed me. I loved her, but later on I realized it was the kind of love that's toxic. I was possessive and paranoid. I was beginning to see shades of my father in myself. The thought of losing Shayna drove me mad, and not being home to see what was happening made me reach my boiling point.

"The week I was supposed to return from my last tour, I was sent on one last mission. It wasn't even supposed to be me out there, but one of our guys had a family emergency so I went in his place. A roadside bomb placed by insurgents took out the first vehicle in our convoy. Seven guys. Dead. Blown to pieces by these motherfuckers. The humvee I was traveling in was right behind; the blast was so strong, shrapnel pelleted our truck, killing the two Marines up front. I was sitting in the back and was spared along with another soldier. The shockwave rocked over us in a violent thrust, knocking us unconscious."

I gasped and stared in horror. "Oh, my God.

"I suffered severe hemorrhaging to the brain and had to be placed in an induced coma for quite some time. Internal bleeding caused by fractured ribs almost claimed my life. Had a broken leg and dislocated shoulder, among other injuries. I was in pretty bad shape, but at least I'd gotten away with my life. Other guys weren't so lucky."

"I'm so sorry. I had no idea."

"I'm not looking for sympathy, Sara. It's part of the job. You know you are sent out there to fight for your country but you can't be sure you'll ever come back. It's something we are prepared to accept. Well, some more than others. Either way, I was hospitalized at Landstuhl Regional Medical Center in Germany for almost four months, healing then undergoing rehabilitation."

"Your family must have been a nervous wreck. Especially your mother. Were they allowed to come see you?"

He smirked at my question before shaking his head. "My mom and James flew to Germany as soon as they heard. Shayna, though, she never came to see me. Not even after I woke up."

I jumped to my feet. "What? Why on earth would your fiancé not come visit you after you almost lost your life?"

"Shayna was having an affair. When she heard about the accident and that I was in a coma with potential brain damage, well, let's just say she saw her ticket out. I learned that tidbit shortly after waking up from my coma. When I tried to reach her back home, she was nowhere to be found. No one was speaking up, but eventually her brother cracked and told me she'd fallen into the arms of another man. So, he said. But I knew better. Shortly after my accident, they eloped, and their son was born six months later. It was Allen, my childhood friend, who got in the middle.

"Jesus Christ. You knew the guy?"

"Can't make this shit up."

"What did you do? Did you confront them?"

Tom jumped to his feet, clenching his fists, black fury shadowing his eyes. "Hell no. I never wanted to see their faces again. When I finally got out of the hospital, I reenlisted and never looked back."

"You haven't been home since then?"

He turned to look at me, his eyes dark with resignation. "No, and I don't plan to. Ever. That place holds too many bad memories."

"Is that why you've blocked love out of your life?"

"How could I trust in another woman after what Shayna did?

He'd loved her so deeply; she'd nearly torn his soul apart with her betrayal. Refusing to let anyone in was his way of preserving his heart. What about now? What was different about me? About us? Could he really love again? My body trembled thinking about the probable heartbreak waiting for me if I chose to stay with this man. He was damaged, jaded.

But wasn't I also damaged?

Unable to meet his gaze, I looked away. What right did I have to expect anything less? When Josh left, I swore I'd never let anyone else in. Love is great, but the pain typically accompanying it is debilitating. Why put yourself through the torture? When I turned to face him, the answer stared back at me, in the depths of his storm-filled eyes.

"So where does all of this leave us?" I asked.

"Us?" He ran his hands through his hair, his gaze uncertain, perhaps trying to find the right words to say. "Baby, up until two weeks ago, I was a man who didn't have a care in the world. I wasn't tethered to anyone. I could come and go as I pleased and not give a shit where or in whose bed I woke up the next day. That was my life ever since I came back from Iraq. Now? I can't imagine my life without you. Am I scared? Hell yeah. But I'm ready to give it another go."

He'd been through so much pain, and although that past was over, the scars remained. I hugged him, wishing I could erase all the sorrow and anger with my touch.

Standing there with him, the early dawn only moments away, I realized it had to be now or never. I wasn't going to run. Not this time. Not again. I reached up to kiss him. I wanted to show him I had nothing to fear and he shouldn't fear me either, but he turned his lips away.

"Tom, what is it?" I asked.

"I don't know if I have the strength to restrain myself from you."

"I don't want you to restrain yourself from me. I want this...us... right now."

"I don't want you to regret this in the morning. To regret me."

"The only thing I would regret is not showing you how I feel."

He stood there, motionless, hands in his pockets. Tense.

"You seem so nervous," I said.

He chuckled. "I feel like a teenager about to do this for the very first time." He smiled at me crookedly.

I grabbed his wrist and yanked his hand out of his pocket then walked back inside toward his bed. The anxiety raking him was coming off his body in waves. I rubbed his shoulders and thick biceps. My hands caressed the slabs of hard muscle on his abs and chest. Everywhere my hands touched, I felt the tension dissipate. "I love how strong you are," I said as I placed my hand over his heart. "In here. You've been through hell and back. But underneath this shell you've built are the true scars."

"I survived by blocking it all away and living a lie. I'm not proud of the man I am, Sara. Yet, here you are. You have no idea what you do to me, do you?" he uttered in a soft whisper. "It's like the walls I have worked so hard to build have all of a sudden come down. I can't hide from you."

"There's no need for walls anymore."

I trailed a path with my fingers to his waist. Eyes closed, his breath intensified with every move my hands made. He remained still, letting me take the lead. Brushing my fingers over his belt, I slowly unbuckled him then proceeded to undo the top button of his pants, unzipping them all the way down. My hand feathered over the stiffness bulging in his pants, making my pulse quicken. It was impossible to avoid the heat of his arousal.

He should have taken me right there, ravaged me like he did that first night at his apartment. Instead, he stood, unflinching, tormenting me.

"You sure know how to make a girl doubt herself. Don't you want me?"

"Is that even a real question, Sara? Did you forget what happened earlier before I stormed away like an idiot?"

"If you want me, what's stopping you?"

He closed his eyes briefly before settling his gaze over me. "Baby, every time I'm near you, this pounding in my chest won't stop, and when I'm away from you, Christ, the anxiety of when I will see you next kills me. It should be enough to make me run, or to make me realize I am heading down a goddamn rabbit hole, but the more time I spend with you, and the more I hold you in my arms, it never feels enough. Tonight, I finally understand what it is I'm feeling, and I'm petrified of what this all means."

"Tom—"

"Sara," he continued, brushing his thumb over my bottom lip, "if we do this, if you let me make love to you tonight, I will lose myself completely in you."

We stared at each other in terrifying silence. His eyes pleaded with me for a response, for some kind of affirmation of the feelings I had for him. This wasn't about an undeniable physical attraction; it wasn't about lust or need. It was about the bond growing between us. The possibility of a love so strong it could hold us together and potentially even tear us apart.

Yes, I was scared. God knew I'd tried to deny it from the first day I saw his face in that coffee shop. The more I wanted to convince myself I didn't want him, the more I was drawn to him.

What use was it to deny it any longer? We both had pasts we couldn't escape, but what Tom made me realize that night was we didn't have to run from our pasts in order to embrace our futures. And it would only be a matter of time before it would be my turn to face my own demons, but that wasn't what was important now. What mattered was that we both cared deeply about each other and together we could heal, we could make it out of the darkness holding us in the tentacles of its shadows for too long.

Of one thing I was certain. The moment I stepped foot on that plane and flew to Santa Monica, I'd plunged deep into his rabbit hole. I reached up, and cupping his face in my palm, I committed to my destiny. "I'm ready to lose myself in you too."

Twenty-Four

SARA

Gripping the hem of my nightgown, he lifted the delicate fabric up and over my head, his fingertips soft as rose petals on my skin. Dressed only in white, satin bikini bottoms, I stood before him, his hot gaze lingering over my naked breasts, electrifying me, making my body vibrate with anticipation.

He tipped my chin up, his lips gently brushing over mine. "I want to feel the warmth of your body as I go inside you."

"Are you asking me what I think you're asking me?"

"Only if you're one hundred percent okay with it. I'm clean. You're the first woman since Shayna that I've even considered doing this with."

"I've only ever been with one other man my whole life besides you, and we never had unprotected sex."

"What about…"

"I'm outside my ovulation window."

He quirked a brow. "You're certain it's okay?"

"If you must know, I'm very regular. Trust me. We're okay."

Tom's eyes shone with dark amusement as he scooped me up in his arms and laid me down on the bed. He climbed on top of me, stretching his body along mine, holding his weight on his forearms so as not to crush me. A wolfish grin twitched at the corners of his mouth as his fingers danced over my skin, seeking my center. The thought of having him inside me without protection—the heat of his cock filling me completely—made me even wetter.

His mouth carved an ardent path from my lips, across my jawline, to my ear lobes and neck. "I want to show you all the different ways I can love you," he growled in a low rumble as he licked my skin, his breath making me quiver.

He pressed against me with the rhythm of his kiss, leaving no inch untouched as he traveled down my body, taking extreme and prolonged care on my chest until my nipples were diamond hard buds. He tickled my navel with his slick tongue. Every nerve ending on my body was a slave to his mouth and hands.

He parted my legs, pushing down on my thighs, silently instructing me to keep them spread. All I could do was arch my back as his fingers trailed from my toes, up my calves, to my knees and thighs, and finally to the apex between my legs. He rubbed the pad of his thumb over my mound, circling around my clit until I was soaked. My hips moved in tune to his touch as I urged him to roll off my underwear. His delay was a clear indication of his intent. Tom's plan was one of torturous pleasure and not just release.

He must have felt how swollen I was because he rubbed at it harder.

"Tom...please."

Hearing my plea, he finally grabbed hold of my underwear and slid them off. His fingers found my clit again very quickly; the invasion was met without resistance as I slowly gave into his expert touch, spreading my legs even wider as he buried two fingers inside me and pressed on my bundle of nerves with his thumb.

Tom knew my anatomy like no other and he played with me until my body was ready to surrender. "Tom..." I exhaled deeply. It was all he needed to hear to push him to massage my walls with more determination, coaxing me to a shuddering orgasm.

I tensed, my body rigid with aftershocks. I needed him now more than ever. He undressed and lowered himself over me again, his warm and velvety erection pressing against the cleft of my sex. I gasped as he sheathed himself inside me slowly, giving me time to adjust to his size, entering in unrushed strokes. His length and girth took up every inch of me, making my body cry out in ecstasy.

I yielded completely to his love for me, losing myself entirely to the man who would forever change me.

Our tempo hastened, our bodies battling each other as we chased relief. His groans were intense, reverberating through my bones. "Christ, Sara," he panted, "I can't hold it any longer. I need to come inside you, baby."

I wanted nothing more than to have him flood me with his passion, but I wasn't ready for this to end. I wanted to prolong the thrill my body was experiencing for as long as I could. "Not yet." Pushing him over onto his back, I straddled him in one quick move, startling him.

"Whoa," he said. "Plot twist."

"I'm not a total novice, you know..." Once on top, I was able to control our pace, slowly riding down the wave. I smiled as I ground my hips over his pelvis, my eyes drinking in the sight of his body splayed underneath me. "It's time for me to show *you* the many ways I can love you, too."

He smiled back, perhaps enjoying the hint of mischief in my eyes. I arched my back as I sensually drove him to the hilt. His hands slid up my thighs as he sat up, my legs wrapping around his waist. Out gazes locked like chains, anchoring us to one another.

Tom wrapped his arms around me as we rocked against each other. His cock was buried deeper than I'd ever felt it, pushing on my G-spot with hard pressure. I'd never been so close to anyone; it was as if our souls were finally whole. His arms tightened around me as his hips pushed deeper and harder. He was about to lose control, and his ragged breaths and growls overpowered my senses, driving me to climax. I wanted to keep riding the stream of pleasure, but I forced myself to push him back down on the bed. I didn't want to unchain myself from him, and heavens knew I wanted him to fill me with his cum, but a different kind of hunger came over me, and I decided to claim his release another way.

I slid off him then took him in my hands before he had a chance to protest. I stroked him long and hard, feeling the throb of his length and the strain in his pelvis as he approached his orgasm. He was completely under my control and the feeling was exhilarating. His massive frame lay vulnerable to me, his eyes shut and arms stretched out, every muscle in his neck and body flexed. He couldn't have looked more beautiful. Not able to contain my appetite, I lowered my lips and licked the head of his cock in a swirling motion before slowly guiding it deep inside my mouth.

I had never enjoyed this type of intimacy before, not like this. I licked and sucked until the skin on the head of his cock was so tight it could have ripped. He grew so hard it had to hurt, but it was painfully good to hear him moaning and feel him quivering until in one final thrust, I tasted the warm, bitter sweetness of his semen.

Cursing my name out in a scream, his palm cradled my head as he continued to pulse inside my mouth.

I swallowed every drop, relishing in the fact that he was all mine and I was absolutely and undeniably all his.

Twenty-Five

SARA

FULLY SATIATED, WE LAID IN EACH OTHER'S ARMS, watching through the open patio doors as the sun warmed the early morning back to life. Tom sealed our lullaby with a kiss. It was a touch of melodic sensation that rocked me harmoniously to a slumbering peace.

A few hours later, I awoke to an empty bed.

Just when I was about to jump out of the comfort of his crumpled sheets, I noticed a folded piece of paper on his pillow. I rolled my eyes as I reached for it, clearly expecting another sappy love note. What I found was a pencil sketch of me sleeping. Scripted on the bottom, he wrote:

I wanted you to see how beautiful you are to me.
Tom

Jeez, he was so corny. But he was my sappy cornball, and I wouldn't have him any other way. I clung to the piece of paper and held it against my chest in silent glee. The sun shone bright through every window. The digital clock bleeped eight-thirteen a.m. on its screen. The last thing I remembered was me encased in Tom's arms at the early dawn.

I didn't want to leave his bed. Memories of our bodies tangled together and making love swam through my head. It had been so amazing. What moved me, though, was his sincerity and how he opened up to me. He'd shared things with me he hadn't with anybody. Love was coming back into my life and I wasn't petrified anymore. I beamed and must have looked like an idiot if anyone had seen me at that moment, but I couldn't pretend I didn't know what I was beginning to feel. I was falling for Tom.

Hard.

Not bothering to check where *Mr. Charming* had escaped to, I trotted naked to the bathroom for a refreshing shower. Eyes closed, I blissfully enjoyed as the water splashed on my face and trickled down my body in rivulets. It was a rain shower that quenched my skin of its thirst. Blindly, I reached for the washcloth, but when my fingers found nothing but air, I opened my eyes and almost screamed.

Stark naked, Tom stood in the large shower with me. It was an open, all-stone shower with only a half-glass wall. He'd walked right in and I hadn't heard him. I wanted to punch him, but his broad smile disarmed me.

"Exactly how long have you been standing there?" I asked accusingly.

"Not long enough," he said, his eyes narrowing over me, crackling with lust as he skimmed my body up and down with his gaze. "I was thoroughly enjoying watching the water slide off your naked body."

I glanced down to his groin with a smirk. His long cock was already aroused. "So, I see."

He walked over and showed me the washcloth in his hand.

"Turn around," he uttered in a soft command that left no room for negotiation. His voice was deep with seduction.

My eyes widened as the blood in my veins simmered beneath my skin in response to the heat of his gaze. I swallowed hard; the look in his eyes was feral, raw. If he ever wanted to consume me, this was it. We'd made love mere hours before, yet his cock was harder than I'd ever seen it, engorged and greedy for more.

When we were both under the stream, the warm water dripping down our faces, he leaned in close to my ear, and sending shivers down my body, he whispered, "I said turn around, baby."

I obeyed and pivoted, planting my hands on the wall, feeling the fire of his body as he brushed against mine.

"Good girl," he continued near my ear. "Now part your legs."

He poured soap onto the washcloth and lathered my body, starting at the neck and down my chest. Soap slicked down my front as he cupped both my breasts, caressing each one in circular motions. My back arched in response. He held my neck back with one hand while the other continued to wash my abdomen, hips, and thighs. My legs trembled, wishing for his hands to reach between them. Tom knew what I wanted, my body nearly screamed for it, but he slid the washcloth down my legs, scrubbing every inch of skin, ignoring my silent plea.

I reached down to grab his hand and led it to my center, but he waved his finger at me. "Nah ah, I didn't say you could take your hands off the wall."

"But—"

"On the wall," he replied sternly.

I had no choice but do as he said and continue to endure his cruel but tantalizing game. He made sure my calves, ankles, and toes were well scrubbed. Even the soles of my feet received their own personal attention.

"I think you are all clean now," he drawled behind me.

"Actually, I think you missed a spot."

"Is that so? Hmm, I thought I scrubbed everything…"

"Nope. Not everything." I turned around and looked straight at him, my eyes piercing and demanding. I took his hand and gently guided him between my legs where my other wetness showed him exactly how much he had missed. He closed his eyes, water beading on his long, dark lashes as he released a growling moan.

With a smirk, he said, "Seems I did in fact miss a spot." He parted me before sliding his finger inside. In a few moments, the familiar circular motion almost brought me down on my knees, and as I felt my release about to peak, he pulled out.

"No," I gasped, but he was kneeling in front of me and lifting my right leg in an instant. He placed my foot on the stone ledge carved out of the wall for seating. There was no time to react. His tongue was already buried in my cleft, licking and flicking the hard nub of my sex. I braced myself on the shower handle and the wall, trying not to collapse.

As I neared my orgasm, he stood and picked me up, my legs wrapping around his waist. I straddled him as he stood, then he slowly lowered me onto his cock. Our bodies raged with need for each other. He gripped my ass firmly as he thrust fast and hard. With my arms roped tightly around his neck, our rhythm synchronized.

Tom was relentless as he drove his dick deep. I'd given him so much of me, I barely had the energy to hold on. He lowered me back on the shower floor and planted a hot kiss on my lips. "I'm not done with you." He turned me around, bent me over the stone ledge, and slapped my ass. The sharp sting sent a surge of sexual pleasure up my spine.

My hips gyrated in circular motion, inviting him to take me from behind.

"I like it when you do that," he said.

"Yeah?"

"You look so hot, baby girl. Spread those fucking ass cheeks for me."

I reached behind me with both hands and spread my ass further apart, showing him everything he wanted to see. "I want you to fuck me hard, Tom. Like I've been a *bad girl*..." Oh, my God. I didn't know what came over me. Why did I say that? I wanted to hide under a rock, but also...I wanted him to do exactly that. Fuck me hard.

I reached underneath between my legs and touched myself, giving him a full view of what I liked to do with my fingers, moaning as I pleasured myself.

"Sara, I'm gonna come just watching you do that."

"So why aren't you inside me yet?"

He laughed. "Bratty much? Get on your knees."

As I did what he asked, he came around me and pressed his dick against my mouth. "You want me to fuck you like you've been a bad girl, is that it?"

I nodded yes as I wrapped my lips around his cock and sucked on the head real slow.

He gathered all my hair in one hand and palmed my head with his other as he gently pushed his dick deeper in my mouth. "You like that, don't you?"

I reached up with my hands and squeezed his shaft up and down while my tongue swirled around his head.

"Oh, baby, the way you do that. Fuck. But I'm not coming in your mouth this time."

As I smiled triumphantly, he pulled out of my mouth and moved behind me. He parted my legs then slid two fingers inside my silky flesh and finger-fucked me until my pussy was so wet, it dripped. Then he penetrated me, but this time, he didn't prime me. He just pushed his hard shaft completely in with one thrust.

I gasped in shock as he wrapped a hand around my hair and tugged. My scalp tingled as he thrust hard and fast, flesh smacking against flesh, both of us breathless and moaning.

"You like being fucked like this?" he asked as he pushed deeper into me.

I couldn't even form a coherent answer as he drove me into bliss. His cock hurt but the pain dripped with ecstasy and all I wanted was more and more.

He reached for by breasts and squeezed as he thrust from behind. "God, you're so hot."

"I'm...almost there."

His hand tightened around my hair, and he beat so fast into me, my whole body shook, my orgasm ready to crest. I pushed into him as well, demanding his release. Our bodies went rigid as we both came, the sounds of our moans reverberating off the bathroom walls. I felt his warmth spilling into me, filling me, and I nearly orgasmed again knowing he'd come inside me.

Spent, I stood, legs shaking and slick with his cum as it slid down my thighs. "I think," he said, kissing me. "That you need another shower."

We washed each other in silence, making sure to lather and rinse thoroughly, several times.

After another round of shower sex followed by another shower, I sat on his bed wrapped in a luscious cotton robe, towel-drying my hair. My eyes feasted on Tom's naked ass as he prowled around his room, looking for his clothes and getting dressed. I'd never tire of looking at him, not when he was the embodiment of pure physical perfection.

To my dismay, he pulled on a pair of black boxer briefs, a pair of dark-wash denim jeans, and a slim-fit gray shirt. I preferred him in his birthday suit. He scurried over to the bathroom where he brushed his teeth and barely combed his hair before rushing back out. Our eyes met as he exited the bathroom.

"What's so funny?" he asked, noticing my smirk.

"You," I replied quickly. "Have someplace to go? You seem to be in a hurry."

"Actually, *we* have someplace to go," he replied, looking in drawers for socks.

"Mind telling me exactly where we're going?"

He sat next to me and put on his white designer sneakers. "Breakfast. You make me work up an appetite. I know this great little hole in the wall that makes the best waffles." He jumped to his feet, kissed me on the forehead, and ran out the door, but not before turning and pointing to his watch. "Twenty minutes."

"That's not enough time to get ready," I yelled after him.

With no time to waste, I threw on a pair of jeans, a cute white shirt, and a pair of silver flats. I hauled my hair up into a messy bun with a clip and dotted on a bit of make up just as Tom came in from the garage.

"Ready to go?" he asked.

"Where are we going?"

"Patience. I'll tell you on the way." We took off in the Maserati and ten minutes later, we pulled into the famous World of Pancakes lot.

I pitched an eyebrow. "Wait, this is your hole in the wall?"

"Okay, so technically it's not a hole in the wall...but they do make the best waffles."

"Technically?"

"You have something against breakfast at WOP?"

"No."

"Then quit your yapping and let's go. I'm freaking starving."

The waft of maple syrup and sizzling bacon permeating the air made my stomach grumble, and reminded me why everyone flocked there. We were quickly seated at a booth.

"So, you love waffles, huh?" I started.

"Just the ones from here."

A petite older lady, probably in her late sixties, greeted us. Her silvery, short hair was held in place by a hairnet, her blue and white uniform was spotless and crisply ironed. "Welcome to WOP, my name is Betsy and I'll be your server," she said as she handed us the large laminated menus. "Can I start you off with something to drink, coffee perhaps?"

"Yes, please," I said eagerly. I didn't realize how much I missed coffee until I walked in and nearly fainted from the aroma.

"And for the gentleman?" she asked.

"Coffee is fine and a glass of orange juice, too, please. Thank you." He flashed her one of his charming smiles.

Once she walked away, I leaned in and quietly chided him, "You should be ashamed of yourself."

"What are you talking about?"

"You could have given her a heart attack. You really have no idea what you do to women when you show them those pearly whites of yours."

"Sara, she could be my mother for Christ's sake."

"It doesn't matter. You really should know when to turn off that overwhelming charm."

"Are you done?" he teased. "I'd like to look at my menu."

"You already know what you are going to order."

"Do you?"

Good point.

I grabbed the menu and struggled to decide. Everything looked way too scrumptious. After perusing the pages for a few minutes, two scrambled eggs, bacon, hash browns, and a short stack of pancakes topped with strawberries and whipped cream seemed like a good choice. Tom barely looked at his menu. He had his mind already made up on the steak and eggs with a stack of his favorite waffles.

Betsy placed our coffee pot down followed by the milk and sugar. Her hands trembled a little. Finally, she took our order and left. Tom reached for the steaming pot of coffee and poured us each a cup. "I know it's not fancy shmancy, but—"

"Tom, please, it's breakfast," I said as I dumped two teaspoons of sugar in my coffee and lightened it with some milk. "By the way, I have no idea how you stay in shape after seeing the way you eat lately."

"I work out every morning." Tom took a sip of his coffee, showing no interest in sugar and milk. I'd forgotten my lion liked to drink crude oil.

"And speaking of morning, is that where you were today, working out? I hate waking up and not finding you there."

He leaned back on his seat and gave me an easy smile. "You looked so peaceful sleeping. I didn't want to wake you."

"What time did you get up?"

"Well, usually I'm up by six, but today I actually slept 'til seven. I was kind of shocked, really."

"We didn't go to sleep 'til late."

"It doesn't matter what time I go to sleep; I can't go past six. Probably ingrained in me from my military training. We were always up at the crack of dawn. I don't sleep much anyway, so I'm sort of used to functioning on limited sleep." He tried to say it nonchalantly, but I had a feeling there was something else he wasn't telling me.

"Is that all?" I asked, circling the rim of my cup with the tip of my index finger.

"What do you mean?"

"The reason you don't sleep much?"

"Kind of early for so many questions, don't you think?" His tone was short, his gaze detached from mine.

"I'm sorry. I was simply trying to understand."

He snapped his eyes back toward me. "There's nothing to understand, Sara. Everybody knows about it. Soldiers coming back from war, dealing with post-traumatic stress."

I paused, realizing his trauma went even deeper than I'd thought.

I'd been through this before. With my father. It wasn't easy. "My dad suffered from it."

Tom scoffed, a tinge of bitterness hiding behind his narrowed eyes. "You say it like it's some kind of disease afflicting us. You know what? Maybe it is. You can't experience the horrors of war, see the shit we've seen, and come home and be normal and act like nothing changed. Everything changes. Life is never the same. But doctors want to stamp a label on you and give you a prescription for happy pills."

"Does it help?"

"The pills? I took them at the beginning, and they helped with the recurring nightmares. I haven't had to take them in a while." He shifted in his seat and picked at some invisible fuzz on his shirt before looking away.

I reached for his hand. "Tom, I...I'm really sorry. I can't even imagine what—"

He pulled his hand away slowly and ran it down his face. "It's not you and I'm a jackass for letting it get to me. It's just...I'd rather talk about something else."

Although his words had a frosty bite, I let it slide. This was not the time or place to dig up demons. "Okay, so where did you go workout this morning?"

He sighed, hopefully relieved to be talking about something else. "I went for a run along the beach. It's my morning routine. I usually take Bax with me when I'm back home."

"It's a shame you didn't bring him with you to Santa Monica. I'm sure he'd love running through the water on the beach."

"Yes, he would, but I travel back and forth too frequently."

"Who watches him when you're not home?" I asked, taking a sip of my coffee.

Tom played with the paper napkin on the table, folding it into triangles as he talked. "My neighbor looks in on him and takes him out on walks."

"Well, that's a very nice neighbor." I was curious to know who this friendly neighbor was, but Tom didn't seem too chatty. Talking about his military life still hovered over him like a storm cloud.

Our breakfast finally arrived, piping hot and delivering a mouth-watering aroma. The mood suddenly lifted. He cracked his knuckles like he was about to enter a fight. "Let's dig in," he said, then he took his fork and knife and cut into his steak.

I shoveled in a mouthful of eggs and hash browns smothered in ketchup. "So, what you got planned for today?"

He took a bite of his steak, chewed, and swallowed, smiling as he took a gulp of juice.

"What's so funny?" I asked.

As he prepared to answer, his phone rang. He frowned as he checked the screen.

"What is it?"

"It's Jake. I have no idea why he'd be calling this early or why he wouldn't text. I don't typically like to answer my phone while eating, but it must be urgent. Just give me a sec." Annoyed, he took the call. "Jake, what's up, man?"

I couldn't make out what was being said on the other side, but it sounded like a frantic male voice.

"Jake, slow down. What happened? You're where? No, I'm not home. Out to breakfast with Sara. Jake, you gotta calm down, man. I understand. Okay... just tell me what happened." His tone went from annoyed to worried, his brow creased with several lines. I didn't know what was happening, but whatever was going on with Jake wasn't good. Tom placed a finger over his ear to drown out the din of the restaurant.

"Wait, how much? Listen to me, you are going to be fine. Tell him you'll get the money; you just need to buy more time. Well, make time. Look, you don't have to remind me. All I'm saying is you better start getting your act together. 'Cause I'm tired of bailing your ass out every fucking time you screw up. Get your shit together. I'll call you when I get back to Santa Monica." He hit the end button and dropped the phone on the table. "Fuck!" The ire erupting in his eyes was incendiary.

The young couple sitting across from us with their two little kids heard Tom's expletive and shot us a dirty look. I shrugged and offered a silent apology on our behalf then turned back to Tom. "What's the matter?

"Well, there go my plans."

"Plans for what?"

He sighed and looked down. "I wanted to drive you up the coast and show you the views of the cliffs, stop and get some lunch at a local restaurant, maybe stay anywhere there's a vacancy. Make love to you all night." He raised his gaze and gave me a seductive look that awakened my body in all the right places.

I chewed my eggs and hash browns as the heat radiated throughout my body, thinking about how I'd always wanted to drive up the Pacific Coast highway, in a convertible, with a hunky man at my side. Inside my head, it played out like a movie, and I was the starlet of my own flick—*Love by the Sea*. "Well, why can't we still go?"

He nodded toward his phone. "Jake."

Seemed this guy loved ruining my time with Tom. I took another sip of my coffee and peered up at him as I held the cup close to my lips. "I guess you don't plan to elaborate?"

"It's nonsense."

"If it's nonsense, then why are you so upset?" I asked, putting my cup down.

"Don't worry about Jake. I'll handle it." He reached for my hands and puffed out a breath.

I didn't like how blanched his face looked. Whatever Jake told him, plagued him.

"Tom, you can trust me. What's going on?"

He forced a mirthless smile. "I know. It's just..." He paused, and the hesitation worried me that he'd change his mind about confiding in me. "Just wanted to make today one of your most memorable trips you've ever taken."

"You *are* making this trip memorable. I'm fine spending the whole day with you back in your bed."

His eyes widened with interest and the glum smile morphed into a wolfish grin. "Now, *that*, my beautiful woman, is a helluva proposition."

Twenty-Six

SARA

We spent the rest of the day making love, eating naked in bed, and were pretty much on rinse and repeat until nightfall, though Tom did disappear into his office for a few hours. He apologized for having to work, but I knew it had to do with whatever trouble Jake was in. I didn't bother asking him again about what was going on with his friend. In truth, it wasn't any of my business. Though, it did rattle me a little to see Tom so upset.

Sunday morning came too fast, and I didn't want to roll out of bed. As I stretched, I realized that Tom had once again gotten up before me. I found him in the kitchen, cooking breakfast. The French doors to the beach were wide open, and I plopped on his leather couch wearing jean shorts and a white tank top, watching the waves crash, enjoying the warm ocean breeze as it gently swirled through the living room.

As Tom continued preparing breakfast, my phone pinged with

an incoming text. I'd left it on top of the kitchen counter since who knew how long and I hadn't even bothered to check it for notifications. I'd been completely lost in Tom world for two days and forgotten the rest of the world existed. I picked it up from the counter and my heart sank when I read the text.

"Shit."

"What's the matter?" Tom asked as he walked out to the deck with a stack of pancakes.

"It's Rebecca. Apparently, she's been trying to reach me since yesterday, but I guess I never heard my phone ring. Something happened at the studio. She's freaking out and Alexei seems to be pissed off about God only knows what."

I followed after him and sat down on the outside table. Tom sat down across from me and made us both a plate. "That asshole is still causing issues?"

As I took a mouthful of my pancake, my brows pinched. "When is he not?"

"You sure nothing else is bothering you?"

There was. I didn't like how easily I had disregarded everyone back home. As much as I wished I could get lost in this fairytale book, real life existed. I never wanted to lose sight of that.

"This was simply a reminder that life doesn't stop just because you take a detour."

"Am I the detour?"

"Maybe," I groaned.

"You say it like it's a bad thing."

"No. I just need to remember it's not always like this. Vacations in Santa Monica, spending full days in bed, eating like my triglycerides aren't gonna kill me one day." I took another bite of my pancake and stuffed my face.

He laughed, one of those big and guttural laughs that can make your stomach cramp. It was so infectious, it momentarily made me forget why I was so mad.

Once the laughter stopped, he walked over to me and knelt down, taking my chin in his fingers. "Baby, yes, it can. I can give you the world, minus the high triglycerides."

I smiled and cupped his cheeks in my palms. "Can you stop being so perfect for once?"

He leaned in and kissed me. "I just want you to be happy," he whispered, his breath hot and heavy on my lips.

"I *am* happy," I told him, brushing my mouth against his and savoring the sweetness of his maple-syrup soaked breath. "You make the best pancakes."

With a toothy grin, he kissed me once more then he went back to his chair. "So, what does the gorgon want?"

"Gorgon?" I choked on my OJ as I burst into a giggle. "Oh, that's a good one."

"Maybe you should call her back and get it over with."

I sighed. "I guess it will be worse on Monday if I don't." I grabbed my phone off the table and dialed.

She let it ring several times before picking up. "Well, look who remembered she has a job."

I sat back on my chair and sucked in a deep breath. "Sorry I missed your calls, Rebecca."

"You know, Sara, you have some fucking nerve. I've been trying to call you since Friday night. Have you any idea what's happened?"

"No. I'm in California, remember? I'm coming back tomorrow."

"Shit's hitting the fan."

"What are you talking about?"

"What am I talking about? Your fucking choices that's what. We lost four more dancers on Friday, Sara. Four. Alexei is fuming, and he's threatening to quit. Have you any idea what's at stake? The shows are sold out. And we have four weeks to find replacements. Four fucking weeks to teach four new people the routine."

"Rebecca, calm down."

"Don't you tell me to calm down. You picked these people. This is all your fault."

"I didn't pick them, Alexei did."

"He gave you a very strict list and you gave him garbage."

"All the dancers who auditioned were well qualified. He's the problem, not me. No one is ever good enough. Are you sure they left or did he fire them?"

"Who the fuck cares? Get your ass back to New York and find me four new dancers, Sara. And not the shit you dragged in here last time, or I swear you'll be looking for a new job." She hung up on me.

"Bitch!"

"What's going on?" Tom asked.

I jumped off my chair. "What's going on is I work for idiots, that's what. Fucking Alexei managed to fire four more dancers in a matter of days. I mean, what does he think, that I freaking grow dancers on a tree or something? Yeah, there are tons of starving dancers out there dying to land the next gig, but no one meets his criteria. No one. Ugh, I'm so pissed I could rip his head off."

"Sara, just sit back down. What happened?"

"Basically, he needed dancers. I couldn't find anyone to audition because no one met the criteria. He wanted years and years of experience; only people who'd gone to the most reputable dance schools and those who had worked not only in the U.S. but who had experience in overseas productions. I mean, those people don't want to come to work for Alexei. Those dancers already have jobs. They are probably choreographers themselves or running their own dance companies. He may be a master at his craft, but he is a horrible person.

"The point is, Rebecca came into my office a week ago and basically said I needed to bring in new people or get fired. I scanned through tons of applications and portfolios. I looked at video after video entry and selected who I thought would be great. He chose four dancers, but apparently, they weren't good enough because he got rid of them on Friday. Now they are both demanding I come up with four new people who can learn the routine in less than four weeks. That's impossible. Literally impossible."

"Quit."

"Quit? That's your solution?" I said, not able to hide my disappointment. "In case you haven't noticed, not all of us are billionaires. And don't even bring up the whole you'll give me some job at your company or take care of me shit. We are together, but nowhere near that stage yet. I simply can't quit. Not again."

"What do you mean again? When did you quit before?"

This was not the time or place to get into this conversation. "It's a … long story. Maybe another day?"

"Sara, I've shown you my skeletons. You know more about me than I know about you. And I'm okay with that, there's no rush to fill a lifetime into a couple of days. I'm just worried about you. This job is really stressing you out. Especially this fucking guy, who I'm ready to punch in the face. I'm just trying to see how I can help."

"You wouldn't understand."

"Try me."

It was there, the aching need to tell him what was raking through me; the words sitting at the tip of my tongue. As I looked back at him, tears ran down my face. For a long moment, he said nothing, he just walked over and waited until I was ready to talk. I didn't need to tell him anything. It was like he had a tapped line into my soul and he understood something lay hidden, a tormenting secret I could not dig up, not here, not yet. He leaned in and kissed me. "I'm sorry. When it's time, I'll be here to listen."

"It's not that I don't want to tell you…it's just so hard for me to talk about it. I just need a little time, that's all."

"Take all the time you need, baby."

We cleaned up after breakfast and Tom spent a big portion of the afternoon in his study again, talking to people on the phone and managing business on his computer. He apologized for leaving me alone, but I didn't mind too much. Sure, it was great spending so much time together, but a little *me* time didn't hurt. I laid on the beach for a while, even took a dip in the ocean.

Though he was flying be back home on a private charter again, I was leaving on a red-eye flight that night. I still needed to get to the airport two hours early. So around five, I picked up my beach towel and went inside to shower and pack my things. When I came out of the bathroom, towel drying my hair, the sounds of a familiar voice coming from Tom's study startled me. Too nosy for my own good, I pried my door open and listened.

"Who're those men in the car outside?" Tom asked, the tone in his voice harsh.

"Carlo's guys," Jake replied.

Twenty-Seven

TOM

"You brought his thugs to my house?" I nearly jumped over my desk and strangled my best friend.

"I had no choice."

"You had no choice?" My jaw muscles clenched so hard, I thought I would crack bone. He had some fucking nerve showing up to my house while he was being tracked by one of the most dangerous loan sharks on the West Coast.

"I guess he wanted to make sure I wouldn't bail."

"He's got you on a leash."

"Listen, you think I like coming here like this?"

"This is the last time, Jake. You know how many strings I had to pull this morning to get this money? I had to yank the bank manager from a family outing on his day off. It's a good thing he's my friend. I don't have millions of dollars in cash lying around my house for every time you have a run in with these guys."

"I'll pay you back. You know I always do."

"For Christ's sake, man. This isn't about the goddamn money. It never was, not even for you. But you're not going to stop until you end up in some ditch with a bullet in your head."

"I can handle myself."

"Yeah, you think so? These are dangerous people you're messing with, and they don't take kindly to people who screw with their money."

"You think I don't know that? Once I get Carlo this money, I'll be done with my debt."

A loud noise boomed outside my office, like someone knocking into a piece of furniture.

"What was that?" Jake asked. "There's someone else here?"

"It's probably Sara."

"Wait. You actually brought that chick home?"

That chick? After what he did the other night, he had some fucking balls talking to me about her in that way. I rushed to close my office door then spun toward him. "Who I bring home is none of your business."

"The hell it isn't. Since when do you bring women home?"

"Like I said, it's none of your business."

"Those were your own fucking rules," Jake shouted.

"I made them, I can break them."

"For her?" Jake seemed beside himself.

Fucking prick. Who the hell does he think he is?

"Men like us," he continued, "we don't bring women home. Not women like her."

Like her?

I walked up to him and grabbed him by the collar of his shirt, yanking him off his chair. "Fuck's that supposed to mean?"

"I saw the way you two were with each other at the party the other night. You can't fucking be serious. You have feelings for this chick."

I shoved him off. "Her name is Sara, and what's it to you anyway?"

"What's it to me? Have you forgotten what happened to you? Did you forget the fucking mess I pulled *you* out of? Women screw with our heads and turn us into idiots. You know that better than anybody."

"It's different now."

"Different how? They are all the same. Lying whores."

"You shut your fucking mouth, Jake," I said gritting my teeth. "Sara is not like that, and you better start getting used to the fact she's not some chick off the street. If you disrespect her again—"

"Wow," Jake interrupted. "I can't believe I'd ever see the day Tom Wright would be getting all soft and cuddly. So now you're in love or some shit? Does Tiff know about her?"

"She knows."

"No, bruh, I mean does she know how you feel about Sara? She's not going to take this laying down."

"Tiffany has no say in what I do or don't do in my life. Who I choose to date is none of her fucking business."

"That woman is still in love with you. Even after the shit you pulled, she fucking hangs around you like a puppy dog. You don't think she's gonna question why you didn't change your rules for her? Why you're changing them for Sara?"

"I've already told you, Sara is different. This time, things are different. And I'm done explaining myself to you. Listen to me very closely. You're my best friend, you've been like a brother to me, but do me a favor and stay the hell away from Sara. You're lucky I don't kick the shit out of you for the stunt you pulled on Friday at your fucking party."

"So that's how it's going to be?"

I said nothing.

"You're joking. You would choose a woman over me? Over us?"

"You see me smiling? Now take your money and get the fuck out of my house. And don't ever bring those thugs near here again."

I made sure he left and that the men trailing him were gone too before closing my front door. "You know, it's rude to snoop," I said, knowing Sara had been listening the whole time.

Still wrapped in a bathrobe, she descended the stairs. "Was I that obvious?" she said, shrugging, trying not to look as guilty as she was, though still managing to look adorable as hell.

"Obvious? Let's just say you'd make a terrible spy."

"I didn't mean to eavesdrop," she said, biting her lower lip.

"You didn't mean to eavesdrop or you didn't mean to get caught?" I wasn't really mad at her, I was simply enjoying making her squirm. I walked to my fridge and took an orange juice container out, opened it, and chugged.

"Don't you own a glass? It's gross to drink from the container."

"Not to me." I took another gulp of juice.

"Are you mad at me for snooping?"

"No. I'm mad at him."

"For what?"

"For being a fucking idiot."

"So, who were those men you were talking about?"

"The less you know the better."

"That's mysterious."

I put the OJ back in the fridge and walked over to the stairs where she stood. "It's getting late. I should drive you to the airport."

"Jake doesn't like me very much, does he?"

"He's not used to this version of me."

She hiked an eyebrow. "There should only be one version of you."

I took her by the hand and guided her back up the stairs. "Now, there is. C'mon, nosy girl. Let's get you packed and ready before you miss your flight."

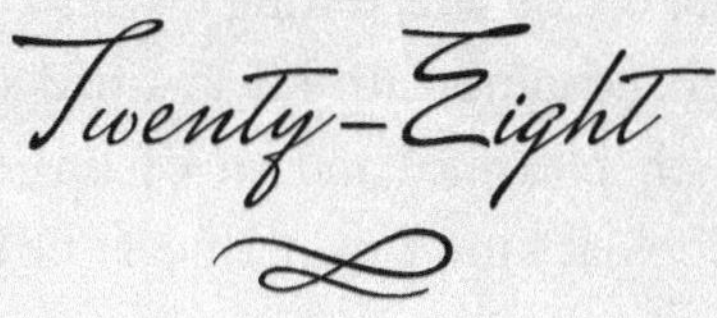

SARA

So much for packing. We barely made it back into his room before he stripped off my bathrobe. The man had an insatiable appetite for sex, but I wasn't complaining. He could give me all the orgasms he wanted. I would never grow tired of his body, especially when his chest felt like the safest place in the world.

Afterward, I lay in bed, curled into him, watching as the minutes ticked down on his clock to the moment I'd have to leave. The thought of separating from him twisted a knot in my stomach.

"What's his name?" he asked out of nowhere.

I pushed up on my elbow and looked at him with a furrowed brow. "Who?"

"The guy who hurt you."

I looked away and rolled out of bed. "Why do you need to know his name?"

"Just curious, I guess."

I found my clothes and dressed. "Not good enough." I tried to sound playful, but dread lurked behind those words. Tom had been so open about his past, yet I still couldn't bring myself up to talk about mine. I was such a hypocrite and I hated myself for it.

Tom rolled over on his side, resting his head on one hand. He was so breathtakingly handsome with his just-had-sex hair, his lion eyes still swimming with pleasure, and those lips swollen with heated blood. It hurt to look at him. I would never be able to resist the way his eyes sparkled when he smiled at me. I simply didn't deserve such adoration.

"Well, what's his name?" he pressed, a mischievous shadow crossing his eyes.

"You're not serious, are you?"

"Yeah, I'm serious. I want to know his name. I think you owe me as much."

He had a point.

"Josh."

"Josh..." he repeated contemplatively, then he rolled onto his back, tucking his arms behind his head and staring at the ceiling fan spinning above.

I finished putting on my silver flats and combed my hair with my fingers. "What are you thinking?"

"Nothing."

I put my hands on my hips. "Don't tell me nothing. I saw a thought cross your face."

"Oh, you can see thoughts?"

"I can see when you're thinking, so spill it."

"I don't like him. I don't know him, and I don't like him." There was stillness about his voice that sent a cold shiver down my spine.

"He's in the past, Tom. And not a big deal anymore."

"I don't like the idea of anyone hurting you."

I smiled. "He can't hurt me anymore." I turned and walked toward the bathroom.

Josh was hundreds of miles away on another continent, in jungles and savannas, hunting wildlife with his camera. He was completely out of my life. Had been for a while. Perhaps, it was time to let go.

I peered up at the vanity mirror, and as I dotted pink gloss on my lips, thoughts of a past long gone bled through, and in the mirror, I saw Josh's face staring back at me. I hadn't thought about him, at least not like this, in a very long time. I shut my eyes, trying to erase his icy blue eyes and pale blond, curly hair. The image wouldn't dissolve. His face still glowed with the sun's rays, highlighting a dust of freckles on each cheek. His smile had always been so radiant.

I took a deep breath and exhaled his memory from my mind. This time, the images faded back to the dark corners of my past.

Where they needed to stay.

Permanently.

We made it to the airport with only forty minutes to spare before my scheduled flight. Before take-off, I dialed Jen.

After two rings, she picked up. "Hey, Ms. California. When are you returning to the world of the common folk?"

"My plane is going to start taxiing soon. I just wanted to tell you my flight is on schedule, so hopefully, I should be arriving on time."

"I'll pick you up."

"It's okay. Tom's got a car service already scheduled to pick me up."

"Of course, he does. I'll be waiting for you at home then, with your favorite cup of joe."

"I'll need it."

"You can stay awake by telling me about your trip. I'm anxious to hear everything. By the way, did you talk to Lisa?"

"Josh's sister? Why would I be talking to her?"

"She called me asking for you. I told her you were in Santa

Monica and she got all excited. She asked for your number, something about wanting to talk to you about work. She lives in L.A., so she figured you guys would meet up or something."

"That explains the missed unknown call on my phone. Look, I gotta go. Tell you all about my trip when I see you."

"Can't wait."

"And, Jen. Make sure we're stocked on ice cream."

"Ooh...bad news binge or good news gorge?"

"Tons of good news gorge. Bye..." I crooned sweetly.

Twenty-Nine

SARA

Jen and I sat on the couch, talking after arriving from the airport. "Sounds like you had a lot of fun out there," she said as she stood up from the couch and grabbed my empty coffee mug. "But what did you guys really talk about? Did he tell you about his time in the war? Has he ever had a long-term relationship?" She walked into the kitchen and washed our dirty dishes.

Exhausted from my flight, I didn't feel like following after her, so I put my arm over the sofa and faced her. "He mentioned the war very briefly, and he did have a serious relationship once. Engaged, even."

Her eyebrows climbed up her forehead. "Engaged?"

"Didn't end well between them. Long story," I said noncommittally, not wanting to elaborate on the details. It was his story to tell, not mine. Boundaries were necessary sometimes, and I needed to keep Tom's past protected. I knew the burden of carrying secrets and

Tom had struggled with his, yet trusted me enough to share them with me. I couldn't betray his trust, even for my best friend.

Jen must have caught the dismissiveness in my reply and dropped her sponge, a weepy look in her eyes. I didn't want to shut her out, but right now was not the time to have this conversation. She opened her mouth to utter something, but closed her lips as if she'd caught herself about to say something she shouldn't.

When I saw the hesitant look in her eyes, my mouth became dry. I knew exactly why she'd stopped herself. And I wished she'd listened to her conscience.

"Did you tell him about the...accident?" she asked, the last word in a whisper, as if the word itself was a sin to be spoken.

I turned my gaze away. She knew very well what talking about the accident did to me, even mentioning it gave me anxiety. Straightening, I rotated completely from her and crossed my arms. I pursed my lips and took a couple of deep breaths through my nose. My heart rammed against my chest.

"Sara?"

"No. I didn't," I replied coolly.

"Don't you think it's important he knows?"

If anyone knew how marrow-splintering those memories were, it was her. It wasn't something I could blurt out in conversation. It wasn't a box with a lid. Once the container housing all my nightmares was ripped open, there would be no putting them away again.

I heard as she turned the faucet and the water stopped. Her sneakers squeaked on our hardwood floors as she walked over to the couch and placed her hands on her hips. I wouldn't look up at her.

"Sara—"

"—Jen, I know what you are going to say, but I don't know why it's necessary to tell him anything right now."

She sat down next to me. "Honey, what happened to you wasn't some insignificant event in your life."

I turned to face her, my brow pinched in frustration. "My

mother died because of me. You don't think I know the weight that carries?"

"That's not what I meant and you know it. Don't you think he needs to know?"

I breathed heavy, trying to remain composed. "He knows my mother is dead. There's no need for more."

"It wasn't just about your mom dying, Sara."

When I said nothing, she gasped. "He doesn't know, does he?"

I rubbed my temple, trying to keep calm, but knowing if we kept having this conversation, I was going to end up in a crumpled mess. I purposefully hadn't told Tom about my failed dancing career. I didn't want him probing into what happened or why I stopped danc-ing. Nothing good would come out of that conversation. What was the point of talking about something that never was? Dancing was my past. Tom was my present. End of story.

I shook my head, my gaze now glued to my hands resting on my lap, picking at my nails. "I know you mean well, Jen. Thank you for that, but I can't do this, not right now. Someday...maybe."

After another long moment of silence, she stood up and paced, her hands clenched. "First of all, your mom did not die because of you. She died because she was in a car accident."

What was the point in rehashing the past? Why bring this up today? Did she think after all these years she'd get me to see things differently?

"She died because I didn't stop her from getting in my car, Jen. It was my fault and everyone knows it. I'm responsible, and every time you force me to talk about it, you force me to relive it. So please, do me a favor and leave me the hell alone. Please." I pushed up to my feet and stormed into my room, slamming the door behind me. My chest filled with anguish as I tried to stifle back tears, but my eyes betrayed me and my grief poured out in rivers.

"Sara," Jen uttered softly across the closed door, "after you healed from your injuries, you told everyone you couldn't dance anymore. That the injury to your spine affected your balance and movement."

Oh, God. She's not going to stop.

"It did. So, what?" My voice cracked.

"Maybe at first it did, but I saw you months later, right here, in this living room. We'd just moved in and we still didn't have all this furniture. It was early in the morning and I woke up to the sounds of loud thumping, like someone was jumping hard in our apartment. I peered out of my room and there you were, dancing in the middle of our living room. Headphones on and completely lost in the music. You didn't even notice me peeking through the open crack of my door.

"You moved like the dancer I knew before the accident. Nothing was holding you back. So, stop telling yourself the reason you are not up on that stage is because of your spinal injury. You are not up on that stage because you choose not to."

I sank to the floor in sobs.

"I know it hurts, Sara. I know you miss your mom more than anything in this world. That you still blame yourself for her death. You stopped dancing because you wanted to punish yourself for what happened. I know this is hard for you, but I can't watch you keep doing this to yourself anymore. And I'm sorry for bringing this up today, for pushing you to talk about it. Perhaps it isn't the best time, but it was the only time. Please, Sara. Open the door."

They say the truth hurts. Well, in my case, it was a jagged knife digging into my heart, tearing me up as it ground my flesh to a pulp. I sat on the floor, holding my knees, trembling, my face soaked with grief. I never knew she saw me that day. She never said anything. It was my dirty secret and now it shamed me.

"I only want what's best for you, Sara. Please open the door. I don't want to leave things like this."

I wiped the tears from my eyes and stood, facing the door, a hand on the knob. Opening it meant shattering the façade I had erected four years ago. It meant facing the reality that I had chosen to give up on my dreams because I didn't feel I deserved to be happy. It meant accepting that while my mom lost her life, I hadn't suffered a single consequence.

"It wasn't fair. I should have been the one to die that day. What right did I have to go on living, Jen? What right did I have to go on dancing? What right did I have to be happy when she was six feet below ground?"

She had no reply.

And I could not open the door.

Jen didn't press me anymore. At some point she walked away. She did know me like no one else. But even with her, whenever this topic came up, I automatically shut down. I couldn't talk about it, even when I knew I had to.

Now she wanted me to tell Tom? If three highly certified therapists and a very persistent best friend hadn't been able to crack my shell, how would Tom?

The answer lay buried in my chest, inside my aching heart. Tom had seen me when he looked in my eyes. He'd seen the pain that throbbed inside my soul. Without having to utter a single word to him, he had known. *When you're ready*...he said to me.

I shuddered. Would I ever be ready?

As if on cue, my cellphone chirped in my pants. I pulled it out and my breath caught as Tom's name popped up on my text screen.

Tom: *Hey beautiful, wondering if you got home safe.*

Tears pooled at the corners of my eyes as all the anguish melted away. I smiled and before I knew it, I was crying and laughing at the same time. It's like he knew when I needed him. I wiped my tears before replying, a wet grin etching across my face.

Me: *Yeah. Sorry for not texting earlier.*

Tom: *Miss you :(*

Tom: *My bed is cold without you.*

Tom: *Hugging your pillow.*

Tom: *Smells like you.*

Me: *Aw, I miss you, too.*

Tom: *:)*

It was a simple smiley face. But what I saw in my mind was his brilliant smile, the one that brought utter joy to my soul as it sewed up my torn heart back together.

Me: *Tom...*

Tom: *Yes?*

Me: *I love you. So much.*

Tom: *I love you, too, baby girl. More than you know.*

I couldn't believe I'd just uttered those three words over a text message. After such a short amount of time. It was crazy but it was true. I just hated that I hadn't told him in person. Still, to see him type the words back filled me with so much joy and relief, I held the phone tight against my chest. He brought such peace to my life; I couldn't imagine myself without him. Jen was right. Tom needed to know the truth.

He deserved it.

Later that morning, I strolled quietly into the office a bit early, trying to stay under the radar as much as possible. I left my door slightly ajar, and had just placed my cappuccino on my desk, and was sorting through my emails, when there was a slight tap on my door. Before I could answer, Alexei walked in.

"Got a second?" he asked.

I looked up from my desk wearily.

Alexei crossed his arms over his chest, leaning his shoulder against the door frame. "We need to talk."

I pointed to the brown leather chair in front of my desk. "Okay, have a seat."

"In my office." He walked away, obviously expecting me to follow after him like an obedient little puppy.

He was waiting for me at the entrance to his large corner office and directed me to enter and sit. Closing the door slowly, he strolled to his desk in his most arrogant stride and sat down. With his back to me, he reclined in his black leather chair, his hands folded behind his raven-haired head while he stared out the window at Times Square. I waited a whole minute in silence, watching him regard the city like he was admiring a Van Gough at the Met.

"You had something you wanted to talk to me about?" I asked, not being able to conceal the tone of annoyance in my voice.

"I don't think I'll ever get used to it, you know. New York City. The city that never sleeps. So many people out there, pursuing their dreams."

Is he kidding me?

"Get to the point, Alexei. I have actual work I need to get done.'"

He spun around on his chair and arrowed his gaze into mine. "Have a good weekend with your boyfriend, Miss Hart?" he asked, a forced grin smeared on his face.

I blinked hard. Who the hell did he think he was, asking me about my personal life and pretending he had the right to form an opinion about it? "Excuse me?" The miff riding my voice couldn't have been more obvious than the ire flashing in my eyes.

Unwavering, his obsidian-colored eyes showed no interest in my reaction. He wasn't fooling me. I could feel the heat of the choler simmering beneath his frigid stare. He leaned forward and dug his spiny gaze deeper into mine. "You heard me. The reason you didn't show up to work on Friday." Every word he spoke was frosted with ice. He didn't care about my actual trip; he was pissed I hadn't been in the office when he had his hissy fit.

"Personal. Leave. Of. Absence," I barked at him, my upper lip curling at the corner. I think I may have snarled.

He sucked in a deep breath and leaned back on his chair, never once taking his eyes off me. He glared at me for a few silent moments, perhaps realizing I wasn't easy prey.

I glowered back with similar bile. He wasn't going to intimidate me.

Resting his hands on his desk, he cocked his head to the side, and with a flat tone asked, "Miss Hart, do you like working here?"

I tilted my head slightly and slit my eyes. If I knew anything about the slithering vermin, it was that things were never how they appeared. His seemingly unthreatening question wrapped in passivity sounded precisely like the minacious sound of a coiled rattlesnake.

I heeded the warning and ignored his question. "Can we please get to the reason you asked me to your office?"

He raked his hands through his thick, black hair. Normally he'd have it tied at the nape, but today he'd left it resting right atop of his shoulders. His eyes matched the darkness of his mane, and he pinned me with their chilled distaste. There was no depth to them; two solid marbles made of coal against the pale white of his skin.

"Do you know what it's like to be up on that stage?" The steel in his voice scraped against my skin. "The music moves through your veins like it is part of your blood. Your muscles, every single one, responds absent of thought. Your soul carries you across the dance floor. Freed. Dancing is living, Miss Hart, don't you agree?"

Blood drained away from my face. He spoke as if he knew about my past, knowing his words could pierce my soul with the sorrowful reminder of my failed career. Perhaps it was my indignation at his slimy intentions, or maybe it was my guilty conviction about the rubble I'd left in my wake, but my body felt cold, rendering me unable to move or speak. The only sound in the room was the raggedness of my breath.

A baleful smile slowly traced across his chapped lips; he'd received the reaction he wanted. He narrowed his eyes. "But you do, don't you? You know exactly what I'm talking about."

There was no need for words. My eyes told him everything he needed to know. He had my full attention, and finally, he was in control.

"I know about you, Miss Hart," he whispered, accompanied by an overly dramatic wink. "Rebecca let me in on your little secret."

The harpy. Should have known.

Leaning back on his chair and planting his crossed feet up on his desk, his fingers pressed against each other, forming a tent. "The Juilliard dropout. I couldn't believe it," he mocked with a surly laugh. "You used to have dreams. Big dreams. What happened?"

No doubt he'd already been made privy to that information. The effing ogress betrayed my trust. I had to think hard about my reply. A million options jostled for first place. One included me walking up to him, grabbing his wooden name plaque, and smashing it across his face. I leaned forward in my chair and eyed the small wooden block sitting on his desk for a good moment before peering up at him. It took every ounce of my body not to follow through with it. This guy was a bona fide jerk and he was trying to get a rise out of me. He was close to getting a full dose of my unhinged dark side.

A deranged, batshitcrazy feline tried to claw her way out of my mental cage, but that was exactly what he'd hoped for.

Nah, Alexei. Not gonna give you the pleasure.

I sat firmly, and grimly uttered, "Have a nice day." And with that, I pushed up from my chair and attempted to walk away.

"Sit. Back. Down. Sara." His angry tone stopped me in my tracks. As much as I wanted to fight it, he struck a chord of fear down my spine. I clenched my jaw in anger, but did as he commanded.

Dammit.

I need a stronger backbone.

His stone-cold gaze pushed me hard against my seat. His intent was clear. I was not leaving until he said I could. With a slight tilt of his head, he urged me to answer his last question.

I tried to chill my exterior, hoping to hide the unnerving tremors shivering inside. There was no way I was going to give him a single gram of my vulnerability. "Spinal injury," I replied coolly.

He shook his head. "Ah yes, the accident. What a shame." He shrugged with a blank affect, as if he were referring to a fender bender where I'd merely busted the bumper on my car.

This time I couldn't hide the pained disgust curdling in my gut. "Are you serious?"

He sucked in a deep breath and rolled his eyes. "I know. You had raw talent. At least that's what my colleagues said. A real future, it seemed. A career full of promise you were forced to abandon. Pity," he sighed with feigned sadness.

It was Alexei. I knew he was cruel and volatile. Taking his bullshit and intolerance was a daily occurrence. I'd grown accustomed to it; sometimes his outbursts were so comedic I had no choice but to laugh them off. This, though, was a personal attack beyond anything he'd ever done. He'd pried open my ribcage, stuck a grenade in my chest cavity, then closed me back up before it exploded, shredding me open and spilling my guts all over his office. I could see my innards sliding off the glass on the windows behind him.

Yes. It was a gory metaphor, but that's how I felt—exposed and destroyed. Not only had he dug up my past and ridiculed me, but he'd also mocked the suffering I endured for the loss of my dance career. He didn't even acknowledge that the biggest tragedy had been my mother's death. He swept that fact under the carpet as if dropping out of Juilliard had been the only thing that mattered, reducing my mom to mere collateral damage.

"I lost my mother in that car accident, you heartless prick." I pushed up off my chair and charged toward his desk. "How dare you sit there and act like you have any right to talk to me about my life?"

He leaned back on his leather chair and smiled. "Heartless prick?" he scoffed. "I've been called worse."

"What the hell is wrong with you? Why do you even care about my past?"

He pushed off his chair so quickly I lurched back as he spat his venom. "I don't give a fuck about your past, Miss Hart. What I do care about is the shit you pulled off last Friday. I know Rebecca hired you because she knew about your past as a Juilliard dropout. She didn't care you couldn't dance anymore, she cared you had the knowledge and intuition for finding true talent. You may not be a great dancer any more, but I know you can spot one when you see one. Yet with mere weeks until this performance you left me with mediocre—"

"So that's what this is really all about, the fact you weren't happy with the dancers I sent you? I know how to do my job, Alexei. There was nothing wrong with those dancers, but no one is ever good enough for you. Trust me, if this show fails, it won't be because of me."

"If this show fails? You better pray it doesn't. I've seen the way you look at my dancers. You think I don't notice when you sneak into the back of the studio to watch us rehearse? I know now why you took this job."

"Why are you telling me all of this?"

"Because I want you to understand very clearly that I'm not going to let you ruin *my* career. You want to keep nursing your pathetic wounds on my stage, then you better find me qualified dancers or I swear I will get your ass fired so quickly you won't know what hit you. I'm well connected. I'll make sure you never find another job working at a dance company, not even as a fucking clerk."

"You have no right to threaten me. You are not my boss."

"That, Miss Hart, is a matter of technicality."

I said nothing. Rebecca was just a puppet and he held the strings.

"Are we clear?" he demanded.

Turning on my heel and walking away, I didn't bother to offer a reply.

"Do you think your mother would be proud of what you've done with your life?" the flippant asshole rasped behind me as I reached for the door knob.

A cold sheet of ice wrapped around my body. For a split second, I stood frozen in place, my fingers clasping the knob.

I should have swung around and dashed to clamp my hands around his throat. The slimy bastard surely deserved more than a verbal lambaste. What good would it have done? Demons had an upper hand. They were immortal and everlasting evil. They thrived on punishment, and he'd bask in the glory of owing the reason for my fury.

I took a deep breath, opened the door, and walked away, wanting to slam the door shut behind me, but choosing to not let an ounce of defiant anger seep out of my pores. That rage would be better served elsewhere.

Once out of his office, I let the wrath broiling me from the inside erupt. I stormed down the hall, zeroing in on one particular target. That deceitful, back-stabbing, soulless husk was not going to get away without receiving a few lashes down her back. I barged through her door, not giving a damn if she was in there alone. She looked up from her computer screen, startled and confused.

"Sara, what's gotten into you?"

"Really?" I roared. "You're gonna pretend you don't know?"

Leaning back on her chair, she rolled her eyes and sighed. "Oh. That," she said casually.

My eyes bulged. "That? Sharing my personal life with a blood-sucking leech in an effort to crush my heart and belittle my life choices is a *that*? You have some fucking nerve, woman."

"Oh, Sara, sit down. And stop seething," she uttered dispassion-ately. "You are practically foaming at the mouth, darling." She was wholly unperturbed by the torrent of animosity gushing from my body and rushing to stampede her. Were it not for the roots of reason planting me on the floor, I would have jumped across her desk and squashed her puny head like a grape.

"Come on now, there's no need to have a conniption," she quipped, a sardonic smile twitching at the side of her mouth.

"A conniption?" I uttered, unamused. The roots of reason were slowly getting chopped away by the axe of lunacy. Soon, I would lose all restraint.

"Look, Sara. He demanded I fire you. I was merely trying to protect you."

I blinked fast and shook my head, stumped at her reasoning. "How did telling him about Juilliard and the accident help me keep my job?"

She folded her hands over each other on her desk and regarded me with restrained contemp. "Sara, I may not like you, but regardless of how I feel..." She swallowed hard before proceeding, the words painful to utter, it seemed. "...honestly, pretty simply, I couldn't afford to lose you, not when the show is merely weeks away. I had to give him something to make him rethink his impulsive decision. Telling him you used to be a dancer at Juilliard and that you have an unmatched eye for catching talent did the trick."

"The trick? You mean you gave him the ammunition he needed to threaten me. Next time, don't do me any favors."

She narrowed her eyes and pursed her lips. "You ungrateful little bitch. You should be thanking me for not putting your ass out on the street. How dare you walk into my office and speak to me like this!"

"How dare I? With the same vile, unapologetic predilection you have toward being a loathsome hag!"

She straightened in her chair, ready to spew wickedness through her mouth, but I stopped her before she had a chance to part her lips. "Hush, Rebecca. I'm done hearing you talk. I will find those dancers, but I am not doing it for you or him. I am doing it for the dancers who have already given their blood, sweat, and tears for this thankless company." I stalked closer. "If you or Alexei ever try to threaten me again, you can go ahead and find those precious dancers your fucking self."

I turned away and yanked open the door then marched out. My heels echoed down the hall as I stomped back to my office, my heart pumping flaming blood through my veins. As I slammed the door shut behind me and reached my desk, my rage finally began to simmer down.

The whole morning replayed inside my head. From the moment Alexei stepped foot inside my office to the instant I barged out of Rebecca's—the entire thing seemed like a script out of a movie. After several minutes, when I was done cooking my brain in my own stew, I had the time to ponder about the actual thoughts causing my head to spin. Alexei's last words wouldn't stop orbiting around my brain.

Would my mom be proud of what I'd chosen to do with my life?

That, as he insinuated, was my true torment.

Thirty

SARA

Out of all the virulent comments those two barnacles had vomited out of their mouths, it was Alexei's barb about my mother's disappointment that tightened its noxious vice around my heart. I sat on my swivel chair and sullenly stared out at Manhattan through the tall windows, my ego licking those broken-dancer wounds Alexei had aggravated with his acid-dripping words.

I sighed. It seemed so long ago since I'd danced on any stage. The memory struck a ping of regret in my soul. The ache throbbing in my chest made me wonder if I had made the right choice. After all of the sacrifices my mom made to get me into the best dance schools and to push me to always be better than the last version of myself, I had chosen to toss it all away.

But how could I go on dancing without her? She'd been my rock, my biggest fan. Without my mother, I was no one. If she was out there somewhere, watching over me, she had to understand.

Right?

I breathed heavily again, still reminiscing about a future I never had.

If only...

I pushed up off my chair and paced. If only what? If only the accident hadn't happened? If only there hadn't been a storm? If only there hadn't been an audition? If only we hadn't gone up to visit Nana? If only. If only. Life was a series of regrets and questions without answers. The more I thought about it, the more frustrated I became—the hotter the rage inside me flared. Anger boiled inside me like an infected cut, spreading toxic gunk throughout my body. It depleted me of my inner peace, stealing away the courage I needed to get back on that stage.

It even lied to me about being able to find love again.

It needed to stop. Allowing rancor to rule my life was vacuuming my drive to live.

As I plopped my ass back down on my chair, I sucked in a deep breath and closed my eyes, trying to summon the strength to finally drag myself out of the pit of despair. Something deep inside me roared, a primal need to survive. Thoughts about my childhood, my family, and my years as a dancer, all clawed their way back to the surface, forcing me to see things differently—for the very first time since the accident.

With trembling anxiety, I reached for my last memory of my mother; the one I had buried so long ago and wished to never relive.

It happened four years ago. We'd been having dinner at grams— Nana's famous pot roast and homemade mash potatoes—the family recipe she'd sworn to only share with the Hart sisters once we were married. My mom knew the recipe, but she was a terrible cook, and she'd misplaced it anyway. Gram said she would only share it once, after that, we were shit out of luck if we lost it.

We sat at her dining table, right off the kitchen, with unobstructed views of the New England seas, watching the snow coat the sandy shore off Gram's backyard.

"Sara, honey, I really don't think it's a good idea for you to drive in this weather," my mom said.

"Your mother is right, Sara," Gram called out from the kitchen as she prepared to bring out her also famous key lime pie. "No need to put your life at risk for an audition."

"—or that of others," Megan chimed in from across the dining table.

I raised an eyebrow at my sister. As if she'd never done stupid things before. "It really doesn't look that bad out there, guys," I assured them. "Plus, I have four-wheel drive. I'll be fine."

Mom stood up and reached for the TV remote resting on top of the kitchen counter. She aimed it at the flat screen in the living room and tuned it to the news channel then hiked up the volume.

...Governor of Massachusetts has deemed it a state of emergency. All civilians are advised to stay off the roads. Only emergency responders are permitted to be out...eighteen to twenty-four inches expected to blanket the area by dawn. This could be the first big storm of the season...

"That's just for Massachusetts, Mom. If I leave now, I'll make it to New York before it starts to get bad. The city is not expected to get as much snow as here."

My mother shut her eyes in frustration before she looked back at me, her eyes flashing with dread. She knew I was being difficult, and no matter what she said, I was going to do what I wanted. But that wasn't going to stop her from trying to dissuade me from going. "Sara, didn't you just hear? It's a state of emergency. Dangerous conditions out there."

I looked away from her, not wanting her to notice the glint of apprehension probably shining in my own eyes. She was right; it was stupid and dangerous. But did I really have a choice? This audition was potentially the most important one of my career. It was an opportunity to become part of the most highly regarded company in New York.

"Mom, you know I can't miss this audition. This is what I've trained for all my life."

"Just wait 'til the morning. The roads will be cleared by then."

"I can't take that chance. The audition is at noon. What if we get snowed in? It's better if I leave now, while it's just starting to come down."

Megan took a bite of Gram's pie. "White-out conditions are going to make visibility impossible on the interstate. You really should stay."

The table trembled; I bounced my knee so hard it made everything vibrate. Fierce anxiety raked through me at the thought of missing this audition. They didn't get it. This was a lifetime opportunity for me. I was at my prime and God only knew when this company would have another audition. By then, there might be a younger, more beautiful, and maybe even more talented dancer than me.

No. I couldn't take that chance.

I pushed my uneaten pie away and headed for the stairs to my guest room.

"Sara, where are you going?" Gram called out after me.

"I'm getting my things before it gets worse out there."

"My God, she's really leaving..." I heard my mom mutter in disbelief.

Curious to hear what they were going to say about me, I stood at the top of the stairs and listened.

"This is your fault, you know," Gram said in a whisper.

"Why would you say that, Mother?"

"She's always been excessively competitive, and that's what you've nurtured—an entitled brat."

"Her talent is a gift, Mother. Why shouldn't she be competitive?

How else could she be where she is now? She's a strong, young woman and I couldn't be prouder."

She'd always told me how proud she was, but that was the first time I'd heard her defend me. Gram appreciated my dancing, but she never shied from sharing her true feelings, telling me I should get a real education and job. She resented my mother for supporting my dream.

"If being strong-willed and determined makes you a brat, then so be it. I have a beautiful daughter who dances like an angel, and I'll be damned if I'm not going to help her spread her wings and share her gift with the world."

"Where are you going?" Gram asked.

"To pack. You think I'm going to let her drive to New York by herself?"

She'd never once missed any of my competitions or auditions. She'd been my lucky charm. I couldn't deny that a huge part of me hated the thought of doing my first big audition by myself, but I wasn't about to ask her to come. I knew the risks. When she came tromping up the stairs, I held her back by the shoulders. I told her she didn't have to, but she cupped my cheek with her palm, and said, "Baby, I would never miss this for the world. Now come on, we need to go."

Gram grumbled while Megan sulked and fretted about poor visibility. During the entire time Mom and I dragged our suitcases to the car, she complained and argued about our decision. There were at least five to six inches on the ground, and from the look of things, the roads hadn't been plowed much. My hands trembled as I held onto the wheel. Looking over at my mom, the dreary clouds in her eyes didn't aide in my trepidation.

As we skidded around the local streets, I questioned my decision and prayed the highways had been cleaned better, but as we pulled off the ramp and entered the interstate, my heart sank.

Then, my world was obliterated.

Thirty-One

SARA

Life became a blur after her death. By the time I was out of the hospital and done with rehab, I had already decided I couldn't go back to New York. My grief was too intense. I moved back home, but after learning of my father's affair, I couldn't bear to live there anymore. There was nothing left for me but hard memories. Then there was Megan. She couldn't stand the sight of me. Being in the same room was a struggle. She never said it, but I knew she blamed me for our mother's death. Not that I could argue with her; I blamed myself too. It didn't surprise me when I found the note one day, telling me she was moving to Seattle with her boyfriend. She apologized for not saying goodbye in person. It was easier that way, she said.

Perhaps, it was.

It was on a cold doleful day when I finally said my goodbyes to the ghosts haunting me in that home. My bags were packed and waiting at the door. My mother's bedroom was a place I hadn't been able to enter since coming back. But on that day, when I was ready to leave it all, I walked into the quiet, lonely room and sat on her pink, paisley arm chair underneath the bedroom window. The shades were half drawn and a dim light penetrated the room through the pale curtains.

Her brass bed was neatly made in a matching duvet. I stared at the empty mattress for a very long time. I wanted badly to cry. I wanted to feel the deep sorrow I had seen in my sister's eyes. I wanted to miss her, but the only emotions I was able to conjure up from inside me were guilt and anger.

You left me! I shouted to her inside my head.

As if she'd had a choice.

I couldn't see reason. The accusations kept spilling out—at her, at me. Why did she have to come with me that day? Why did I let her get in the car? Why didn't I listen? Why didn't she fight harder?

Tears rolled down my cheeks. I thought I would feel relief, but crying fueled the anger I'd bottled up since the accident. If she hadn't died, I might not have been so guilt ridden. I might not have given up on my life. I was mad at her for dying and driving me away from dance. I blamed her for my misery. I thought I would never be able to forgive her for leaving me the way she did—alone, scared, destroyed.

I could have been mad at God for taking her from me. I could have been angry at life for messing up my world. Yet, I chose to be mad at the only person who had ever truly loved me. Lord knows those heartless thoughts haunted me for years. I was not able to look at myself in the mirror and not remember what had gone through my mind that day. I sank into the deepest and darkest corners of myself.

I let hate and pity consume me.

Now, four years later, as I sat in my office, digging through my past, another memory sprang up at me. I always thought enduring the fact that I survived the accident—when I wished I'd been the one below ground—might have been more bearable if at least Josh hadn't left me. I guess it made perfect sense why Josh *would* leave me. I went numb after my mom died. Happiness was a foreign concept. With the blinds drawn shut in my room, I'd stay in bed for days, sleeping away my life. It was the only peace I ever enjoyed—being doped up on pain meds I knew my body didn't need, yet my mind and heart craved with ferocity.

For years, I remained perturbed as to why he would choose to abandon me at the worst time in my life—without telling me why or at least saying goodbye. I'd always understood Megan, but for some reason, accepting Josh's rejection? That just hadn't been in my realm of possibilities.

Thinking back on it now, maybe I was so shutoff from the world, I missed the signs. Perhaps he *did* try to tell me, and I was simply not listening. Still, I could not help the sting in my heart every time I remembered the day I found out he'd packed his bags and taken off to Africa to pursue a dream I never even knew he had.

The day I found out, I had awoken from a three-day fog of pain killers and vodka. It was the first time the clouds in my head dissipated enough to give me the clarity to want to get out of bed. I'd risen with the resolve that had eluded me for months. As soon as I opened my eyes, I rolled over, picked up the phone, and called Jen.

"Sara, is everything okay?"

"I...need a shower."

"I'll be right over."

A half hour later, Jen was sitting on my bed, waiting for me to get out of the bathroom. As I came out, an uneasy smile stretched on her face. I guess she wasn't sure what to expect, but the look in her eyes told me she was hopeful I was finally coming out of my depression.

"Do you want to go somewhere?" she asked.

I shrugged. "I do miss the sun."

She opened up my closet, picked out a pair of sweats and a T-shirt, and gave me my sneakers. "Let's go for a walk."

We must have done about ten laps around the track at the park behind my house. I told her the last few days had been rough. My body felt feverish and I'd woken up in cold sweats, fragments of nightmares still splintering in my brain. Every time I woke up, I simply took more pain killers chased with a shot of vodka.

She gasped.

I assured her I wasn't trying to kill myself, at least not consciously.

I told her about my latest dream.

In the dream, I'd been walking aimlessly through the hospital halls. I knew I was looking for something, or someone, but I couldn't figure out what or who. Confusion set in, followed by panic. Before I knew it, I was running in slow motion, the sound muted. All I could feel was a deep sense of agony in my soul, a longing for something I might never find.

Then it happened, I stopped short in front of a door. I couldn't remember how I'd arrived there, but whatever it was I was looking for, lay beyond the threshold. The air grew icy; my breath a vapory fog around me. I stared down at my feet and noticed I was bare-foot, and as I scanned the rest of my body, I saw I was still wearing my hospital gown. Bandages covered many of my extremities, and an IV dripped blood from where I had apparently pulled out the feeds.

I pushed the door open and walked into a dimly lit room lined with empty metal tables. I stood in the middle of the hospital morgue. The air smelled of death; the room was impregnated with the faint tang of iron and rot tinged with traces of sterilized medical instruments.

Then the lights began to flicker, accompanied by the sound of strained electricity trying to push power through. The blood chilled in my veins when my eyes caught sight of the body lying on top of one of the metal tables in the center of the room. That body had not been there before. My bones trembled, ice dripping down my spine.

Every instinct in my body urged me to bolt. Still, I walked closer toward it, my feet stinging from the ice-cold floors.

As I approached, my chest constricted. It was my mother's lifeless form, her blue eyes staring blankly at me. I wanted to scream, but the sound was stolen from my lungs when I heard her disembodied voice speak to me.

"It's time, honey." The sweet tone reminded me of Sunday morning pancake breakfasts at the house.

My heart throbbed at the memory. This eerily haunting scene was a sorrowful contradiction to the warmth of our kitchen every weekend. "Mom?" I uttered in a whisper, wishing for her eyes to light up with life, and the frozen, blue lips on her face to flush with the rosy luster of her smile.

They didn't.

"It's okay, baby. It's time to let go," her voice echoed in my head, as her lips remained sealed.

"I don't want to let go. Please, come back. Please."

"Wake up, Sara. Wake up!" she urged in my mind.

"No. I don't want to. Let me come, too."

A single tear rolled off one of her eyes. "Where I've gone, you can't follow. It's not your time."

"I'm so sorry."

"It's okay. I love you. Always."

As I prepared to tell her I loved her too, her dead body sprang up into a sitting position, her arm extended, a finger pointed at the door. "Wake up!" she yelled in a screech, causing me to jolt awake.

Jen stopped in her tracks and rubbed her arms. "I literally just got goosebumps throughout my body." She looked at me with puzzled eyes. "You think she was trying to communicate with you?"

I shook my head. "I don't know. The dream is still very foggy, but at the same time, I can still hear her voice very clearly."

"I know you'll always blame yourself for what happened—"

"Look, nothing you can say is ever going to change how I feel about it. I know I've been living half-dead for the last few months, hiding like a hermit—too cowardly to show my face. I get it now. I shouldn't have the luxury of escaping my pain by numbing my body and sleeping forever."

"You have to stop punishing yourself at some point. That's what she was trying to tell you."

"Perhaps. But I can't let go. Now, I just gotta go on with my life, knowing I'm responsible for her death. Knowing I lost the most important person in my life because of my selfish needs."

"Dancing is not selfish."

"That day it was. And I have to live with my decision, but at least I know I never have to step foot on a stage again."

"What are you talking about? You're not quitting dance."

"It's too late. Even if I wanted to dance, because of my spinal injuries, doctor said I'd probably never dance again. Not like I used to."

"Christ, Sara. You never told me."

"There was no need. Even if I could, I wouldn't. I lost her because of dance. It would simply be a constant reminder of her loss. Plus, I don't deserve to be happy."

She caught up with me, grabbed me by the shoulder and turned me around to face her. "Honey, you don't mean that, do you? Your mom would never want that."

I shrugged her hand off my shoulder. "She's not here, is she?"

"Sara, don't think like that—"

"Jen, I'm moving on. The best way I can. Please, just let me."

She stared deep in my eyes, understanding washing over her. It was the only way she was going to get her friend back, at least the remnants of my old self. "Okay," she said.

I took a deep breath, silently thanking her for allowing me to deal with my grief the only way I knew how. After a long pause, I said, "Time to call Josh, I guess. I haven't talked to him in days. He must be so worried about me, but I just haven't been ready, you know. I'm so blessed to have him. After all the shit I've put everyone through, he's stuck around. The way I've been treating him…God knows I don't deserve him. But at least he understands."

Jen's gaze dropped.

"What is it?"

She closed her eyes and finally uttered, "Honey, Josh left."

Thirty-Two

SARA

The moment Jen told me Josh had left, my heart was permanently scarred. That day, Jen and I walked the track for hours, stopping often when I broke down into inconsolable sobs. She explained how she and Josh had grown closer since the accident. Their mutual concern for my wellbeing helped them cope with losing me to depression. They would have lunch at least once a week to catch up on things and talk about how I was doing.

The week prior to me finding out he'd left, she'd gone over to his house to pick him up as usual, but his mom answered the door. She told her Josh had left the night before. His mom hadn't known either until she found the note he'd left her, telling her how he needed to get out of town for a while and not to look for him. It wasn't until years later when, through his sister, Jen learned he'd been living in Africa, freelancing as a wildlife photographer. Happily, it seemed.

At the time, though, no one knew what happened to him. The

idea that he would leave me at the lowest part in my life without even saying goodbye put me through a meat grinder.

"Sara," Jen had said, "maybe he didn't want to hurt you anymore. You were already in so much grief."

"So, I'm dying inside because of the loss of my mother and the best decision he makes is to leave me in all this mess—because that's better than actually talking to me about it?"

"Sweetie, he's been hurting too. We all have."

I said nothing.

"He tried talking to you. He visited you practically every day—stood by your side while you slept twenty-four hours a day."

"Then he should have told me it was too much for him."

"Maybe saying goodbye was hard for him."

"He didn't even leave me a note, Jen."

"Look, I'm not trying to defend him. He should have at least said something to you. But you weren't the only one he left in the dark. His mom. Me. We all felt betrayed."

"I'm so stupid."

"Why do you say that?"

"Because love is supposed to transcend everything. Because if there was anything I still believed in, anything that still gave me a little hope, even in my self-induced sleep-coma, was the fact someone still loved me, that maybe not everything was lost.

"You do have people who still love you. What about me?"

"I know, Jen. You've always been my constant. But Josh? He was supposed to be my soulmate. He was supposed to be my happily ever after, 'til the day we died. We promised it to each other. I believed every word. We were going to get married one day, have children..."

Jen reached for me and hugged me tight as the tears spilled from my eyes again. "I'm so sorry, hon. I know it hurts. I wish you didn't have to go through this."

I pulled away from her. "I don't know how I'm going to go on. Without my mom. Without Megan, and now...him?

"Together. I'm still here, remember?"

It was shortly after that day when I decided to move out of my house and in with Jen in the city.

Now, even after all this time, my past was showing its ugly head again. Alexei was making me doubt my choices. Tom was making me want to be in love again.

Dear Lord...

A storm was definitely coming. I just prayed I could survive it.

Trying to get work done while being an emotional mess was nearly impossible. The last thing I needed was to get another speech from those assholes. If I was to leave that place, it was going to be on my terms.

By the end of the day, I was burnt out. I could have stuck needles in my eyes and it would have been less painful than sifting through hundreds of applications. At last, I found a couple of really great dancers who somehow had slipped through the cracks the first time I reviewed their portfolios.

I scheduled them for auditions then zombie walked out of my office.

Finding my apartment absent of my best friend was a relief. Jen didn't need to see me that way. She'd want to comfort me with hugs and ice cream. All I wanted was to be alone.

Skiddles snored away while I lay flat on my bed staring at the ceiling. It had been an hour and my mind wouldn't stop racing. Putting away my clothes and rearranging my closet seemed like a good idea to help keep my mind occupied and away from clouded thoughts. As I reached above my head to retrieve a box of shoes, another much bigger box, slightly tucked behind more clutter, slipped, fell, and bounced off my head before flopping to the floor.

"Shit!" I rubbed the sore spot on my forehead. Organization was not my forte. My stomach lurched when I finally realized what had fallen out of the box. Scattered by my feet were a few articles of clothing I had forgotten still lingered in my closet.

I thought I'd thrown everything out.

Still folded neatly in between random clothes was my favorite pair of knit, purple leg-warmers my mother had given me on my eighteenth birthday. There was also a pair of sling-back half socks, a pair of worn, footless black tights, a nude camisole leotard, and a pink wrap-sweater.

My breath caught in my throat and my heart stopped. I braced myself for what I thought would be another sting to my soul. It should have been like pouring salt into a wound, instead, a soft smile crept to the corners of my mouth. A warm feeling enveloped me, and I stripped off my clothes and suited up. All of it still fit like it did years ago, the fabric soft against my skin.

My eyes widened as I stared in the mirror. I looked like a dancer. My face glowed and my heart leaped. The joy was short-lived. As I regarded myself intently, reality hit. I wasn't a dancer. Not anymore. Not for a long time. What I saw reflected was only a shadow of who I had been and the life I had left behind.

Putting this on was a mistake.

My joy quickly turned to pain, and it dropped me to my knees. The dam inside me broke, and all the sorrow I'd tried to conceal all these years poured out of me without cease. Minutes ticked by, or maybe hours, it didn't matter. My life caved again. I no longer wanted to be alone. All I needed was to be held by someone. I needed someone to tell me it was all going to be okay. That the pain wasn't going to kill me. That I was going to make it through another day.

In between my muffled cries, I heard Jen's soft voice whisper my name, "Sara?"

I couldn't say anything. My hands cradled my sunken face, collecting puddles of hot tears. When I didn't answer, she rushed to my side and knelt beside me, pulling my face up to look at her, tears rolling down the side of my cheeks.

"Oh, honey, what's the matter? What happened?" She searched my eyes for some indication of what occurred. "Sara, why are you crying?"

"Jen..." I struggled to say her name.

"Sara, please. What happened? Why are you dressed like this?" She continued to look at me, trying to understand why I was dressed in my old warmups, crouched on the floor crying hysterically.

"I...I miss her," I moaned. And it was all it took to send me over the edge. I latched onto her in a powerful embrace and cried into her shoulder. "Oh, God, Jen. My mom. I miss her so much."

"Hey, it's all right, sweetie." She hugged me tight. "It's gonna be all right." She held me there, letting me cry until, at last, the waters receded.

Soon after, she had me on the couch drinking a cup of sleepy-time tea.

"No ice cream?"

"I don't think ice cream is going to help this time." She sat next to me, pulling her feet under her legs. "You want to tell me what this is all about?"

"I wasn't ready for all this."

"Tom?"

"I'm falling head over heels for this man. After everything that happened, I really thought happiness was not for me. I really thought I was okay with it. Until...now. I can't imagine not having him, and it scares me to think I could lose it all again."

"It's not everything that's bothering you." She looked me in the eyes, knowing full well I was hiding something from her. Jen always knew the issues with my mother's death went deeper than I let anyone know, but she never pressed. This time, I feared she wouldn't back down.

"Jen, it's complicated."

"I'm tired of you brushing me off. What is really eating you up?"

"Guilt," I barked.

"We've talked about this before, hon. We all experience it one way or another when a loved one passes."

"No, Jen. The guilt I've been carrying goes deeper."

"Tell me."

"I squandered my life, all right?" I placed my cup on the coffee table as I prepared to empty out my cluster of regrets. "Everything she fought for me to have. I know if she knew what I've done, she'd be so disappointed in me." I choked and my eyes began to tear up again. "For what?" I continued. "What did I gain from it? I've been punishing myself, all for nothing. Now? I can't go on living like this anymore. I want Tom in my life. And…"

"And what?"

"I think I want to dance again, Jen." I lowered my head, ashamed of what I was feeling. "I don't think I'm strong enough to stave it off. I'm so angry with myself. This is not how it's supposed to be."

"And just how is it supposed to be? Are you supposed to spend the rest of your life locked up in your room alone? With no one and nothing to bring the light back into your eyes?"

I angrily wiped the wetness from my cheeks. "I swore to myself I'd never set a foot on a stage again. Am I just supposed to forget that?"

Jen scooted closer and wiped my tears. "Why would you even think you had to make such a promise?"

"I swore it to her. My mom. It was all I could do. The only thing I had."

"Why, hon? You think that's what she would have wanted? Her death wasn't your fault. What's done is done. And it's over. Your mother died almost four years ago. You have to stop this self-loathing. Your mother wouldn't want the life you've chosen for yourself. She loved you too much. And now you need to make things right."

"How do I get rid of this guilt?"

"What would she tell you to do?"

I paused to think. My mom's face slowly shone through the storm clouds of my desperation. Her brilliant smile and glowing eyes embraced me with all her love. I looked up at Jen, and with a quivering smile, I said, "She'd tell me to dance it off."

"Well, hon, maybe it's time you listened to her again."

The next morning, I trotted to work ready to embark on my journey to become a new woman, determined to make things right. Auditions went perfect. Thought I might have hit a goldmine actually. Alexei would be a happy man. If the words Alexei and happy could coexist in the same sentence.

Catarina Dimitelos and Francesco Bernardino. She was a Greek Goddess and he an Italian sculpture. Their dancing skills were impeccable and they looked fabulous together, as if they were simply made to be dance partners. It was a match made in heaven. My work was done.

Two hours later, Rebecca tapped on my door, forcing me to lookup from my computer screen.

"You did it." There was an incredulous tone to her voice, the words tasting of venom.

"I take it Alexei approved?" I asked.

"*We* did. Although, we weren't as impressed. Nevertheless, they should do."

Arrogant asses.

"They will make a great addition to the company," I added.

"Oh, dear, that's yet to be seen. They need to survive Alexei's boot camp before we make such claims. And I asked for *four* dancers."

"Be glad you got two. We will need to go on without understudies and pray nothing else goes wrong."

She stared at me in silence, trying to come up with some vile retort. Apparently, nothing came to mind.

"Was there anything else, Rebecca?"

"I assume you are already working on all other details?"

I lifted my gaze off my computer and looked up at her, expressionless.

"I never doubted you," she said through a forced smile.

"There never was a need to," I spat.

She turned and walked away.

After all the dancers and staff left, I stalked to the dark, empty studio. It was late, and the crew tried not to linger past closing unless it was crunch time. Tonight, the expansive space was quiet, and thankfully, all mine. I flicked on the lights. The walls were lined with floor to ceiling mirrors and the hardwood floors gleamed from a recent wax.

I couldn't believe I was actually going through with this. I took a few deep breaths before entering the studio. I paced a hundred times before finally making up my mind. Eventually, I placed my shoulder bag down on an empty chair and slowly took out its contents. I held them in my hands, trembling with fear.

You can do this.

Two minutes later, I stood in front of the wall of mirrors, dressed in clothes that should have felt foreign to me, but now felt as familiar as my own flesh and blood.

I'd been reborn.

This time, to dance again.

Thirty-Three

TOM

Unfortunately, I'd had unfinished business in L.A. and wasn't able to accompany Sara back home. I'd been so bummed about her departure, I didn't even bother going into the office on Monday and just worked from home. When Tuesday morning came, my mind was still a jumbled mess of thoughts, but I couldn't hibernate inside my house any longer. They needed me back for some in-person meetings. Still, no matter how hard I tried concentrating on business, I couldn't stop thinking about her. Images of Sara's soft naked body against the hard planes of my chest pushed the already growing tightness in my groin to a throbbing ache for the warmth nestled between her legs. The wait to see her again was more than I could bear.

"Tom?" Jake's annoyed voice snapped me back to earth.

I'd forgotten he was sitting across from my desk, discussing a recent business dilemma. Absentmindedly, my eyes still swimming with visions of Sara in my bed, I turned to face him. "Sorry, what?"

"You listening to anything I said?"

Raking my hands through my hair, I uttered, "You were saying..." The memories of Sara's naked body quickly dissolved, although the side effects still lingered underneath my dress pants.

"Seriously?" Jake shot back. "What the fuck is wrong with you?"

"It's nothing. What *were* you saying?"

"I was *asking* you if we are going to make an offer or not? If we don't jump on this right now, we are going to lose this property."

"Right..." Slowly, I recalled the conversation. "Not going to pay the asking price if that's what you are implying."

Jake leaned in closer and placed his index finger down on my shiny oak desk. "Look, I know we've talked about this before, and we both agree this property is highly overpriced, but this building is valuable real estate—"

I leaned in as well, meeting his gaze. "Don't doubt it is, but three-and-a-quarter million is more than highly overpriced for a vacant, run-down warehouse."

Jake threw his head back and growled, "There are other interested parties, Tom. This property is not going to be on the market very long."

I shrugged unapologetically. "Don't know what you want me to say. Not paying the asking price. The place is barely worth two mil. We had agreed to negotiate starting at one and that's generous."

Jake ran his hands through his hair, a disgruntled breath escaping his lungs. "For fucks sake, one mil is hardly an offer."

"Other comparable properties exist."

"I've put feelers out there. Possible investors."

"What are you talking about?"

"There's big competition for the next big nightclub. I know a few people ready to write me out a check if I can get the wheel turning. I need this property."

"I know your kind of people. Not interested."

Jake ignored my barb. He knew I didn't approve of his *investors*. Last time he pissed off one of Carlo's cronies, I found Jake bloodied inside his apartment and the place trashed like someone had gone apeshit with a bat.

"If I don't jump on it, someone else will," he continued, his voice charged with anxiety.

It could only mean one thing. I sucked in a slow and heavy breath, hoping to reel in the ire ready to burn through me. "You've already promised him this property."

He dropped his gaze, his jaw muscles twitching.

"Oh, my God, are you fucking crazy?" I slammed my fist down, making the pen laying on my desk bounce.

Jake's gaze darted back up, but before he could answer, Tiffany trotted into my office wearing a red silk blouse tucked neatly inside form fitting black pants. As she made her way from the doorway to my desk, Jake, not bothering to disguise his lascivious gaze, tracked and scanned Tiffany from her red flowing hair down to her six-inch black heels. His stare lingered on her round ass.

She circled around until she stood next to me, nonchalantly bumping her hip against my arm. She placed a file on my desk and asked for my signature. As I drew in to examine the documents, Tiffany tucked a red lock of hair behind her right ear, and placing her hand on my shoulder, she leaned lower and slightly brushed her chest against my body.

Jake couldn't have cared less that Tiffany hadn't greeted him. I stared back at him before placing my pen to the paper and followed his stare to the voluptuous mounds openly visible now that she was bending over my shoulder. The top two buttons of her blouse were undone, revealing a lacy black bra. I would have missed it, but Jake had a way of announcing his thoughts with his bare eyes.

She had a nice pair of knockers, but there were other ways to stare at a woman's tits without making it so damn obvious.

"So…Tiff," Jake started, "have you noticed it, too?"

"Noticed what?" She didn't look at him as she gathered the documents and walked back toward the door.

"Tom's new female friend has turned him into a drooling idiot."

She froze mid-step, then slowly turned to face me.

"Don't listen to him," I said, taking a pen and darting it at Jake.

As I looked back at Tiffany, I noticed she swallowed hard. Shaking her long locks off her shoulders, she said, "You mean you're still playing around with that little brunette?" She tried to sound uninterested but royally failed.

Jake smirked at her with a taunting chuckle. "Oh, Sara is no plaything. At least not anymore. Isn't that right, Tom?"

I shot him a sniper bullet with my eyes.

"Oh?" Tiffany's voice cracked.

"Seems our little playboy has finally found his soulmate."

Tiffany drilled into me with her gaze, trying to find confirmation of Jake's accusations, but I avoided her eyes.

She turned to Jake and tried to hide the sting I knew was pounding in her heart. "Tom has no soulmate. He has no soul, remember?"

"Ouch," Jake uttered, with a laugh.

"It's different now," I said.

Wide-eyed, she whipped her neck toward me. "Oh, how's that?"

"Well, for starters," Jake interrupted, leaning forward on his seat, seemingly jubilant. "She stayed at his place this weekend. Can you believe it?" he scoffed.

Tiffany's eyes spit fire at me as her face flushed. Biting her bottom lip, her voice trembled. "You…brought her to your house in Santa Monica?"

Pissed at Jake for broaching the subject with Tiffany, and annoyed at her reaction, I dismissed them both. "You know what," I said, "this is none of either of your business."

She sucked in a deep breath. "You're right, I'm sorry." Tiffany turned on her heels and stormed out of the office.

Once the door closed behind her, I stood up and stalked toward Jake, intent on snapping his neck. "What the fuck is wrong with you? Why would you tell her that?"

His arrogant grin disappeared, replaced by a defiant stare. "Because she needed to know the truth." Jake rested back on his chair and crossed one leg over his knee, his hands cradling the back of his head.

"I was going to tell her. When I was ready, and not like this."

"Spare me the melodrama," Jake snapped, rolling his blue eyes. "She'll get over it. At least now, she'll finally stop looking at you like you're the only one with a sizable dick around here."

I walked back to my desk. "Since when do you care so much about how Tiffany feels anyway? You're not exactly Mr. Sensitive."

"I care..." he said, sarcasm spewing from his lips.

"Then ask her out on a date." I wasn't being serious.

"My interests are not exactly in...dating her." His sinister smile twitched at the corners of his mouth.

I shook my head. "On second thought, just leave her alone. Take it from me. That kind of relationship doesn't work. It won't end pretty."

"What's the matter, I'm not good enough for your sloppy seconds?"

"Have a bit of decency and stop talking about Tiffany like she's not our friend. I couldn't care less who the fuck you sleep with, just do me a favor and keep it out of the office. I don't need any more drama."

"Yeah, about that..." Jake could barely contain his haughty smirk. Clearly, it was too late for office rules.

"You're a fucking prick."

"Had me a taste of her peachy nipples."

I palmed my face, fed up with his crudeness. "Like I mentioned, I don't care who you fuck, just don't let it interfere with work. There's already enough tension between you two."

"Didn't know the thought of Tiffany fucking another dude would upset you."

"That's not what upsets me and you know it. Now, please, go do some work. Or at least pretend."

"Whatever, man. I'll leave. But don't think I've forgotten about our conversation. I want that warehouse." Jake stood up and left.

After that fiasco, I locked myself in my office, but there was no way for me to focus on work. My veins thrummed with worry. I didn't like being so far away from Sara. My male instincts seemed to be on overdrive. Something was wrong, something she hadn't been willing to share and it unnerved me.

Walking over to the floor-to-ceiling windows behind my desk, I stuck my hands in my pockets and stared out at Los Angeles.

What the hell am I doing trapped in this high-rise office building?

Peeling my gaze from the skyscrapers, I walked back to my desk and pressed on the intercom. "Tiff, do I have any appointments scheduled for the rest of the day?"

"Um, lemme check...just a three o'clock with Mrs. Brentmire."

"Cancel it."

"This appointment has been scheduled for weeks."

"I'm taking the rest of the day off. Route any calls to Jake."

"Is something wrong? Are you sick? Are you going home?"

"Unless it's a dire emergency, let Jake handle it. Can you do that for me?"

"I...um...okay. But what if—"

I let go of the buzzer before she had a chance to finish.

By the time I made it home and parked the Maserati, my body itched to get out of my monkey suit and into a wetsuit instead. An afternoon low tide made for an easy paddle to the Santa Monica Pier. The mix of the warm salty air and the cool calm waters was the best type of therapy to ease my rattled mood.

When I arrived back from the beach, a hot shower seemed to be the last of the medicine I needed to knead my tight muscles. Yet, everywhere I turned, I saw her. In the shower. On my bed. Tangled in my arms.

Shit.

My body tensed. This primal need was unlike anything I'd ever felt. Everything male about me buzzed with desire for Sara. I would have ravaged her if she stood in front of me, naked, mewling, and soaking ready.

Fuck it.

There was no way I could wait until Saturday. No fucking way. I needed to see her and today was already too late. As I walked out of the shower, I quickly threw on a pair of black briefs and gray sweatpants, and did not even bother with a shirt.

My mind was made up. I'd catch the earliest charter back to home. Screw the business meetings. That's why I had a partner. Jake needed to pick up the slack anyway. Needing the sweet sound of her voice, I grabbed my cellphone and strolled into the kitchen as I dialed her number.

"Hello?" Came the soft voice on the other end.

"Hi, baby girl," I said, perhaps a bit too urgently, but unable to control my need to hear her voice.

"Hey, love. Happy you called," she replied.

"Really?"

"Yes, really. I've missed you."

"Me too. You sound better today."

"Yesterday was just a shit day. Alexei has a way of getting under my skin."

"I swear, if he continues to harass you, I'm not gonna be able to stay quiet."

"Babe, I don't need you fighting my battles. I can handle him."

"I'm certain you can handle yourself, but that doesn't mean he doesn't need a beating."

"Can we not talk about Alexei? That man gives me heartburn."

"Fine. Well, I'm anxious to come home and see you. Maybe we can plan something for the weekend."

"I'd actually prefer to just stay in."

"I'm cool with that. We can order in and watch movies all weekend."

"That sounds delightful."

"It's a date then."

I reached for the fridge and pulled out a half gallon of orange juice and was about to take a slug directly from the carton, but thought better of it. I shouldn't have cared. After all, it was my home, my juice. But dammit, I pulled a glass out from out the cabinet and poured myself some OJ.

"Know what I just did?" I asked her.

"What?"

"Poured myself a glass of orange juice."

"Aw, I'm so proud of you."

"Don't mock me. It took a lot of manly courage to abstain from drinking from the carton. In my own house. That's what you do to me."

"Turn you into a Homo sapien?"

"Turn me into a mush for you. A ball of clay for you to mold however you please."

She broke into laughter. "You're such a cornball!"

God, I loved it when she laughed like that. It made my heart melt. It was loud and screechy. She didn't think it was her most attractive quality, but it's what made her distinctly her. I'd live in a cornfield for the rest of my life if only to hear her happy squeals.

"A corny cornball, prancing through a field of corn, holding a bag of popcorn. Get it right," I told her.

We both burst out laughing.

Then the doorbell rang.

"Shit, someone's at the door," I grumbled as my smile faded.

"Are you expecting somebody?"

"Nah. I bet it's Jake. I left the office early today, leaving him in charge. He's been calling me nonstop. Had to turn my cell off for a while. I'm tempted to not answer the door and leave him out there."

"No, Tom. Get the door. You can call me back later."

"Hold on, I'm gonna tell him to fuck off. He's been an intolerable prick lately." I stalked to the door ready to tell Jake to leave, but when I yanked it open, the hairs on the back of my neck stood up. "Ah...Sara, I'm gonna have to call you back."

Standing at my door, dressed in a floor-length turquoise, spaghetti-strap dress with a plunging neck line, was Tiffany. I stared, speechless and confused, nearly dropping the phone.

"Well," she said, "aren't you going to invite me in?"

She didn't wait for a formal welcome.

Thirty-Four

TOM

Her hair smelled freshly washed and citrusy, but the intrusion of her scent in my home left a sour taste in my mouth. She caught me completely off guard. I was annoyed, pissed even, Tiffany had showed up unannounced. She knew how particular I felt about visitors, especially women I'd been intimate with. Holding onto the doorknob, I remained like a statue on my front door. I wasn't certain I wanted to close it. Wasn't sure I should be under the same roof with this woman.

"I could never get tired of this view, Tom," she said as she strolled through my foyer, passing the kitchen and walking into the living room. She entered with an air of familiarity, as if she felt she belonged in my house.

With a sigh of resignation, I closed the door and followed behind her.

She laid her purse down on the brown leather couch and stood in the middle of the room. She turned from the ocean views and plastered her wistful gaze on me, eyeing my naked chest with a suggestive smile, pleading with me for a reciprocal response. My spine tightened, the voracious look in her eyes sent me off kilter.

Although we had grown accustomed to volleying flirtatious innuendos, always smiling at secret jokes and even entertaining playful—and perhaps at times inappropriate—touching, it had been a very long time since we'd flirted with true intention, and even longer since we'd acted on impulse. The intensity of her penetrating gaze made me struggle to make eye contact, and with sweat beading down my back, I yearned for a second shower.

She'd suited up in full sensual armor. The flames in her hair were combed into curvy waves, and her white porcelain-like skin glowed against the bold contrast of her turquoise dress. Harder to ignore were her braless breasts jiggling to their own tune as she walked. Luckily for me, I'd mastered the art of noticing without noticing. The old me might have felt my cock rise to the invitation just thinking about her large chest. Tonight, the only fevered blood running through my veins was the one rising to the surface of my face.

I crossed my arms. "I thought I was clear about giving everything work related to Jake."

"Um, this isn't about work," she replied coyly.

I clenched my jaw and swallowed hard. "Then it could have waited 'til tomorrow."

Her eyes widened with shock. If the brashness of my voice wasn't enough to warn her of my irritation, the tension in my face and body made it crystal clear her visit wasn't welcomed.

She frowned then looked away.

If it had nothing to do with work, I could only guess why she was here.

Jake.

Fucking dickhead.

His callous comments earlier in the day probably still percolated in her brain, especially since I'd told her numerous times when we were fucking I would never fall in love. She'd accepted it, resigned to the fact I was damaged goods, and that much to her dismay, she could never fix me.

Then Sara happened. Now, Tiffany wanted answers.

"Tiff," I said, "coming here wasn't a good idea."

She turned, but as soon as we locked eyes, she began to cry.

Ah, fuck.

Thank you, Jake. Much appreciated, buddy.

I didn't need this melodrama. Then again, I couldn't ignore the fact it was my fault she was here. I'd screwed with her head and her heart. Even though I presumed we had ended our arrangement before she could get hurt, deep inside I'd known it was too late. She'd been head-over-heels for me, and I, well, I'd simply been a prick.

With a sigh, I dropped my arms and planted my hands on my waist. "Don't do this."

She turned to face the beach behind the glass doors. "Tom... why?" she finally asked.

Here we go.

She walked over to the balcony doors and stared out to the frothy ocean. "Why didn't you ever ask me to stay here with you?"

I said nothing.

"The only time you even invited me here was after you bought the house and you had the team over to celebrate. That night, I sat on the balcony, imagining what it would be like to sit here with you at dusk, holding hands." She turned to face me once more, but this time, when her eyes met mine, she dug into me, silently demanding an answer she knew she didn't want to hear. When I said nothing, she continued her reproach. "I don't understand. I did everything right. Everything you wanted. I only longed to make you happy, but it wasn't enough."

"I don't know what you want me to say. You knew my rules."

Her eyes narrowed over me, blazing with fury. "Fuck your rules, Tom. What about Sara, hmm? The rules don't apply to her?"

I swallowed hard. Sara made me break all my rules, and I was still trying to figure out how. "Things are different now."

Tiffany's body shook, her hands clenched to her sides. "Different how? What does she have that I don't?"

I didn't know how to answer her. Falling in love hadn't been in my plans. When I broke it off with Tiffany, she'd been cool about it. She'd pretended, at least. Knowing this type of outburst would simply push me further away from her, she'd accepted we were better off as friends—without the benefits. It was clear now that she'd bottled it all up.

I didn't want to see her cry, so I grabbed her by the shoulders, pressed her to my chest, and hugged her. I cared for Tiffany. She was a great girl and an amazing friend. I should have never dragged her into my mess. I knew it was a mistake from the first night we spent together. Back then, she'd been hard to resist. Tiffany was a drop-dead gorgeous redhead with curves in all the right places. I'd lusted after her cream-colored skin from the moment she stepped into my office for an interview.

The first thing that caught my eyes as she strolled in was her blood-red, heart-shaped lips. She moistened them as she reached over my desk to shake my hand, a glint of satisfaction shone in her eyes as she watched my wide-eyed approval of her beauty. She must have been wearing a figure-hugging dress. I couldn't even remember. Keeping my eyes focused on her face and away from her perfectly round and naturally large breasts was an arduous task, even for my experienced gaze.

As she'd sat down and crossed her long legs, her hands folded at her lap in a professional manner, waiting for her interview to start, I drew a blank. The last thing on my mind was offering her a job. My primitive instincts already had her undressed and bent over my desk. With my dick throbbing in my pants, concentrating on business was nearly impossible. After a few moments of awkward pleasantries, we got the interview underway. Needless to say, she got the job and became my personal assistant. Tiffany was very confident in her assets and she skillfully used them to her advantage that day.

Her resume was good too, of course.

A week later, she lay naked next to me in a hotel room. She was amazing when it came to fucking, and I indulged my hungry cock to the hilt. Yeah, it was unprofessional, but she didn't hide her attraction to me and I certainly didn't intend to ignore it. I wasn't proud of my ways, but I wasn't about to make apologies for them either. It was a mutual arrangement, and I'd specifically laid out my rules to her. I simply didn't do the relationship thing. Then one night, after messing around, she told me she loved me.

It was a slip—so she said—but it was enough to knock some sense into me. I liked Tiffany. We worked well together, had fun when we hung out, and when we fucked, well, we fucked, but that was it. I looked into her green eyes that night, and I felt nothing. I didn't love her, and it hurt me to know I would crush her heart. Other women, I couldn't care less what they thought of me when I walked out of their lives. But Tiff?

I couldn't do that to her. It was the reason I usually tried not to mix business with pleasure. Before Tiffany, I'd never fucked one of my employees. Especially since the women I usually messed with were in an out of my life fairly quickly. I'd gotten to know Tiffany very intimately, not just physically. As my personal assistant, she accompanied me everywhere, including my business trips. I became very familiar with her background, why she'd come to New York from Los Angeles, the money struggles with her family, and her burden with her drug-addicted brother.

If we continued on that path, it was only going to end in heartbreak for her, and she didn't need any more pain. She agreed and said she'd rather preserve our friendship than end up resentful and hating me. She said she appreciated my honesty, but the gloom in her eyes told me that, despite my efforts to save her heart, I had already shattered it.

Holding her in my arms now, all I felt was guilt. I should have never let our relationship go beyond the office.

I guided her toward the couch and asked her to sit. My chest was wet from her tears. As she looked up at me, she wiped her eyes and sniffed.

"Tiff," I said, tucking a loose strand of hair behind her ear, "what we had was fun while it lasted. I told you then and I'll tell you now. I wasn't ready to start a relationship. I couldn't give you what you needed from me."

She pinned me with sodden eyes. "And you are ready now?"

"Things are different now."

"You keep saying that," she snapped, pushing away. "But I don't get it. What did I do wrong? I was ready to give you my heart, but you said you could never fall in love. Then Sara comes along and you offer her your home, the one place you said you'd never bring women? I'm confused. I guess it wasn't that you could never fall in love. You just couldn't fall in love with me. Is that it?"

"I didn't plan this."

"So, what now? You are finally ready to give someone your heart?"

I dropped my gaze, shamefully hoping what I was about to tell her wouldn't wound her even deeper. "I already have."

Her lips sucked in a small gasp of air. She held it a few seconds before she breathed again. I knew it wasn't what she wanted to hear, but it was the truth and I couldn't lie about it.

Not to Tiffany and not to anybody.

I pulled away and stood.

Eyes damp with tears, she gazed up at me.

"Look," I said, "no matter what, we'll always be friends. I was about to make dinner, if you want to join me?"

~

I worked on the skillet while Tiffany sat on a barstool watching me cook.

"It smells delicious," she said, sniffing the air. "You were always such a great chef. I could have lit scented candles in my apartment, but I preferred the smell of garlic and herbs. It always lingered even after dinner and after, well, after you left me in my bed, happy as a kitten full on milk."

I smiled, knowing she was trying to bait me. If she only knew the memory of us together in bed didn't summon lewd thoughts of her. It only made me miss Sara. "Hope you're hungry," I said as I poured us each a full plate of linguini in clam sauce. Grilled scallops also made the menu for the evening.

"Tom, this looks amazing. Can't wait to dig in."

I nodded in the direction of the wine fridge below the kitchen counter as I took our dishes and walked toward the balcony. "Grab some wine and meet me outside."

Tiffany jumped off the stool, picked up a bottle of Sauvignon Blanc and skipped out behind me.

As I finished my meal, I glanced at Tiffany's plate.

"Well, I'm stuffed," she said.

I motioned at her dinner, an eyebrow raised. "You barely ate."

"I have a small stomach. You know that. It was delish, though. Love your cooking." She ran her hands through her long red locks several times, cocking her head to the side and flashing me her perfect smile before bursting into an exaggerated laugh. It was the boisterous side of her she wasn't shy to expose once she'd poured alcohol into her system.

I forced a tight grin and pressed two fingers to my temple. It could have been the wine giving her back some confidence, but I knew her too well, and I had a hard time buying it. I blew out a long breath and tried to avoid making eye contact. The woman shamelessly tried to flirt with me, and I had no patience for it. I was not interested in her advances, and she, more than anyone, should've remembered once I was done with something—or someone—there was no going back.

As I stood and gathered the dishes, she leaned forward on the table and rested her chest over her folded arms, practically pushing her breasts out of her low-cut dress. She blinked softly as she brought the glass of wine to her lips and took a shallow drink. "C'mon, we can clean up later," she uttered in a raspy voice, winking and smiling at me.

I pretended I didn't notice the desperate cleavage tactic, and completely ignored the hidden message behind her words. The trick might have worked in the past, but these days my cock hardened for another woman. Did she really think she'd get me to drop my pants simply because she showed me some skin? She could have taken off her dress and stood stark naked in front of me, it wouldn't have mattered. I *could* control my cock—except when it came to Sara. That woman was a whole different ballgame.

Yawing and rubbing my hands together, I said, "It's late. Let's call it a night."

She blinked quickly and looked away. "Oh..." She stood up, her gaze avoiding mine, and tried to walk back into the house, but stumbled as she knocked into the table.

I grabbed her by the arm to keep her from falling. "Are you okay?"

"I'm fine," she shot back as she yanked her arm away. "I'll see myself out." She zigzagged through my living room, trying to make her way to the front door.

Fucking perfect.

I slid a palm down my face. I had a scorned, drunk-off-her-ass woman in my house—because I needed that shit. What was I supposed to do, let her drive back to the hotel when she couldn't even walk straight? "Tiff, you're not going anywhere."

She perked up at the sound of my words and turned around, a gentle smile on her lips. Part of me wondered if this had been her plan all along. "You can sleep off the alcohol in my guest room upstairs."

I shouldn't have let her drink so much wine. And I probably should've just driven her home and taken a cab back.

~

After phoning Sara, I undressed and lay in my bed. A wide smile stretched across my lips. Wanting to surprise her, I didn't tell her about my plan to come back home early. I couldn't wait to see the look in her deep chocolate eyes when she saw me.

Unfortunately, having to wait until the following day to fly did mean I'd have to spend one more night sleeping in my bed alone.

Alone.

Shit, this means I might have an episode again.

A few months back, the nightmares started up once more, only showing up sporadically, but always with a vengeance. They had become more intense and vivid. The terror I felt in these dreams was agonizing, violently bolting me awake. Yet, I hadn't experienced one since I met Sara.

That is until two nights ago when she left.

I closed my eyes and prayed for peace.

How long will the ghosts continue to haunt me?

How long will I have to carry the guilt?

I failed my team. My comrades. My friends. My brothers.

They were all dead now.

Because of me. Because I failed to pull the trigger.

I sat up and planted my feet flat on the floor. Anxiety ripped through my body. I was petrified to relive that moment and see their burning faces, hear the bone-shattering cries. I stretched my neck and rubbed my shoulders as I walked to the bathroom and opened up the medicine cabinet. I hated taking the pills; didn't want to be a slave to them. My pride drove me to think I could recover on my own, not wanting to admit my own weakness, but it had begun to take a toll.

I wanted to rest.

Needed it.

I opened up the bottle and poured a white pill onto my palm, letting it sit there for a long time before picking it up and holding it between my index finger and thumb.

Shit.

I simply couldn't do it. A part of me still believed I deserved the nightmares. The pain kept their memory alive. It was my duty to honor it even if it meant losing my sanity.

I flushed the pill down the toilet and went back to bed.

Thirty-Five

TOM

I JUMPED OUT OF BED IN A DAZE, HANDS SHAKING, BODY still pulsing with pure adrenaline, and soaked in a cold sweat. I shook my head, trying to understand what was happening. A fog trapped me, my senses flooded with images of war and gore. My gaze darted around the room as I struggled to regain my bearings. Amongst the muffled sounds of screams and gun fire still ringing in my ears, I heard the strained moans of a woman.

Slowly, the fog cleared and all other sounds, but the female coughing, drowned out. When my vision finally focused, all I saw was Tiffany lying naked on my bed, curved into a ball, clutching her chest and grasping her throat.

"Tiffany?"

She didn't respond

I ran to her side. "Shit. Tiff? What's the matter? Are you okay? What happened?"

She coughed some more, releasing her grasp on her throat. Red marks lined her neck, some already turning blue. I rushed over to my nightstand where I'd left a glass of water and handed it to her. "Here, drink this."

She took the glass and gulped.

Finding my sweatpants lying on the floor, I quickly dressed, but not before noticing a bathrobe at the foot of my bed.

What the...

Then it hit me, why she was laying naked on my bed, grasping her neck. I grabbed the robe and threw it at her. "Cover up," I said as I walked toward the balcony. The cold air welcomed me, cooling the anger blazing inside my chest.

A moment later, Tiffany joined me.

I stared at the ink-stained sky, fighting not to snap. "What were you doing in my room, Tiffany?"

"Tom...I'm sorry." She began to whimper.

With my back turned to her, my jaw clenched. "Again. What were you doing?"

"I snuck into your room earlier while you slept."

I swirled around, eyes flaming with outrage. "What in God's name possessed you to do that?"

She looked down at her clasped hands, tears running down her cheeks. "I wanted to be with you."

"I almost killed you!"

She looked back up, panic streaking her eyes. "Nobody has to know. I won't say anything, I promise. It was an accident. You didn't know what you were doing."

I shook my head and pinched the bridge of my nose. "Tiff, I almost fucking killed you. You understand how grave that is?"

"It was my fault. I shouldn't have tried to...It was stupid of me, I know."

My insides coiled, tightening in my stomach with consternation at her foolishness. "Stupid doesn't even begin to explain what you did. Christ, Tiff, any longer and I could have—" I paused. "Why? You knew about my past."

"Tom, please. I didn't know you still had the nightmares or I wouldn't have—"

"What did you think was going to happen in there? That I'd forget I'm with someone else?"

"You asked me to stay, I thought maybe—"

"What I should've done was drive you back to your hotel."

"Why? So, you can keep denying what we have?"

I paced. "Christ. Listen to what you're saying. This is why things would never work out between us. You are stuck in your own little delusional universe. Oblivious. You can't stand that I actually let someone else into my life." I scoffed. "Your so-called love for me didn't spring up until you heard about Sara. I mean, weren't you just fucking Jake up until a few weeks ago?"

Her eyes widened at the revelation. "Jake means nothing to me. You have to believe that."

"Tiffany, I don't care who the fuck you sleep with. I'm done with this conversation and I'm done with you." I stalked back inside my room, barely missing knocking her over.

She ran in after me.

Sitting at the edge of my bed, I held my head in my hands, my body raging with anger.

Tiffany knelt down in front of me, tears still streaming down her face. "I'm so sorry. I don't know what went through my mind. I guess...I thought coming here tonight might remind you of the good times we shared. If we had one more moment...If you remembered how good we felt together, maybe, you'd forget about her."

"I'm in love with Sara. Accept it and move on." I stood and walked away.

"I'm not giving up on us!"

"I want you out of my house immediately. Get dressed. I will call you an Uber."

"I drove the company car here."

"I'll arrange for someone to pick it up. Right now, I just want you gone. And don't bother showing up for work tomorrow."

"You're firing me?"

"I'm telling you to take the day off, Tiffany. Now leave."

She lowered her gaze and stomped out of my room.

Thirty-Six

TOM

By three p.m. the next day, I realized coming in to work had been a waste of time. The night replayed inside my head and every time I arrived at the moment where I almost choked Tiffany, my insides twisted with fear.

I closed my eyes and shuddered.

It could have been Sara.

I gathered my things and prepared to leave. My flight wasn't departing for Teterboro for several more hours, but I wanted an early start, anything to keep my mind from spinning nightmares.

What the hell was I thinking last night?

Out of nowhere, Tiffany barged through my door and slammed it closed.

Speak of the devil.

The red scarf around her neck highlighted the thoughts I'd been attempting to shake out of my mind.

"I heard you're leaving. What's going on?" she demanded.

I didn't look up at her and continued to stuff my briefcase with documents. "I thought I told you to stay home today."

"Yeah, well, I didn't."

Reaching for the mouse, I closed down window screens on my laptop. "I'm leaving for Jersey."

She approached closer, the scent of her musky perfume assaulting my nose as she neared my desk. "Stop pretending you're doing something important and look at me. Why didn't I know about this sooner?"

I lifted my gaze from the computer and met her eyes with a cold stare. "It was a last-minute decision. And, well, as you are no longer my personal assistant, I didn't see the need to inform you of my itinerary." I looked away, dismissing her wide-eyed reaction as I shut down my laptop.

She placed her hands on my desk. "What are you talking about?"

I looked at her stiff fingers pressed down on the oak tabletop then peered up at her face. "You've been reassigned as office manager for this location."

Stumped, she shook her head in disbelief. "Greg's already the office manager."

An exasperated breath escaped my lungs as I rubbed a hand down my face. "Greg is my new personal assistant, and it seems he will need training regarding visitors into my office. If you'll excuse me, I'm in a hurry." I packed my laptop and reached for my suit jacket.

"You can't do this to me."

"Sure, I can," I replied coolly.

"Tom, why are you leaving? Is it because of me? Because of what happened last night?"

I shook my head as I put on my jacket. "Me leaving has nothing to do with you. Your reassignment, however, that's a different story."

"You can't reassign me here."

I slammed my briefcase on the desk; the sound making her jerk back. "After the stunt you pulled last night, you are lucky I didn't fire your ass."

"What about my apartment in New York?"

"Sell it. Stay at your L.A. hotel as long as you need. Until you find a new place here. Greg can assist you with the details later."

"My friends? My life?"

"I don't know what to tell you, and frankly, I don't care what you have to do to get your life together." I grabbed my briefcase and walked around the desk to leave.

She reached for my arm as I passed her on my way out the door. "I won't let you do this to me."

My eyes froze over her gripping hand. "Accept the relocation or consider yourself terminated from this company." Raising my eyes to meet hers, the stern look forced her to let go of my arm. Then I walked out.

After boarding my private charter, I plopped down into my seat. My body pulsed with uncomfortable energy. Telling Sara about what happened with Tiffany didn't sound like a bright idea, but I'd promised her I'd never lie. I had no clue how she'd handle the news.

Trying to shake the nerves, I raked my hands through my hair a thousand times. The flight attendant strolled by my seat holding a tray of scotch and tumblers. My mouth felt like ash all of a sudden and my fingers trembled.

Not again.

I'd been able to keep the illness under control. Aside from Jake who knew about my troubled past, no one guessed I still battled with alcoholism. Masking the problem hadn't been difficult; always pouring myself a glass of wine at dinner, holding a drink in my hand at parties. No one cared or noticed the liquid never entered my mouth. It took a hard level of self-control, but I'd mastered it. Everything had been fine.

Until now.

Forgetting about the acid churning inside my stomach, I rested my head back and focused on Sara's brown eyes and her soft smile. Soon she'd be wrapped in my arms and I would feel at home and at peace.

Soon.

Thirty-Seven

SARA

As I flicked the dance studio lights on, the room sparkled to life. It was Wednesday and my second night there—alone. The first night hadn't gone quite as I'd expected. I'd foolishly hoped that by simply strapping on my old dance warmups, I would glide through the dance floor, twirling, bending, and rolling as if I never stepped off the stage. Yeah, well, I should have known better. Reality hit me hard when I tried my first leap and fell flat on my ass. Luckily, it hadn't been my face.

I deserved it.

Years of training taught me that even a couple of weeks, or just days, without dancing or working my muscles, affected my ability to move. Seemed four years absent of dance hadn't only affected my skills, but also my brain.

Even after rigorous stretching, I was stiff as a board. I had no depth of reach, no straight lines. Aghast, I stared at my winded and sweaty self in the wall mirror and nearly wept. Defeat was not something I took lightly, and right about then, I was feeling pretty beaten. Yep, I was no longer the polished dancer who took people's breath away.

Once upon a time, I could dance with my eyes closed.

Now look at me.

I wasn't completely delusional. I knew my skills weren't going to make a comeback out of nowhere. Still, the harsh reality of how badly out of shape I was broke my morale. Crushed it. All my years of training lay by the wayside. I'd been reduced to a beginner. It was a brutal truth that ripped through my soul.

I was beyond rusty.

I was appalling.

Last night, I'd grabbed my things and stormed out of there, ready to give up again.

Tonight, I was determined not to. Fierce determination coursed through my blood. I wasn't doing this for me. It was for my mom. Last night had been about reminiscing, but this was the start of something different, and I refused to be weighed down by my past.

As it'd always been, I began by focusing on my reflection.

Wearing black, form-fitting stretch shorts and matching midriff shirt, I imagined a new routine forming behind me. I saw a specter of myself, gliding across the dance floor. A pirouette here, a grand jeté there, maybe even a pas de chat. I carefully calculated and recorded every movement to memory until it felt as real as if I had danced it. I plugged the headphones into my ears and let the routine take over my body.

The long stretches helped, but they hadn't been enough. My legs no longer reached beyond my waistline. Pointing my toes triggered constricting tentacles around my calves, excruciating cramps that dropped me to the floor in seconds. The imagined routine dissolved into a discombobulated mess. I felt the music in my veins. I heard the beats pumping with my heart. I knew what I wanted to do, but my body simply did not respond.

The perfectionist in me couldn't handle the failure. I didn't want to do something unless I knew I could excel at it. Dancing had been no different than breathing. I'd never struggled so much to accomplish one roll. Everything now took too much effort.

Maybe it's too late for me.

After several more floundering attempts at a weightless land from a leap, I called it a night. My ass was bruised and my legs were sore. Tomorrow would be another day. I threw my sweat suit over my dance clothes, grabbed my bag, and left.

Before shutting off the lights, a chill ran down my spine. A shadow moved and disappeared through the back door of the studio. My blood iced. Rather than go inspect, I exited the studio through the entrance behind me and hurried home.

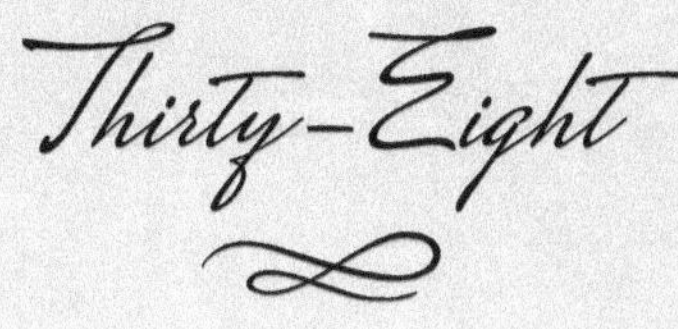

TOM

Somewhere in the Midwest, due to severe weather, my flight made an emergency landing. According to the flight crew, we would be delayed until Thursday morning.

Nothing was going according to plan. The memory of Sara's touch and the soothing feeling of her soft fingers on my skin placated the tension in my chest. The thought of tasting her rose-colored lips was enough to make my head spin. And her eyes, the way she lit up when she looked up at me, hell, I could die after one glance.

Just one more night in some random city, in some lonely hotel room.

I could do this. I hoped.

Thirty-Nine

SARA

I spoke to Tom later that evening. I wished nothing more than to tell him about my day and how the last two nights had been so frustrating my hair was falling out. How could I explain why I never told him anything about my past as a dancer? I'd had several opportunities to confide in him, to share my deepest secrets, and I'd chosen silence.

There was no way I'd be able to keep doing this without it blowing up in my face. It was a matter of finding the right moment. Perhaps when he returned that weekend I'd finally lay it all out?

When I woke up Thursday morning, I was so sore my ribs ached with every breath. Still, I was not about to let a little pain stop me. I was going to hit the studio again and again until I finally got it right. The pep talk did little to push my body out of bed. I struggled to even open my eyes. The sun shining with a vengeance through the tall windows didn't help. Eyelids partially glued shut, I managed to maneuver out of bed and slowly walked into the kitchen still wearing my boy-short pajamas.

Jen looked me over as she packed her lunch. "You look like someone beat you with a stick."

I flinched as I gently placed my tender gluteus on the kitchen stool. "I'd forgotten how unforgiving hardwood floors can be."

"You didn't wake up one day with the grace of a swan, you know. You worked your butt off for many years. It's gonna take time to bounce back. You should take it easy. Stop pushing yourself so hard so soon."

I exhaled deeply, grabbing my throbbing side as I breathed, wincing. "I didn't get to where I was by slacking either. I drove myself to the ground. Sore or not, I practiced every single day. I have to keep that mentality if I'm to go anywhere with this."

"And exactly where is it you want to go with this?"

"Don't know. Back then, becoming a famous dancer was it. Everything was geared toward one goal. Now? Who knows if I'm even good enough—don't know if it even holds the same appeal. It used to be about accomplishing something grand, about making it all the way to the top, as far as I could possibly reach. Things were so much different. I had dance and I had Josh. We had a life planned. Marriage, children. The white picket fence.

"After the accident, I lost all sense of direction, goals, purpose. It wasn't just the loss of my mother or never dancing again. Everything dissolved. I've been walking around for the last few years with no purpose whatsoever. Getting up every day and going to work—that's been my life."

I slowly slid off the stood and gently walked to the couch, my thighs burning as my worn muscles flexed to sit. "Oh...that feels better," I said as the soft cushions welcomed my bum. "With Tom," I continued, "there's brief glimpses of faraway fantasies where maybe I could have a happily ever after. I don't know if he even pictures us having a life together. And what about dance? Where does it fit into the picture?" I looked at her, hoping to find the answers in her eyes.

All I saw was ambivalence reflected back at me. When she said nothing, I dropped my gaze. "Why am I pushing myself so hard? I have no audition to prep for, no dance school I'm trying to impress, no show to rehearse for, or future to work toward. I still have no purpose." I rested my head back in silent desperation.

She stopped packing her bag and walked over, sitting next to me. "Sara, so what if you can't pick up where you left off," she began as she placed a hand on my shoulder. "Life changes and we have to change with it, even if we don't want to. You are a different person now and it's okay for your dreams to be different also, but it doesn't mean there is no room for your passions. God knows where this may lead. Tom, you. Picking up dance again. Who cares? It's not about the destination. It's about the trip there. The journey is what matters."

I raised my head, hiking an eyebrow as I looked at her. She loved to use clichés. As annoying as it was, I loved her for it. She always managed to be my voice of reason, regardless how corny it was. "I know it's about the journey, it's just that..."

"Don't worry about how hard you have to push yourself," she said. "Look, the beautiful thing is, you don't have an audition; you don't have the stress of impressing some school or being in a show. You can do this at your own pace, on your time, and you don't have to do it for anyone but you."

"I have to do it for my mom."

"Your mom would want you to do it because you love it. Because it's what makes you happy."

"What about Tom?" I lowered my gaze, thinking about his reaction.

"Why wouldn't he support you?"

"He doesn't know...anything." Hopelessness tightened around my heart as I thought about how I should have confided in him sooner.

"Then, it's time." She kissed the top of my head and gave me a big hug. "Promise me you will do the right thing."

I nodded. It was the closest thing to a promise.

Forty

SARA

I should have listened to Jen's advice and taken it slow; allowed my muscles to heal, but I was stubborn, even when my body clamored for mercy. I took some ibuprofen, and a couple of hours later, I was able to walk around without wincing. After everyone had gone home for the night, I finally had the studio all to myself.

Fall after fall, I got up and pushed myself harder until I had no more to give. "Shit!" I ripped off my headphones and fiercely flung them across the room. Frustration took the best of me. I tried practicing without music. I concentrated on the counts. I shouted them one by one, hoping my body would somehow respond better.

Nothing.

It was simply another fall and countless bruises. I growled out my desperation, completely agitated and ready to cry when a familiar voice echoed through the studio. "You're thinking too much," the voice said in a thick Russian accent.

I pivoted toward the back of the room. "Alexei?"

There he was, leaning his lithe body against the doorframe. Dressed in his black button-down shirt and trousers, his coal-colored eyes scrutinized me.

"What are you doing here?" I asked.

"Your problem, Miss Hart, is your brain. You're letting it do all the dancing." He walked toward me, his movements smooth and fluidic; a snake dancing in trance.

I stared at him in disbelief.

Oh, God, how long has he been standing there?

He stalked closer. "I guess our little talk motivated you?" He eyed me greedily from head to toe.

I wiped sweat off my brow with the back of my hand. "So, that was you the other day, lurking in the shadows?"

He clasped his hands behind his back as he walked a slow circle around me in some type of authoritative manor. It forced me to rotate along with him. "I was intrigued," he started. "You. Rehearsing in my studio after hours? You can imagine why I couldn't walk away."

"I didn't invite an audience."

He ignored my comment. "The first night was awful," he uttered, shaking his head, a sardonic grin pulling at the corners of his mouth. "Your lines were hideous, your movement stiff, and the complete lack of coordination..." His eyes rolled to the back of his head.

"I didn't ask for your critique, Alexei," I retorted, embarrassed he had witnessed my shameful comeback.

Alexei. Out of all people.

I wanted to pick up my things and go hide under a rock somewhere. I couldn't stand the prick, but I respected his talent and his professional opinion. I sucked. I knew it. But to hear it from the lips of that arrogant ass? I wanted to disappear.

It was a sucker punch to the chest. He was right, though. I was atrocious and probably an unfathomable idiot for even trying. As I turned to grab my things, he said, "I'm sorry. I shouldn't have spied on you."

I froze and peered up at him, unable to hide the disbelief blazoned across my face.

"I was curious," he said.

I scoffed as I slid into my sweat suit and pulled the hood over my head. "Nothing much to see. Sorry to disappoint."

"You're wrong, Miss Hart '"

"Sara is fine."

"Sara, I can help you."

My brows fixed into an exaggerated pinch. "Excuse me?"

"I have your routine memorized. It's simple, but has great potential. First, you need to stop letting your brain dictate your movement. Second, you need a partner."

"Counting is how we learn steps."

He threw his hands up in the air and blew out a strong breath. "Counting. Counting. You dancers can be infuriating. Yes, it's important, but you need to dance from the heart before you can focus on choreographing a routine. You need to get your body used to movement. You need to let your body feel the music and let the muscles do the dancing, not your brain."

"I haven't danced in four years. I'm out of shape. You can't expect me to jump back in the game like nothing happened."

"I didn't expect anything, Sara. I especially didn't expect to find you here two nights ago. Let me help you. Technique can make you really good, but raw talent is what separates the good from the great."

"Why do you care?"

"Do you want my help or not?"

Perhaps it was my desire to dance again and to be good at it that had me second guessing my own intuition. Something told me it wouldn't be a good idea. Alexei was a cold man. He could be hostile and toxic.

What could he possibly offer me?

I repeated the phrase in my head, trying to convince myself the decision I was about to make was a good one. I placed my gym bag back on the floor. "I don't know if this is a good idea."

He cocked an eyebrow with amusement. "How about you let me show you what I can do for you right now?"

"Now?"

"You're warmed up."

"I...don't know." I was reluctant, but not entirely opposed to the idea. The fact that I was even considering this repulsed me. I hated this man. He was abusive. He'd practically coerced Estella into having sex with him, yet there I was, about to accept his proposition to dance with him. About to let him coach me. What was wrong with me?

"Sara, let me help you. Here." He reached for my hand and brought me close to him. I didn't resist. We stood face to face, our noses inches from touching. "Your routine needs the support of a partner. The lifts will complete the missing pieces; my strength will provide you with stability." A shimmery sparkle rippled across the dark pools of his eyes. A partner *would* make things easier, and Alexei was offering me what I desperately needed.

A nervous string rode the length of my spine as I walked to the stereo system and hit play. Was I really that desperate that I was willing to forget everything this man had done all for the sake of getting a semblance of who I used to be back? I stripped off my sweat suit as the song that had been burning in my ears for the last couple of days now piped through the speakers in the studio. Swallowing hard, I convinced myself that I was doing this because I needed a stepping stone and if I was going to step on someone to get to the top, why not Alexei?

"I'll give you what you need out of this routine, Sara. Let the song and the emotions behind it guide your movement. Let me handle the rest."

Alexei guided me through every chord. He held me when I needed to reach beyond my means and lifted me up when I needed to soar. He added dimension to the piece, investing himself completely into the song, the lyrics, and emotion. I did not count a single step or thought about what came next. The music moved me and we were free.

I descended from a lift while Alexei held me up under the arms. I reached high above as I slowly slid down his chest. Our eyes met as I touched the floor. The piece ended with me in Alexei's embrace. We were both slightly winded. Breathing deeply, our gazes stayed glued to each other. For a short moment, I didn't see the stern-faced Russian who prowled our hallways with a heart of stone, but a man filled with vitality. His love for dance was every bit as infused with passion as was mine. We would never see eye to eye on everything, but this, dance, was our common ground. I smiled briefly, but before he could return the gesture, we were interrupted by the sound of hands clapping.

Startled, we both turned toward the sound.

Sitting on a folding chair, in the back of the studio, was a man bathed in darkness. He stood and walked out into the light, still clapping.

As soon as I recognized his face, my heart turned into a lead ball that free fell into the pit of my stomach.

Forty-One

SARA

"Bravo," Tom said. The sarcasm in his voice was all too palpable. He walked toward Alexei and me until he was merely a couple of feet away. "You two looked great. I'm no expert, but that was fascinating to watch." He turned to lock gazes with me. "Interesting though, Sara, how well you danced. I mean, given you're not a dancer." He grinned, yet his eyes remained impassive.

"And who might you be?" Alexei asked, almost defensively.

"How rude of me," Tom replied, looking back at Alexei. He reached his hand across to the Russian. They shook hands. Firmly. "I'm Tom, Sara's boyfriend."

Alexei sensed the heated tension. We'd both been so startled by Tom's impromptu appearance that we hadn't realized we were still standing close. Tom's scrutinizing gaze didn't alleviate the situation.

"I'm Alexei, the company's choreographer." He stepped away from me, releasing some of the uncomfortable intimacy left behind from the dance. "I'll leave you two alone." Alexei walked out of the studio, leaving an eerie silence behind.

This was life blowing up in my face as I'd feared it.

I swallowed hard. I still couldn't put together the words that could possibly begin to explain what Tom had just witnessed or why I had lied.

Tom crossed his arms as he settled a steely gaze over me. "So, care to elaborate?" His voice scraped like sandpaper against my skin.

"Aren't you supposed to be in California?" I blurted out, still in shock.

His face scrunched into a scowl. "You're gonna make this about *me*?"

"This *is* about you," I shot back at him, annoyed. He'd caught me in a lie, but why hadn't he told me he was coming home sooner? This was the second time he'd showed up unannounced at my office, and it irked me he felt the need to check up on me. "What is it with you and showing up unannounced? Do you not trust me or something?"

"You're going to question *me* about trust? Now? After finding you like this?"

I knew being mad at him wasn't the proper reaction, but he'd caught me completely off guard. I'd had every intention to tell him when he returned that weekend, just not like this. Things looked worse than they were, and I had no way of explaining what he witnessed without sounding like an ass. "Why didn't you call me to tell me you were coming?"

"I did call," he replied sternly, tamed anger brimming in his eyes.

Last time I'd seen him this mad was back in Santa Monica after I'd confronted him about his best friend's comments. I'd accused him of treating me like one of his hook-ups. He didn't take it too well.

I crossed my arms in the hopes the nervous energy vibrating

through me could be contained. "When did you call? And why were you sitting in the shadows, anyway?"

"Sara, stop trying to avoid the real issue."

My body shook. He was right. I'd been caught lying and I was failing miserably at trying to deflect. I panicked and instead of owning up, I dug a deeper hole. "You should have told me you were coming home sooner."

He sucked in an exasperated breath. "That's what's bothering you? Not the fact you've been lying to me from the beginning? I mean, you had me convinced this Alexei guy was an asshole. That he was making your life a living hell, yet here you are, after-hours, dancing alone in this studio like you've been dance partners all long. What gives? What other lies have you told me, Sara? Is anything you've said to me about your life true?"

I blinked hard. His words were the walls of a spiked cage closing in on my heart. My chest constricted. The accusation was an acid burn. Shame continued to wash over me, covering me in guilt. Not only had I not told him I was a dancer, I'd painted a virulent image of the man I was intimately dancing with. Tom had every right to be upset.

Seemed all I knew was how to screw things up.

I looked down at my crossed arms for a brief second then gazed up at him, trying to find the courage I needed, the strength he'd always been able to give me. All I saw reflected in his eyes was anger bathed in sadness and soaked in disappointment. My heart fractured. His anger I could bear—I deserved every ounce of it—but to see him slowly blink away the moisture in his eyes made my universe crumble. I'd broken our trust, the one thing he'd lost in women and only recently been able to restore. I felt his pain and was no longer able to hold back the tears beginning to trickle down my face. "Tom, I can explain—"

"Explain what?" He dropped his arms and placed his hands on his waist, his face taut with frustration. "There's nothing that can justify why you've been lying to me about dancing or why I found you here. Alone. With Alexei."

My spine tightened. This wasn't how I'd wanted to tell him about my past. I needed to salvage the situation, but his harsh attitude and the disapproval in his eyes unraveled me. "Tom, I was going to tell you when you got back."

He paced. "That's not the point, Sara. You should have never lied in the first place. Baby, there was never a need for you to lie to me about this. It doesn't make sense." He paused, confusion dimming the glow that always sparkled in his eyes. He looked away as if trying to conceal his thoughts. "Unless..."

"Unless what?"

He was silent for a long moment before he replied, "Unless you didn't want me to know about Alexei." His poignant stare cut through my core.

I shook my head in disbelief. He couldn't have been farther from the truth, and the insinuation I could stoop so low made the ice in my blood turn arctic. "How can you accuse me of such a thing?"

He sucked in a deep breath as his nostrils flared, pressing his lips into a tight line. "I'm ending this conversation before either one of us says anything else we'll regret."

He turned to leave but I called after him. "You don't get to decide when this conversation is over. You can't leave."

"Watch me."

"Not until you tell me why you came here."

He stalked back toward me and pinned me with an unflinching stare. "I came to make sure you were okay. You're alive and breathing. I can go."

"Why wouldn't I be okay?"

"Listen to your messages."

"Tom, please. You have to let me explain."

He looked back, his eyes liquid fire. "Where's the girl I had in my arms a few days ago? Because it sure as hell isn't the person standing in front of me now. I...I can't believe I was so wrong about you." He shook his head in disbelief as he continued to walk toward the back door.

"What are you talking about, Tom?"

He stopped for a second, his back still to me. "Sara, it's obvious you didn't want me to know about this." He opened his arms wide, showing me he meant the studio. "After everything we've talked about and shared, I don't know why you would lie to me about it. And then to find you so intimately close with Alexei...I mean, all the stuff you've said about him. I don't get it. And to tell you the truth, I no longer care." He kept walking.

"Where are you going?" I ran toward him, fear crawling up my skin. As I caught up to him, he stopped to look at me one last time.

"Sara, I don't want to do this. I don't have time for bullshit in my life. I know I told you I'd wait until you were ready, but finding out like this..."

"You weren't supposed to find out like this. Just give me a chance to explain. Please."

"Sara, stop," his voice quavered as he held back the pain he was clearly trying to cover up with anger. "I'm done. It's over. It's not even that you lied, it's all this other shit. The fact you can't own up to what you did."

Something inside me cracked. It was like watching your most precious porcelain treasure slip from your hands and fall to the ground, shattering into a million pieces. There's this moment of awe, disbelief. Then this feeling of helplessness settles in when you know there's no way of putting it back together, and even if there was a way, the porcelain would be full of nicks and craters. Never perfect. Never whole.

What have I done?

"Tom..."

"Save it. Don't bother calling." He walked out.

I could have followed after him, but I had no right. My body was numb. A meteor had collided with my world, obliterating me from existence.

I'd been exposed for what I was.

A hypocrite.

A shameful liar.

I was a foolish girl standing alone in the place where I had sought redemption, but where all that now remained was humiliation and self-reproach.

And too many regrets.

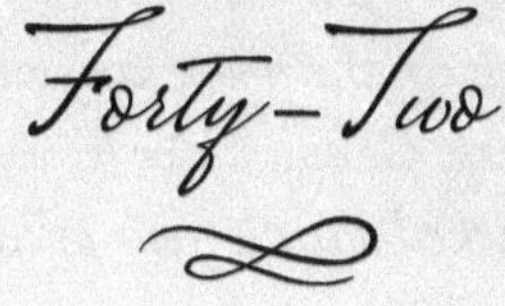

SARA

Walking back home seemed to take a dreadful eternity. What made it worse was that I couldn't stop listening to his messages or reading his texts.

6:00 p.m. Missed Call—Voice Message: *Sara, baby, where are you? I'm back in New York. I wanted to surprise you. Just left your apartment. Doorman said you hadn't come back since you left this morning. Running late from work? Call me, okay. I'm dying to see you.*

6:04 p.m. **Text:** *Where are you? Call me.*

6:30 p.m. **Missed Call—Voice Message:** *Still haven't heard from you. Hope everything is okay.*

7:01 p.m. **Text:** *Call me.*

7:15 p.m. **Missed Call—Voice Message:** *I'm sorry to keep calling. Did you forget to charge your phone again?*

8:00 p.m. **Missed Call—Voice Message:** *Now I'm really*

starting to worry. Baby, please call me back. I just want to make sure you are okay.

8:16 p.m. Text: *Seriously, Sara, why aren't you calling me back?*

9:00 p.m. Missed Call—Voice Message: *Stopped by your apartment again. Hoping maybe Jen was home. Tried to call her but no answer. Does anyone pick up the phone anymore? Sara, please. It's not like you not to call me back. Gonna drive by your office just in case.*

9:25 p.m. Text: *Parked outside your office. See some lights are still on. Guess you guys are working late?*

9:35 p.m. –Missed Call—no message left.

9:45 p.m. –Missed Call—no message left.

That was the last missed call I had from him. By then, he'd probably come into the studio looking for me, followed the music, and found me and Alexei.

I couldn't imagine what he must have felt seeing me dancing with Alexei. I had told him I was just Rebecca's assistant. I'd told him I wanted nothing more than to rip off Alexei's face. Yet, there I was, gliding through the air in none other than Alexei's arms.

The confrontation replayed in my mind over and over again. I didn't know why I said the things I did. I danced like I hadn't in four years and had been running on a serious high. I was still caught up in all the emotion, and when I looked into Alexei's eyes at the end, I saw approval, satisfaction. I wanted to hold on to that feeling forever.

However, as soon as I saw Tom's face, guilt covered me in a slimy coat. I hadn't cheated on him with another man, but for some reason, it felt like I had. I had shared an incredibly intimate moment with Alexei—not the dancing—the thrumming in my veins, an elation verging on ecstasy that made me feel like I was on top of the world.

That moment should have been Tom's.

It wasn't even the lie that cut him; it was my inability to own my mistake, the erratic reaction and senseless anger spewing from my pores. He had every right to walk away from me, to leave me alone in the studio.

I deserved his rejection.

Wanting to avoid Pedro, I rushed past the front door and lobby of my building. He yelled after me, trying to give me the message that Tom had stopped by looking for me. I waved him off with a brief thank you and scurried into the elevator.

Still wiping tears from my eyes, I walked into my apartment, my hands streaked with mascara. Jen was in the dining area getting ready to sit down and eat when she saw me. "Sara, what's wrong? Why are you crying?"

As soon as I looked at her, I began sobbing again and covered my mouth. Trying to choke back my anguish, I rushed to my room and laid on my bed, weeping into my pillow.

Jen sat down on the floor next to my bed. She brushed loose hair away from my eyes. "Sara, what happened?"

"It's...over."

"What's over?"

"Me and Tom. He broke up with me."

"What? Why?"

"It's my fault, Jen. I screwed up."

"What are you talking about?"

"Not now. I just want to be alone for a little while."

"Okay, hon. I'll be in the kitchen if you need anything."

I cried myself to sleep and awoke two hours later. I walked out of my room in a daze. It was almost one a.m. and Jen was in the dining room studying. I sat next to her, my mind still in shock at everything that happened. It all ended so suddenly.

"Tom found me dancing with Alexei," I blurted out.

Jen snapped her head toward me. "Wait, back up. Why were you dancing with Alexei? And isn't Tom supposed to be in California?"

I told her everything. How Tom had wanted to surprise me.

How he had tried to reach me, but I missed all his calls. How he'd tried to come find me, and then the confrontation in the studio.

She rubbed her temple. "Of all people, it had to be Alexei."

"I should have listened to you. I should have told him about it sooner."

"It's not like he gave you an opportunity to explain."

I buried my face in my hands and sobbed, my chest tight with sorrow.

Jen placed a hand on my shoulder. "You deserve a chance to explain your side. If he still wants to end things, well fine. But he needs to know the truth first. He owes you that much."

"He said not to even bother calling."

"Since when do you do what people tell you?"

"He won't listen."

"Are you ready to give up on him?"

I peered up at her, sniffling and wiping away the wetness from my cheeks. "I don't want to lose what we had."

"Then fight for what is important to you, hon. If he chooses to give up on you after you tell him the truth, well, maybe you guys were not meant to be after all. But if you don't do this, if you don't try to explain, you'll never forgive yourself. You will always think, what if?"

What if?

What if he absolutely never wants to see me again and I make a fool of myself?

What if he never forgives me?

What if?

Forty-Three

SARA

I TRIED TO CALL HIM—A MILLION TIMES. THE PHONE stopped ringing after a while. It went straight to voicemail.

He shut me out.

I left him messages, asking, begging him to please call me back. I cried hysterically, trying to explain it was all a big misunderstanding. I didn't know why I said the things I said. I told him I loved him and wouldn't be able to go on without him.

Oh, God, I sounded so desperate.

At the time, I was.

I never thought I'd lower myself so miserably as to beg for forgiveness. That probably wasn't what Jen meant for me to do when she told me to seek him out. But I was so consumed by despair, I was willing to do anything to get him to call me back.

By the following Friday, I was at my wits end. Still at work and staring at my phone, I silently prayed for his call or even a text. Any hope of him calling me back began to dissolve into thin air. Panic bubbled inside my chest. Was I really going to lose the man I loved because of dance? My life was falling apart all over again because of a bad decision, because dance seemed to cloud my judgment. This had to be a sign.

Accepting my dismal reality was the easiest way to get to the place where I was no longer hurting, but somehow it didn't work. I wanted Tom and I wanted to dance.

I refused to give up on both.

Things couldn't end like this. Tom needed to hear me out. I tried calling one last time, but it rang once then an automated voice stated the mailbox was full and couldn't accept any more messages. My heart sank into the empty pit of my stomach.

Now what?

That night, I actually wished he'd pull one of his unexpected visits. I stood and walked up to my window, longing to find him in the crowd, walking toward my building. I shook my head at my nonsense. What was I gonna do, sit at my desk all night and keep praying Tom would miraculously change his mind and come looking for me?

I yawned and rubbed my eyes. Getting sleep the last few nights had been a task. Even though my body pleaded for rest, my mind could not find peace. I'd been up until the early dawn every night since the incident. It was taking a toll on my body and my sanity as well. As I continued to look for a man that was not going to show, a knock at my door drew my attention. "Come in."

The knob turned and Alexei poked his head in. "Working late?"

"Probably gonna head home soon," I replied as I sat back down on my chair.

"It's seven. Don't stay too late."

We paused to look at each other for a brief moment. We both knew there was unfinished business between us, but neither one of us was willing to breach the topic. I wasn't ready to talk to him about what happened. At least not until I'd had a chance to talk to Tom.

As he turned to leave, I leaned down on my desk and rested my head on my arms, stalling.

It frightened me to go home and stare at four walls, watching as the minutes ticked down, waiting for a call that would never come, until it got so late—or early—sleep would finally beat me.

I can't do this anymore.

Tom was not going to end things like this. He had to hear me out. He owed me that much. With resolve, I pushed off my desk, grabbed my things, and hurried home. Rain pelted the city, as if Mother Nature knew how badly my heart was aching. As soon as I arrived at my apartment, I changed from my soggy clothes into a pair of jeans and a T-shirt, rummaged through some old items, and pulled out pictures, newspaper clippings, dance school memorabilia, and a DVD of my favorite movie.

Before heading out the door, I went to the freezer and a pulled out the Margherita pizza I had ordered from Thomasina's before the blow up with Tom. He'd told me they could deliver a frozen pie anywhere in the country overnight. I'd wanted to surprise him that weekend since we'd talked about staying in and watching movies.

Throwing everything into a box, I ran out the door, jumped into my Jeep, and drove to Jersey, the rain falling even harder.

I must have been beyond delusional thinking the measly peace offering was going to do much, but I had run out of options. My guy wasn't taking my calls, and I was pretty much done waiting. I stopped at a grocery store nearby and picked up some popcorn and a box of candy just in case the pizza wasn't enough.

Did I think all this stuff would win him over? Not really.

But I had to try.

I had to do something.

I arrived at his place shortly after nine and parked a block away. The rain hadn't let up and I had to run with my box of memories under one arm and the pizza in the other. As I arrived, dripping wet, I told the doorman I was there to visit Tom, but when I walked toward the elevators, he asked me to come back to the front desk.

He eyed me and my pie suspiciously. "Mr. Wright is not expecting any pizza."

I smiled. "I'm not delivering the pizza. I'm his girlfriend."

The doorman grinned, mirthless, trying to be polite, but his gesture teetered on rude. "Mr. Wright is not expecting any visitors."

"Please, call him and let him know I'm here."

"Mr. Wright left clear instructions with the front desk that he does not want to be disturbed. By anybody. I'm sorry, but I'm afraid I'm going to have to ask you to leave."

"Listen…" I paused to look at his name badge, "Derrick, I'm sure you are simply doing your job, and I don't blame you for trying to send me away, but I'm not going anywhere. Buzz Mr. Wright and tell him his girlfriend, Sara, is here."

"I don't care who you are. Mr. Wright does not want to be bothered. By anybody. That includes crazy women holding pizza boxes who claim to be his girlfriend."

I lurched back at his comment. "Claim? Listen, buddy, if you think Tom is going to flip because you buzz him to let him know I'm here, what do you think he is going to do when he finds out you refused to let his girlfriend upstairs?"

Derrick stared, unflinching, not buying my ruse.

"Fine," I said as I pulled out my cellphone and pretended to look through my contacts.

"What are you doing?" Derrick asked, his stoic expression melting into a frown.

"Texting Tom. I'll make sure to tell him to thank you for ruining his surprise."

"No, don't!" Derick must have weighed his options and caved. "I'm not letting you go upstairs until he says okay, though." He picked up the phone and dialed Tom's unit. "Mr. Wright? Sorry to bother you," Derrick began. "I know, sir, and I'm extremely sorry. I would not bother you if I didn't think it was extremely important. I'm afraid we have a situation in the lobby. In the interest of not making a scene, I was hoping you could help me. There is a young lady who says she is here to see you...I know, sir. I am quite aware of your instructions." Derrick eyed me as he spoke. I could tell he was getting an earful from Tom.

"Tell him it's a damsel in distress," I whispered at him.

Derrick stared at me with wide eyes.

"Tell him. Please. I'm his damsel," my voice cracked with dread, thinking Tom would actually send me away.

A glimpse of sympathy crossed Derrick's gaze. "Mr. Wright, she says...she says she's a damsel in distress." He was hesitant as he spoke. Perhaps fearful and embarrassed at sounding stupid.

Then there was silence.

Derrick put the phone down. "Mr. Wright is on his way down. He didn't sound too thrilled to hear about you, by the way."

"Thanks. I owe you."

Derrick looked worried. "Thanks to you, I'll probably be delivering pizzas soon."

I tried to give him a warm smile, but my heart beat a million miles a minute as soon as the elevator pinged. I walked over as the doors glided open.

Tom leaned against the back of the elevator, arms folded tightly across his chest. He wore a pair of dark gray sweat pants and a white T-shirt. Despite his haggard look, he was still breathtaking. Bloodshot eyes and a week-old scruffy beard told me he'd been miserable, too.

He pressed the stop button on the elevator, but remained inside. He had no intention of joining me in the lobby. "I didn't call you back for a reason," he said dryly. "I thought you'd be smart enough to take a hint." His voice was devoid of the velvet that usually washed over me every time he spoke. The words were biting and cold, nails puncturing my flesh.

My heart bled. But I had to stay strong. "I...deserve that. I know."

"Then why are you here, Sara? When I said it was over, I meant it."

"Look, I know I screwed up. But you need to know the truth."

"I don't have time for this." He went to press the button on the elevator, intending to leave me in the lobby without giving me a chance to explain.

I stuck my arm out and stopped the doors from closing. I didn't think my heart could ache much more. I was wrong. How could he be so harsh after being so warm? Trying to ignore the sound of my heart breaking, I continued. "Once, I had the opportunity to leave you behind, to leave us. But I chose to stay. Because I cared about you and I was not ready to give up on the only thing that mattered to me in a long time. You wanted me to listen and I did. Now, I need *you* to listen, but I know I can't make you. So, if you really want me out of your life forever, then tell me now. You said once you'd never lie to me. Look me in the eyes, baby. Tell me you don't feel anything for me anymore. That the love you had for me is gone."

He looked away in silence.

My heart lost its last drop of blood. The dead look in his eyes confirmed my fears.

"Okay," I said, resigning to the bitter truth spoken by his silence. "I hear you." I pushed the soggy pizza into his arms, plopped the popcorn on top of the box, followed by the candy, and finally, the movie. "These were meant to be a peace offering. I guess...I thought everything we shared was enough for you to at least give me a chance to explain. I was wrong. I don't care what you do with them. Eat the pizza, chuck the popcorn down the chute, or give them all to Derrick. I don't care. I just can't take any of it back with me."

Turning from him, I rushed to the exit and pushed through the large revolving door and into the rain, praying to God the self-imploding despair pressing on my chest would cease, because this time, I would not be able to survive the searing pain coiled around my heart. I headed back toward my car, hoping the rain could wash away my sorrow.

It didn't.

"Sara, wait," Tom shouted after me.

I swung around. "What, Tom? You made it very clear you no longer feel anything for me. I can't hear you say it anymore."

He rushed to where I stood and cupped my face in his strong hands, rain soaking his hair and dripping down his brow. "You think this is what I wanted for us? You think it didn't tear my heart out to leave you there alone in that studio? You think my love for you could really end so easily?"

Words escaped me. I didn't know what to say. I simply stared at him in total confusion.

"You still need me to prove to you that I love you?" He crashed his lips into mine, taking me up in his arms as the rain continued to soak us. He kissed me hard and demanding, as if he wanted to tattoo himself on my lips. Roping my arms around his neck, I answered him with an equally fevered kiss, needing him to know how badly I'd ached thinking what we had was over.

When we finally pulled away from each other, our breaths steamed around us. He pressed his forehead against mine. "Don't you ever doubt how much I love you."

"I don't understand," I said pulling back, pointing back to his building. "What happened in there...the things you said..."

"I've been falling apart, Sara. Not having you in my life was like a piece of me was torn away."

"Then why didn't you let me explain?"

"Pride. Anger. You have no idea what seeing you in Alexei's arms did to me. I wasn't jealous of him. I was jealous that he knew a side of you I didn't. Baby, you...you looked amazing. You dancing—it was one of the most beautiful things I'd ever seen. But it hurt me so deeply you hadn't shared it with me, that you'd chosen to lie, to keep that part of your life hidden. I didn't know how to react other than to close myself off." He lowered his chin.

I shivered in the cold rain. "I was angry at myself for keeping it a secret, for not confiding in you sooner. But I guess, I was scared you'd leave me once you learned the truth."

He caressed my cheek. "Baby, why would I leave you?"

"Because it's a part of my life I'm not proud of." My tears mixed with the rain as the image of my mother's lifeless form flashed in front of me.

"We all have ghosts we want to keep buried, but I never want you to feel like you need to hide them from me." He took my hand and placed it over his heart. "I will always be your safe place. I need you to believe that."

Roping my arms around his neck, I let him pick me up in a hug so tight, it felt like we were melding together. "What's in the box?" he asked.

"Everything," I said in a whimper, as he lowered me back down.

"Hey," he intoned softly. "No more tears, okay? I'm ready to listen. Let's get back inside and dry up, then you can show me what you brought."

We arrived at the entrance to his building, looking like soaked cats. Before we pushed through the revolving door, he looked at me once more and lowered his lips to mine again. This time, it wasn't an ardent kiss filled with passion and desire, but one laden with warmth and forgiveness.

Forty-Four

SARA

BACK IN HIS APARTMENT, TOM CHANGED INTO DRY sweatpants and another muscle-hugging white t-shirt. Nothing of his would fit me properly, so he just offered me a hoodie that I wore as a short dress. Thankfully, my underwear was still dry, though I had to throw my bra in the dryer. I sat on his black leather couch, my legs folded under my butt, trying to keep warm. Bax plopped his head on my lap as I patted his soft brown hair, his eyes slightly closed. Tom prowled in the kitchen, warming our pizza.

"Hey," I called out to him, "So, what changed your mind about me? What made you follow me out into the rain?"

He threw a dishtowel over his shoulder and looked up at me, leaning his hands on the kitchen counter. "I remembered what a prick I'd been back in Santa Monica. I couldn't stand seeing the pain in your eyes. They mirrored what I was suffering, the nightmare of losing you. When you walked away, my heart shattered. I didn't have the strength to lose you again."

I never wanted to remember the pain of losing him either. As if sensing the sting in my heart, Bax licked my cheek. Looking up at me with those big amber-colored eyes, Bax gave me the warmth and comfort I needed. "I never thought I'd be a dog person, but how can you resist these eyes?" I said, rubbing under Bax's chin.

"He likes you." Tom placed the warm pizza on his coffee table accompanied by plates and some napkins. He sat next to me and tried to shoo his pal off the couch, but Bax wouldn't budge. "Apparently, he likes you a lot."

"I don't mind him sitting next to me."

"Well, I mind. *I'd* like to sit next to you." He planted a wet one on my lips.

My box of memories sat on the floor next to the coffee table, the movie I'd brought lying on top. Tom reached for the movie. "I thought I was the only one who still owned DVDs. So, what are we watching?" he asked, then he hiked an eyebrow. "Top Gun?"

I grabbed a Margherita slice as I took the DVD from his hand. "Everyone loves this movie."

"Yeah, back in 1986. But why are *we* watching it tonight?"

"Okay, this is going to sound weird, but after my mother died, whenever this movie came on, I was a mess."

"Naval officers remind you of your mother? This I gotta hear."

"My mom had wanted to be a ballerina when she was young, but her dreams ended when she got pregnant with me. Teen romance, and all that. She had to marry my father and became a housewife and mother. She never really could let go of dancing entirely, so at a very early age, she put me in dance. Ballet wasn't really my thing, so she didn't push me. She let me try all other forms of dance. My interest in jazz and contemporary dance grew when I started high school. My mother immediately recognized my talent for those styles. She saw the joy it brought me and was convinced I was going to be a famous dancer one day.

"Dance was my life. I ate it and breathed it. It was all I ever did, and my mother was there with me all the way. She was like a drill sergeant, but she was also my support. She never once tried to live her dream through me. She was my biggest fan. She was there to pick me up every time I fell, encouraging me and motivating me."

"She sounds like an unbelievable person," Tom said as he took a bite of his slice. "You never told me how she died."

My eyes swelled with tears as I thought back to the accident. The chest-piercing memory dried up my mouth. I looked away from Tom, afraid to relive that day.

Tom reached for my chin and turned my face toward him. "If you don't want to talk about it..."

I burst into tears as I leaned into him and wrapped my arms around his neck.

Tom tightened his arms around my body and held me close, knowing I needed his strength to get through this. "Listen, we don't have to do this today."

I loosened my hold and sat back on his couch. "There's no point in keeping it a secret anymore. It happened. It was my fault and I just have to learn to live with my mistake."

He put his half-eaten pizza slice down and stared at me. "What was your fault?"

I bit my bottom lip, trying to keep it from quivering. "My mother died because of me."

"Sara, what happened?"

I sucked in a deep breath and pushed off the couch, walking over to the tall windows. As I looked through the glass, the clear summer night of the New York City skyline dissolved into a wintry mirage that transported me back four years to when my mother died. "It was the night of my biggest audition and a snowstorm was creeping in. We were up in Cape Cod visiting my grandmother and my mom begged me to stay, which would mean I'd risk missing the audition versus risking my life on the road. I should have listened."

In the next thirty minutes, I told him how my gram, mother, and Maggie begged me to stay. How, against her better judgment, my mom decided to join me instead of letting me face the audition alone. With a heavy heart, I admitted the foolishness of my actions. Blinded by ambition and cold determination, I refused to listen to reason. All I'd cared about was landing a spot in the company. I'd jumped in my car and headed back to New York in the middle of one of the biggest snow storms of the decade. I should have stopped her from getting in my car, but I didn't and she paid with her life.

"Sara, accidents happen," Tom began.

I turned to face him, fury in my eyes. I'd heard the same sorry-ass consolation a million times from everybody. It wasn't their fault and it sure as hell wasn't Tom's. What else could they say? *Yeah, you fucked up and killed your mom?* Our natural instinct is to try and comfort, but nothing made me feel better. Nothing ever could.

I didn't want to lash out at him for something beyond his control, so I paused and inflated my lungs with a deep breath. "You don't have to make me feel better. No matter how we try to spin it, the reality is, I could have prevented the accident. I didn't have to go to that damned audition. If I'd stayed, if I'd listened to them, my mom would still be alive."

"Okay, fine. You fucked up."

I stared at him in shock. No one had ever said it, at least not to my face. Not even Jen, whom I had a no-bullshit agreement with.

"Isn't that what you want to hear? The truth?" he asked, somewhat rhetorically.

I said nothing.

"You were reckless and stubborn and selfish. But who isn't when it comes to chasing their dreams? You were doing something you thought was right, and tragically, it ended in a terrible accident." He cut straight to the core of my guilt.

"And that's exactly why I didn't want to tell you. Who wants to be with someone who risked everything for a dream? I lost my mother, my career, and the man I was going to marry because of my reckless love of dance."

"You were a kid, Sara. I'm not going to judge you by the mistakes of your past."

"Why shouldn't you judge me?" I shot back. "I'm making selfish mistakes all over again. Look at what just happened with us. I was so consumed with getting back on stage that I didn't consider what lying about my past would do. I didn't even care that I chose to let Alexei coach me."

"What happened between us was stupid. I blew it out of proportion, and well, you have a right to your secrets. It's not a requirement for you to tell me everything."

Was he for real? I'd just spilled my dirty secret, explained I was still that same selfish girl, and he was taking the blame for our breakup? Could he possibly love me that much? I dropped to my knees, my hands covering my face as I cried.

Tom rushed to my side. "Sara?"

"No more secrets," I ushered between sobs. "I'm tired of carrying the weight of my past. I can't do it anymore."

"Oh, Sara..." he sighed as he sat down on the wood floor and leaned his back against the glass wall, pulling me toward him. Both of us sitting on the floor, I pressed my back to his chest as he cradled me in his arms and ran his fingers through my hair. "I know there's nothing anyone can say to help wash away the blame," he continued. "I may not be able to lessen your guilt, but I can wipe your tears away, baby. And you won't have to carry those regrets by yourself anymore, either. I'm here with you."

My chest was ready to rip open. I could not contain so much emotion. His love for me was so immense, it blotted out the sun and became my new star. I knew I didn't deserve his kindness, but I didn't have the heart to pull away from him. How could I when his chest was a soft pillow and his arms a warm blanket?

I was finally able to tell him the rest of the story.

"Making it big in New York as a contemporary dancer was the only thing that mattered to me," I started. "Owning the big apple—that was my dream. I look at the city now, and it all seems so trivial. None of it is of real importance. The worst part of it, though, is the fact I never accomplished anything. All the hard work. The sacrifices she made, even my selfishness, was all for nothing. She died and I didn't even finish school."

"Why did you quit dance, Sara?"

I looked up at him, sadly having to push away from his arms. "The accident damaged my spine. I was bedridden for months, barely able to walk."

His eyes widened in shock. "Shit. I had no idea."

"It was the excuse I needed to never step foot on a stage ever again."

His brows knit as he cocked his head to the side. "You wanted that?"

"Her death made me realize how self-absorbed I had been. I hadn't cared about anything or anyone else. The only thing that'd mattered was my success. But realizing she was gone, that she was never coming back? Dance was never going to be the same for me. Knowing she'd never get to see me dance on stage made me realize she had been the reason I started dancing in the first place—my dream of making it big had all been to make her proud of me. In the end, she died thinking I was a terrible person."

"What makes you say that?"

"What kind of daughter does what I did, knowing the risks? That's why I didn't want to tell you. Because I was afraid you'd see me for who I really am."

"That's not who you are."

"It is. My foolhardy decision caused someone their life."

"Shit. Now it makes sense. The death of the best friend..." He realized then why the movie touched so close to home. He rubbed the scruff on his chin.

"After a year of physical therapy, my doctor told me I'd made a miraculous recovery. I may have been able to make up for all the lost time, plus my instructors told me the door was always open, but I didn't even want to think about it. It was the perfect way out. I was tired of everyone telling me the accident was not my fault, that there was nothing I could have done. It was easier if I said damage to my spine kept me from dancing again. They wouldn't be able to question that."

Tom stood and offered me a hand, helping me to my feet. "Everyone bought it?" he asked, guiding me back to the sofa.

I sat down on the leather sectional and leaned back as I rested my feet up on the ottoman. "Well, up until Monday, I thought no one knew, but Jen told me she'd seen me dance in the apartment back when we first moved in together. She'd kept quiet. She knew how traumatized I was about the whole thing and didn't want to stir up trouble."

A gentle smile began to trace across his lips as he rested a playful gaze over me.

I smiled back, not really knowing why he was looking at me like he'd just figured out the final clue of a riddle. "What is it?" I asked.

"You can't deny who you are, Sara. That's all. Not then and certainly not now. You've been dancing in the shadows for too long, don't you think?"

I let out a labored breath. "I wish it was that simple. What Jen saw was a shell of the dancer I used to be."

He reached for a soggy pizza slice and chomped down. Between swallows, he asked, "So what happened to inspire you to get back on stage?"

I straightened and stared at him. "Are you kidding? Isn't it obvious?"

He stopped chewing and shook his head no.

"It was you. You inspired me."

He almost choked and had to gulp down a whole bottle of water to clear his throat. "Me?"

"Since I met you, my whole universe has uncoiled, opening up places I'd locked down long ago. After the accident, I fell deep into depression and was self-medicating with booze and painkillers. Josh couldn't deal with my shit and left. I was so devastated I closed off my heart and I've preferred it that way because the slightest touch of happiness would dredge up my past. The thought of losing everything all over again...It consumed me with fear."

He narrowed his eyes. "So, tell me again why me uncoiling your universe is a good thing?"

I reached for his hands and held them close. "Because this time, I am not running. I've wanted to, but that strong, unexplainable attraction to you won't let me. And as memories from my past have surfaced, my desire to dance again has grown even stronger. You're right, I can't deny who I am. Jen convinced me it was the right thing to do, that I needed to tell you, I just didn't know how." I looked down, embarrassment washing over me. "I lied to you from the beginning. I was a coward for hiding it in the first place, and instead of fessing up, I dug a deeper hole."

He raised a hand to my face and pulled a lose strand of hair behind my ear, caressing my cheek, drawing my gaze to his. "That's in the past now. I get why you lied. Finding out how I did was just poor timing."

I peered into his green eyes. Twinkling like a star-speckled night, his eyes told me he loved me more than I could ever imagine and he'd forgiven me for my mistake a million times over. "Thank you," I told him, encircling my arms around him. "For being so understanding and for loving this damaged girl."

After ten seconds that felt like the length of an orbit around the sun, he peeled me off him. "Okay, baby girl, I love you, you love me, but can we please finish this cold-ass pizza?"

~

We were done enjoying our cold pizza when Tom stood up from the couch and walked over to his sound system.

"What are you doing?" I asked.

He smiled at me over his shoulder. "I want you to dance."

My eyes bulged. "Are you crazy? Here? You are nuts if you think I'm going to break out into a dance number right in your living room."

"I meant...I want you to dance with *me*." He pressed a button and the song began to play. "Ever since I saw you dance to this," he continued, "the song has been circling in my head. I want you to know that I know I was wrong for leaving you, and, well, I'm never giving up on us again." He stretched his hand out to me.

My heart melted. Moments like these were why I had fallen in love with him. I took his hand and followed him toward the tall windows. His apartment floor was our stage, and the twinkling New York City lights our audience.

"There's a small disclosure, though," he said, giving me a twirl with his hand.

"Oh yeah, and what's that?"

"I can't dance as well as fucking Alexei. Don't have any fancy moves or anything. But I think I can pick you up in my arms if you'd like."

I smiled. "I don't need fancy moves. I just need you."

We swayed in each other's arms, tightly cocooned until the song ended.

And that was the best dance I'd ever had.

Forty-Five

TOM

AFTER OUR DANCE WAS OVER, I WATCHED AS SARA PICKED up the dirty dishes and paraded her sexy ass to the kitchen. Dressed in that hoodie that brushed against her bare thighs, she looked like a fucking wet dream. I followed after her, and as she rinsed the dishes off, I snaked my arms around her waist. "You know, there's this really cool invention called the dishwasher. Have you heard of it?" I asked, taking a nibble of her earlobe.

"Smartass."

Unable to contain myself, I reached under the hoodie, lifting it up to her waist, exposing her black, lacy underwear. But what I was more interested in was further up. I slid my hands up her silky skin until I cupped her naked breasts. She moaned as she tried concentrating on washing the plates, but the suds were rising with the water; She was clearly not paying any attention to what she was doing.

Perhaps my fingers were too distracting as they traced circles around her hard nipples.

"How's that feel, baby girl? I whispered over her ear, my breath summoning goosebumps to the surface of her skin.

"I've missed you," she said.

"Not nearly as much as *I* have."

"Should we be doing this right now? We're supposed to watch Top Gun. You're supposed to make popcorn."

"Fuck the movie and popcorn. I'm so fucking hard, I want to take you right here. Right fucking now." I pressed my cock against her ass, wanting her to feel exactly how hard she made me. She gasped. Even though I was dressed, my sweatpants made it difficult to hide my raging erection.

She continued to pretend she was trying to wash the two measly dishes, but I knew it was because she was enjoying the game. I lowered my hand down the front of her body and slid it inside her underwear. She parted her legs without me having to ask her, and I moaned when I felt how slippery with arousal she was. "Good girl. You're already wet for me."

"I need to finish cleaning the dishes."

I shut the faucet off and ran my tongue along the side of her neck. "What dishes?"

Her chest heaved as I swirled my finger around her clitoris, soft moans spilling from her lips. "That's it, baby. I want you to feel how badly I've needed you these past few days. How much I fantasized about storming to your apartment and punishing you with my cock for keeping secrets from me."

"I'm so sorry..." she panted as she spread her legs wider.

My fingers were so soaked, I couldn't wait to satisfy my cock with her wet pussy, but first, I needed to remind her that I owned her. "I don't want you to keep secrets from me anymore," I said as I put a finger inside her.

"Tom...I want you to..."

"Hush, baby girl," I said, playing with her clit. "If you want my cock, I need you to promise me. Promise me you won't keep things from me again. That I can trust you."

"I..." but her words were swallowed up by her moans as I pushed my finger as deep as it could go.

"Go on, baby girl. I need to hear you say it," I said harsher, hooking my finger inside her, pressing on that G-spot."

"Fuck," she clamored, arching her back. "I promise not to keep secrets from you."

"That's it. Now you're getting it." I pulled her underwear to the side and made her bend over. Kneeling behind her, I buried my tongue inside her cleft, licking her end to end. "You taste so fucking good." I flicked her little swollen clit with my tongue until I knew she was ready to come, then I pulled away.

"No. No. Please don't stop."

"Get on your knees."

She turned around, her rosy lips plumped into a pout, those brown sultry eyes alive with lust. Keeping her gaze locked on mine, she did as she was told despite looking annoyed that I'd denied her the orgasm I'd been coaxing from her body.

"Now lower my sweatpants and pull out my cock."

Again, she did as she was instructed, her eyelids growing heavy as she reached between her legs to rub at her pussy while stroking me.

"I didn't say you could touch yourself. This time. I'm going first, baby girl. That's your punishment for making me feel like a fucking lunatic these last few days. Now open that pretty mouth of yours."

She obliged, licking her lips in the process. Damn brat. She knew exactly how to tease me, but I intended to punish that bratty mouth of hers with my cock until tears streamed down her face. I needed to punish *her* for driving me mad since I saw her dancing with that fucking asshole. Needed to punish her for making me feel like the ground had collapsed beneath me.

I slowly glided my cock between her lips, remembering how

expertly she'd used her mouth back in Santa Monica. She used that tongue like a fucking pro, lapping up my precum like she couldn't get enough. "You like that, don't you?"

"I love the way you taste," she said, swirling her tongue over the tip of my cock. Fuck. I had to wrap my hand around her hair to keep myself under control. Looking down on her, with her eyes anchored to mine as she sucked on my head, had me ready to blow my load inside her mouth. I wanted to prolong my orgasm, but I wasn't able to hold back, and needing to remind her she was mine, I fucked that mouth so fast and hard, she gagged, those tears I wanted to see running down her cheeks.

Fucking hell. She didn't protest. She took that dick like a good fucking girl. Shit. Sara looked so divine with that pretty mouth full of cock, I erupted, shooting my release to the back of her throat. She moaned and moaned as she licked off every drop of cum from my shaft, and I swore I could erupt all over her again just watching her do that. Wiping a milky drop from the corner of her mouth, I said, "Now, it's your turn."

"You're ready to go again so soon?"

I hiked a brow. "Are you challenging me?" Stroking myself, I showed her I was more than ready.

Turning her over onto all fours, I practically ripped her underwear off her in half a second. I could've told her to take the hoodie off so I could watch her tits bounce in the foyer mirror directly in front of us, but I wanted my clothing on her as I claimed her body. I gave her no warning as I penetrated her. This time, I had no plans to ease myself into her. Tonight, it was about taking back what was mine. It was about fucking her brains out, not making love.

She quivered in pain and delight all at the same time as I rammed into her, one of my hands grabbing onto the hoodie as I thrust. My mind swam with thoughts of taking her in the ass, but I knew she'd never done it, and this was definitely not the time and place to do it, but fucking hell, I wanted that tight little asshole. Unable to dampen my depravity, I simply teased the rim with the tip of my cock, watching her hole pucker, inviting me in.

"Oh, Tom," she whimpered. "That feels so good."

"I know, baby girl. But not tonight."

"Please. I want to feel…"

"Full?"

"Oh, God. Yes. Please."

"Fuck. I love hearing you beg. But that's part of your punishment—making you want it so bad it hurts."

"Go in a just little?"

I chuckled, loving how greedy her ass was for me. "That was meant to be just a tease of what I can make you feel, baby. Remember that. But you're not ready. Right now, I'll make you come a different way."

Knowing her knees were probably killing her, I flipped her on her back, and this time, I lifted the hooded sweatshirt, needing to see her breasts as I spread her legs open. She smiled as I licked her pussy, and I forced her to lift her hips off the floor to seek that release. Right when she was at the summit, I placed my palm over her pelvis and brought her hips back down, denying her that orgasm once again.

She let out a stream of curses, but I climbed over her and lowered my mouth to her lips, inhaling her words as I slid my length inside her pussy and ravaged her. She moaned, wrapping her legs around me.

Sara dug her nails into my back and I knew she was ready for me to get her over the edge. I'd tortured her long enough, so I reached between us and gently brushed my fingers over her clit as I thrust in slow circles. She spread her legs and I grabbed onto the back of her thighs, pushing her feet above her head. I smiled to myself. The perks of dating a dancer. She was fucking flexible as hell and I was enjoying every second of it.

I was nearing the peak myself and that's when I realized we'd been so consumed by lust, we'd forgotten about protection. "Fuck, Sara. I don't have a condom."

"Too late for that...luckily, I went on the pill as soon as I got back from Santa Monica."

"Smart girl. So you want me to come inside you?"

"Fuck yes."

"Keep those legs above you like that, baby. I fucking love this position." I rammed into her as I circled her clit, rocking her body and watching those tits bounce. Shit. The instant she screamed my name, covering my cock in her release, I wasn't able to hold it any longer and came inside her so hard, I thought I'd never stop spilling into her. The sight of her pussy full of my cum was utter beauty. I knew then that when it came to sex with Sara, there was no way I'd ever get enough.

Forty-Six

SARA

Around two a.m., I awoke to a cold and empty bed.

This was starting to get annoying.

I tried not to get too upset, though. The man had done incredible things to my body all night and I was still reeling from the erotic bliss. He was insatiable when it came to sex and had managed to turn me into a bit of a minx, making me crave things I'd never imagined I could enjoy so much. Stars, I'd begged him to fuck me in the ass, something I'd never even dreamed of doing with Josh. I felt a bit embarrassed afterward when Tom explained that it was something he'd need to ease me into if it was something I truly wanted, especially given his size.

He promised to make it as pleasurable as possible and said it was something we could explore for a bit before going all the way. The idea both thrilled and scared me. But it also made my lady parts clench with the need for him to fill all of my holes with his cock. I squirmed, pressing my legs together, wishing he were next to me right now so I could straddle him.

Slightly miffed about his absence, I climbed out of bed naked and freezing, my lips trembling. I found a fleece throw on a nearby chair and draped it over my shoulders before venturing out to look for him. Spotting him lying down on his couch in the living room, his arms crossed over his shirtless chest and only wearing his gray sweatpants, I tiptoed out thinking he was asleep, but as I approached, I was startled to find he was wide awake.

"Why are you out here instead of in bed with me?" I asked.

"I couldn't sleep."

I sat at the end of the couch by his feet. The apartment was an ice box, cold as hell from the central air. I wrapped myself tighter in the blanket. "What's going on?"

He sat up, resting his elbows on his knees. "I told you I wouldn't lie to you."

"Yeah..."

"Well, there is something we need to talk about."

"Go on," I said, not knowing where this conversation could possibly lead.

He pressed his lips into a thin line and took a deep breath. "This is not going to be easy, so be patient, okay?"

I nodded.

He shook his head. "Shit. I've been laying here for hours, thinking about what I was going to say. Now, I don't know where to start."

"The beginning is always a good place."

He scratched the scruff on his jaw, breathing heavily as he gathered his thoughts. "Okay. Here goes. I was an expert marksman for the Marines when I was asked to join MARSOC as a sniper in the MSOR 3rd Battalion."

I put a hand up. "You lost me. What is Ma...zork?"

"MARSOC is the Marine Corps Forces Special Operations Command."

My eyes widened and I leaned in closer, intrigued. "You mean like the Seals?"

"Seals are Navy, we are Marines."

"That's still special forces. Incredible."

"It's not like the movies. There's nothing glamorous about what we do, and I'm not telling you because I wanna impress you with a war story."

"I'm sorry. I didn't mean for it to come off that way. Look, I know it's not easy to talk about this stuff. Like you said earlier, there's no need for you to tell me all of your secrets."

"You need to know *this*." He walked over to the windows. "During my last tour, my scout platoon was dispatched on a special recon mission in Afghanistan. There was critical intelligence present and we needed to recover everything we could. Things were going according to plan and then...Jake spotted him."

"Jake?"

"Right," he said, turning to look at me over his shoulder. "I never told you. We were stationed together in Afghanistan. That's where I met him."

"I never realized."

"It's okay. We don't talk much about it. As I was saying, our guys were moving in on our target, and that's when Jake saw him. In an attempt to destroy what we had gone in to recover, the enemy sent in a suicide bomber." Tom lowered his head and rubbed his face with his hands. "Those sons of bitches are constantly using innocent people." He paused again. Anger mixing with the anguish in his eyes.

"He came out of nowhere. It should have taken me less than a second to take him out, except, as soon as I had him in my scope, my finger froze over the trigger. After years of training and executing countless missions, I'd never flinched. Never once did I ever hesitate to take out a target, but this time…" He looked away with dismay, shaking his head in disgust.

"Suicide bombers," he went on. "You know how many of those guys we took out while stationed there? I had my orders. Shoot to kill."

"You missed?"

"He detonated his vest before I had a chance to pull the trigger."

"Christ."

"He was a kid, Sara. A God damn kid. Probably thirteen. The fucking explosion killed all six of our men."

"Oh, my God."

"I was a sniper. My job was simple."

"Killing an innocent life—a child for Christ's sake. They can't possibly train you to do that. Order you to kill children?"

"It's a war zone out there, Sara. He was the enemy. And that bomb was gonna go off anyway. He was already dead. My job was to protect our guys from that fate. All my years in the fucking military carrying out missions like this and my conscience decided to make an appearance at the precise moment. That split-second cost six men their lives. Sons, husbands, fathers, friends. The rules of engagement are different when you are in the middle of war— behind enemy lines. I should have taken him out without the slightest hesitation. Those men would still be alive if it weren't for my mistake."

"Is that why you left the Marines?"

"It's why I never went back. Shit happens. Mistakes are made and men die. But we keep forging on, fighting the war. It's the ugly truth most people choose to ignore. *I* couldn't. Those guys were my brothers. Facing their families wasn't easy. Not when I knew I was responsible for their loss."

"Did anyone know what really happened?"

"The aftermath of that mission debrief was a complete debacle. It wasn't pretty. Not only did we lose six good men, we lost all that intel. It was a complete set back to everything we had gone there to do."

"Is that why you can't sleep?"

"I've never stopped reliving it. Since I've come home, I've been haunted with images from that day. Nightmares."

"I'm so sorry."

"In my dreams, all I hear is the bone shattering explosion and the screams of men dying, burning. Limbs scattered everywhere. Sometimes, I'm right in the thick of it, dying with them."

Tom sat next to me on the couch, grasping my hands. "Sara, the reason I told you all of this is because after I came back from the war, I wasn't the same. I had seen too many men die, soldiers, civilians, but the death of those six guys...it was too much. I had to take medication to help me with the trauma. And for a while, the dreams went away. I decided to stop taking the pills and focused on my new career and my new life. Things seemed to be going good for me, but just a few months ago, the dreams came back. With a vengeance. Happening almost every night. They are more real, more vivid. Visceral. Even after waking up, I can still hear the screams. I can still feel my own flesh burning."

"You told me you had a hard time sleeping. I never guessed it was this bad."

"When I wake up from one of these things, I'm not myself. It takes me a bit to gather my bearings, to realize I'm not still back in Afghanistan fighting a war. I can be dangerous. I can potentially hurt someone."

"You haven't once woken up from a nightmare like the ones you are describing while you've been with me."

"Not with you, no," he said with caution.

"Oh? Then with who?"

"Sara, please understand. I didn't mean for it to happen."

I stood up from the couch, wrapping the blanket tighter around me. "For what to happen?"

He closed his eyes and clasped his hands together, preparing to answer. "After you left on Sunday—"

I gasped. "Oh, my God, that recent?" I paced as I ran trembling hands through my hair.

"Sara, calm down. Just listen, okay?"

I snapped my head toward him. "You've been sleeping with someone else?"

Tom pushed up from the couch. "What? No."

I sat back down, my mind swirling, my body seething, anger bubbling in my gut.

He sat across from me on the ottoman. "The night you left," he began, "I had a nightmare. It was the first one I'd had since I met you. I panicked. If I continued to have these dreams, it could potentially affect our relationship. I still had some pills left, but I couldn't take them. Part of the reason I stopped taking them also had been because I thought I deserved to have those nightmares. I needed them to keep their memory alive. I didn't want to ever forget. After a while of not taking them, the dreams just stopped. Until a few months ago."

My knee bounced as I waited for him to tell me what happened after I left.

The muscles in his jaw twitched. "Look, I refused to take the pills because the side effects are not pleasant and I didn't want to become a slave to them."

I didn't know what to say. I understood everything he was saying. I wanted to be sympathetic. I wanted to be a support, but I also knew there was more to his story—the part that he was working up to tell me. And knowing there was something he was going to tell me that I wasn't going to like, had my heart ready to jump out of my chest.

"Sara, Tuesday night when we were on the phone I told you someone was at the door. I thought it was Jake."

"I remember that."

"It was actually Tiffany."

My eyes bulged and I gasped as if an elephant had sat on my chest.

He put his hands on my shoulders. "Sara, nothing happened. I didn't sleep with her."

"What happened then?" I asked, my lips firm.

"Tiffany confessed she still had romantic feelings toward me."

I rolled my eyes and shook my head. "I could have told you that. Oh wait, I did."

"Look, that afternoon, Jake told Tiffany about us—"

He touched a finger to my lips to silence what he knew I was going to say. "I know, she already knew," he continued. "But what she didn't know was that you had been staying with me at my house. When I told you I had never brought another woman home, I meant it. She took me by surprise when I found her standing at my door."

"What did the viper want?"

"She wanted to know why I never invited her in and why things didn't work out between us. Why I had chosen you."

I should have figured she'd try to get between us.

"I told her I loved you. It wasn't what she wanted to hear, but it was the truth," he said, apologetically.

I dug my spiny gaze into him. "Why do you sound like it hurt you to tell her that?"

He blinked in surprise. "What? No. It's not like that. You need to understand, Sara. I hadn't been ready to give anyone my heart until I met you. I didn't think I ever would fall in love with another woman. When I broke things off with her, she didn't care who I fucked, as long as I didn't care for them. To her, seeing me with you and realizing how deeply I fell for you...it made her feel like she was the problem."

"But that is all ancient history. Why the hell is she stirring up trouble now? You fell in love with someone else. End of story. You don't owe her any explanations."

"I know. I tried to get her to understand that."

"How did she take it?"

"I thought she had taken it well, but…"

"But what?" I asked, nearly snarling at him. "What do you mean you thought she was going to take it well? What happened?"

He sucked in a deep breath and looked away. "She drank a little too much wine."

My breath froze. Nothing good ever follows the words…*too much wine*.

"That's when I told her she could stay the night," Tom continued slowly, expecting another explosion from me.

"She stayed the night?"

"Sara, she was too drunk to drive. But I never imagined she'd do what she pulled later that evening, after I had fallen asleep. She snuck into my room. Naked. Then rolled into bed with me."

Forty-Seven

SARA

My stomach cramped and felt acidic. "I'm gonna throw up." I ran toward the bathroom.

"Sara, what's the matter?" he asked, following after me.

I dry heaved several times over the toilet before pushing the lid down and plastering my naked ass on it. Tom stood at the entry, leaning a shoulder on the doorframe.

I looked at him, my face contorted from the sick feeling still clinging to my stomach. "And I guess you didn't realize she was sleeping next to you naked?"

"I was asleep. I had no idea she was even in my room."

"Right."

"Are you insinuating that I'm not telling you the truth?"

"I don't know, Tom. I mean, how the hell does a naked woman just walk into your room? Wasn't the door locked?"

"I never lock my doors. I hardly ever close them. It's not like I thought she'd pull that crap."

I scoffed. "You have to be fucking kidding me, right? I met her for two seconds and even I know she'd be the kind of woman who would pull that kind of stunt."

"Believe whatever it is you want to believe. You're going to anyway." He stormed away and disappeared into his bedroom.

I followed after him and found him lying on his bed, hands behind his head, staring at the ceiling.

"I'm sorry," I said.

He remained silent.

"I jumped to conclusions before I let you finish."

Still, more silence.

"I over reacted. Tiffany just—"

"Baby, I was sleeping," he uttered. "I had no idea what was going on. The next thing I knew, I had her by the neck, choking her. I almost killed her."

My heart stopped. "What?"

"She thought she could seduce me while I slept, perhaps that I'd wake up mid-something and then we'd conclude what she started. The only thing I remember is jolting awake from one of my night-mares, still in a fog. I'd been in close combat in the middle of gun fire and men yelling. When I finally came to, I was squeezing her neck so tight she nearly lost consciousness. A few more seconds and I would have crushed her wind pipe. She would have died in minutes."

I could have been pissed at Tiffany's sneaky tactics or angry she tried to take advantage of him. The probability something could have happened was all too palpable. But what I saw in Tom's eyes quickly took my anger and fears and reduced them to ashes. Tom was utterly horrified, and it was more concerning than anything else I could be feeling about that woman.

I laid next to him, offering him my warmth as I placed my head on his chest.

"The first thing that went through my mind," he said, "when the nightmare began to dissolve and I realized what'd happened was, what if she had been you?" He turned to face me. "Sara, her neck was black and blue, I was squeezing so tight. She would have died. She could have easily been you. I just... I wouldn't be able to live with myself if I ever hurt you. If I ever..."

I reached over and cupped his cheek. "You wouldn't."

He turned his face away from me. "You don't know that."

"You can take the pills. Maybe see a doctor."

"It takes a while for any treatment to work. It's a risk I don't want to take with you until I'm certain I won't have an episode."

"So, what's going to happen? You can't live like this, not sleeping in your bed while I'm around."

"I'm okay with sleeping on the couch or in the other room."

I blinked. "You are being ridiculous. I'm not keeping you from your own bed."

"I'll do whatever I have to until I can figure out how to control this." He spoke calmly, but his soft words were not able to hide the dread seeping into his eyes, saturating the ambivalence holding him captive. I'd never seen him so worried.

I placed my head on his chest again. "We'll get through it. We'll figure this out. Together."

He squeezed me tight and placed a kiss on my head. "I reassigned her, you know. She's no longer working as my assistant," he added out of nowhere.

I jolted up. "Say what, again?"

He sat up next to me. "She betrayed years of friendship. I can't work with someone I don't trust."

My spine tightened. "Yeah, but what do you mean you reassigned her? Why didn't you just fire her?"

He shook his head, a twitching smirk pulling at the corners of his lips. "I knew you were going to say that."

"Clearly. So, why didn't you fire her ass?"

"Look, aside from what she did that night, Tiffany has been a good friend and a good employee. I didn't want her to lose her job for something so stupid. She did what she thought she needed to do to get what she wanted. It backfired. What matters is that I reassigned her to our L.A. branch as the office manager. My new assistant is some geeky dude. Nothing for you to worry about, okay?" he said as he tucked a strand of loose hair behind my ear. "Tiffany is out of the picture."

I shimmied away from his touch. "Until you visit the L.A. office. She is never going to be out of the picture until she is no longer working for you—in any capacity. She's shown she is willing to do anything to get you back."

"She never had me, Sara. I'm serious. There's nothing for you to worry about."

"I don't like it."

Tom looked at the clock. "It's late. You should be getting some sleep."

I hated it when he did that, dismissing what I was saying because he was done talking about it. I didn't have the energy for another argument, so I let it slide. "What about you?"

"Don't worry about me, all right? I'll stay up and watch TV."

"Don't leave me in this bed alone."

"Baby, please try to understand, it's not that I want to leave you here. God, it's the last thing I want."

"Watch TV here instead." With puppy-dog eyes and a playful pout, I pleaded with him to stay.

He looked at me and cocked an eyebrow. "Who taught you to do that?"

"Do what?" I said, rolling my eyes and pretending I had no idea what he was referring to.

"Get whatever it is you want just by looking so adorable?"

I smiled coyly. "I have no idea what you're talking about."

He smirked. "I'll stay with you until you fall asleep."

"Deal." I giggled as I slipped under the comforter with him. Like the gravitational pull of a planet, his body snatched me into its atmosphere and slowly dropped me into his world. The safest and only place I ever wanted to be in.

A couple of hours later, I awoke to a heavy and sloppy tongue licking my face. I opened one eye and saw a pair of anxious amber eyes staring right at me. I was lying flat on my stomach with my arm dangling off the bed.

"Bax, what gives? Shouldn't you be bothering your daddy for this?"

Bax sat down on his hind legs with his tongue sticking out. He whined, putting his paws back up on the bed, licking me and nudging my arm.

"Okay, okay. I get it. I'll get up. Where's your dad? Did he forget to take you for a walk?" As I turned around to rise, my hand hit a bulk.

I smiled. Tom was still lying next to me. Passed out.

And for the first time since I'd met him, I'd finally not woken up alone in his bed.

Forty-Eight

SARA

After breakfast the following morning, I sat on the couch snuggled up next to Tom as he read the morning paper. I wanted to spend the rest of the day with him, but I'd been on a mission to recondition my body. There were no days off when it came to dancing. I peeled away from his warmth and stood up.

"Where're you going?" he asked.

"I need to hit the studio."

He placed the newspaper on the couch and crossed his arms. "It's the weekend. I just got you back and now I'm gonna lose you again?"

I didn't want to separate from him either, but there were things I needed to get done. "I need to talk to Alexei."

He grunted. "I get a strange vibe from that guy. You couldn't stand him, now you are going to dance with him? I don't under-stand." He shook his head and looked away.

"Tom," I said, "would I rather it be someone else? Yes, of course.

399

But right now, I don't have much of a choice. He offered to help me train."

"Yeah, but at what cost? You think he is doing this out of the goodness of his heart?"

"No, but he is one of the best in the business. If anyone can get me back to where I was, I think it's him."

"You can't just go back to school? Reapply to Juilliard?"

"I don't want to think about going back to school at this point. And I'm not good enough to make it into Juilliard again anyway. I'd have to train for years. Plus, I don't even know what it is I really want."

"What do you mean?"

"Back then, the plan was simple. I'd graduate and become a brilliant dancer. That's it."

"So why can't you continue to pursue that dream?"

"I don't know if I want that. Dancing on the big stage, it doesn't hold the same appeal anymore. Without my mother, it isn't the same. It will never be."

"You don't mean that."

"I do. I want to dance again, yes, but it's not because I have this drive to make it big. Dancing just makes me happy," I said, drifting into thought.

"What are you thinking?"

"My mom always thought about starting up her own dance school. She wanted to teach ballet, but she was so busy with me, she was never able to accomplish her own personal dream."

"You want to open up a dance school?"

"I don't know. Maybe...someday, I guess. I'd love to give others the chance I had to fall in love with the art. Especially young children. First, I need to get my life back in order. Can't be a dance instructor if I can't dance."

"You're sure there is nothing I can do to make you stay with me?" he said, flicking his tongue in the air.

"Oh, you're the fucking devil," I said, laughing.

~

Hours later at the company, I decided to tackle a little bit of work before hitting the dance floor. It was Sunday and no one used the studio on the weekends unless it was crunch time. I was sorting through email when I saw Alexei pass my door. Perfect, just who I need to see. "Alexei!"

When he didn't answer, I went after him, but he'd already locked himself in his office. I gently knocked on his door. "Alexei, I'm sorry to bother you, but I really need to talk to you."

Still no answer. I knocked again. "I know you're in there."

Finally, he opened the door, his face expressionless.

"Can I come in?" I asked.

We walked back to his desk and sat opposite each other. His eyes filled with impatience.

"This won't take long. Just want to discuss what happened the other night."

"Nothing happened," he responded.

"No need to conceal my embarrassment."

"What do you want, Sara?"

"Well..." I wasn't sure I wanted to continue the conversation. This was the Alexei I knew, stoic and rough. It shouldn't have hit me like an ice-cold bucket of water.

"I don't have all day, Sara."

"Well, you said you'd help me."

"Right. Look, I thought about it and it's not gonna happen. I'm too busy, especially now. Plus, really, Sara, what's in it for me? What's in it for *you*? Have you thought about that?"

"I'm not sure I understand."

"You were great once. But that was four years ago. New talent— fresh talent—that's what people want. The dancers now are lightyears ahead of you. You'd need to be retrained. I don't have that kind of time."

I nodded, my head bent down while I looked at my fingers resting on my lap. What he said was true. I was still a good dancer, but I wasn't great, and you needed to be great to make it anywhere. More than great, actually. You needed to be phenomenal. But I wasn't interested in joining a company or of making it big on Broadway.

"I'm not looking to land a spot on your show. I just want to recoup a semblance of who I used to be—until I can figure out what it is I really want to do."

"If you're not looking to pursue a dancing career, then you definitely don't need me. I'm a renowned choreographer, not a dance instructor."

"So, what are you saying? That I shouldn't pursue dance unless it's to join a company?"

"I'm saying I can't help you. Practice or go back to school. You could always do it as a hobby."

I raised my gaze, my heart heavy with disappointment. "Hobby? Dance was my life, Alexei."

"I'm sorry to say your decision to quit four years ago was a huge mistake."

I stood up, thanked him, and walked away.

"Feel free to use the studio whenever you want," he said, his voice trailing behind me.

I was such an idiot. Believing I'd actually been given a second chance? I plodded back to my office, feeling like a fool. And to have trusted in Alexei? That was even more asinine. What had I been thinking? I should have known he would never agree to help me unless there was something in it for him. I almost couldn't blame him. He was right. My train had arrived four years ago, and I stood on the platform, watching it pull away. Now it was too late.

~

I didn't tell anyone about my conversation with Alexei. Not even Tom. I was humiliated, dispirited, and in no mood to talk. Tom was freakishly sensitive to my moods, though, and called me later that night just as I was going up the elevator to my apartment.

"You finally going to tell me what's been bothering you all day?" he asked.

"Nothing's bothering me," I droned as the elevator door opened and I hurried to my apartment.

"Try again."

I stopped and leaned my back against the wall next to my apartment door. I held the phone to my ear, not knowing how to respond. When I hurt, I curled into my cave. That was me caving. "I don't know what else you want me to say. I told you nothing is wrong." As much as I loved him and wanted to confide in him, tonight I needed to be by myself with my own thoughts. I had to figure out what the hell I was going to do with the rest of my life. I reached into my bag to look for my keys and cursed.

"What's the matter?" he asked.

"God dammit. I must have left them on my desk back at work."

"Left what?"

"My keys."

"Changing the subject?"

I growled as I marched back to the elevator. "No. Why would I lie about my keys?"

"Jen's not home, I guess?"

I huffed. "Would I be this upset if she was? Now I have to go back to that place, as if I needed this shit tonight."

"Hang tight. I'll come get you and drive you over to the office."

"Don't be ridiculous. I'm already in the elevator. I'll call you when I get back."

He sighed on the other end and grumbled something inaudible.

Great. He's frustrated with me.

I'm frustrated with myself too.

He was right to be upset. I was taking my anger out on him.

"Can I see you tonight?" he asked. Seemed he wasn't ready to give up on me yet.

I shouldn't have been so difficult on him. Tom was only trying to help. His persistence made me realize perhaps a night out with him was the remedy I needed to get out of my slump. "I need to freshen up first," I said as the elevator descended to the lobby.

"Take your time. I'll pick you up later."

I popped into a cab and headed back to the office.

Music echoed from the studio as I walked through the corridors of the building. I figured the new dancers were rehearsing so I decided to take a peek. As I approached the studio, my jaw dropped, the air trapped in my lungs. My body trembled with shock and fury. Gliding across the floor in graceful synchronization, Caterina and Francesco worked on their new routine.

My routine.

Alexei counted beats as they pushed through every single step.

My steps.

"What's the meaning of this?" I shouted.

All three of them stopped mid-dance to look at me. Alexei was particularly startled.

"Take five," Alexei ordered as he tried to usher the dancers out of the studio.

"No." I pointed to the couple. "You wait right there. I need an explanation."

"You don't tell my dancers what to do, Sara."

"I do when it's my routine they are dancing."

Caterina and her partner looked back and forth between Alexei and me, perhaps trying to decipher what I meant.

"Your routine?" Alexei tried to play stupid, but I was not about to let this jerk make a fool out of me.

I scoffed. "This is the big secret, hmm? The number you've been rehearsing all week behind closed doors?"

He turned to the dancers once more. "Caterina, Francesco, please leave us."

"No." I put my palm out to them. "Stay. You should see for yourselves what a sneaky, slimy phony your choreographer really is." I looked back to Alexei. "This is what you do? How you made a name for yourself? By stealing intellectual property from others?"

"That's enough." He grabbed me by the arm, squeezing my flesh until it burned. He dragged me out of the studio toward his office.

"Let go of me." I tried to pull away, but his grip was too strong. I almost tripped trying to keep up with his pace. "I said let go of my arm. You are hurting me."

He shoved me through the door of his office, followed behind, and closed it.

I turned to face him. "What do you think you're doing?"

"I've had enough of your attitude, Ms. Hart. I think it's time someone taught you a lesson."

"What are you talking about?"

He smiled, his lips dripping with menace.

My heart raced. I didn't like the look in his eyes and I certainly didn't like where this conversation was headed. "You better open that door, Alexei."

"Nah."

"I'll open it." I walked toward him, feigning confidence in my ability to defy his intentions, but he blocked me with his frame and grabbed me by the shoulders as he pushed me into him, my back to his chest. He put his arms over mine and squeezed tight, forcing the air out of my lungs.

"Let go of me. Sick bastard!" I tried to break loose, but his hold on me only grew stronger.

"Ms. Hart, is that anyway to show your appreciation?"

"Appreciation? For what?"

He sniffed my hair, nudging my neck with his nose and inhaling deeply. "Bet your boyfriend likes the way you smell."

"What is wrong with you? Let go of me!" I squirmed with all my might, trying to at least free one arm or an elbow.

He pressed his lips to my ear. The hotness of his breath was revolting. His arms wrapped even tighter as I tried to get loose. He lifted me higher off the ground; I was barely standing on my toes as he whispered his venom. "Let me tell you something, Ms. Hart. What you saw in there...that was me doing you a favor. I took your mediocre routine and turned it into something worth seeing. You should be thankful. It's about the closest you will get to a stage ever again. Show a bit more gratitude."

"You are sick."

He licked my cheek. "I haven't really shown you how sick I can be."

"You want the routine? Keep it. Just let go of me."

"Giving up so easily? I thought you'd have a bit more fight in you, Sara." In one quick move, he turned me around to face him, then he pinned me to the wall, his body pressing hard against mine. I was inches from his sweaty face, but I refused to look him in the eyes and turned away.

"You can pretend you don't want me to touch you, Ms. Hart, but your body said otherwise the other night when we danced. Look at me."

"No."

He reached up and wrapped his hand around my neck forcing me to turn my face. Instinctively, I tried to pry his hand off me, but he was much too strong. Breathing heavily, I dropped my arms, and with defiance, arrowed my gaze into his. "I knew agreeing to dance with you was a mistake."

He bared his teeth and gripped my neck harder, causing me to gasp. "You didn't resist," he gritted.

"I was desperate and you took advantage," I croaked.

He inched closer to my lips. "Oh, you are going to be fun." He laughed deeply. The sinister intent made my bones tremble.

"You are not going to get away with this."

"Sara, I'm not going to take you. At least not until you beg me to."

"Never gonna happen." I spit on his face.

He didn't bother to clean it. "You will beg—that I promise you," he threatened.

A knock at the door startled both of us.

"Alexei!" Caterina shouted. "We are leaving."

It was my moment. "If you don't let go of me now, I will scream."

He didn't need me to utter another word. His grip loosened and I pushed off him with anger, running for the door. I yanked it open to find Caterina and her partner standing outside. Turning to Alexei, I said, "You will regret this." Then I stormed off, almost knocking over the two dancers.

Back at the apartment, I sat on my couch holding a warm cup of tea, my hands still shaking. Jen paced back and forth, her hands fisted at her sides. "You have to call the police, Sara."

"And tell them what?"

"Exactly what happened. That asshole can't get away with this."

"Stealing someone's routine is not a crime."

"I'm talking about the way he attacked you."

"Nothing happened."

"Are you blind? Have you seen the red marks on your neck? If you hadn't been interrupted, who knows what he might have done. He is dangerous, Sara. You need to report this guy. God knows how many other women he has violated."

"You think I don't want to report him? I could lose my job."

"Who cares about your job. How could you go back to work after what happened?"

"I don't know. I can't think right now."

"Since when do you care about losing your job? You've hated that place ever since you started working there. The only thing keeping you enslaved is the fact you felt you didn't deserve any better. Well, that's over and done with. You are not going back."

A frantic knock on the door turned my attention. "That's probably Tom."

"Thank God. Maybe he can knock some sense into you." Jen walked over to the door to let him in.

"Where is she?" he said as he pushed through the door. He nearly ran Jen over to get to me. He kneeled, cupping my face in his hands and raising my chin. "Let me see your neck." His voice was unusually calm until he saw the marks. "That asshole did this to you?" He pushed to his feet, his breath ragged. "He's fucking dead."

"Tom, I'm fine."

He snapped his head toward me, "Fine? Are you serious?"

"Please tell her she's not going back," Jen told him. "She's worried about losing her job."

He shook his head, his face scrunched in disgust. "You plan on going back?"

I placed my tea on the coffee table and stood. "If I quit, he wins. I'm not going to let that prick drive me out of there. He thinks he can threaten me, and that like a scared little bird I'm going to fly away? No. I'm facing him tomorrow, and I'm going to show him he can't intimidate me."

Tom turned toward the door. "The hell you are."

I rushed after him. "Where are you going?"

"To pay Alexei a visit."

"Babe, no. I can handle this."

He turned around and put his hands on my shoulders, holding me back. "As can I." He looked at Jen. "Make sure she gets some rest. I'll come back later." He walked out of the apartment and headed for the elevators.

"Tom, please!" I chased after him. "You are going to make things worse. He may not even be there."

As he waited for the elevator to open, he said, "You don't understand, do you? What he did..." he paused, "I won't let him get away with it."

"What are you going to do, beat the shit out of him?"

"Yes." The doors finally glided open.

Forty-Nine

TOM

I STORMED DOWN THE HALL OF THE DANCE COMPANY, hunting for Alexei's office. Every muscle in my body tensed, ready to confront the motherfucker. If I remembered Alexei well, it was going to be no effort at all to give the prick a lesson. I rolled up my sleeves. Face tense with anger, my teeth almost cracked from the tightness of my clenched jaw.

The hallways were dark, but like a beacon, the dim light from his office guided me right to my prey. I barged in without warning, startling the creep.

"What the— How the hell did you get in here?" Alexei demanded.

"You don't remember me?" I snarled.

"Do I need to?"

I slammed the door closed behind me.

"What do you think you're doing?" Alexei asked, standing up from his chair, his gaze trembling with fear.

"We need to have a little chat," I growled, cracking my knuckles and trying not to dash toward the vermin to crush it under my boot until all that remained was its pulp.

Alexei reached for the desk phone.

"I checked. Security is gone for the night."

"I'm calling the police."

"By the time you hit the first number, I'll be done with you already."

Alexei pulled his hand away from the receiver. "What do you want?"

"I'm here to deliver a message from Sara."

Recognition swiftly came back into Alexei's eyes. The tension in his neck relaxed. He smiled at me mockingly and sat back on his leather chair. "Oh, now I remember you. You're the boyfriend. The little bitch thinks she can send her bulldog to intimidate me?"

"Watch your fucking mouth, Alexei."

"Or what?"

"Or you'll be needing a new set of teeth."

"You don't frighten me."

"You like preying on young girls and their dreams?"

"Is that what this is about?" Alexei laughed, placing his feet up on his desk. "Please, Sara's dreams were over four years ago when she decided to give up on them."

"That gave you the right to steal her routine?"

The jerk scoffed and rolled his eyes. "Is that what she thinks I did?" He sighed as he stood and stalked toward me.

Bad idea.

"I gave it life," he continued. "Sara knows she will never perform on a real stage again. The people she'd be competing against have been training rigorously for years. She wouldn't stand a chance as a professional dancer out here in this city. She should be thanking me for putting her measly routine up on display for people to see ."

I didn't move, but my body vibrated with anger. "You didn't tell her you were planning on making it a number in your production."

The idiot continued to draw closer. "She wants me to tell everyone she's responsible for the choreography, is that it?"

I clenched my fists. "She doesn't want anything from you."

Alexei's gaze drifted to my hands, his eyes narrowing in suspicion. "Why *are* you here?"

My lips twitched with a humorless smile, my eyes sharp as razors.

Seeming to sense my intensions, he began to back away from me. "Hmm, as I see it, all you've done is cost Sara her job."

I cocked my head as I took one step toward him. "Firing her?"

He sucked in a deep breath, puffing his chest. "Gone. That little cunt is never going to find another job working in this city for any dance company. You can tell her that's my personal parting gift."

In one breath, I rushed toward him, grabbing him by his shirt, and hauling him off his feet. Still holding on to him, I pushed him backward before slamming his spine onto the wooden desk. Alexei let out a grunt of pain as his bones cracked. His feet tangled beneath him as he struggled to break free. My adrenaline spiked, pushing my anger past the boiling point as I stared at the quivering worm beneath me.

"Let go of me," Alexei shouted.

"I told you to watch your fucking mouth."

"Fuck you, asshole."

"You think you are so slick, don't you?" I said, gritting my teeth. "Walking around here like you're big shit, like you're somebody who should be worshipped or feared. I'll give you something to fear." I coiled my right arm and jabbed a fist into Alexei's face three times before finishing him off with a hook.

By the fourth punch, Alexei's left eye was swollen shut and bleeding. Several teeth fell from his mouth. I'd busted his nose too.

"You're gonna pay for that..." he mumbled out of his broken lips.

I grinned and delivered another blow, knocking him out momentarily. Then gripping him by the collar, I lifted the asshole to his feet, his head wobbling. My breath inches from his bloodied face, I said, "Looks like you're going to need a new set of teeth after all. How's *that* for a parting gift." I let go of him then shoved him back against the desk.

I opened the door to the office, but before leaving, I looked back at the slumped form hunched over the desk. All Alexei could to do was hold his broken face. "One more thing, Alexei. If you ever lay your hands on her again, I'll kill you. That's a fucking promise."

I jumped back into the car and quickly put it in drive then peeled off. When I arrived back at the apartment, adrenaline still raced through my veins. Sara screeched when she saw my bloodied hand.

"You're done with that place," I told her as I plopped on her couch.

She sat next to me, her hands on her forehead. "Oh, my God. What did you do?"

"I handed in your resignation."

"With your fist? Christ, Tom."

"He hurt you. He's lucky he's still breathing."

"What if he decides to report this to the police?"

"He won't if he knows what's good for him."

"But what if he does?"

"He does. I don't care. Not the first time I've punched a guy. He deserved it. I'll do it again if I have to."

Sara's body trembled, her eyes wide with dread. "I'm worried about you. What if he retaliates against us? Against you?"

Seeing her so shaken made me realize I hadn't given the situation much thought. There could be repercussions to my actions, and I didn't think about how this could affect her. I leaned closer, letting the fire in my blood simmer down. "Baby," I said, caressing her cheek with the fingers on my uninjured hand, "there's nothing to be frightened about. I will make sure nothing happens to you."

She took my bloodied hand and cradled it in hers. "Look at your knuckles. You could have been seriously hurt."

I chuckled. "I've dealt with worse."

She peered up at me. "What about Alexei?"

"He'll need to see a plastic surgeon. Probably won't be showing up to work for a couple of weeks."

Sara shook her head, puffing out a breath. "I guess now I have a bigger problem."

I leaned back on her couch. "What's that?"

She shrugged. "Finding a new job."

Fifty

SARA

Eight weeks later...

Needless to say, I didn't return to the dance company. The show had to be cancelled and apparently, Rebecca had a breakdown. Still, they managed to recoup from the disaster, and from what Martha told me, Rebecca hired a new assistant. It seemed the new person probably wasn't going to last long. I was the only idiot willing to put up with Rebecca's shit as long as I did.

Surprisingly, Alexei did not press charges, but I had a feeling he simply didn't want the truth getting out about his sleazy behavior at the company. I also decided not to report him. I knew what would happen if I tried. He'd serve minimal time in jail for assault, if that. If I wanted to take him down for good, I would need the support of all the other women at the company. Problem was, I was forbidden from stepping foot back there.

Tom felt zero remorse for bashing Alexei's face in, though he hated the fact I was still trying to find work. Alexei had kept his promise, and no one seemed interested in hiring me, despite my background. I was living off my savings, which were quickly dwindling. Tom offered for me to move in with him and told me I didn't need to worry about money, but how I could possibly accept that?

I hated feeling like a mooch. That didn't stop him from randomly showing up at my apartment with bags of groceries, or from sending me periodic gift boxes filled with designer clothes, which I knew Jen had helped pick out. Zelle transactions also mysteriously appeared in my bank account weekly. The man was relentless in his need to help me. Probably because he felt responsible for me losing my job.

Then he strong-armed me into accepting his Black American Express card. I tried handing it back, but arguing with him when he wanted something was a losing battle. He told me that if it made me feel better, I could pay him back once I got a job.

As if he'd take my money. I seldom used the credit card if ever, though I did take him out to eat at his favorite restaurant one night and paid with the credit card, which he found amusing. About the only good thing that came out of the whole fiasco was the fact that I got to spend a lot more time getting to know him. Even though I hadn't officially moved in with him, I split half my time between his apartment and mine.

Oh, and there was also the fact that Tom let me use his apartment as a makeshift dance studio. His living room was so large, I could literally fly across the room leaping and twirling.

During one morning after he'd left for work, I had been dancing when nausea hit out of nowhere. I had to run to the bathroom and heaved into the toilet until I puked my entire breakfast.

That day, I figured I'd simply pushed myself too hard. Or maybe something I'd eaten hadn't settled well with my stomach. But when the feeling returned a day later and a day after that, I knew something wasn't right. I'd been on the pill so I didn't think I could be pregnant, but when my period was late three days, then five, then seven, I began to worry.

Then, day fourteen came. My period didn't. I stood in my shower until the hot water ran cold, trying to figure out how this could've happened. I tried not to panic, but there was no other explanation. I sure as hell wasn't ready for this. And probably, neither was Tom.

All I knew once I finally exited my bathroom was that my whole entire world was about to change.

Tom and Sara's love story is not over.
The road to their Happily Ever After continues in...

Available on <u>Kindle</u>

Acknowledgments

Wicked Dance was originally conceived eleven years ago as an escape after I'd given birth to my twins and I was home on maternity leave. I never imagined it would ever be published or that so many readers would fall in love with this story as much as I did.

After almost seven years of being under contract with The Wild Rose Press, the rights for book one were reverted back to me this past April 2023. While my debut novel will always hold a special place in my heart, I've grown as an author in the last seven years, and I realized that my old manuscript needed a little TLC.

Thus, Falling for Mr. Wright was born. The core of the story remained the same, but I added the finishing touches that now make this story the version I always dreamed of telling. If this is your first time reading Tom and Sara's love story, then welcome to my universe of spicy romance with heart wrenching angst. If you've returned... lucky you! You've experienced this rollercoaster of a romance for a second time.

Thank you to my family and friends for supporting me during this relaunch. I'm also grateful for all my readers, old and new. So happy to have you on this journey.

Love always,
Liv

About the Author

REAL LOVE AS IT IS. MESSY. COMPLICATED. AND SINFULLY ADDICTIVE.

Olivia Boothe is a contemporary romance and fantasy author.

Born in Colombia and raised in New Jersey since the age of eight, Olivia always dreamed of becoming a storyteller. Now, she enjoys crafting novels with deep, layered plots because romance is not just about the first kiss and the happily ever after, it's about everything in between.

In addition to writing, Olivia loves reading across all genres, binge watching her favorite TV shows, and hanging out on Tuesday nights with her girlfriends for wine, snacks, and junk-TV therapy. Olivia lives in Northern New Jersey with her hubby, three boys, and a mini Aussie named Rosie.

To read more from Olivia, visit her website and follow her on social media:

https://www.oliviaboothe.com

www.ingramcontent.com/pod-product-compliance
Lightning Source LLC
Chambersburg PA
CBHW020323010826

48973CB00005B/1103